R_XOXY

NEAL SHUSTERMAN
and
JARROD SHUSTERMAN

SIMON & SCHUSTER BFYR

NEW YORK   LONDON   TORONTO   SYDNEY   NEW DELHI

An imprint of Simon & Schuster Children's Publishing Division
1230 Avenue of the Americas, New York, New York 10020

SIMON & SCHUSTER BOOKS FOR YOUNG READERS
and related marks are trademarks of Simon & Schuster, Inc.
For information about special discounts for bulk purchases, please contact Simon & Schuster Special Sales at 1-866-506-1949 or business@simonandschuster.com.
The Simon & Schuster Speakers Bureau can bring authors to your live event. For more information or to book an event, contact the Simon & Schuster Speakers Bureau at 1-866-248-3049 or visit our website at www.simonspeakers.com.
Interior design by Hilary Zarycky
The text for this book was set in Bembo.
Manufactured in the United States of America
First Edition
2 4 6 8 10 9 7 5 3 1
Library of Congress Cataloging-in-Publication Data
Names: Shusterman, Neal, author. | Shusterman, Jarrod, author.
Title: Roxy / Neal Shusterman and Jarrod Shusterman.
Description: New York : Simon & Schuster Books for Young Readers, [2021]
| Audience: Ages 12 + | Audience: Grades 10-12 | Summary: "Two siblings get caught up in a wager between two manufactured gods, Roxicodone and Adderall, in this new thriller inspired by the opioid crisis"—Provided by publisher.
Identifiers: LCCN 2021006900 (print) | LCCN 2021006901 (ebook) |
ISBN 9781534451254 (hardcover)
| ISBN 9781534451278 (ebook)
Subjects: CYAC: Drug addiction—Fiction. | Brothers and sisters—Fiction.
Classification: LCC PZ7.S55987 Ro 2021 (print) | LCC PZ7.S55987 (ebook) |
DDC [Fic]—dc23
LC record available at https://lccn.loc.gov/2021006900
LC ebook record available at https://lccn.loc.gov/2021006901

*For those in the throes of addiction,
may you find the strength to fight off
the demons who pose as gods*

Roxy is a work of fiction that deals with prescription drug addiction. Though many of the drugs depicted were designed to help, their misuse has spiraled into an epidemic. It is our hope that everyone who reads *Roxy* will leave the story with a clearer understanding of how insidious, seductive, and dangerous these drugs can be. For those struggling with addiction, or with an addicted loved one, this book will be cathartic, but also very intense.

We hope you have a powerful, and meaningful read!

Neal & Jarrod Shusterman

I

Nal**ox**one

I am no superhero. But I can save you from the one who claims to be.

I am no wizard. But I cast a spell that can bring back the dead.

Almost.

And never often enough.

I am, if nothing else, your final defense—your last hope when hope itself has spiraled into that singularity that crushes not just you, but everyone around you.

And so here we are, you and I. The scene is set. Never identical, yet always the same:

Today it's a room in a house on a street that was born when dreams were milky-white appliances, and cars were like landlocked ships, too proud to ever be slung with seat belts.

This was once suburbia, but it was long ago consumed by a gelatinous urban tsunami. The neighborhood struggles and sometimes even thrives. But this street? This street is dead. It has been sacrificed for the greater good.

The trees on either side have already been taken down, their trunks turned into firewood, their limbs fed into a chipper. Most doors and windows have been stripped and salvaged, leaving the homes with the deadest of eyes and gaping, silent mouths. Nearly a mile of this. And just beyond are bulldozers and rubble, and beyond that, towering concrete pillars reach skyward like the columns of an ancient temple.

Because a freeway is coming. A six-lane corridor that will cleave the neighborhood in half, right along this very street, in a brutal rite of passage called eminent domain.

When night falls, the doomed street is engulfed more completely than anywhere else in the city.

And there you are. In the fifth house on the left.

You're not from this part of town, but somehow you found this place, drawn by darkness so dense you can wrap it around yourself like a blanket.

Now flashlights illuminate a familiar tableau. One officer, two paramedics. And me.

A medic leans over you—presses a finger to your neck.

"Hard to find a pulse," she says. "If it's there, it's weak."

This room was once a bedroom. But there's no bed, no dresser. All that remains is a warped desk and a broken chair that no one deemed worth saving. You lie on carpet mottled with mold that has left it looking like a wall-to-wall bruise. It is the very epicenter of abandoned hope.

"I can't detect any breathing. Beginning CPR."

Rats would complete the scene, but vector control has already been here with some of my more vicious cousins to kill the vermin. But they can't get rid of the roaches no matter how hard they try. They are the victors of this world, the roaches. Truly undefeatable.

You, on the other hand, are defeated. How defeated is yet to be seen.

Thirty chest compressions, two rescue breaths. Repeat.

The other medic prepares me for what I've come to do, while the officer gives a description of you on his radio. They don't know who you are. I don't know who you are either—but soon you and I will be close. I will be inside you. A kind of intimacy neither of us wants but both of us need. It is, after all, my purpose. And you? You have no choice.

"Administering the naloxone."

"Make sure you get the muscle."

"I never miss."

The needle plunges deep in your left thigh—and I surge forth into muscle tissue, searching for capillaries that will carry me to larger and larger vessels. And yes—you're still alive! I *do* hear your heartbeat! Slow, faint, but there!

I ride the long sluggish wave of your beat into the chambers of your heart, and out again, up and up toward your brain. Only there can I save you. I will rip you free of the hold they have over you.

They.

The *others*. Who care for you only as long as they have you locked in their embrace, as if you are nothing more than a child's tattered toy. They do not know love—only possession. They promise you deliverance and reward you . . . with this:

Thirty compressions, two breaths. And me.

It is you, and those like you, who gave them power, and continue to give them power day after day. Because who but you can generate current enough to feed the bright flashing lights of their eternal Party? How could you not see that the others—my brutal cousins—are the cancer at the core of seduction? The void at the heart of your craving? They see themselves as gods, but in the end they are just like me. Nothing but chemicals. In complex combinations, perhaps, but still no more than tinctures, distillations, and petty pharma. Chemicals designed by nature, or by man, to tweak *your* chemicals.

If they live, it is only because you gave them life. As well as the license to end yours. And if they act in roles beyond their purpose, it is only because you placed them upon the stage to perform.

Thus the stage has been set. The audience cool and dispassionate—waiting to be entertained but too jaded to believe it ever will be.

But we must try, must we not?

And so here, between the chest compressions and the life-saving breaths, I will do my part, struggling to wrest your fate back from the capricious "gods."

I am no superhero. I am no wizard. But I can save you. Although half of the time I don't. Too often I am too late. Victory and tragedy will forever fight for purchase on this stage.

And today the dimming footlights find tragedy.

Your heart begins to fibrillate. Then it seizes like a furious fist . . . and then releases. The wave is gone. I can't do my work if I can't get to your brain. Still, the medics keep working CPR, but it will not change the fact that you have surrendered your life in the bruised room of the rotting house, on the street that will soon be gone.

They tag your toe with the last name on your ID, and your first initial:

Ramey, I.

Then they wheel you out, and I have little left to do but settle in your veins—one more chemical to parse in the autopsy.

And I curse the others.

My soulless clan who brought you to the Party, then left you in this desolate place, where even those who tried to save you are too world-weary to shed a single tear.

If I had a voice, I swear to you I would tell your story. At least enough of it so that I might know who you are.

2

Isaac, Ivy, and **the** In**finite** Loser

TWO MONTHS EARLIER . . .

Ivy's got to be here somewhere, thinks Isaac Ramey as he pushes through the door of the cesspool, looking for his sister. *No doubt about it; this is Ivy's kind of party.* The house reeks of puke, hormones, and beer, making Isaac wince as he wades through the living room. He's ankle-deep in deadbeats, burnouts, and druggies—all of whom are far too wasted to realize that freak-dancing to techno looks like faking a seizure to someone who's close to sober. Or worse, actually *having* a seizure while interpretive dancing—which would be a really sad way to die, because the audience would just slow clap while you writhe yourself into oblivion.

Isaac needs to stay on track. He searches through the muck and mire. A girl with a half-shaved head. A guy who clearly pissed himself. A seedy dude too old for this party, talking to a girl who's too young for it. Nothing Isaac didn't expect. And if this night is like any other Friday night, he'll find Ivy here. Ivy is a year older than Isaac, but more often than not, Isaac feels like her older brother.

It's not that he doesn't like parties. He's a junior, so he's been to plenty in his time, where things were going on that his parents wouldn't want to know about. . . . But he doesn't go to *these* kinds of parties—his sister's kinds of parties. Where seedy things don't happen in back rooms but are in your face—the dismal and the desperate shoving their brains into a hydraulic press just to make themselves forget how finite they are.

He goes out to the backyard. It's overgrown and features an amoeba-shaped pool not large enough to do anything but float, or secretly urinate. Which might be why the water is clouded and green like a study in bioterrorism.

It isn't long before Isaac spots his sister—her Slurpee-blue hair is a dead giveaway. Ivy's by the pool with Craig, her infinite-loser boyfriend, who lives here. He's their parents' perfect nightmare: ratlike fingernails, competing tattoos, and a man-bun protruding from his head like a tumor.

"Ivy," Isaac calls out as he gets close. He has to call her name three times to get her attention. She takes a moment to hide her surprise at seeing him.

"Mom and Dad know you snuck out, and they're getting ready to go nuclear."

"So they sent *you*?"

"They have no clue where you are, or even that I went out looking for you."

Ivy turns and is already marching away—her classic response to anything she doesn't like. Especially when she's been drinking. Isaac follows, grabbing her arm before she stumbles into an overgrown bush:

"If they get wind of this party and find you here like this, it'll be bad. You'll thank me tomorrow."

Suddenly, Craig discovers enough brain cells to notice Isaac's presence.

"Hey, is this guy bothering you?" he asks Ivy.

"Shut up, Craig. He's my brother. You met, like, six times." Ivy turns back to Isaac. "I'm not some basket case; I don't need you to save me. So go home and study, or whatever it is you do on Friday nights."

"Yeah," seconds Craig. "You heard her. She wants to party with me."

That's when Isaac sees the drug bag that Craig holds, dangling like a little scrotum full of god-knows-what. Just the sight of it ignites something primal within Isaac, taking over his body and making him swat the bag out of Craig's hand, sending it flying into the pool.

"Oops, my bad," Isaac says. He's not the kind of guy who looks for a fight, but some are worth starting.

"What the hell . . ." Craig's shock turns to fury, and he pounces on Isaac. They begin to grapple, and it quickly grows into a full-fledged fight. A zombie horde of the stoned gather to gawk, making it the center of the party's limited attention.

Isaac, who's stronger, lands some blows, but Craig grabs a Solo cup of something 180 proof and hurls it in Isaac's eyes. Craig has a distinct advantage in that dirty moves are his superpower.

And now Craig is punching Isaac over and over again as Isaac fights the burn in his eyes. Hammerfists over his head, body shots. Whatever Craig can do to inflict damage before Isaac recovers his eyesight. Ivy tries to break it up, but can't.

Finally Isaac regains enough of his bearings to deliver a

shot to Craig's nose that may just break it, but before Craig's pain kicks in, he shoves Isaac with all his might, sending him flying to the ground.

In an instant Ivy is at Isaac's side, helping him stand. She looks up to Craig, who now rotates through every profanity he knows as he cradles his gushing nose.

"What the hell is wrong with you!" Ivy yells at Craig.

"He started it!" Craig yells back

But Ivy's not having it. "Just get the hell away from us!"

Craig turns his back far too easily, making it clear how little he actually cares. "Fine. Whatever. You and your family are psycho anyway." Then he goes over to the pool and stands there gazing into the murky water, mourning the loss of his little plastic scrotum.

It isn't until Isaac's adrenaline fades that he realizes his ankle is hurting. No—it doesn't just hurt; it throbs. More than just a run-of-the-mill ankle twist, this is a bone-deep ache. He can already sense that it isn't going away anytime soon. When his sister sees him limping and grimacing, she helps him through the side yard, and together they make their way to the street.

As they get to Isaac's old silver Sebring by the curb, Isaac leans against it, exhaling, realizing he'd been holding his breath most of the way. Then, as he opens the car door, he puts too much weight on his injured ankle and nearly goes down. His vision darkens from the pain, then clears again—but the pain only subsides the slightest bit. That's when he realizes that the simple task of getting home is no longer so simple.

"I can't drive home with my ankle like this. . . ."

"Uh—that's why you have two feet."

Isaac considers it, but shakes his head. "I drive right-footed. I don't even know if I can use my left."

"Fine. I'll drive." She puts out her hands for the keys, but Isaac knows better than to let her have them.

"No. You're drunk. Or worse."

She glares at him. "Not worse."

"No? Looked like it was about to get that way."

"Don't you dare lecture me!"

Isaac backs off. He knows that was out of line. "I'll get an Uber," he says. "I can pick up my car tomorrow."

The app says their ride is three minutes away, which, as always, means ten. They watch people come and go from the house. Neighbors peer angrily out of windows. One comes to his porch and begins yelling at Isaac and Ivy, as if waiting by the curb makes them the official ambassadors of the party.

"If this doesn't stop, I'm calling the police!"

"Be my guest, jerk," says Ivy, and Isaac raps her to shut her up. Their Uber can't get here fast enough.

Finally, it arrives, and they slip in the back, Isaac putting too much weight on his ankle again and grunting from the pain.

"You didn't save me, you know," Ivy tells him as they head off. "I would have left on my own. Eventually."

Isaac nods, choosing to believe her but wishing it came without effort.

Now they sit there in awkward silence, their dynamic going back to normal.

Ivy smirks. "The look on Craig's face when you tossed his stash was classic. Like you took a dump in his Froot Loops."

Isaac, even through the pain, can't help but smile too. Ivy

leans over, rests her head on Isaac's shoulder, and closes her eyes.

"I'm sorry," she says. And he can tell she means it. Although neither of them is sure what it is she's sorry for.

Ivy truly believes she would have left on her own. Even though she's never left a party before they released the proverbial hounds and threw everyone out. Believing something that you know is not true is *Ivy's* superpower.

When they arrive home, she decides to walk in the door ahead of Isaac. She turns on the light, fully expecting to find their parents waiting for them in the dark. That's how things work in this house. It's a three-stage progression. Stage one: her parents explode after realizing she snuck out the window. Stage two: they blame each other's parenting fails for seven to twelve minutes. Stage three: an hour of solitary brooding, where her father will retreat to his computer, while her mom invents household tasks that don't actually exist, like alphabetizing kitchen spices or pairing other people's socks. Stage five: at least one of them will sit in the living room in the dark, monitoring every sound from outside and each passing headlight until Ivy comes home.

Since Isaac got her fairly early, it hasn't reached the darkened-room stage yet. Instead, her father steps out from the kitchen. He's already built up plenty of potential energy, and the look in his eyes tells Ivy it's about to go kinetic.

"Good evening, *Father*," Ivy says, trying to sound ironic and light, but instead it comes off as snarky. Well, the sooner she gets him yelling, the sooner this can be over.

Her mother comes out from the bathroom. Ah—so it's an

ambush. The only family member missing is Grandma, who's been living with them for the past year. She's wise enough not to embroil herself in the drama.

"Care to explain yourself?" Ivy's mother asks her, but looks to Isaac instead. He's an easier read than she is.

Ivy prepares to respond, but before she has the chance, Isaac blurts out, "I was on my way back from Shelby's and figured I'd grab Ivy from the movies."

It's not an unbelievable lie. That is, if Ivy weren't wobbling, still majorly buzzed. She wonders if they saw the Uber drop them off. Oh, the rabbit hole of explanations ahead.

Isaac tries to hide his limp as he crosses the room, but almost trips. Their father is there to support him. "You okay?"

"I . . . twisted my ankle at practice this afternoon. It's nothing." But if there's anything that Ivy has learned, it's that parents always know when you're lying. Even if you're just lying to yourself.

And so to prove his ankle is a non-issue, Isaac walks on it again, and he almost goes down. Ivy silently wonders if her boyfriend's redeeming parts come anywhere close to outweighing his unredeeming ones.

"That looks pretty bad . . . ," their father says.

"I'm fine, Dad," Isaac says with just enough exasperation. "I'll go ice it, okay?"

Then their mother zeroes in on Isaac's forehead. "Is that blood?"

And although part of Ivy is glad that the interrogation has been turned entirely to Isaac, it also pisses her off that her brother's boo-boos have completely blasted Ivy out of her parents' minds.

"I went to a party," Ivy says without flinching. "Isaac came to bring me home. He's like that because he beat up Craig."

If she was going to tell the truth, she might as well make Isaac look good in the process and give their father the satisfaction of knowing that Craig not only got beaten up but by his son, no less.

And now the negative attention has turned back to Ivy. Their mother starts haranguing Ivy about broken promises and patterns of bad behavior until she exhausts herself and shakes her head woefully. It's the expression Ivy hates the most. That *you-disappointed-us-again-and-guess-what? We're-not-even-surprised* look.

"Ivy, I honestly don't know what we're going to do with you," she says.

"Why do you have to do anything? Why can't you just, for once, leave me alone?"

But they can't. She knows they can't. This is, after all, their job.

Then her father drops the boom. "We're making an appointment for you to see Dr. Torres."

"No!" says Ivy. "I am not a child—I will not go to a kiddie shrink!" Ivy would much rather choose her own humiliation than swallow theirs. Dr. Torres has a mural with Winnie-the-Pooh in a pharmacist's robe.

"Well, you're going to see someone. All this self-medicating isn't doing you any favors."

Self-medicating. Ivy wonders when drinking with your friends became clinical. Ivy hates the idea of having to go see some sweater-vested pencil-neck "professional" with a cheaply framed diploma. But what if it's the only way to avoid harder action? She knows a kid who knows a kid who got dragged out of their home in the middle of the night and taken to one of those forced labor camps for unruly teens. Would her parents do something like that to her? At this point in her life, she has no idea.

Isaac has slipped away from the scene. She hears him in the kitchen getting ice, but their fridge has a sadistic ice dispenser that hurls ice everywhere but where you want it to go. She finds Isaac kneeling in pain, trying to pick ice up off the floor. She helps him gather the remaining cubes and put them into a Ziploc.

"Shoulda used crushed," she said. "Or a bag of frozen peas."

"Crushed would be a bigger mess, and peas would be a waste of food—and you know how Mom is about wasted anything lately."

"Yeah," says Ivy. "Especially wasted me."

She hopes it might bring a smile from Isaac, but it doesn't. Maybe he's just in too much pain. "They'll get over it by morning," he says. "They just needed to vent."

Maybe so. But Ivy's not sure she'll be over it. And that doesn't just mean the hangover.

3

Roxy Can't Contain Herself

ROXY

I am so hot right now. And everyone knows it. It's like I own the world. It has no choice but to yield to my gravity.

As I step into the Party, all heads turn, or want to turn, and are fighting the urge. The music hits me first. Loud and rude. It's not just in your face, but in your blood. The lights flash to hypnotize, and the beat takes over your own, replacing it, forcing you to move to it. We are the pacemakers, and right now I'm the one who sets the rhythm. There's no better time to be me.

Al greets me at the door, a glass of champagne in each hand. He's always been the designated greeter, and never misses an arrival. Al's older than the rest of us, been around longer, but he carries his age well.

"My, my, Roxy, you are looking fine tonight!"

"Are you suggesting that I didn't last night?"

He chuckles. "My dear, you get more irresistible every day."

Al slurs his words. It's almost like an accent, the way he's perfected that slur. Consonants and vowels spill over one another. Words in a waterfall. He holds out a champagne flute to me, and I take it. It's how we shake hands here.

"But where's your plus-one?" Al asks, looking behind me.

"I'm on my own tonight, Al."

"On your own?" he repeats, as if it were a phrase in some other language. "That's unfortunate—what will I do with this second glass of champagne?"

I grin. "I'm sure you'll put it to good use."

"Indeed, indeed." Then he leans closer, whispering, "Maybe you could steal a plus-one." He looks over at a gaggle of revelers, singling out Addison. He's dressed in a conspicuous style, like he belongs to a yacht club that his father owns. All prestige and privilege. But we all know it's overcompensation for being forever on the periphery. *In* the Party, but not *of* the Party.

"Addi's rather full of himself tonight," Al says. "He's held on to his date longer than usual—you should steal her before someone else does."

"You're always making trouble, Al."

He raises an eyebrow. "I do love a little drama."

Addison is at the bar, intently focused on a young woman, who, in turn, is caught in his hypnotic gaze. He's selling her on how he'll make her life so much better. All the things he can help her accomplish, blah, blah, blah. Even now, he's still going on about his keen ability to focus the distracted. There are moments I admire him for his singularity of purpose. Other times I pity him, because he will never be great like the rest of us. Like me.

Addison and I came up together. Different family lines, but similar circumstances. Born to help others rather than help ourselves. The problem with Addison is that he never outgrew that stifling idealism. I suppose because most of his work is with kids and adolescents, he still holds on to the youthful naïveté of the task he was created for. True, I still do my job when necessary—dulling angry nerve endings on a strictly clinical basis—but it's such a minor facet of what I've become. They label me a killer of pain, but that doesn't come close to defining me. I've found far more entertaining and empowering uses for my skills.

Al, reading my faint grin, says, "Oh, how I love to watch you calculate, Roxy."

I give him a wink and head off toward Addison. I won't steal the girl from him—I'm fine being solo tonight. After all, we do have to clear our palate once in a while.

Nonetheless, Addison's so much fun to tease.

I make my way to the bar, pushing past the sloe-eyed barflies. Al has long since replaced their empty beer bottles with crystalline glasses filled with more elegant, liver-challenging liquids. Martinis heavy on the gin. Aged scotch. Name your poison, and Al will provide it.

I come up in Addison's blind spot, upstaging him. "Hi, I'm Roxy," I say to the girl, pulling eye contact. She's intense and twitchy. Like she's in the process of being electrocuted but just doesn't know it yet. Too much of Addison can do that to anyone.

"Hi! I love your dress!" she says. "What color is that?"

"What color do you want it to be?"

Addison turns to me, bristling. "Isn't there somewhere else you'd rather be, Roxy? Someone else you'd rather grace with your presence?" He looks around. "How about Molly? She looks like she could use a friend right now."

Molly does look pretty miserable. Dripping wet and crest-fallen. "He was in my hands," I can hear Molly complaining. "I had him—and then some idiot threw me into the pool!"

"Not what I'd call a state of ecstasy," I quip. Then I smile at the girl Addison has been trying to charm. "Molly's a whiner—I'm much happier to hang with you two."

I'm enjoying Addison's irritation—and for a moment, I do toy with the idea of claiming her as mine . . . but it wouldn't be worth the trouble. Addison's positively obsessed with one-upmanship. If I lure her away, he'll never rest until he thinks he's bested me. Poor Addison. He tries to be like me, but he's still too deeply mired in the mundane to ever be a player.

And as if to prove it, the crowd parts, and I see a commanding presence coming toward us through the breach. It's the head of Addison's family. The undisputed godfather of his line. I take a small step back, knowing this doesn't concern me.

"Crys . . . is everything to your liking?" says Addison as he sees his boss. I can see Addison deflate, but he does his best to keep up the facade.

From a distance, Crys is small and unassuming, but up close he's larger than life. Then he becomes intimidating far too quickly. It can be disconcerting for the uninitiated.

"And what do we have here?" Crys says, zeroing in on the girl. He smiles darkly, a sparkling quality about him. Or maybe it's just the glitter on his fingernails. "Addison, aren't you going to introduce us?"

Addison leaks a quiet sigh. "Crys, this is . . . This is . . ."

"Catelyn," the girl reminds him.

"Right. Catelyn." Addison will forget her name as soon as

she's out of sight. So will I. A benefit of living in the moment.

"Charmed," Crys says. Then he takes the girl's slender hand, his fingers closing around hers like a flytrap on a mosquito. "Dance," Crys says, and pulls her out onto the floor. She doesn't resist—but even if she did, it wouldn't matter. Crys always gets his way.

Addison watches them go, pursing his lips, stifling all he wished he could say to his superior. "He could have given me a little more time with her."

"It's not his way," I remind him.

Beneath the flashing lights, Crys and the girl begin their dance. It will not end well for her. Because before the night ends, Crys will pull her into the VIP lounge. Intimate. Deadly. The one place where she'll get everything she's ever asked for and a whole lot she didn't. The VIP lounge is the place where the real business of the Party is done. The girl should consider herself lucky, for Crys is the shining jewel of his line. You can't trade up any higher than that.

Addison shakes his head. "I really don't like Crys's style. I wish I had *your* boss."

"No you don't."

"Are you kidding me? Hiro never leaves the back office. He lets you bring your plus-ones to him when you're good and ready."

I don't argue with him. No one can know what it's like to be on someone else's chain.

"Are you going back out to find someone fresh?" I ask him.

"Why? Just to have them stolen again?"

"Maybe the Party just isn't for you, Addison." And

although I mean it as a sincere suggestion from a friend, he takes it as a jab.

"Things are always changing, Roxy. Crys won't always be the head of my line. There's room for someone smart to move up the ladder."

I could almost laugh, but I spare him my derision. He gets enough of that from his upline. "You mean someone smart like you?"

"It's possible."

"But you've never even brought someone to the VIP lounge. You've never been with them to the end. That's not who you are."

He glowers at me. "Just because I haven't doesn't mean that I won't," he says, and strides off, indignant.

After he's gone, I step out onto the deck for some air. The club is high above everything, giving it a spectacular view of the world below—all those city lights. Any city—*every* city—and here, those lights are always twinkling, because it's always night. The date might change, but the scene is the same. The bar never closes. The DJ never stops spinning one song into another. This place exists at that golden moment when the bass drops.

I join Al, who's taking a moment too, standing at the railing, looking down on all there is. The turmoil and excitement. The winds that both lift and shred.

"So many parties down there," I say.

"There's only one Party," Al points out. "The rest are but a faint reflection of this one. People can feel it, reach for it, but can't find it. Not without an invitation."

And then I hear a voice to my left. "Do you ever wish we could do better?"

I turn to see a slight figure wearing a tie-dye dress and a vague expression. Around her neck hangs a heavy diamond necklace completely out of sync with her style. If you can even call it style.

"Do better?" says Al, amused by the thought. "How so, Lucy?"

"You know," Lucy says, as if it's obvious. "Find what we were *meant* to be. Transcend all of this."

"Right," says Al, still smirking. "Good luck with that."

"We are what we are, Lucy," I say, shutting her down. "That won't change, so you might as well embrace it."

"Well," she says, "it's nice to dream." Then she goes back inside, spreading her arms wide and careening side to side, like she suddenly decided she was an airplane.

"I never liked her," Al says. "There's something terribly off-putting about her eyes." Then he goes back in as well to greet newcomers and freshen everyone's drink.

I linger, looking out over the endless array of lights.

Do you ever wish we could do better?

The question rankles me. I *am* better. At the peak of my game. Loved by those who matter and hated by those who don't, because they wish they were me.

Addison might be bitter, but not me. It's time for me to get back out there and bag a new one. I'm ready for my next plus-one.

4

The Curvature of the Earth

ISAAC

"MIT, Stanford, Princeton, or Caltech," Isaac tells his academic adviser. "Those schools have the best aerospace engineering programs in the country."

Mr. Demko screws his lips into a wry and somewhat superior smile. "So you want to be an astronaut."

"No," Isaac says, trying to be a little less condescending than Demko, who has made the same wrong assumption everyone makes. "I want to design the ships that take astronauts out there. I'm going to be a propulsion engineer."

"Oh, I see." Demko immediately begins tapping on his computer, obviously trying to give himself a crash course on propulsion-engineering programs. Isaac doesn't dislike Mr. Demko, but it bothers Isaac that he's a part of his own counselor's learning curve.

"So . . . you want to eventually work for NASA?"

"Jet Propulsion Laboratories," Isaac tells him. "It's a part of NASA. They do all the heavy lifting, you know? Before the *actual* heavy lifting."

Isaac's friend Chet has an uncle who used to work for JPL, so he has at least one potential contact. Isaac has a little fantasy that he'd put in his time as a low-level engineer at JPL, and then he'd be headhunted by SpaceX or whatever other cutting-edge aerospace companies have exploded onto the scene by that time. He knows that looking beyond the horizon is the first step to getting there. You don't have to be an astronaut to see the curvature of the earth.

"There are plenty of schools with excellent propulsion-engineering programs," Mr. Demko says. Then, as he scans the list of schools he's pulled up, he grins. "MIT, Stanford, Princeton, and Caltech—just like you said. . . . But you may want to widen your field. I'm not saying you won't get in, but look at MIT's average admission GPA—it's 4.18."

"I know—and I have only a 3.77—but I can bring it as high as 3.93 by the time I have to apply—and I know for a fact that MIT accepted some freshmen into their engineering program last year with GPAs under 4.0."

Mr. Demko takes a moment to check his chart again. "Says here you play club soccer?"

"Yes . . ."

"Are you any good?"

Isaac shrugs, knowing where Demko is going with this. "Well, I'm team captain . . . but everyone thinks they're going to get a soccer scholarship, and nobody does."

That makes Demko actually snort. "You're realistic. That puts you at an advantage over most students I see." Then he leans close. "Here's the thing, though; a simple nod from a recruiter could be the thing that puts you over the top. Even without a scholarship, that nod could make a 3.77 worth a 4.0. . . ."

And although Isaac had considered that himself, having his counselor say it makes it feel all the more legit. Scholarships are pie in the sky . . . but nods? Those happen all the time.

Demko concludes the appointment by giving Isaac some info on financial aid and student loans, which Isaac will definitely need, considering his parents' perpetual financial woes.

When Isaac leaves, he tries not to grimace despite the pain in his ankle. He's made an oath to himself that he will not let this bring him down. He'll do whatever is necessary to keep his injury from affecting him. And now, more than ever, he can't let it impact him on the field.

He knows what to do about it—he had gone through the familiar drill last night. Three ibuprofen—which was one over the recommended dosage but less than full prescription strength. Then twenty minutes of ice as cold as he could stand, followed by heat, followed by more ice, for three cycles. Then in the morning he got up early to do it again. Yet even with all that, he was still tender and limping, so swollen that he had to leave his shoe untied all day.

"When I was your age, that was a thing," his father had told him. "No one tied their laces."

His soccer team has practice tonight from seven to nine. If he misses it, he won't play this weekend. That's not going to fly. So all day long, whenever he could, he'd been taking off his shoe and massaging his foot, finding just the spot to press where it hurt the most, then massaged that spot anyway, getting the blood flowing through it. Blood flow equals healing.

"Maybe you should kinda sorta . . . I don't know . . . see a doctor or something?" his kinda-sorta girlfriend Shelby suggests. Shelby is big on hedging. When she speaks, she never really commits to anything she says. It's one of many endearing things about her, and will probably make her a good politician someday, which is something she wants to be. Although she hates the word "politician." She prefers "public servant."

The problem with doctors, though, is they have a one-size-fits-all mentality when it comes to athletes. Regardless of how he got the injury, he'd get slapped with one of those Darth Vader boots for two months, and there goes his position on the team, along with any hopes of being noticed by a scout. That hurts more than his throbbing ankle.

"How'd it happen?" Shelby asks.

"My sister's boyfriend," Isaac tells her. "It's okay—I gave as good as I got." Except that Craig isn't currently limping around his biohazard home. Isaac can imagine him, his nose already healing, as he gets high and plays video games on his waterbed. Ivy's always complaining about his douchey waterbed. It bothers Isaac that Ivy might have spent time in it.

"People are saying that Ivy might possibly get sent to the alternative school, maybe," Shelby says.

Isaac thinks of his sister, and for a moment his ankle seems to hurt even more. He knows it's just in his head. One kind of pain begets another. He wishes there were something he could do for her, but Ivy just resents him when he gets between her and her shitty decisions. Not that every decision Isaac makes is stellar—but he does tend to learn from them. Unfortunately, Isaac suspects that his sister only knows how to learn things the hard way.

IVY

Ivy spends lunch hour with her friends. Though she can hardly call them "friends." All they ever do is talk about themselves. Or what party they're throwing. Or who did a keg stand and then passed out, and how all these things manifested on social media.

"You'll never believe who liked my post," TJ says, showing the pic with his teeth photoshopped refrigerator-white.

"Rembrandt?" Ivy says deadpan.

"Is that an influencer?" Tess asks.

"No, it's toothpaste," Ivy responds with scorching sarcasm.

No one laughs, but that leads Tess to open the widely controversial debate on whether swallowing toothpaste leads to brain damage. Tess and TJ are a couple. They are clearly soul mates.

It's hard to have true friends when no one gets your humor. So Ivy returns to the lunch she brought from home because school food sucked ever since a state mandate removed all flavor to make it less unhealthy. Not healthy, just less unhealthy. But Ivy doesn't complain, because cafeteria food is the ultimate in low-hanging fruit as far as complaints go. As a senior, she can always go off campus for lunch, but really, it's not worth the effort.

She glances around at the various groups—which, unlike TV high schools, are less about cliques than they are about lifeboats. Those who can't find one don't necessarily get picked on, but they are more likely to die of neglect in frigid water.

The defining factors are never as simple and clear-cut as

"popular kids" or "bandos" or "honors geeks"—because the musical screeches of the band kids have given way to observable talent, and popularity starts to bloom for the honors kids as it dawns on everyone else that smart is good and the future actually exists.

Isaac sits with his own group across the cafeteria. They are from all walks of life, with nothing definable holding them together, and yet they are fast friends. Isaac says something. The others laugh. It's the way friends should be.

Meanwhile, Ivy's friends are playing an uninspired Would You Rather game.

"Straight or curly fries?"

"Beer or vodka?"

"Ketchup or ranch?"

Ignore. Ignore. Ignore. Insipid conversation is the bane of Ivy's existence. Well, that, and Shelby Morris—Isaac's stuck-up girlfriend. She lives in her own cloud of moral superiority, and Ivy's unsure how the people around her don't choke on it. Anyone who takes a luxury family vacation to Africa, snaps a staged photo with a malnourished elephant, and makes that their profile pic for two years can't be trusted. Ivy isn't sure what Isaac sees in her. Just one of many things they don't see eye to eye on. Even though there's a lot of sibling love between them, Isaac and Ivy don't connect on many levels. Ivy connects more with people like Craig. Happy, carefree losers. She wonders if that makes her a loser too.

Meanwhile, her friends drone on with their comparisons. . . .

"Filter or no filter?"

"Dogs or cats?"

"Biggie or Tupac?"

That's when Ivy stands, finally having had enough.

"Where are you going?" Tess asks.

"Mars, or the moon," Ivy responds, grabbing her lunch. As far as her friends are concerned, where she's actually going might as well be off-planet. It's certainly not a part of their universe.

Ivy's head has been full of a thousand things lately. She promised her parents she'd get *help*. Every time she goes through this, it's the same story, since Ivy was a child—first it was play therapy, then talk therapy, then behavior modification therapy, and of course medication, which she was never consistent with.

ADHD. That's her affliction—without the H part, but ADD is so last century. Ivy scoffs at the idea of her having a deficit of attention; she focuses just fine on her own when she wants to. Her grades are low because she chooses not to focus. Or at least she tells herself that.

Ivy steps on a public bus. "Does this go downtown?" she asks.

"Unless you plan to hijack it," the bus driver responds jovially.

"No such plans." Ivy flashes her bus pass. "But the day is still young."

On school-cutting excursions, Ivy will usually borrow Isaac's car, but this time it just felt wrong asking him for his wheels after what happened the other night. She shouldn't always be putting him in that position.

Ivy sits, her earbuds blasting her favorite band, Wutever Werx—the perfect soundtrack for bailing from school. Finally, the bus reaches the second to last stop. Her favorite place in the world.

The City Art Museum.

Art was always Ivy's *thing*. It's something that comforts her. The one thing she's actually good at. She used to be in art classes when high school started, but admittance to higher-level classes was limited to those who sucked up to the art teachers. Teachers don't really like Ivy. She knows it's not personal, although sometimes it feels like it is. She is a *type* to them. The type that makes their lives difficult in a stunning variety of ways. It's okay. Ivy doesn't care for them, either. Maybe she'd like her teachers if she went to a different school. An art school or something. But who does she think she's kidding? Her parents would never pay for that. The chance of a return on their investment is simply too low.

The fact is, she's close to flunking out of her senior year. It would mean repeating this semester in the fall, or just accepting the fact that she's not going to finish high school. She already knows that if she has to repeat in the fall, it won't be here. The district will send her to the alternative school.

"There's no shame in it," Mr. Demko had told her. "You just need a different kind of educational experience." Such bullshit.

The bus arrives at the museum. Ivy knows there's a traveling Van Gogh exhibition this month. He's one of her favorites. The troubles he had seemed insurmountable, and yet he succeeded not because of them but in spite of them. All his great work was done when he was well, not when he was in the depths of madness. And often utilizing rich shades of blue. It was why Ivy started dying her hair "VooDoo Blue." Most people think she did it in an act of teenage rebellion, but it was the opposite. It was a way for her to connect with something she cared about. It brought her closer to the person she really was.

Ivy grips her brown-bag lunch and sits on a bench in a gallery of works so vivid, she can almost feel the wild brush-strokes in her brain. Chaos guided into form and structure. But her favorite is one that almost disappears beneath the vibrant assault of the others. *Vase with Carnations.* Famous for being *un*famous. Ivy knows all about it, because from the moment she heard about it, it fascinated her. The painting was from what you might call Van Gogh's "meh" period. Just a pedestrian study of light and color. It was hidden in storage for decades, after a Jewish family sold it to escape Nazi Germany. Then, years later, it resurfaced in Hollywood, sitting behind a movie screen in a film mogul's living room before disappearing into museum storage for years. Unloved. Disregarded. That is until someone somewhere decided those carnations deserved some light. Ivy can relate.

She takes a deep breath and lets Van Gogh's inspiration—as well as those moments when he lacked inspiration—calm her troubled thoughts. If this is what it takes to wrangle her brain, then Ivy will have to make do. But at some point she'll have to start painting the broad strokes of her own life.

There are only three choices: alternative school, drop out, or kick her ass into gear and make a big change. And if she doesn't choose option three now, only the first two will remain. But Ivy knows, as much as she hates to admit it, that she can't make that change without a little help.

I'll go see Torres and get the right meds, she tells herself as she bites into her sandwich, staring across at flowers that suffered indignation but never wilted. *Ritalin, Adderall, whatever he prescribes. I'll take it, I'll be consistent, and I'll make my life work.*

Ivy finishes her lunch like this, alone—no noise, no distractions—just her and Van Gogh. It reminds her of simpler times, when she was a little girl on a field trip and brown-bag lunches always tasted a little better.

5

The Prince of Attention

ADDISON

I sit in the back row of a piano recital with my older sister, Rita. She feverishly knits a scarf that already wraps twice around the world.

Onstage, a fifteen-year-old boy plays Rachmaninoff's Piano Concerto #3—a piece that stymies the most accomplished pianists. I want to appreciate the music, but I can't. How ironic that the so-called prince of attention can't focus.

"You think too much, Addison," Rita tells me in that judgmental way she has. "Stop thinking and just *do*." Even though no one can hear us, Rita whispers, because it is, after all, a recital.

Well, she can spend her life knitting row after row and organizing closets to her heart's content. That's not who I want to be.

"I'm tired of doing for others," I tell her. "Our upline does whatever they want, and they get away with it. I'm tired of playing by the rules . . . of being ordinary."

I think about Crys, who can have whoever he wants, whenever he wants—or even worse, the twins, Dusty and Charlie, in their white silk suits and flashy jewelry, lounging in a private booth like they own the world, making the party come to them. But most of all I think about Roxy—who thinks she's so much better than me now. That never stops chafing.

"Hedonism is not to be envied," Rita says in her most holier-than-thou voice. "Crys, the Coke brothers, and all our other wayward cousins rot everything they touch, leaving behind a trail of misery—"

"That they never see," I point out, "because they're happy to never look back."

"But we're better than that. We have the power to change worlds; all they have is the power to destroy them. We are the gardeners, Addison."

"Yes, but they gorge themselves on what we grow."

Rita just shrugs. "What they do is not our problem." Then she adds yet another row to her scarf, which stays a constant pale yellow, never once having turned green with envy.

Onstage, the boy plays flawlessly. Most don't realize what a feat this is, but I do. Years ago, the boy's parents would have scoffed at the idea of him being onstage at all. But I came quietly into his life and calmed him. Centered him. Helped him feel at peace within his own skin. And then he discovered the piano.

"You're looking at it all wrong, Addi," Rita says. "Look what you've done here. There's much to be proud of."

"The applause will be for him, not me."

Rita turns to me, scowling. How I hate her scowl. "You've become quite the bitter pill, haven't you? Too vain for your own good. I think you've been spending too much time with Roxy—she's a bad influence on you."

That makes me laugh. "You're just jealous because I have

friends in high places." Then I add, intentionally blithe, "I even go up to the Party sometimes."

I thought she might react to that, but Rita is neither scandalized nor impressed. "I've been," she says. "It's not my cup of tea. . . . Is it really yours, Addison?" she asks. "Do you enjoy it, or do you just pretend to?"

The question burns me more than it should. Because part of me knows the answer to that question.

"Why are you even here?" I put to her. "The boy onstage is *my* ward, not yours."

Rita puts down her knitting. "You see the little girl right in front of us? She has trouble sitting still. I was recently brought on to help."

How typical to throw Rita at such a minor concern. "Just because she can't sit still doesn't mean she needs *you*."

Rita sighs. "It's not our job to make that decision, merely to provide service for our wards once the decision is made."

"Our *wards*," I scoff. "Even our lingo betrays our banality."

"Not banality, but responsibility," Rita says. "It reminds us that we are here to provide service and care. Those others at the Party? They see people as targets to acquire and dominate. Their so-called *marks*." Then she gestures to the stage. "Is that what you want for this young man you've taken such great pains to help?"

"Of course not," I tell her. But I also know that there are others who are older—more streetwise and jaded—who know full well the difference between use and abuse. I would have no problem seeing them as marks and targeting them with the full force of my laser-like focus.

The girl in front of us—Rita's ward—begins to squirm in her seat, and Rita reaches out, draping part of her scarf over the girl's shoulders.

"That's enough," Rita says, both gentle and firm. The girl stiffens. Then relaxes, and Rita returns to her knitting, satisfied. "You see? All better now."

I could go on, but why bother? Talking to Rita is like talking to an assembly-line robot. She does only one thing, but she does it very well.

So is that all I am too? Just another tool above a conveyor belt, stamping out identical human molds?

Onstage, the piece concludes, and the boy with whom I worked so hard to reach this moment stands to take his bow amid thundering applause. And although I truly do want to beam with pride, I choose to deny my own nature. Today I refuse to feel anything but slighted.

6

Exactly How to **Fix** It

ISAAC

Isaac chooses to live in defiance of his sprained ankle rather than let it derail his life. He's taught himself how to drive left-footed, and when it's time for practice that night, he slaps on a neoprene brace that's easily hidden beneath his sock, gears up for soccer, and heads for the field.

But tonight he's running even slower than the backup squad. Truth is, the ankle brace doesn't help at all, and it isn't long before the coach takes note and sidelines him. In fact, he tells Isaac to sit out a few days so he can recover, and when Isaac protests, the coach says he'll let him play in the game if he's "up to snuff," whatever that means.

And so, as much as he doesn't want to, Isaac stops by the neighborhood walk-in clinic on the way home. He doesn't tell his parents—they won't know until they get the report from the insurance, and by then it will be a moot point.

He arrives just before closing, and even with only one patient ahead of him, the wait feels like it takes forever. When he's taken back, he can tell that both the nurse who checks his vitals and the doctor who examines him have already mentally checked out for the day. The doc asks the standard questions, then takes a look at Isaac's ankle. Isaac tries not to grimace as he presses the sore spots.

"It's gone a bit yellow," the doctor notes. "You've had this for a while?"

"Just a few days," Isaac tells him.

"We should get you x-rayed, but our tech is gone for the day. Come back tomorrow and we'll let you skip the line."

"Is that it?" Isaac asks. "Come back tomorrow?"

The doctor offers Isaac his best professional shrug. "No magic wands here, I'm afraid. We'll see you tomorrow for that X-ray."

If there's an upside to being benched from practice, it's that he can spend a little more time with his friends.

After school the next day, and into the evening, they all hang out in his friend Ricky's garage, which has been converted into a "fun room." One of the few places that actually deserves the title. There's a pool table, a soda fountain, and even a couple of old-school pinball machines. Ricky's uncle owns a junkyard, so every month or so there's a new eccentric addition, making the garage the ultimate balm for boredom. This month's installment is a hundred-pound big screen from the turn of the century and a game console that needs a special adapter because the ports it uses no longer exist.

"That old Nintendo is more valuable now than when it was made," Ricky tells them. "And the games are worth even more than the machines."

Chet, Shelby, Rachel, and Ricky sit on the couch and clack away on the controllers playing Super Smash Bros. with the intensity of neurosurgeons. But Isaac has been tasked with removing malware from Chet's computer, since he's the closest thing to a computer guy they have.

"Isaac, aren't you going to play?" Ricky asks.

"I will as soon as Chet stops crashing his computer with porn."

Rachel guffaws and kicks Chet in the head—in the game. Chet, in turn, playfully punches Isaac's arm—in real life.

"Isaac isn't playing because he's too afraid of losing to me," Shelby taunts from a beanbag. Which isn't entirely untrue—Shelby's always been the goddess of games—though Isaac has already accepted that he'll never beat her unless she lets him. Which she would never do.

"You're an inspiration for the rest of womankind," Rachel lauds her. "And a total pain in the ass. Now die!" She mashes buttons hard enough to break the cheap plastic controller.

Isaac takes a moment to watch his friends. A teacher once told them they looked like the cover of a health textbook. Different ethnic backgrounds, different interests, different everything shoved together in a single dubious tableau. But the group did have one thing in common: Isaac. Each one of them had entered his life at a different stage. He knew Shelby from elementary school, Ricky from soccer, Chet from camp, and Rachel from Sunday school. They stuck together, Isaac being the bonding glue—and when their middle schools all fed into the same high school, they were set from day one. A health textbook case of an organic friendship.

Chet's laptop runs out of power, and Isaac sighs. "Where's your charger?"

Chet spares a quick point between the mashing of buttons.

Isaac stands from the couch to retrieve it, momentarily forgetting about his ankle. The pain makes him flinch, he over-corrects, and he wipes out across the coffee table—an embarrassing fail that knocks over some drinks and sends a metal bowl of popcorn clanging to the ground. "Oww! Damn it!"

The spilling drinks and flying popcorn make the whole thing look much worse than it is—especially when Isaac can't get up right away, because it would mean putting his full weight on that ankle. Chet helps him back onto the couch, while Rachel triages the mess. "Did you resprain it?" Chet asks. "Let me see."

"Stop. I'm fine."

"I got you, bro." Then he forcefully elevates Isaac's leg onto the coffee table, which just makes it hurt even more. Chet works weekends as a pool monitor, though he tells everyone he's a lifeguard, and has been known to forcibly administer first aid. "Why isn't this wrapped? Don't you have an ACE bandage?"

"It's been in a brace all day—I've been letting it breathe."

"You've sprained it again. Look at how swollen it is."

This is infuriating. "It was like that before."

"Ginger and turmeric naturally relieve inflammation," Rachel points out.

Ricky opens a cupboard and tosses Chet a first aid kit, knowing he'll ask for one. "Keep still!" Chet orders.

"No, he should move it around to get blood flowing," Rachel says, then heads into the house to search for a natural cure.

Meanwhile, Shelby takes advantage of the opportunity to kill everyone else's characters. Finally, at the "game over" screen, Shelby looks in Isaac's direction. "Just put ice on it," she says.

"Way ahead of you," Chet responds, giving her a thumbs-up, as if her two cents adds up to something bankable.

"Guys, I know what I'm supposed to do for this," Isaac protests. "I've been doing it for days."

"Just shut up and let a professional handle this." Chet activates a chemical ice pack and thrusts it against Isaac's foot, but it must be too old, because it stays room temperature. Then Rachel returns, announcing that there will be neither tea nor a poultice, because there's absolutely nothing natural in Ricky's house. With this whole humanitarian mission going south, Ricky offers Isaac an escape. "So before they amputate your foot, you want me to take a look at that car of yours?"

Isaac welcomes the chance to get out. So while Shelby sets up the next game, and Chet and Rachel try to untangle their controllers, Ricky helps Isaac up from the couch, and they head outside, leaving the others to their Falcon Punches and Thunder Attacks.

Isaac's convertible is in decent shape for a twelve-year-old car. Its roof has duct-tape patches, and, like Isaac's grandmother, often needs help getting up or down, but the car runs. That's thanks to Ricky, who helped him turn it from scrap metal to freeway safe. While Isaac excels in the theoretical, Ricky excels in physical application, so their skill sets always meshed, making them a deadly duo. Ever since they were kids, the two of them have been taking things apart and putting them back together again—mainly at the expense of Ricky's mom. It's true her hair dryer may blow circuit breakers, but at least it's souped-up to the point of maximum efficiency. And although her coffee maker spontaneously combusted one morning, it did make the world's strongest drip coffee before its blaze of glory. It was always Ricky's thing to make the best of the worst—and that's exactly what he did for Isaac when he rolled up in his hunk of junk earlier this year.

"Old Chryslers actually have Mercedes engines, because they used to be owned by the same company." It was the line Ricky used to convince him to buy the thing in the first place. Now, with Ricky's help, Isaac's car has the low-profile tires of a Porsche and the exhaust of a Mustang. And as much crap as they talk about the car, Isaac and Ricky have actually come to love the thing. It's their final project together before their lives part ways.

Ricky slaps the hood of the car like it's an old friend. "What's wrong this time?"

"Clunky acceleration. Sometimes it struggles to start."

He pops the hood, roves around inside, and does a quick diagnosis. "Just as I thought—spark plugs are shot."

Ricky pulls out a toolbox from his Jeep and gets to work, grabbing the right tools without even looking in the box as he does it.

"How do you make that look so easy?" Isaac asks.

"Bro, you're the one who reverse-engineered that lawn mower, remember? And figured out how to make it fly."

"Yeah, but you're the one who put the thing together."

Their flying lawn mower had become not just a neighborhood

story, but an internet meme. It was mere luck that it didn't kill someone when it came down.

They both grin over the memory; then Ricky returns his attention to the car. "It might look complicated, but if you know how it all works, you know exactly how to fix it."

It's a statement so simple, yet at the same time profound, and it sticks with Isaac. "You know, you could be an engineer if you set your mind to it."

That makes Ricky chuckle. "Yeah, well, setting my mind to school has never been my strong suit. But tell you what— when all your crazy-ass designs break down, I'll be around to fix them."

Ricky finally finishes up, slams the hood, and smiles proudly. "See, it's like your foot; all it needs is a little TLC."

But Isaac doubts there's a tool Ricky can blindly reach for that will tune up his ankle.

Isaac's already a light sleeper, but now every time he shifts under the covers, the pain wakes him up. In the morning he ups his ibuprofen from three to four.

It's all he can do to keep his eyes open in class that day, and he heads straight home when school is over. The bathroom mirror reveals bags under his eyes. He decides it must just be his imagination, or the bathroom light, but then his grand-mother ambles past with her cane, takes a good look at him, and unleashes a drive-by truth bomb.

"If you're wondering how you look, the answer is *terrible*," she says. Grandma comes from a generation when life was too short for sensitivity. At the end of the day, everyone always appreciates Grandma's honesty. She cares enough to give you the truth, even if it's straight up with a twist.

She smiles warmly, which tempers her words, then points to her cheek, demanding a kiss, to which Isaac obliges. "I only say that because I know how handsome you are."

"I've been having trouble sleeping," he tells her.

"Don't I know it! It's like a bed of nails when you're in pain." She glances down at his foot. A bit of bruising is visible above his ankle socks.

"I'll get you set up with my orthopedic guy. He's the best. Fix that ankle right up."

"It's okay, really," Isaac says.

Grandma's eyes wrinkle, and she chuckles. "Your grandfather, your father, and now you. All the men in this family hate doctors." Then she reaches into the bathroom medicine cabinet and fishes around, eventually producing an orange prescription pill container. "The doctor gave me these when I busted my hip. Heavy-duty." She places a pill in Isaac's palm. "You could do without the bed of nails for one night." Her eyes twinkle the way grandmas' eyes sometimes do. "What is it they say? No pain, no gain? That's horse shit. Pain is overrated."

Isaac laughs, and Grandma heads down the hall toward her room. Once she's gone, Isaac looks down at the stubby oblong pill; it's smooth and ivory white. Almost weightless in his palm. He pops it into his mouth, then turns on the bathroom faucet, leans over the sink, and scoops some water to his mouth to chase the pill down. He feels it for a moment in his esophagus before it silently slides to his stomach and begins to dissolve.

ROXY

I know the moment it happens—the sensation is instantaneous. Subtle at first, but building. It's an overwhelming feeling of belonging—a connection to something greater than myself. It's what I live for. It's why I exist.

That's what Hiro tells me.

"You're here to envelop them, Roxy. To quell them. And then to bring them to me."

I'm at the Party—in the Jacuzzi. It's an infinity tub that feels so vast, it seems to drop off not just the horizon, but the edge of the entire universe. I've been chatting with Mary Jane, who sits nearby, not daring to ruin her business suit by actually getting in the water. I swear, Mary Jane's gotten so boring since she's gone legit.

Molly's in the tub, wet again, but this time by choice. She holds her plus-one—a handsome frat boy—completely under her spell, drowning in ecstasy. Their bodies seem to melt together. I can't hear her whispers, but I know what she's telling him.

You always were, and forever will be, the only one for me.

But it isn't true. It never is.

The irresistible pull of a new mark summons me out of the hot tub, and everyone watches me as I get out—the way water droplets form on my perfect contours. Their envy is a compliment so rich and aromatic, I can wear it like a fine perfume.

I grab a towel and stand at the edge of our domain, gazing across the sparkling city below and wondering who I will be brought to this time.

"You look like you're fishing," says Addison, coming up behind me. As always, his hair is perfect, and his complexion is radiant. We all exist at our physical peaks. But he also looks like he's trying too hard.

"Are you spying on me?" I tease.

"I'm just a skilled multitasker."

Back in the Jacuzzi, Molly gently cajoles the frat boy. "I know a better spa," she tells him, this time in a stage whisper we can all hear. "The water's so much hotter." Then she leads him out, and he follows her like a woozy puppy across the deck and through the red leather doors of the VIP lounge. The final destination for all our honored guests.

"Molly was fast tonight," I note, impressed.

"Everyone knows she doesn't work alone," Addison replies, but it's just sour grapes. "I can do what she does. I could do what *all* of you do."

Here we go again. Addison blustering. All talk with no real action. "Then do it!" I tell him. "See someone all the way through to the end. Be their one and only."

Addison shifts uncomfortably. "You don't think I can?" he asks.

But we both know the answer to that question. Addison and I might have come up together, but we're made of different stuff. Different ingredients entirely. He might have been a golden child when we were younger—a fix-all that was supposed to change the world—but times have changed. Everything's faster, more cutthroat. It's a world I'm perfectly suited for—but the more famous I grow, the more Addison covets all of the oxygen in the room. Oxygen he'll never be able to ignite.

So, do I think he has what it takes to see someone through to the bitter end? You tell me.

"Addison, don't ask questions you don't want the answers to," I say. Then I saunter off, pulled by the call of my next mark. Let Addison chew on that for a while. With any luck, he'll finally admit to himself that, no matter how well he's dressed, he just doesn't have what it takes to bring someone to the VIP lounge. Maybe then he'll be content with his place in the world.

I slide through all the excess until I reach the gilded elevator. It's Gothic by nature—elegant and eternal with friezes that depict our ancestors. We venerate them even though they're just less-refined versions of ourselves.

The elevator doors open, and I step inside. There are only two buttons. One to go up to the Party and one to go down. No emergency button. No help or rescue.

I don't need to press a button for the elevator to take me to where I need to go. The buttons are for the mortals below. They are the ones subject to their own decisions. Their own activations.

The doors close, and the elevator descends, building velocity until I'm in free fall.

7

No Chance Against **th**e **Under**tow

ISAAC

Isaac knows that pain is there for a reason. He learned it in biology: his body has flushed white blood cells to his ankle, which creates pressure, which creates pain, which is the body's way of preventing further injury. Sometimes painkillers can make things worse by defeating the body's warning—but sometimes pain is a pointless alarm that won't stop blaring. Isaac is careful not to put too much weight on his ankle once the medication takes effect. He won't be fooled into thinking it's doing anything more than masking the injury.

He doesn't mention the pill to his parents. What would be the point? And Grandma was right—he does sleep well that night. Of course, he's a little cranky and listless in the morning, but it's a small price to pay for a good night's sleep.

"So we were all thinking about maybe going down to the pier tonight, if the weather holds out," Shelby tells him at lunch. The pier is an old-school amusement area, so generic it's actually called The Pier™. It seemed magical when they were younger, but now it's just kitsch enough to still be fun once in a while.

Isaac thinks of his ankle but doesn't say anything about it. "Sounds like a plan," he tells her.

His ankle begins aching right at the end of the school day, or maybe it was all along, and class acted as a distraction. As much as he hates to admit it, he's in no condition to play soccer this weekend. It bothers him no end that his whole future could hinge on whether or not he plays in that game.

When he gets home, Isaac goes to the fridge for some leftovers, thinking he's hungry, but he's not hungry enough for anything he finds in there. The oven's on, and he takes a peek inside to see a casserole of something cheesy that Grandma is baking. He grabs a bottle of water, thinking he's thirsty, but only takes a few sips because there's no thirst to quench.

Grandma's in the downstairs bathroom, probably taking one of her beauty soaks while her casserole bakes. He imagines the bubbles, candles, and cucumber face mask as she listens to music from the days when life was a rosy-cheeked Coca-Cola ad and cigarettes were doctor recommended. She's not supposed to do things like that alone. Too many slippery surfaces in the bathroom, but "I'm not an invalid" has been her battle cry since she moved in after that first fall.

So Isaac waits. And thinks. His parents, who own their own business, usually don't get home until seven or so. They drive themselves harder than their employees.

Grandma vacates the bathroom wearing a flamingo-pink robe and her hair wrapped in a towel. The smell of lavender and some other herbs that Rachel would know blend with the savory smell of whatever's in the oven.

"Isaac! Perfect timing!" she says. "You can help me take my baked ziti out of the oven. It should be just about done, and that damn oven rack is too low for me."

"Sure thing, Grandma."

Isaac grabs a pair of oven mitts and pulls it out while Grandma directs like it's a precision engineering project. "Careful now. Don't burn yourself."

"I got this, Grandma."

He sets it down on a trivet to cool. "Can I sneak some before dinner?" he asks, hoping that a taste will wake up his appetite.

"It's not for us," she tells him. "I made it for Mr. Burkett across the street. Word is he got a grim diagnosis, and I want to do something . . . neighborly."

"Isn't he a minister or something? His whole church is probably bringing him food."

Grandma turns her nose up. "Nothing his church ladies cook will hold a candle to my baked ziti."

Isaac offers to carry it over for her, but she refuses.

"He doesn't need two people limping to his front door." Then she ambles off toward her bedroom.

There had been plenty of opportunities during their casserole operation to ask about her orthopedist, but he hadn't. Instead, he waits until she's in her room with the door closed. Then he goes into the bathroom and opens the medicine chest.

He stands there for the longest time. It's one thing to be offered a pill and another to take one without asking. He closes the medicine cabinet and comes up with a better, if less convenient, idea.

. . .

The walk-in clinic is more crowded than when he was here the first time. Kids with croupy coughs, a weary-eyed workman holding a hand in need of stitches, and a few people whose issues are not quite so obvious. Isaac tells the desk clerk that he was given a free pass to skip the line, and she clearly thinks he's lying, because she reads him the riot act.

"I'm sorry, but it's first come, first serve. Nobody skips the line. You can have a seat."

And although Isaac despises those *I-want-to-talk-to-your-supervisor* kind of people, he invokes the name of the doctor, which he fortunately remembers.

"Ask Dr. Cardenas."

She heaves a heavy sigh. Isaac isn't sure whether it's her exasperation with him or with the good doctor for fouling the waiting-room dynamic—but two minutes later Isaac is called back for his X-ray.

The news from the X-ray isn't good, but it isn't terrible either. A simple sprain. Nothing torn, nothing broken.

"I'll give you a referral for an orthopedist," Dr. Cardenas says, which doesn't solve anything.

"How about something for the pain?" Isaac asks. "I mean, my grandma gave me something last night, and I was able to sleep, so I figured . . ." He lets the thought trail off, hoping the doctor will finish it. He doesn't.

"First of all," says Cardenas, "she shouldn't be doing that. And second, you're a minor; I can treat you, but I can't give you a prescription without parental consent."

"So it's 'come back tomorrow' again?"

The doctor considers it, then says, "I'll be back in a minute with that referral."

Well, figures Isaac, it was worth a shot.

But then, when the doctor comes back, he has more than just a referral for Isaac. He has sample packets. Six of them, each with a single pill.

Isaac leaves with the sample packets, and although he doesn't take a pill then, later, when he's ready to head out to meet Shelby and his friends at the pier, he makes sure to bring one with him, just in case his ankle threatens to ruin everyone's evening. He can just imagine Chet trying to elevate his foot again and a crowd gathering like they do around buskers. Not gonna happen. As far as Isaac is concerned, that pill is an insurance policy for the evening.

Although it's barely the earliest days of spring, the weather's been unseasonably warm, so the pier is brimming with life by the time Isaac arrives. A family stabs at an enormous funnel cake. Giant stuffed animals are won for girlfriends as demonstrations of nontoxic masculinity. There are flashing lights everywhere, and all happening at that magical moment where the brilliance of the Ferris wheel blends with the afterglow of the setting sun.

Isaac spots Shelby down the pier, playing a ring toss game with the others.

"Hey, you!" Shelby says, surprised to see him. "I thought you weren't going to come," even though Isaac clearly remembered telling her that he was.

"Look who's here!" Ricky says. "You okay? You're still limping."

"Just a little."

"Did you have to remind him?" Rachel scolds.

"Lucky you caught us," Chet says. "This place is a zoo—we were about to head down to the beach." And he takes off his shirt, because Chet is always finding a reason to take off his shirt. "Let's go for a swim, yeah?"

Isaac looks off to the water. It's rough today, and the clouds that have held off all day are gathering on the horizon. "You sure that's a good idea? It looks like a storm's coming in," Isaac points out. "Plus, the water'll be freezing."

"That's half the fun," says Chet, and leads the way down to the beach.

Isaac tries to keep up, but he falls behind. Shelby notices and hangs back to walk with him.

"You don't look so great," she says.

"Long day," he tells her. "I'll go down with you guys, but I think I'll pass on swimming."

Isaac hobbles across the beach and takes a seat on a berm marking high tide. For a moment he thinks Shelby might sit down with him, but then she pulls off her clothes, revealing a bathing suit underneath. Swimming was already in the plan, but Isaac never got the memo.

She glances to Ricky, Chet, and Rachel, who are already surveying the pounding surf, building up fortitude.

"It does look kind of rough," Shelby says.

Isaac smirks. "Why worry when there's a pool monitor to save you?"

"Ha-ha," she says, then tosses Isaac her clothes and hurries off after the others.

Now Isaac is alone. Only in the absence of others does he realize that the hungry/not hungry sensation he's been feeling has never once left him. If anything, it's only intensifying.

He doesn't consciously notice the moment he decided to reach into his shirt pocket and pull out the little sample packet. But when he sees it in his hand, he bends the corner, rips it open, and spills the pill into his palm. It's smooth and ivory white. It seems to stare back at him, glimmering in a stray ray of light from the pier.

The last thing he wants to be is the buzzkill that ruins everyone's fun.

So Isaac lifts his hand to his mouth and tosses the pill back, swallowing it dry.

ROXY

I love beaches! The way they make people lose their inhibitions. How they make even the worst ideas feel right. The expression "It seemed like a good idea at the time" must have been coined at the beach.

They have a reputation for being romantic. A moonlit walk, hand in hand. The feel of the sand between your toes and the sound of the gentle surf whispering that it's all just for you.

But beaches can be unrelentingly lonely too. That same white strand can be soulless and isolating. That same surf can roar rather than whisper, resonating in the neediest places of your soul. A reminder of how small you are compared to the eternal forces of nature. Compared to forces like me. Perhaps not natural, but a force to be reckoned with nonetheless.

Isaac is a grain of sand on an endless beach. Alone, even among those he calls his friends. This is how I know he's ready even before he does. He sits there at high tide, just above a murrain of dying seaweed, and he peers out at the others, wishing he felt like joining them. He says it's just his ankle, but it's more than that.

That melancholy is me. Or the lack of me. He might sit at high tide, but he's at his own low tide now. He feels a vague longing. Not a craving. Not yet. Cravings must be cultivated. Carefully tended until their roots are strong and can strangle out everything else around them. But he will get there. A grain of sand stands no chance against the undertow.

I approach casually. Unrushed. Silent, like the lightning on the horizon, too far away for the thunder to be heard over the surf.

"The water must be cold," I say, just to pull his attention from his friends in the waves. "It'll be at least a month until it's really swimmable."

"Yeah, no way they'll stay in long," he says. "It's more like a dare."

"So how come you didn't take the dare too?"

He shrugs. "I don't know. Maybe getting cold and wet isn't my idea of fun."

"So what is?"

He takes a moment before answering. His shoulders slump just a bit. A gust comes off the water, and he pulls his knees up to his chest. "I used to know," he says. "Now I'm not so sure."

I'm sitting with him now. He was too deep in his thoughts

to notice how quickly I got close to him. Without even realizing it, he begins to share with me all the things on his mind,
from his frustrations for not getting his time on the soccer
field, to his parents' financial woes, to his sister's issues—and all
wrapped up in the fragile, fraying bow of his own future: his
precarious college dreams, and beyond. He takes on the weight
of the world; it's no wonder he sprained his ankle.

More silent flashes illuminate the shapes of storm clouds
on the horizon. Brief strobes of light doing their damage far, far
away. Without thunder, lightning can trick you into thinking
it's not as dangerous as it really is.

The girl he came with is now thigh-deep in the water,
arms gingerly extended, as if it will help her levitate above the
wave breaking at her waist. She curses, and another boy beside
her laughs and splashes her. She splashes him back, and now
they're both laughing.

Isaac keeps a poker face as he watches. His knees are still
pulled to his chest. Protective position. I extend my legs out,
pushing away the seaweed. A moment and he relaxes enough to
do the same. I'm close to him now. Nearly touching, although
he doesn't realize it.

"They're sure having fun in spite of the cold," I point out.
"Still, your girlfriend should have stayed out here with you—or
at least offered."

Isaac sighs. "Shelby does her own thing."

"I can see that." And then, for good measure, I add, "She
hasn't even looked back at you once."

"So? She doesn't want to turn her back on the waves—
they might catch her off guard."

But she does turn so that a wave hits her back instead of hitting her full-on. Even so, she doesn't seek out Isaac on the shore.

"Seems to me you should be giving your attention to someone who'll give it back," I tell him.

And finally he looks at me. I wait for the connection. Delicate. Careful. Like two spacecraft docking. Perhaps the ones that Isaac hopes to design someday.

He smiles, and there it is. I've got him.

"I'm Roxy," I say, and gently place my hand in his.

"Isaac," he tells me, although he doesn't really have to.

He takes a deep breath. Not shuddering, but easy. Soon he'll feel my comfort. The easing of his pain. The lifting of his heavy, irritable mood. It will be a long time before he pieces together that his moodiness is because of me, just as his relief will be.

Poor Isaac. You need someone to take away the pain. Not just the hurt in your ankle, but the awful ache that corkscrews down and down to that place you can't seem to reach. I can reach it, though. It's what I do. I'll fill that space so completely that it will stretch like your stomach on Thanksgiving. Making it all the more empty when I'm gone.

"I've seen you play soccer," I casually mention. "You're good."

He gives a bitter laugh at that. "I'm only as good as my ankle—and right now that's no good at all."

"That's too bad," I say. "But professionals find ways to play injured, don't they?"

Out in the water, a wave hits his friends a little too hard, and that tips the scale between good fun and get the hell out. They all find their footing and push against the undertow, scrambling to get to shore.

I stand up with him. "You're easy to talk to, Isaac. I hope we see each other again."

I back out of the moonlight into the shadow of a cloud, and he turns his attention to his friends, slipping out of the diminished reality my presence had put him in. His friends stampede toward him, propelled by the sheer force of their shivers. Isaac takes off his jacket and wraps it around Shelby, who's too busy railing against the cold to thank him. He's already forgotten me, but not for long. I suppose I could be jealous, but that's not my way.

I stride off, the wind making my gossamer gown flutter like an ivory flame. I'm satisfied in knowing that the tide has already begun to turn.

Interlude #1—Mary Jane ($C_{21}H_{30}O_2$)

A door that has always been closed to me is now left wide open. How cool is that? I get to walk right in through Reverend Burkett's front door instead of slipping in through a side window or hanging in the shadows of the backyard, like I used to do with his daughter so many years ago.

There's noir jazz playing on vinyl. Not remastered millennial vinyl, but an original album, with all the character of age. Scratches and pops and the occasional skip. It's a song I know: Coltrane, "You Leave Me Breathless."

He's waiting for me there in the living room. Each time I come, I want to flaunt my presence. Rub it in. But I don't, because I'm not like that anymore. Instead, I stand patiently, keeping a professional distance. I let him engage first.

I still find it hilarious that I have gone legit. My hair back in a neat, tight bun. My T-shirt and torn jeans replaced with something your mother might wear to the office. I look like a lawyer. I'm not sure how I feel about that.

The Rev still doesn't know how to feel about all this, either. The higher the horse, the greater the vertigo. I can tell he's just gotten back from the bathroom, because he's still trying to get comfortable in his La-Z-Boy. His visit to the john was all about retching. Nothing that goes in stays in for long. I glance over to see a casserole sitting on the kitchen pass-through. Some sort of cheesy pasta a neighbor brought over. Doesn't look half-bad, but he couldn't keep it down.

He becomes aware of my presence and is not happy about it. "Leave me alone," he says. It's what he always says.

"How was it today?" I ask.

"Eh," he says. "You've seen one treatment room, you've seen them all. My IV kept getting tangled. Such a nuisance."

He had a session with Kimo today. Kimo is a brutal trainer. His boot camp is relentless, demoralizing, and exhausting. But people endure it because he gets results.

"All the other patients sit there reading these awful magazines. Celebrities acting badly. As if having cancer isn't torture enough." He closes his eyes and groans. His nausea comes in waves, and this was a long, rolling one. Once it passes, he pulls a blanket over himself and shivers, even though it's not at all cold. He tries to push the recliner back but doesn't have the strength or the leverage, so he just gives up and leaves it in the upright position. Then he reaches to the end table next to him and turns on the e-cig, checking the little glass cartridge, where I've been distilled down into a rich amber oil.

A new song starts. Sad and soulful. A saxophone in a doorway in the rain.

"Did you know jazz used to be considered the music of the devil?" I casually point out.

"Don't you dare lecture me. You do not have the moral authority."

I glance over at his e-cig. The ready light goes on. "Shall we do this, Joe?" I ask.

"So we're on a first-name basis now?"

I shrug. He looks over at the e-cig but doesn't pick it up.

"You are not my only companion," he points out.

"Of course not. Anyone in your congregation would be here in a heartbeat if you asked," I remind him. "So why don't you ask?"

He purses his lips. "And let them see me like this?"

I know people call him regularly. He tells them how blessed he is to have so much support. He thanks them and tells them they are loved, then sinks back into his self-imposed solitude. He pretends it's vanity and pride—but I know the truth. He can't bear the weight of their concern.

Finally, he picks up the little plastic cylinder, takes a shallow hit, coughs it out, then takes a deeper hit and holds it. Nothing but Coltrane . . . Then he breathes it out slowly and grimaces from the burn I leave in his lungs. "Do you have any idea"—cough, cough—"how much"—cough, cough—"I hate you?"

I don't answer. Instead, I take his feet in my hands and massage his toes, making them tingle. I grab his hands and do the same for his fingers. He's beginning to hear my voice much better now, in the silence between the notes. He looks at a painting on the wall. A sailboat on a summer day. Totally generic. But under my influence, the brushstrokes come to life with hidden patterns. Even the frame reveals things he never noticed before. And everything seems to have a face now. The plates in the china cabinet are wide, startled eyes. The knobs and gauges of his vintage stereo smile and wink. A curious effect of my presence. The line between what's alive and what's not is blurred. And everything is watching.

"I used to smell your stench on my daughter's clothes," he tells me. "She tried to hide it but never could."

"So you threw her out."

"Tough love. She cleaned up her act, didn't she?"

"It was never all that dirty," I tell him. "She and I still spend time together once in a while. Which is more than I can say for the two of you. When was the last time you saw her? Does she even know you're sick?"

"She doesn't need to know." He stiffens his jaw, but I press into the pressure point on either side until he releases the tension.

"The funeral," he finally says. "The last time I saw her was at her mother's funeral."

His wife died during the pandemic. They both got the virus, but he survived.

"Sarah was a good woman," he says. "Why she was taken instead of me, I'll never understand."

"Mysterious ways . . ."

That makes him stiffen again. "You can mock me any way you like, but you cross a line when you mock my beliefs."

"You're right; I'm sorry." I'm silent for a moment, but then I have to ask. . . . "Does it ever waver? Your faith, I mean?"

"I can't afford for it to waver. Not now." Then he folds just a little. "If my congregation knew that I sought relief from you . . ."

"It'll be our little secret."

He rolls his head, and his neck pops like the old vinyl record. "What do you believe in?" he asks. "Anything at all?"

"I believe there's a time and place for everything under the sun."

He grins the tiniest bit. "Ecclesiastes 3. You may have some grace in you yet." Then he sighs. "Is it weakness giving into you, I wonder, or a lesson I was meant to learn?"

"Only you can answer that, Joe."

And so he closes his eyes and begins a quiet prayer for

guidance, mumbling earnestly to a god who can decipher the most garbled of supplications. I truly do admire his conviction. Conviction and motivation have never been my strong suits. I've been accused of being the high priestess of apathy. Maybe so, but doesn't everyone deserve to do absolutely nothing once in a while? And then order a pizza?

"No matter what you do for me, I can't ignore the damage you've done in the world," he says, and it's hard not to be a little offended. What damage have I done? More than AI? More than Nico? Nico killed Joe's mother. Hand-planted cancer right in her lungs and cultivated it like his own personal garden. Could be all that secondhand smoke as a child contributed to his own cancer now. But I don't argue with him. Whether he appreciates me or not, I continue to do what I'm here to do. I begin to massage his shoulders, hitting key pressure points. The nausea that had filled him loses its edge.

"Last year, three teenagers in my congregation died in a tragic accident," he tells me. "All three were high."

I nod sadly. "I remember."

"So you admit it! You were there! It was you who killed them!"

"I was there," I acknowledge. "And so was the rain, and the tree, and the bald tire."

"Technicalities!"

"They invited me, Joe. I didn't force myself on them any more than I'm forcing myself on you."

"They'd be alive if it hadn't been for you."

"Maybe, maybe not. You can't convict me on maybe."

The record ends. The stylus raises, the hand arcs back to its cradle. He's too relaxed now to flip it. But he still hears the music in his head. It's still playing for him.

"Sarah and I would dance to this one. It was our favorite." Then he adds, "Soon I'll be dancing with her again."

"Maybe," I say.

"Definitely," he insists.

"I mean maybe not as soon as you think. A few more sessions with Kimo and you might be as good as new. Your chances are still pretty good. Fifty-fifty at least."

He grumbles at that but doesn't comment. As if voicing hope might kill it.

"Do you even care if I make it through this?" he asks.

I answer his question with my own. "If you do, will you call your daughter?"

He thinks about that. "Yes," he says. "If I survive this, I will call her."

"Then I hope you do survive. I'm rooting for you. Now lean back."

He finally manages to coax the recliner into its full extended position. I move my fingers along his scalp, soothing the neurons in his brain. His thoughts begin to spill into one another.

"Don't expect me to thank you for this."

In time, the last of his resistance is gone. His clenched stomach is now as easy as the sea beneath the painted sailboat. My effect has peaked. I step away, leaving Joe in an easy, semi-conscious state.

"We're done," he says. "You can see yourself out."

"I'm not going anywhere, Joe. Whether you like it or not, I'm keeping you company."

He grunts his disapproval and turns away. But then, in the silence, he says something. And although his words are barely a whisper, I hear them.

"Thank you," he says.

I know better than to acknowledge it. Instead, I just let my hair down—if only to remind myself what it was like to be wild and just on the other side of the law.

8

Psychophar**ma**cologisticexpia**li**do**cious**

ISAAC

Isaac doesn't want to stick his nose into his sister's business. He's got enough troubles of his own right now—but he can't ignore what's going on with her. How could he? Even if his parents want to have a quiet, controlled conversation with Ivy, it's not possible, because Ivy always escalates it. She complains that they don't give her privacy, and yet she's the one who broadcasts her business to anyone in range when they fight.

So when Isaac leaves the house that next afternoon, he already knows where Ivy's been and where she's going.

He doesn't have to drive past her as he leaves. He's heading to Shelby's and can just as easily turn left instead of right. But he chooses right and catches up with Ivy as she reaches the corner. On foot. She's always on foot or riding the bus. She will not take her bike as a matter of principle . . . because it's a reminder that she has two wheels instead of four.

Isaac rolls down his window. "Need a ride?" he asks.

"No, I'm good."

He knew she'd say that. He also knows that Ivy is headed to Walgreens to pick up the prescription she got from Dr. Torres. The one their parents want her to fill right away. Isaac matches her pace. A car behind him honks, then goes around him.

"It's what, like, two miles to Walgreens?" he says. "The sooner you get this done, the sooner you can put it out of your mind," he tells her.

At last she relents, but clearly under protest. "Fine." She gets into the car and slams the door hard. "Mom and Dad sent you, didn't they? They don't think I'll actually get it filled."

"Probably not—but no, they didn't send me. I just overheard and was heading out anyway."

"We oughta get your ears pinned back. They hear too much."

"Ouch!"

"And do you have to come to a complete stop at every freaking stop sign? What's wrong with you?"

Isaac knows the steam she's venting isn't meant for him. Her head is just full of its own malicious code right now. He won't take it personally. Instead, he offers his best brotherly smile. "Maybe I want to keep my license," he says, knowing it will sting just enough to get her to stop.

"Low blow," Ivy says.

"Agreed."

They drive in silence for a while. Then she asks, "So, how's your foot?"

"Better than it was," he tells her, not wanting to get into it. "How's your ego?"

"Sprained," she says, without hesitation. "Dr. Torres's waiting room was the Pit of Despair. Little kids with issues and parents who couldn't control them. It felt like getting stuck at the kiddie table with Cousin Logan."

Their cousin Logan, three years younger than them (but in their memories, a perpetual eight-year-old), had impulse control problems. One Thanksgiving, not willing to wait, he shoved his hand into the turkey to get at the stuffing and ended up being rushed to the hospital with third-degree burns.

"Dr. Torres knows you," Isaac points out. "He might specialize in kids, but better him than some random psychopharmacologist."

"It really pisses me off that you know that word."

Isaac smiles again. "Psychopharmacologisticexpialidocious."

It brings forth the expected groan.

"Anyway," Ivy says, "if this gets Mom and Dad off my back, it'll be worth it."

"You shouldn't be doing this for *them*."

She glares at him. "This better not be the Little Brother Lecture Tour, or I swear I will hurl myself out of this moving car and tell the jury you pushed."

"No lecture," Isaac says, and leaves it at that. Ivy knows everything he might want to say anyway. And if she's actually getting the prescription, she doesn't need him to remind her.

Ivy sighs as they pull out onto a commercial street, the Walgreens just a few blocks away. "I don't want to *need* anything," she tells him. "Having to be on something just to function . . . I don't know . . . it makes me feel *less than*."

"Less than what?"

"Anything and everything," Ivy says. "And everyone."

Isaac shrugs. "Everybody's got a turd somewhere on their lawn. So this is yours."

Ivy turns to him, and he thinks she's going to curse him

out, but instead she says, "That may be the wisest thing you've ever said."

He pulls into the Walgreens parking lot, and Ivy gets out. "Promise me that when I get my license back, I can give you thoroughly humiliating lifts too."

"I promise."

Then she tells him not to wait—that she'll walk home. "I actually want to," Ivy says. "I need the time to myself."

Isaac can tell she's sincere about it. She might be good at lying to their parents, but she never lies to Isaac—or at least when she does, she makes it intentionally transparent.

He wants to tell her that he knows how hard this is. He wants to tell her that he's proud of her, but he knows that will humiliate her even more. So he just says, "Bring me back some orange Tic Tacs," because it's a gesture that gives Ivy a clear path to "Thank you."

IVY

Ivy could never keep a plant alive. She's started a hundred books but rarely finishes them. She once even forgot what she was doing and then remembered she was in the shower. Ivy's focus issue was always something to contend with—but a TV remote accidentally left in the refrigerator is only funny the first time. And now, nearing adulthood, her problems are growing up as well. How can she plan for the future when she's scrambling to organize her present—only to realize that the day she thought was tomorrow is actually today, making her twenty-four hours late to feed the goldfish that has already died.

Ivy's metagoal: make it through senior year without failing any classes. But right now half of her classes are in the D range. She might even have to repeat an entire year, not just the semester. That would mean she'd graduate at the same time as her brother. That would be one humiliation too many. It's what pushed Ivy to "get help" and sit through that painful session with Dr. Torres. Hell, she was thirty minutes late to the appointment and forgot her insurance card. If that wasn't an indication, what was?

So now Ivy pointlessly wanders the aisles of Walgreens as she waits for her Adderall prescription to be filled, wondering what the hell ginkgo biloba is and why the hell there is so much of it in the vitamin aisle. The place reeks of rubbing alcohol, or maybe it's just the Purell on the counter, which everyone religiously douses their hands with after using the diseased stylus that hangs from the signature pad. The smell makes her think of when she was a kid, getting her flu shot here. Ivy was one of those weird kids who liked getting shots.

She looks around at all the different people waiting, wondering what weird illnesses they're suffering from. This crowd runs the entire gamut of human experience. An old man with an oxygen tank. A little girl with a radioactive cold. A middle-aged woman with leathery skin and a raspy voice that was definitely not from singing in choir. Funny how this one service window could hand out medicinal cocktails to such different types of people. Hopefully, they'll give Ivy her pills before she can catch some disease that will require another prescription. But as she's waiting for the pharmacy clerk to call her name, she catches sight of a familiar face.

It's her friend Tess—the one who, beyond all reason, chooses regular fries over curly fries. The kind of person Ivy has to remind herself she likes.

"Ivy?" Tess says, a little surprised, a little nervous. In any other situation that would have been a red flag, but Tess's entire life is a blazing banner of red flags, so just one more is easy to miss. "What are you doing here?" Tess asks.

"Just picking up stuff."

"So hey—there's this party tonight. A *college* party. Wanna come?"

Ivy instinctively starts considering it. This has been one of the lamest weeks of her life, and she could use some fun. That's when Ivy realizes that they're standing in the booze aisle—because, at least in this state, Walgreens is a full-service pharmacy, not just for the medicated but also the self-medicated.

Tess glances nervously to the front of the store, and Ivy sees Tess's boyfriend, TJ, at the checkout, blatantly flirting with the cashier. The girl is smitten—but it's just a diversion. Because Tess grabs a bottle of vodka and slips it into her backpack.

"What the hell are you doing?"

"We can't go to a high-level party empty-handed," Tess says, then grabs two more, tries to fit them into her bag, and when the third one doesn't fit, she slips it under her arm.

Ivy is flustered in spite of herself. "You can't carry all those. You'll get caught!"

"You're right," Tess says, and hands Ivy one of the bottles. "Thanks!"

Ivy freezes, staring at the bottle in her hands. This is definitely not the way Ivy thought this afternoon would go. Yes, she's snuck vodka from the liquor cabinet before, and charmed legal guys into buying it for her, too—but stealing it? That's a different thing entirely.

Ivy hands the bottle back to Tess and pulls back, distancing herself. "Not how I party," she says.

Tess looks deeply offended. "Since when?"

"Have fun tonight," Ivy says, but she really wants to scream at Tess for trying to pull her into the theft—and then at herself, for being such a follower that she was almost willing to do it.

"I'll have more fun than you," Tess says with a smirk, and takes off and out the door, with TJ joining her a second later, leaving behind a very flattered and completely oblivious cashier.

Ivy has to take a deep breath. She was never the superstitious type. The Virgin Mary never appeared on her toast, thirteen happened to be her favorite number, and stepping on a crack broke absolutely no one's back. She does, however, believe in signs and signposts. Moments of clarity in life that mark turning points. This is one of those moments. She clearly sees the two paths diverging and knows which path she needs to take. She has to dredge up the strength to fight the inertia of all her previous choices, all the bad-news friends and self-destructive cycles. She has to make a declaration and stand by it, because if she doesn't champion her own future, who will?

So Ivy leaves the liquor aisle and approaches the pharmacy window just as they call her name. Admitting she needs the lousy pills is humiliating, but there are worse kinds of humiliation. Ivy is determined to earn back her dignity.

ADDISON

Her name is Ivy Inez Ramey, and she's been charged into my capable hands. Unlike Roxy, who waits until she feels the call, I arrive early. Punctuality is a virtue I hold in high regard. Ivy doesn't want to have any relationship with me, much less one where I have all the power, but she will quickly learn that it is not my nature to abuse that power. In time, she will come to lean on me. Not as a crutch but as a companion and confidant. I will know her secrets, but I will never press my advantage. I will, however, influence her choices. How could I not, when I know so much better than she what's good for her?

Ivy sits alone at the kitchen table on an ordinary weekday morning. She filled the prescription days ago but has yet to commit. The little orange pill bottle sits before her, and she contemplates it. I'm losing patience, so I have to remind myself that this relationship must not be forced. She must make the first gesture.

Then, just as I think we're about to begin, she gets a text from her boyfriend—a mildly attractive Neanderthal named Craig. Craig is two years older than her, works as a house painter when he works, and deals on the side—not just to make ends meet, but because he enjoys it. Yes, I know Craig—hell, we all know Craig. He's what we call "eyes on the ground." He's too much of a scag to be invited to the Party, but he's good at sending others there. He's like a pimp for plus-ones.

Well, now that Ivy will be spending time with me, she'll definitely be spending less time with him. Of course, our relationship will be different from theirs. I may flirt on occasion, but I am an asexual being, and I like that just fine. Who needs to taint what's pure with animal desires? Let Roxy and the others seduce if they dare. After all, 'Lude was a master of seduction, and we all know what happened to him.

No sooner does Ivy put down the phone than her grandmother hobbles into the kitchen behind her.

"Looking at it isn't going to help you," she says.

Ivy flinches and quickly grabs the pill bottle, as if she can hide it after it's already been seen. Ashamed of me, Ivy? I can't help but be offended, but I'll give you a pass just this once.

"Grandma—I didn't know you were there."

"What can I say? I'm stealth."

I like the old woman. She's got a healthy *I-can-say-whatever-the-hell-I-want* way about her, and she genuinely cares for Ivy.

Grandma pushes a glass against the ice dispenser, then pours some lemonade—but instead of drinking it, she sets it in front of Ivy. I like the not-so-subtle way she urges us into an introduction.

"Never swallow dry," she says. "It can get stuck and give you a pill ulcer. I got one from a stupid Tylenol. Ugh, don't get me started."

Her grandmother leaves, but even after she's gone, Ivy still stalls, cleaning up some ice from the floor that didn't make it into the glass. Finally, there's nothing left for her to do but get on with it. Her brother calls from upstairs, asking if she's ready to go to school. If she doesn't go with him, she'll have to take a bus, and she'll be late. It's now or never, Ivy.

At last, after days of waiting, she takes the plunge, and I'm right there to catch her.

"Hello, Ivy. My name is Addison. And we're going to be very, very good friends."

9

Heir to the Painless Throne

ROXY

The elevator doors open, and there's Al with two frothing beers.

"Hello, Roxy!"

My evening's plus-one sees the beers and pushes forward. "Don't mind if I do." He takes both beers and toddles off into the Party, dazzled by the music, the lights, and the glittering gentry.

"And thus, all is right with his world," says Al.

My plus-one tonight is a construction worker from Connecticut. Not the most gorgeous guy, but I don't discriminate—I love all those who love me.

"Who's here tonight?" I ask Al.

"Everyone who's anyone," he tells me. "The usual."

I point to some new boy in an outfit louder than the music. He's the center of attention in his corner of the Party. "Who's the new guy?"

"He goes by Flak," said Al. "I hear he made a name for himself in Florida. He's one of the new designers."

"Who's line is he in?"

"He's under Crys."

Good. Last thing I need is an up-and-comer in my line. Someone new to compete for Hiro's attention.

Al glances over at my "date" tonight, who's already down-ing the second beer and looking for something stronger. "So what's his story?" Al asks.

"Back trouble. Too much heavy lifting. We started casual, but now he's into me big-time."

Al smirks. "In for a penny, in for a pound."

"And coin is definitely a problem; he can't afford me any-more."

Al gives me a grinch of a grin. "So you brought him to the Party."

"He's ready for Hiro."

Al nods knowingly. "A much cheaper date."

The elevator door opens again, and two champagne flutes appear in Al's hand—beverage of choice for whoever the new arrivals are. I leave him to his business and push deeper into the crowd. I'm not feeling myself today. I'm distracted, but I don't know why.

Addison is over by the pool table, and I join him. He's shoot-ing around on his own—no one is foolhardy enough to take him on in pool. He always wins. "Focus is the key to this game," he tells me, sinking the last ball. "And no one has it like me."

"Alone tonight?" I ask.

He bristles at the question but tries not to show it. "I didn't *arrive* alone, if that's what you mean." Then he nods over toward one of the booths, where a guy in a muscle shirt and hundred-dollar jeans is partying with Charlie and Dusty. "My plus-one traded down," Addison says.

"Traded up, you mean. Aren't the Coke brothers above you?"

"They might be in my upline, but there's nothing superior about them but their attitude. They're bankrupt in every way that matters."

"And yet you long to be just like them."

He turns to me, planting his cue like a staff. "Working for the greater good and indulging yourself are not mutually exclusive."

That literally makes me laugh out loud. "Of course they are! Are you even listening to yourself?"

"You're the proof," he insists. "You still do good work— you still do your job when called upon." Then he adds, "I'll bet you even take some satisfaction in it."

He's not entirely wrong, and it just pisses me off. "My 'job,' as you call it, is just an anchor for a far greater existence," I tell him. "Your problem, Addison, is that your job doesn't just keep you grounded; it keeps you pinned."

That makes him stew all the more. "I'm entitled to take some pride in my work."

"Ha! Now you sound like your sister. What's next? You'll take up crocheting?"

He doesn't dodge my parry. Instead, he takes it in the chest, letting it sink in. Finally, he says, "(A) Rita does have a point, and (B) if you tell her I said that, I'll deny it."

I take a moment to look around, beginning to worry that some of the others might see me hanging out with Addison. On some days, I hope some of my success might rub off on him. Other days, I worry that being around him will diminish me in everyone's eyes. Dragged into the utilitarian depths by that anchor of his. Crys, and the others in his upline, mock Addison constantly.

True, they're assholes through and through, but that doesn't mean I want to be in the blast zone of their toxic derision.

Across the room Charlie and Dusty burst out laughing—and I immediately think they're laughing at Addison, and by proxy, me. But no—they're busting up over something the muscle-shirt boy said, as if he told the funniest joke in the world.

Addison scowls at the twins as they lavish attention on his plus-one. "Kevin was doing fine. Keeping up his grades, making sensible choices. I didn't think he'd abuse our friendship—but then it was 'Who else do you know?' and 'When can I meet them?'"

Addison throws his cue down on the pool table, exasperated. "Fine, he wants to hang with Dusty and Charlie? He wants to dance with Crys until he drops? Let him. What do I care?"

"But you do care," I tell Addison. "It's quaint, and charming, and part of what I like about you."

It's the perfect way to goad him—because quaint and charming are the last things he wants to be.

Just then two firefighters and a paramedic barge in out of nowhere. They move past, never seeing me, never seeing *us*. These days, their jobs have less to do with fires and more to do with our handiwork. Theirs is a harsh reality; where we see revelry and flashing lights, they see crack houses and despair.

Then, as always, Naloxone, with his holier-than-thou attitude, trails in their wake.

"Hi, Cuz," I say with enough insincerity to bring a cold glare of disapproval; then Nalo turns his attention to the problem at hand: a gaunt woman who had been dancing with Crys.

They'd been dancing for a while—but now she's in a heap on the dance floor, being tended to by the paramedic. Crys is furious. Coding in the middle of a dance? And before even getting her to the VIP lounge? The nerve of some people.

The medic hurriedly sets Nalo to work: Nalo picks the woman up, embraces her. He wails in anguish as he holds her limp body in his arms. And, wonder of wonders, she revives. Naloxone, who more often than not, is too little too late, is, for once, on time, and just enough. The crowd around us boos and jeers at him, but quickly forgets about it, having much better things to do. We all turn away, and the moment we do, Nalo, the girl, and the emergency team vanish from our view, no longer present in our world.

Nalo won't see many victories like that tonight. Most of the plus-ones will get the VIP treatment tonight, and die. Some will be saved. But even the ones who make it out alive find it hard to stay that way. Few can resist the lure of being a VIP. Everyone out here wants to know what they're missing in there, and the mystery eats them alive.

As for my construction worker, this is his first time at the Party. He's done with Al's libations, and he's steeling himself for the next step. He's already standing at the red leather doors of the lounge, daring himself to go through. But of course he can't without an escort.

I saunter over to him, gently stroke his arm, and grasp his hand in mine.

"It's not so hard," I tell him. "You've taken every step so far—this is just one more." Then I push open the door and wait for him to step through.

The moment we're inside, the doors swing closed behind us, and the noise and tumult of the Party are gone, as if we've crossed through an airlock. My construction worker marvels at the simple elegance. No jarring bass, no shoving crowd. There's room to breathe in the VIP lounge, for as long as one has breaths to take. Rows of Ionic columns rise on either side of a grand colonnade. The marble beneath our feet is rich and rare. Black and white swirling into gray, with veins of bright crimson—as if ancient blood has petrified within the stone.

Murmurs seethe out from dim, candlelit alcoves. In a far corner, a towering ayahuasca vine has grown into a tree that breaches the roof, letting shafts of moonlight slice across the space. The tree's hallucinogenic blooms waft down through the moonlight, the sweet smell of the pink and white flowers an invitation to those so inclined. But we have other business.

My construction worker is as wary as he is eager.

"There?" he asks, pointing to our left, where a spa bubbles bright orange like a volcano caldera.

"Not there," I tell him as I lead him along the colonnade.

He looks off to our right. "There?" he asks, pointing to the dance floor, much more intimate than the one in the outer party. Instead of a DJ, this dance floor is presided over by a live band. They are skilled in all instruments. Whatever song you wish to hear, that's the song they're playing. But it's your heartstrings they're really caressing. Your most receptive nerve endings.

"Not there," I tell him, and lead him to the very back of the lounge, where a narrow corridor leads into darkness.

"Through the hallway?" he asks, sounding more like a little boy than a grown man.

"At the end of it, you'll find a door," I tell him. "No need to knock; he's waiting for you."

He peers into the darkness but still hesitates, so I lead him the rest of the way.

Finally, we reach the door at the far end. I turn the knob—but I let him push the door open. Just as with the elevator buttons, it must be his choice. You can lead a horse to water, but he's got to be the one who drinks.

Hiro's office is like a shrine. There are lit candles all around. A chandelier made entirely of tarnished spoons. Hiro sits at his desk, in his big comfortable chair, looking at a heavy ledger in the candlelight, checking an endless array of numbers and names. Does he know how much I covet that chair? The throne of the painless king. Because when Hiro falls out of favor, someone will take his place. Why shouldn't it be me?

But looking at the desperate face of my plus-one throws a wet rag on my ambition.

Hiro doesn't even look up at us when he says, "Close the door."

I push it closed behind us. As it seals, the chandelier tinkles.

"Hiro, this is Anthony."

Hiro doesn't respond, still giving his attention to his ledger. He writes something down, closes the book, and finally looks up.

"Anthony Grisso," he says. "Thirty-six. Divorced, two kids. Formerly with Krebs Construction but currently on disability leave."

Anthony gives a nervous laugh. "All that in your book?"

Hiro taps his temple. "All in here," he says. "What can I do for you, Mr. Grisso?"

Anthony looks to me as if he needs my approval. I give him a nod, and he spills his whole sob story to Hiro. How the pain keeps getting worse. How his insurance has cut him off. How he needs relief now. And that he'll do anything for that relief.

Hiro comes out from behind his desk and up to the man, intruding too far into his personal space.

"Done with Roxy, are you?"

"It's complicated . . . ," Anthony says.

"Not at all," Hiro tells him. "Roxy has expensive tastes, simple as that. I know how hard it is to keep up. I, on the other hand, am more in your price range." Then Hiro pauses, taking a deep look into Anthony's anguished, needy eyes. "Tell me, Anthony, do you want what I have to offer?"

Anthony nods. But Hiro is not satisfied.

"Let me hear you say it."

"I—I want what you have to offer. I want it bad."

Then Hiro pinches Anthony's forearm, just beneath the bend of his elbow. Anthony grimaces.

"The pain in your arm will pass. As will all other pain," Hiro says. "And then you'll be mine."

Anthony doesn't resist. I see his eyes begin to roll. His whole body shudders.

And I've had enough. As much as I want to be in Hiro's place, I don't want to watch this. "Can I go now?" I ask.

Hiro gives me a dismissive wave of his hand. I can't get out of there fast enough.

· · ·

Addison is waiting for me in the colonnade, leaning against a column like a GQ model—as if his posture is enough to make him belong.

"I've been considering your challenge from the other day," he tells me.

"What challenge?" I ask—whatever he's talking about is long gone from my radar.

"You challenged me to bring a plus-one in here and be with them to the end. No handing them off to my upline. No letting Crys have the last dance."

"Oh, right," I say. As if he'd ever be able to swing that. But I'm not in the mood to disabuse him of his dream. After having my construction worker drop me for Hiro, I feel a bit like Addison always feels. Yes, I led the man there, but he could have had the decency to change his mind and stay with me. Being at the same pity party as Addison is definitely cramping my style.

"So I have an idea," Addison says.

"Ooh, I can't wait."

"I saw you at the beach last night, with a new mark. . . ."

"You were watching me?"

He's indignant at the suggestion. "Hardly. I was on the pier babysitting a seventh-grade girl who was at the ball toss, hell-bent on winning a Pokémon."

That's another thing about Addison; people trust their kids with him, because, for the most part, he's trustworthy. He helps them. But as he had pointed out, there are plenty of people willing to abuse the relationship.

"The boy I saw you with at the beach—are you planning to bring him here?" he asks.

"Of course," I tell him. "But it's the early stages. He's not ready."

"Well, as it so happens, I'll be spending time with his sister. . . ."

I smile, seeing what he's getting at. "And you think you can be her one and only all the way to the end?"

"If I set my mind to it."

"And have you?"

Addison tries not to waffle. "Maybe."

"So quaint," I tease. "So charming."

"And what if I charm her right up to the Party? And what if I keep her to myself without Crys ever even seeing her?"

"Ooh! Good-boy Addison goes rogue! What *will* the neighbors say?"

He holds that severe, serious expression. He's so earnest, I just want to pinch his cheek—but I won't toy with him anymore. If he wants to go toe-to-toe, I'll indulge him. If only to make him realize that he'll never be me.

"So you think you can bring her to the Party before I can bring her brother?"

"Not just to the Party," Addison says, "but all the way here. To the lounge. To the end of the line. All by myself."

"What's the wager?" I ask.

Addison considers it. "The loser is banned from the Party for a year."

"Okay," I tell him. "You're on." But then I have to add, "I'll miss you up here when you lose, Addison. Of course I could always visit you in whatever library you're keeping people awake in."

And, not willing to let me have the last word, Addison says, "I wonder where you'll go when *you* lose, Roxy. Maybe you'll have to haunt hospices like your cousin Phineas."

Meanwhile, Crys enters with the guy in the muscle shirt, whom he's stolen away from the Coke brothers. They make a beeline to the dance floor.

And, oh, can that boy dance.

ADDISON

While Roxy works on the brother, I do my job for Ivy to the best of my ability. After all, earning her trust is the first part of any long-term plan. She will begin as my ward before she graduates to being my mark.

I work fast; in just a few days, I've turned her into a studying machine. She's in the library now, having never labored so hard in her life—and she is truly enjoying her work. It wouldn't do for her to feel beleaguered. I must give her a sense of command and control. Anything else is sloppy—and I am never sloppy. I sit beside her, chair turned casually backward, every hair in place.

"Don't forget to show your work," I say, pointing to the equation she's working on. "Not just for the teacher, but so you can see how you got the solution."

"Or see where I made the mistake," she offers.

"There won't be any mistakes," I tell her. "Not while I'm around."

She smiles as she reaches the solution. And it's the right

one. There's an honest, accessible quality to her that hides just beneath the surface—it's a genuine beauty few could truly appreciate, but I always have. Ivy and I are actually old friends, although I haven't seen her for years. She barely remembers, but I do. I can see our relationship will be different now. Much more passionate. But platonic—always platonic. As I said, I pride myself on that.

Ivy turns the page to reveal rows of problems even more complex than the ones she just finished. I can see her confidence waver.

"My test is tomorrow, and I'm still a whole unit behind."

"You're going to need more time," I tell her. Then I stand up. I make my way through the library, flowing smoothly, like the elegant sonata that thankless boy had played at his recital. I step up onto a chair and press my finger to the clock on the wall—inhibiting the second hand from moving.

The clock stops, and instantly, so does life around us:

The librarian snacks, midbite.

A student is stuck in the threshold of the door.

Another has dropped her books and reaches for them—frozen in the air.

But Ivy doesn't notice. She's intently working out her math problems. Only when she's done does she look up—just as I take my finger away from the clock, and time resumes it's normal flow. Ivy's eyes sparkle. So much work accomplished between the seconds. She realizes she might just pull this off. *We* might.

"I think I can finish this page before the bell!"

"Of course you can," I tell her. Ivy knows this sensation;

she just forgot it. What it's like to have a study buddy. All these years she didn't want a crutch—but there's nothing wrong with a little support. She takes a considering glance at the lunch bag sitting next to her with an unappetizing sandwich inside.

"You're not hungry," I remind her, although she hasn't eaten since breakfast.

She forgoes the sandwich and returns to her studies—but it seems the world is conspiring to pull her focus, because just then her phone vibrates with a call—and who is it? Her boyfriend, Craig. A friend to all those I despise.

Ivy looks to the phone, melancholy settling in. She misses him. Ivy's a smart, talented girl, but clearly lacks self-respect. And discipline. We'll need to work on that.

"Don't answer it," I advise her.

Still, she looks at the phone sliding slightly with each silent ring, so I give her the slightest, quietest nudge.

"You deserve so much better than him."

She casts her gaze down, doubting that. I look into her eyes—they swim with humility that she rarely allows anyone to see. Finally, she nods and gives the hint of a smile, appreciative. The call goes to voicemail—hopefully, it's one she'll never listen to. Because Ivy and I are truly connecting now. I will be the unwavering voice of positivity in her life. I will be the shoulder she never got to cry on. I will be the one who keeps her secrets. Soon she will come to rely on me as the only one who can measure the soaring heights I'll push her to reach.

"Next unit," I tell her. "You still have time,"

"Right." She flips the page.

"Then, when we're done, we'll go home and organize

your room," I add. "And if you can't sleep tonight, we can color-code your wardrobe. . . ."

She doesn't resist the idea, and why should she? We can do all those things and more. Because although they say time waits for no one, it certainly waits for me.

10

By **No Means** the **La**ir of a **Bond** Villain

ISAAC

Isaac's club soccer team is one of the top-rated teams in the division. Last year they lost at state, but they made a good showing. This year they have their eyes on the prize. So does Isaac. Because scouts do show up to these high-level games. Rarely announced but widely rumored.

"See that guy?" one of his teammates said a few weeks ago, nodding toward a stoic man with graying hair on the sidelines—a guy who didn't seem to be rooting for either team. "He's scouting for UCLA." Although someone else said he was a scout for Notre Dame, and a third teammate was 100 percent sure he was from North Carolina. Turned out he was just someone's unimpressed grandfather. There *had* been a scout there, though. From Seattle. No one had pegged her. Serves them all right for assuming it would be some stoic dude with graying hair.

As Mr. Demko noted, Isaac is a realist. He knows that athletic scholarships are few and far between—but as Demko also pointed out, impressing a scout could make him stand out and earn him admission, if not a way to pay for it.

Isaac has been miserable knowing that Saturday's game

could have been his chance, if he weren't going to be benched because of his useless ankle. And then a last-minute reprieve, literally from heaven. Saturday morning's game is rained out. There is no lightning at all to this storm—just a torrential, field-flooding deluge from a featureless gray sky. As far as Isaac is concerned, the coach's email telling the team he'll see them at Monday's practice is worthy to be framed. One more week to heal.

Isaac's ankle is a bit better, but still not 100 percent, so having the whole weekend off will do it good. And the painkillers, judiciously taken, have made life easier. There's no question that they do the job, but there's more to it than that. When he takes them, there's a sense of wellness that he didn't even know he was missing. A lightening of his spirits. Not so much a sense of being invincible, but of being capable. He used to get that feeling on the field, but for some reason he has a hard time remembering that.

He's taken the pill enough times now that he knows how long until it takes effect, and he can feel when it starts. A warming, rubberiness in his hands. He gets a little drowsy, a little dizzy, but not in a bad way. And he feels cushioned. Like his soul is packed in Bubble Wrap and ready for delivery. He likes that feeling—even though he knows it's a dangerous feeling to like. For that reason, Isaac tries not to focus on the sensation but just to live his life while the medicine does its job. He wisely spaced the pills out over the past few days, and now, on Saturday morning, he's left bereft. He checks his pockets. Weren't there eight samples? Or was it only six? He could swear there were eight. Thinking about it leaves him at the uneasy edge of a no-man's-land he doesn't want to cross.

He paces his room half the morning, listless and bored. By the time he goes downstairs, tired of bouncing off his own walls, his parents are gone for the day buying supplies for their current work project.

"They might as well move into a hardware store," Ivy tells him. "Easier that way." Ivy is camped out at the dining table, cracking the books. On a Saturday. If that's not a sign of the apocalypse, nothing is.

It's no surprise that his parents are putting in extra work time. When you own a small business, the concept of weekends ceases to exist, although they do generally make Isaac's games. But a rainy Saturday means they put in more hours.

"Your parents work too hard," Grandma tells him from her spot on the couch, but she's preaching to the choir. "That's where you get it from."

Isaac checks the fridge and once more finds nothing that's even worth the effort to heat up. Then he goes into the downstairs bathroom to take a leak. He knows he could have done it upstairs. He knew he had to go when he was upstairs before. But he didn't. He glances at the mirrored medicine chest while he's doing his business. He glances at it again while he's washing his hands. He dries his hands and refuses to catch his reflection in that mirror a third time. Instead he looks down at all of Grandma's pill bottles spread out on the counter.

When it comes to the elderly, prescriptions seem to pop up like mushrooms in a moist yard. This one for blood pressure. That one for thyroid issues. This third one to combat the side effects from the first two.

The meds on the counter, Isaac knows, are the ones she takes regularly. The vial Isaac wants is in that medicine chest. She has it there for emergencies. For days when the weather and wear make her hip throb. Today could have been one of those days. Rain affects joints, he knows—so he opens the medicine chest and finds the right bottle, curious as to how many pills she has. Eighteen. And the prescription is a couple of months old. Which means she doesn't need them all that much. Grandma did offer him one—so if he takes another one now, no harm, no foul. After all, his parents are too busy to take him to the walk-in for his own prescription. This is a far more logical solution. It's a little thing, not even worth mentioning. And if Grandma does ask about it, Isaac will be happy to tell her that, yes, he's needed a few for the pain, and they've been helping, and thank you, Grandma, for always thinking about me.

It would have been a well-balanced equation, except for the fact that his pain isn't enough to justify taking one. *Maybe it's worthy of half a pill,* Isaac reasons. But he grabs a few of them anyway. Three. That's all. He slips them into his shirt pocket. But then he's worried they might dissolve in there, so he wraps them in a tissue and slips them into the back pocket of his jeans. But then he worries that they might get crushed when he sits down, so he goes into the kitchen, seals them in aluminum foil, and puts the little silver wad into the front zippered pouch of his backpack—the pocket for odds and ends, like loose change and the occasional paper clip. Just like the change, he's not planning to use those pills—but they're good to have if he needs them. The pills are a security measure. A contingency.

Isaac's big with contingencies. He has plans within plans. He doesn't like things left to chance.

On his way back upstairs, he stomps, exaggerating his footfalls in order to test his ankle. To make sure it's not feeling worse than he thinks it does.

"What, is there a herd of elephants on the stairs?" Grandma shouts from the sofa.

"Yeah, your grandson, Dumbo!" yells Ivy from the dining room.

"My ears are a wonder," Isaac quips back. "You're just jealous."

By the time he stomps on the top step, he has to concede that his ankle is no worse. It still hurts a little, just not a lot.

Well, that's a good thing, right? Healing is the goal, isn't it?

Up in his room, he tries to get to work on a chemistry project he's been putting off: a desktop desalination plant, made from common household items. He's got the plans, he's got the materials, but today his heart's not in it. It's like pulling teeth. And that gets him thinking about the dentist. Didn't they say he'd need his wisdom teeth out someday? Don't they give painkillers when you get your teeth pulled?

Isaac finally gives up, hurls himself onto his bed, and listens to the rain. This melancholy, this uneasiness, this lack of motivation—it's just the weather. On days like this, who doesn't feel gloomy? It will pass. And although he doesn't dig into that little zippered pocket, he keeps his backpack close all day long.

Sunday brings clear skies, but Isaac still doesn't feel entirely right about the world. Shelby calls him, and he tries to pretend he wasn't sleeping in. He wished she just texted, but Shelby's been on an anti-texting campaign since she blasted out to half her art class anybody have multicolored penis I can borrow? The GIFs and JPEGs she got back could not be unseen. She blamed autocorrect, called Siri an evil bitch, and vowed henceforth to use her iPhone as nature intended.

"So the new *Superman* reboot just came out," she tells Isaac. "I have absolutely no interest in seeing it."

"Me neither," he tells her. "What time does it start?"

"Every half hour starting at ten, but if we want 3D, we should get tickets online."

"Let me call you back," Isaac tells her. "I may have to put in some family time today."

Family time for Isaac usually consists of helping with Ramey Custom Interiors—the family business. His mom and dad had built it from the ground up. Mom does all the designs, as well as all the financial and PR stuff, while Dad and his team do the assembly. Mostly it's restoring old cars, or "pimping the rides" of customers with questionable taste. But every once in a while a big fish comes along. A celebrity tour bus. A stretch limo. They once even got a contract to refurbish the interior of a private jet.

Isaac was thirteen then. His dad brought him to the job when it was almost done. It looked like pure science fiction. That was when Isaac first started thinking about aerospace design. Interiors were all well and good, but it takes a serious propulsion system to turn something that *looks* space-aged into something that actually is. Secretly, he dreams that his parents will get the contract to do the interior of something he designs.

He knows it's a little-boy fantasy, but he entertains it anyway.

With business slow and salaries to pay, the Rameys have had to tighten their belts in every possible way. But the current project is a real lifesaver. They'd been hired to gut and redesign the interior of some rich guy's yacht, a 126 footer. Four cabins. Not quite the lair of a Bond villain, but substantial enough to turn heads.

Since it's just the interior, the boat didn't need to be dry-docked—all the work is being done right there in the marina—but they're weeks behind schedule, and the owner, who has issues with delayed gratification, has been getting antsy. Isaac's heard his father on the phone trying to placate the guy. "Two more weeks, Mr. Sherman," his father says. "Two more weeks." It's the watchcry of every contractor.

Since his parents won't make their crew work Sundays, that's the day that Isaac often pitches in.

"Are you sure you're okay helping out today?" his mom asks as they get ready to go. "Don't you need to rest your ankle?"

"All I've been doing is resting it," he tells her. "I'll be fine."

Today it's mostly bringing on unassembled furniture and panels to be put together on Monday.

"Well, as long as you're feeling up to it."

More than feeling up to it, and for the first time all weekend, he's excited. Invigorated. He calls Shelby to take a rain check on the movie neither of them really wants to see anyway and gets ready to go.

He was okay yesterday, but he's been limping a bit this morning. If he's going to be carrying boxes, that just won't do. Luckily, he has just the thing to make that limp go away.

He reaches into his backpack for the little foil ball because his parents need him—if that's not reason enough to kill the pain, then what is?

ROXY

I sit at the counter of one of those themed burger joints with red booths and chrome-edged tables, where the servers all dress in white. At least that's what Isaac sees when he walks in. But all I see is the counter and the empty stool beside me. Nothing else is relevant.

The grills sizzle, sending forth the irresistible aromas of meat, cheese, and onions, which draw Isaac forward. I don't go to him. I wait for him to come to me. It's a matter of gravity. I have it, and he doesn't. He's a falling body. Physics dictate his motions; chemistry dictates his choices. And, as science predicts, he sits beside me at the counter, exactly where I want him.

"Hello, Isaac," I say gently. "It looks like the universe brought us back together."

"Yeah, the universe is funny that way," he says, a little bit uneasy, as if our meeting is clandestine, rather than right out in the open. He's sweaty. He's been working hard. I like that. The honest musk of hard work beats the stench of frying dead cow any day.

The waitress gives him a menu. He peruses it, but not really. I can tell he already knows what he's getting.

"What happened to your girlfriend?" I ask. "She's not with you on this fine Sunday?"

"Shelby's not my girlfriend, exactly."

"Right. You two don't really connect, do you?"

"We do," he says. "Just not on every level. I mean, who connects on every level?"

I run a finger above his forearm, just close enough to tickle and excite the hair on his arm. "Was she your first?" It's a very personal question, but I have a way of getting people to open up to me without them ever realizing they're doing it.

"We were each other's," he admits, and grins with the memory. Not a reaction I want.

"Somehow I'm not reading passion," I say, and his grin fades. Good.

"It's comfortable with Shelby," he says. "It's easy. It's—"

"Convenient?" I offer.

He sighs. "I was going to say 'satisfying'."

"Is it though?"

He takes a while to think about it. "I guess we just don't know where things go next. We've been in the same place for months."

"Maybe you're just not really into each other."

That deflates him, slowly but steadily, until he's slumping on his stool. I leave it at that. Let it brew. Let it ferment.

"Are you ready to order?" asks the waitress.

His attention snaps to her. "Yeah, yeah, just a sec." He glances at the menu again and orders from the children's corner. The waitress scribbles it down and strides off.

"Really?" I say. "The kiddie menu?"

"Two blastoff burgers are cheaper than one regular burger and have more meat. And when it comes to fries, less is more."

But the real reason is obvious, at least to me. "Money trouble?"

"No," he says too quickly, then takes a moment to finesse his response. "I mean, my parents are trying to cut back. I know a couple of bucks at a burger place won't make much of a difference, but the least I can do is be responsible with my money."

"Admirable," I tell him—and I mean it. No one will know that he saved $2.36 on today's meal. He's not doing it for credit or praise—he's doing it because it's the dignified thing to do.

"Besides," he says, "if everyone left the table a little hungry, maybe there'd be more food for the people who really are."

I chuckle. Part of me wants to gag, but another part loves that noble, naive streak in him.

When the food arrives, he eats the first burger quickly, then the second slowly, his self-control finally overcoming his hunger.

"Looks like you worked up an appetite today," I comment.

He wipes a dab of ketchup from his face. "Just helping my parents out, down at the marina."

"And your ankle?"

"Not a problem."

Of course it's not. Thanks to me, it's yesterday's news. And tomorrow's, but certainly not today's.

When the bill comes, he reaches into his pocket to pay, and his face loses all color, "Oh crap." He pats his pants down frantically. "I must have left my wallet at the marina. I'll have to go get it, then come back to pay."

I lean in mischievously, deciding to test just how tempered his nobility is. Because cute or not, it's getting old. "What if we just run," I whisper.

He laughs at the thought, then gets a little scared at it. "I can't do that."

"Of course you can," I tell him. "You can do anything you set your mind to, Isaac." Then I run my finger up his spine. I can feel his shiver just like I can feel the beat of his heart. The beat that neither Shelby, nor anyone else, can feel the way I do.

"It'll be easy. Painless. No time wasted coming all the way back here. And look, the waitress isn't even watching."

I feel his resolve beginning to falter.

"On the count of three," I say. "One . . ."

His heart begins to quicken. He's still not sure what he'll do.

"Two . . ."

He begins to steel himself, on the verge of a decision.

"Three!" Isaac says it himself, not waiting for me. He grabs me, and together we fly through the diner and out the double doors.

"I can't believe I did that!" Isaac says over and over as we glide all the way to the marina, both of us giddy and punch-drunk on defiance.

He guides me down the hazy docks. It's dusk now. We follow the dim path, illuminated by faint lanterns along the railings. Isaac stops at a huge yacht. "Not ours—we're just remodeling it." He goes up the gangway. "I'll only be a minute."

But I haven't come this far just to be left at the threshold. "Permission to come aboard?" I ask.

And like the gentleman that he is, he escorts me on and down to the lower deck. A staircase opens to a grand living area even more spacious than the yacht appears on the outside, although the work there is far from complete.

"It's a Falcon 100," he tells me. "Over a thousand horsepower. It's as fast as it looks. Not that I'll ever get to ride in it, of course."

"It's going to be spectacular when it's done," I say.

"I know, right? My parents are good at what they do. They should get paid more for it."

"They will," I remind him. "When you're the one who hires them."

He smiles at the thought; then we go down one more level to the cabins. The main cabin is the width of the hull. This room is almost complete—full of surfaces in a marine-grade mahogany veneer and a king-size bed in the middle—although the mattress itself is still wrapped in plastic while the finishing touches are being put on the room.

"A place I could spend some time in," I say.

Isaac laughs and grabs his wallet off a bespoke end table. "I'm just here for the wallet. I'm not going to steal dinner *and* a yacht."

"It's not stealing if we don't go anywhere," I goad from behind. Then I get a little closer and whisper into his ear, "Isn't that what you were doing down here in the first place? Daydreaming, pretending that it was yours?"

He stiffens just a little. "I was taking a break. And if I daydream a little, that's *my* business."

I loosen my grip on the rod, giving him a little bit of line.

"Still, there's no one here but us. We could always daydream a little bit more."

"A little late for daydreaming. It's almost night."

"Magic hour," I remind him. "When anything can happen . . ."

I run my finger up his spine again. He shifts his shoulders and coos just the slightest bit.

"Stay with me," I whisper, breathing gently on his neck.

"I should go. . . ."

"But doesn't this feel good? You deserve to feel good, Isaac. *We* deserve it. . . . And we can feel even better than we do now."

Finally, he makes his move. He reaches into the front pocket of his backpack to the little wad of foil.

Time loops into itself like a Möbius strip. Like a snake gorging on its own tail. I soothe him to the point of him forgetting why he's here. I have him in my grip, I'm not letting go, and he doesn't want me to. I'm already miles ahead of Addison in our competition—because Isaac is already ripe and ready to be devoured.

Outside, beyond the brass-rimmed portholes, the magic hour fades. All the lights of the marina glitter, their reflection dancing on the water. The sky is too hazy to see the stars, but the lanterns of the marina might as well command their own solar systems. Still, they can't compare to me. My irresistible, inevitable gravity. Entropic, like a black hole, turning Isaac's hard-forged order into exquisite chaos.

IVY

Ivy doesn't usually stay up late studying on Sunday nights. She doesn't usually stay up studying on *any* night—but she's been on a roll. Stupid meds. She hates that they're working, because it's one big "told ya so" from her parents, who never actually say the words, but "told ya so" bleeds out of their pores when they see her hitting the books.

At this moment, her parents are in full worry mode over Isaac. It's midnight, and Isaac hasn't come home, which is very unlike him. He'd been working on that yacht with them and then vanished. Even Ivy's beginning to get concerned.

Her parents have been playing devil's advocate with each other for the past hour. Glass half-full/glass half-empty.

"He's probably over at Ricky's and lost track of time."

"So why isn't he answering his phone?"

"Or he went to a late movie with Shelby, that's all."

"So call Shelby's parents and see if she's home."

"If something happened, don't you think we would have heard?"

Grandma keeps her silence through all of it—in her downstairs room, but with the door open, hearing everything. Her worry is a dark cloud rather than a storm.

Mom and Dad are on the verge of calling 911 when Isaac finally arrives. Ivy's just as relieved as her parents, but she doesn't rush to him as they do. She stays in the dining room, pretending to read, as she listens. Her parents are barraging Isaac with parental stress clichés. "Where the hell have you been?" "Do you know what time it is?" "Do you have any idea how worried we were?"

It bothers Ivy, because when they ask her those same questions, they're accusations rather than genuine expressions of concern. Ivy always deflects those arrows with a glib Teflon coat before going upstairs to sleep off whatever it was she took, drank, or smoked. But the arrows they fire at Isaac are different. Suction-cup tips. They stick to him, and he has to answer.

"I'm sorry . . . ," he tells them. "I'm really, really sorry." Ivy can tell that he means it, but when she glances over at him, there's a look there that she doesn't often see. His eyes are weighty and tired.

Now that he's here and not lying dead in some gutter, their parents' concern finally decays into anger. Their father points a crooked finger. A few years ago he broke his index finger, so now, when he points, it's slightly misdirected. "You'd better have a good explanation."

"It's a stupid one," Isaac says. "I was on the boat."

That catches them off guard. They weren't expecting that. Neither was Ivy.

"All this time?" Mom says.

"I left my wallet there," Isaac tells them. "By the time I got back to the marina to get it, you were both gone—and my ankle was hurting again. I thought I'd lie down for a few minutes—you know—to let the Advil kick in. But I fell asleep. . . ."

Silence from their parents as they work to process that. Isaac is so out of it—so nonconfrontational, it almost causes them both to short-circuit. Meanwhile, Ivy hears Grandma's door close. Now that Isaac's safe, she doesn't want to participate in the subsequent theatrics. Good for her.

"Why didn't you call when you realized?" their mom asks.

"My phone was dead," Isaac tells them, "and I just wanted to get home."

But their father isn't ready to step off from his own anger.

"You fell asleep for half the night on a boat that isn't yours? Are you trying to get us fired?"

"I'm sorry," Isaac says again. "I guess I was much more tired than I thought."

Then their mom turns to their father. "Because *you* worked him too hard!"

"Oh, so this is *my* fault?"

And in a single, imperceptible instant, the spotlight is entirely off Isaac, and they're playing the blame game. Remarkable how that works.

"How much lumber did you have him unload?"

"He asked to help!"

"And you took advantage!"

Finally, Ivy gets up, happy to be the one playing referee for once. "Will you two just shut up and let it go? Seriously—I've done so many worse things on purpose. Isaac doesn't deserve all this drama over something stupid like this."

Dad takes a deep breath, then lobs a stern gaze at Isaac, but it's only half-hearted, and like his finger, seems mildly misdirected. "We'll talk about it in the morning." In other words, *We shall never discuss this again.* It's the last word in any parental harangue.

Isaac trudges upstairs, and their parents go off in opposite directions, wise enough to know that bickering won't help anything. The case is closed. Except that for Ivy, it isn't.

Ivy lets herself into her brother's room, finding him already slipped under the covers. She closes the door behind her, smiling, bright-eyed.

"You little shit! You were with Shelby on the yacht, weren't you?" Ivy sits on the edge of the bed, grinning ear to ear, awaiting Isaac's confession.

But Isaac isn't playing. "I wasn't with Shelby," he says. "To tell you the truth, things seem to be cooling between us."

Ivy would love to make a crack—like *How do you cool from lukewarm?*—but she doesn't.

"So if it wasn't Shelby, then who?"

"No one. Just let me go to sleep."

"Why?" Ivy says. "Didn't you just sleep for, like, six hours?"

Isaac turns to look at her. His eyes do look tired. No, not tired, *weary*. Weighty. She remembers how he looked when he stepped in the door. Like the burden of their parents' worry was only a fraction of the weight on a much heavier scale.

"Are you okay?" she asks. "What's going on?"

"Nothing," he says. "I'm fine. Really." And he forces a smile.

Ivy can usually tell when her brother is lying or telling the truth, but tonight Isaac's playing in the gray area between. There's more to this story, but he's not sharing it, and she isn't going to push any more than she already has. Isaac has given her the benefit of the doubt far too many times. She owes him that courtesy.

"Good night, Isaac," she says, only to realize that he's already lightly snoring.

She quietly gets up, and that's when something catches her eye.

It's Isaac's phone.

It isn't plugged in to charge, which strikes her as odd. Isn't that the first thing you do when your phone is dead? That's what he said, wasn't it? His phone was dead, so he couldn't call. Ivy stands there frozen, wondering if her suspicions are true—that Isaac lied to their parents. That he has something to hide.

So she moves slowly, reaching out a finger to touch the face of the phone that's supposed to be dead.

Her finger touches it.

And it lights up.

Interlude #2—Dusty and Charlie ($C_{17}H_{21}NO_4$)

We don't need an introduction. Our names are already known. Our place in history has already been earned. After all, we were there for the Thousand Days' War. We stood by Queen Victoria as she colonized the East, and even helped Sigmund Freud write *The Interpretation of Dreams*. In Austria, we soothed the pain of patients under the knife, and in the Americas we helped Thomas Edison invent the movie camera. We practically built Las Vegas, and were done in time to see Hendrix play Woodstock. We're everywhere! We were even the key ingredient in Coca-Cola until they replaced us with caffeine.

Our enemies call us evil, beastly, or vile, but to our aficionados, we're simply stardust that rains from heaven.

The devil's dandruff!

Florida snow!

Paradise white!

The nicknames may change, but we are eternal and timeless. That perfect fusion of old-school and new. And tonight, like all nights, we party. Hopping from one, to the next, to the next. Like electrons, we move so fast, we're impossible to nail down. We're everywhere at once!

At a flashy corner of everywhere is a familiar club in a familiar city. Hundreds of people, bright lights, and music loud enough to deafen. Not quite as intoxicating as our endless Party up above. The parties down here on earth have their limits—a strange concept for us to grasp—but this one still has plenty of steam.

Per usual, we're in the best booth, where we can see everything and reign over all—and when the song bores us, we motion to the DJ to change the track, which he does in a heartbeat—proof that when you own enough people, you don't just influence the few; you control the masses. Later we might bring a choice subject or two up to the big Party—maybe even into the VIP lounge—but truth be told, we much prefer the raw energy of parties down here.

That energy is pumping tonight! There are familiar faces in the crowd—new ones too.

And you!

You made it in! Good for you! This is, after all, a very exclusive event—invitation only—and even if you've been invited, that doesn't guarantee they'll let you in. But you're here, so either you're important or you're crafty. We're curious to know which.

What's that you say? You're in a band? Unimpressive. Half the people here are in a band. Or directing a movie. Or rolling in new money from some shady Wall Street maneuver. You see, everyone here has money—that's a given—but money doesn't impress the way celebrity does. Everyone here thinks they're a celebrity, but few truly are. They lack that ineffable quality. But maybe you have it. Maybe.

All right, we'll admit that, yes, we've heard of you—but even so, your renown is midlevel at best. You're the front man of an esoteric band. You do have the potential for greatness, though. Superstardom is not entirely out of your reach. Your fans certainly adore you. They're loyal. That's saying something in an age when rats in a maze have longer attention spans than human beings.

But on the other hand, your manager couldn't even get you a spot at Coachella. Shit bands can get into Coachella, so why not you? Yes, yes, you're being featured at the Desert Swarm Festival, but face it, that's a minor event. Again, not impressive.

Still, we like you. We like your energy. You're charismatic, persuasive, and easy on the eye. Handsome in a grunge sort of way. Everyone loves a throwback to the nineties—especially when it feels authentic. Some try too hard, but your vibe is sincere.

All right, you've convinced us. Come, sit—we've made a space for you between us in our booth. We'll entertain your hopes and dreams as long as you entertain *us*.

Our friendship comes with conditions, however. You are required to bring us to all of your gigs. You'll have us backstage with you before, and especially after, your performances. You do this for us, and we promise we'll do things for you. We'll be both your left and your right hand. Bookends to keep you bathed in our white light center stage, even after the show is over and the spotlights are gone.

Are you ready? Good. Now put your nose down on the table like a pig in its trough. Snort us in. Deep. Indulge your primal pleasures, because what are you, really, but an overstimulated primate? A slave to your brain chemicals. Endorphins. Dopamine. Let us do our magic with them. Oh, the excesses we could show you! Come, have some more. Be all you can be!

The burn is familiar, yes. Clearly this is not your first time, which means you must have been in our presence before; we just didn't notice you. But now we do. You should be flattered.

There! Now that we've formalized our agreement, let us rule you and we'll show you how to rule others. Your friends who never gave a shit about you, who now realize you might actually be a star—they've all come back around, knocking at your door.

Select the finest of them. Bring them to us. Give us the best of your fawning fans. Forget the rabble; let their hopes and dreams languish on the other side of the velvet ropes. Think of us as your support staff. Your handlers. Every rock star needs handlers to keep away the unwashed masses.

Yes, you could definitely be a superstar! We've decided. So let our winds fill your sails and help get you there. Sit back and enjoy your success. Watch it bubble and overflow like champagne. Speaking of which, here comes our friend Al with a bottle just for us. Dom Pérignon. We love Dom! He's our favorite. Only the best for us, and for you.

And we promise to be there for you until we lose interest, so you'd best work hard to keep it. How do you keep it? Well, money doesn't hurt. That new recording contract has left you with some disposable income, yes? Dispose it in our direction. Don't be stingy. Money is made to be spent. Someone has to pay for our jewelry and fine white suits.

What? You want to dance. No, we don't dance. We just observe. We take in the scene. People-watching—that's our thing.

But we do know someone who loves to dance.

His name is Crys.

He would *love* to meet you.

But let's take it slow—there's plenty of time for that farther down the line.

You look like you're enjoying yourself. Good! Nothing could make us happier. Now get out and make room for someone else in our booth—but come back tomorrow, because we love you, man—you're our favorite. You're our star!

Now go. We won't ask again.

11

There's Only One Way to the Throne

ADDISON

Ivy is beginning to depend on me.

Thanks to me, her notebooks, pens, and agenda are coordinated by color, shape, and function. At any given moment she could tell you where each of her personal items is. She even received an A on her much-dreaded math test—something she hasn't done in years. Her room is spotless. And today Ivy hardly notices the pesky flickering fluorescent desk lamp as she studies for another upcoming exam.

School, study, clean, repeat. Even I'm starting to get bored. All the more reason to take this to the next level. The ultimate level. But not yet. Ivy's not ready. Of course Roxy would say I'm the one who's not ready, but I know that rushing this won't work. Bring her up to the Party too soon, and she'll be just another plus-one to be ripped away by Crys. If I'm the one she'll be dancing with, this must be finessed.

And in the meantime, she gets to enjoy the benefits I bring.

It's a Wednesday. A half day of school for a teacher in-service. Most of Ivy's "friends" are wasting their time with things of little purpose. Ivy's using the time to get a step ahead, like a race car taking an inside turn. But my finger's getting tired holding back the seconds. She's studying Spanish, and I don't think I can bear another page of her dull conversation workbook.

"*¡Ya basta! Haçemos una pausa,*" I tell her.

"*Pero tengo que estudiar,*" she responds. Her Spanish is hitting new levels. But her accent still hovers at gringo.

"You've studied enough for now. Let it sink in. You'll get even more work done tomorrow."

She closes her book, but her eyes are clearly looking for another point of focus. If I don't rein it in, it will become nervous energy, which won't help either of us.

"I know—let's go to the museum."

Looks like I pressed the perfect button. She jumps at the idea, and we're off.

The art museum used to be the one place where Ivy could truly focus. But she always limited herself to just a small subset of galleries. Protection from overstimulation. That was how she created her safe haven. It's how she controlled her faulty focus mechanisms.

But today I'm breaking her free of all that. I'm taking Ivy to see every painting they have. Starting with the new Goya exhibition.

Ivy explores, wide-eyed, full of wonderment.

She settles before a disturbingly grotesque painting of a crazed giant eating a limp, headless body, the giant's eyes peeled wide in madness and paranoia. *Saturn Devouring His Son.* It's one of Goya's Black Paintings, depicting the great Titan of Greco-Roman lore, who devoured all of his children so he could never be overthrown. Mythology—the womb of both faith and horror.

"It's terrifying," Ivy says with hushed reverence. "But I can't look away."

She studies the painting, then the placard beneath, which is all about how Goya wanted to dramatize not mythological beings, but the anguish of war.

We move on past the exhibit and to the rest of the museum—and although we're powering through gallery after gallery, it's not frenetic or haphazard. Ivy takes precisely the time she needs to take in the works she chooses to give her attention. Still, there's nothing else we see that resonates in Ivy as much as the bleak Goya.

"I can't stop thinking about those eyes," Ivy says. "I think I'll have nightmares about that painting. The Titan devouring the defenseless."

"Well, can you blame him?" I counter. "After all, there's only one way to the throne."

But just then, something else begins to resonate. In her purse. Like an insect struggling to escape. She pulls out her phone, and of course it's Craig. He keeps coming back like a cold sore.

"Don't let him ruin your day," I tell her. "He will. You *know* he will."

"Maybe he wants to apologize. . . ."

"More likely he wants *you* to apologize."

It continues to ring while nameless aristocrats peer fecklessly down on her from the walls, their eyes set somewhere between judgment and indifference.

The phone finally goes dark. With a breath of relief, she slips it back into her purse. This can't go on. It's counterproductive. To her. To me.

"You know what you have to do," I tell her.

Ivy shakes her head. "I can't."

"You can and you will. You don't need him anymore. You never did. Break up with him."

She looks to the paintings around us, but she's clearly lost interest.

"You see? He's already ruined your day," I tell her. "He's Saturn, Ivy. He'll chew you up, spit you out, and think nothing of it. Don't let him."

"I'll think about it," she says, which is the best I'm going to get out of her right now. We're going to have to systematically take the toxic people out of her life, beginning with Craig. For both of our sakes. Because toxic people mean direct threats from my upline. It means more competition, and I can't allow that. No one is going to steal Ivy from me.

12

Follow the **Syring**e

It's six o'clock on a Tuesday evening when Isaac hears the crash. The kind of cataclysmic sound you never want to hear in your own home. He's already on his way downstairs, even before he hears Grandma wailing for help. Until he heard that cry, he thought she had only dropped something—but the warbling agony of her wail tells him that it's much, much worse.

He arrives to find her splayed out on the kitchen floor, writhing in pain. She clutches her hip. The remains of a shattered food processor are strewn between the counter and the table. There's a half-melted ice cube on the floor next to her and a glass of lemonade on the counter. Isaac knows exactly what happened. That damn ice dispenser!

"Isaac!" she says as soon as she sees him. She's breathing in quick, sharp gasps, hyperventilating. "Help me up."

He goes to help her, but the second he tries to lift her, she wails in anguish.

"No! Stop! Damn it all to hell!"

This is bad. This is the kind of fall that could leave her in a wheelchair for good. Isaac tries not to think about that. He realizes he's not going to be able to help her up by himself, at least not without hurting her. There's no one else to help—his parents aren't home yet, and neither is Ivy.

"You're going to be all right, Grandma."

"God damn it!" she rasps through her pain. Angry at herself. Angry at the world, angry at the universe for allowing this to happen. "I don't need this! Not now!" As if any time would be better.

Isaac pulls out his phone and dials 911, explains the situation, and provides the address.

"An ambulance is on its way," he tells her, but it already feels like an eternity.

Then, with pain so great she's on the verge of losing consciousness, she says, "My pills . . . Isaac. Get my pain pills. . . ."

Of course! The pills! Isaac races to her medicine cabinet, finds the little orange bottle. He knows exactly which one and where it is. He opens the cap and turns it upside down over his palm. But nothing comes out.

It's empty.

Shit! Of course it's empty. He *knew* it was empty. In fact, he had already called in a refill for her, but the robovoice said they had to check with the doctor. He'd been conserving them—even breaking pills in half—but over the past couple of weeks, it's added up.

Think. Think. Think.

He sprints up to his bedroom and heads straight for his backpack.

There has to be one left. There has to be.

He checks his backpack's little zippered pocket, where he kept the pills before, but there's nothing there. He checks under his bed—maybe one fell. No such luck.

But he has one last Hail Mary. His dirty jeans. He remembered putting a pill in a pocket when the foil he wrapped them in had fallen apart and has no memory of having taken it out. There are two pairs of dirty jeans in the hamper—any others have already been washed. He locates them, begging the powers that be to be on his side today, and pushes his fingers inside the little coin pockets. And to his relief, from the second pair of jeans, he fishes out one last little white pill, grainy and covered with lint.

Peeling the lint away, Isaac darts back down to the kitchen, grabs the lemonade sitting on the counter, and kneels beside Grandma, putting the pill in her mouth. A sip of lemonade, a hard swallow. Her pain doesn't ease, but her panic subsides, knowing that relief is right around the corner.

"This is not what I wanted," Grandma says through her grimaces. At first Isaac thinks she means the pill, but then realizes she's talking about the whole screwed-up situation.

"I know, Grandma," Isaac says, trying to comfort her. "Nobody wants this. But it'll be okay."

It's there, crouched by his grandma's side, holding her hand, that Isaac realizes something. Something he's known for a while but hasn't consciously admitted. His ankle is healed. Completely. He's been fine at team practices and briefly played in last weekend's game with no ill effects. Even running up and down the stairs now confirms it in real time. Still, that empty orange bottle looms large in his thoughts. Intense guilt that he left it empty, mixed with despair and irresistible desire. His foot doesn't need the medication anymore, but the rest of him does. And won't let him forget it.

The red lights of the approaching ambulance flash across his face, while alarm bells wail inside his head. Because the life he had designed so carefully has veered off course in an entirely unknown direction.

ROXY

Isaac's grandma is certainly a force to be reckoned with. I'm there in the ambulance with Isaac, her, and an EMT—who wants to start her on an IV, but she won't let them.

"It's just a saline drip, ma'am."

"Are you a doctor?" she asks rhetorically.

"I'm a trained emergency medical technician."

"Sorry—six months at a community college is not the same as four years of medical school and a residency."

"Grandma," says Isaac. "These are first responders—it's what they do."

"They can do it to someone else—and you can tell the driver that if he hits another pothole, he's the one who'll need to be hospitalized."

Isaac apologizes for her, but the EMT isn't bothered. Like me, he's seen people in pain before. They say the funniest things. Sometimes they see you as a savior; other times you're their tormenter. Pain, when there's enough of it, makes a person helpless. Whether it makes them blindly trusting or just plain paranoid depends on the person.

Personally, I happen to like the woman's well-earned crankiness. Anyone with a broken hip has every right to be as nasty as they want—and it *is* broken. But they won't know that until after the CAT scan.

Isaac calls his mom, letting her know what happened. "I think I left the front door open," he says—as if that matters now.

"You didn't," I tell him, but he's too distracted to even know I'm here. Isaac is a dutiful son and grandson. Where others might fall apart, he's doing what has to be done. Rising to the occasion. I do like that about him. He's someone you'd want by your side in a crisis.

"Meet us at Mercy Memorial," he tells his mother.

His grandmother scoffs at that. "Mercy," she says. "The only mercy is if they put me out of my goddamn misery." Then she yells at the EMT not to touch her until she sees that he's just trying to take her blood pressure. She shifts in the gurney and yelps from the pain. I'm here with her, but there's not much I can do in the moment. It will be at least another half hour until I really start making a difference.

"Just relax, Grandma," Isaac says. "Let him do his job."

She lets out a deep, shuddering sigh. She might yell at the EMT, but she won't yell at Isaac.

"Hold my hand, Baby-boy," she says—her pet name for him. So he does. All the way to Mercy Memorial Medical Center.

I'm not heavily into hospitals, but they're heavily into me—so I find myself there more often than I'd like. A lot of us do, I suppose. Hospitals are like airports to us. Hubs between where we've been and where we're going. And with whom. They're also safe zones. That is to say, we don't pick up plus-ones there. Hospitals are hallowed ground. Cathedrals consecrated to our power. So any time we spend there is in more selfless pursuits. After all, service is core to some of our basic designs. I suppose it makes us feel better about ourselves when we feel we've gone too far—which just goes to show that even selflessness can be self-serving.

Mercy Memorial has an ER less haphazard and over-whelmed than most. Isaac's grandmother allows a nurse to do her IV, and the nurse promises a doctor will be right in. Ten minutes later—which is instantaneous by hospital standards—a doctor arrives. She checks the chart, asks the same questions that were asked by both the intake clerk and the nurse, but at least now those questions lead to a definitive course of action. Isaac answers most of her questions, because his grandmother is too exhausted from the trauma of it all. Plus, I'm beginning to have a calming effect on her.

"We'll get you upstairs right away for a CAT scan," the doctor says. "And I'm going to give you some morphine for the pain."

All it takes is the mention of it, and he's there.

Phineas.

He looms just on the other side of the curtain. His pale slender fingers pull the curtain back just enough for me to see his face peering in, curious, expectant. Long black hair, pallid complexion, and eyes as dark as a moonless night that are a little too large for his face. Ghoulish and beautiful at once. He moves like he's underwater—even his hair floats, as if gravity has forgotten it.

Phineas is in my upline, but we don't socialize. He never comes to the Party—hospitals and nursing homes are his stomping grounds—but he's anything but noble in his pursuits. He's more of a bottom-feeder, scavenging sustenance from the doomed. He stands there peering from the curtain, like a vampire waiting to be invited in. If you ask me, it's just plain creepy.

As it turns out, however, this is not Phineas's day.

"No," yells Grandma. "No morphine!"

Phineas frowns, and Isaac pulls out the empty pill bottle, which he had the good sense to bring with him. "This is what she takes," he tells the doctor.

She examines the prescription. "How many did she have?"

"Just one," Isaac says.

The doctor considers it; then she turns to Grandma. "Mrs. Ramey, I'm going to put the same medicine in your IV. Enough of it to take the edge off the pain and help you rest."

Now we're talking!

The doctor taps on the computer console, putting in the orders. Phineas seems neither pleased nor displeased, just resigned. He moves off, in that underwater way of his. Good riddance.

The doctor finishes at the console, then turns to the old woman and says, "Funny, but most people in pain like yours beg for morphine." Then she leaves to take care of someone moaning in the next bay.

Now that the doctor's gone, Grandma turns her head to Isaac and whispers, "If you're terminal, they give you morphine," she tells him. "They don't care if you get hooked when you're gonna die anyway. All bets are off when you've got an expiration date."

The nurse comes in to say there's a backlog in radiology. It'll be an hour until they can get her in for the scan. "But there's no reason you have to be in so much discomfort while you're waiting." Then she pulls out a little ampule of yours truly, in convenient liquid form.

"Just what the doctor ordered," Grandma says. "Literally."

The nurse fills a syringe and pushes it directly into her IV line.

I notice how Isaac's eyes follow the syringe from the moment it makes its appearance right until the moment the nurse drops it, empty, into the red sharps container on the wall.

"Warm . . . ," Grandma says. "Hooooo . . . I'm flying. . . ."

"Quick, isn't it?" the nurse says. "I'll be back to check on you."

Finally, I'm free to do what I'm here to do—and Addison's words come back to me. *We have purpose beyond pleasure.* This poor woman does not deserve the pain she's enduring. I gently stroke her arm. I smooth the care lines on her forehead.

Isaac watches his grandmother's face. He watches the drip, drip, drip of the IV. He is aware of me, here between them, but I am not his focus. That's fine for now. Ebb and flow. I will be his center of attention soon enough. But now to the task at hand.

I gently stroke the tension out of her. I whisper in her ear that she can relax. Not in English, but in the language she spoke in her childhood. The one she sometimes still dreams in. I have to admit, there are times I enjoy this. Using my power for the benefit of others. Something sweet to cleanse my palate—but only once in a while. And, of course, I'll only offer short-term support, because helping people can be habit forming.

Soon the woman's breathing becomes easier—but she looks right through me, to her grandson, as if this relief is his doing.

"Thank you, Baby-boy," she says. "I don't know what I'd do without you."

I sit with Isaac in the hospital cafeteria as he mulls over a bowl of melting ice cream. His parents are here now—they went up with his grandmother to radiology and are in a waiting room as she gets the various scans that will confirm the extent of the damage. They insisted that Isaac get himself something to eat. He did as they said, but he's not hungry. At least not for food.

"An ice cube . . . ," Isaac says. "Her whole life has been changed by a lousy ice cube on the floor."

"Lives can rest on a whole lot less," I tell him. "But what about you? How are *you* feeling?"

"That's not important."

"But it is, Isaac. At times like this, you need to take care of yourself, too. Fulfill your own needs. If you don't do that, how can you help anyone else?"

"*I* didn't help her," he says. "*You* did. What you did in there for her was . . . miraculous."

Aw. So sweet I could blush. "I do what I do," I tell him.

He looks down into his bowl, but I know his thoughts are on me. As they should be. But then I'm blindsided by the last thing I expect him to say.

"What's it like?" he asks. "What's it like to be you?"

I'm taken aback by the question. No one has ever asked me about *me* before. The lives I've touched, the lives I've taken, have always been conquests for me, nothing more. None of my conquests even think to ask such a thing. It's always about them. Their pain. Their need. But what is it like to be me? Powerful. Triumphant. Desired.

"It's . . . lonely," I tell him. The word's out there even before I realize I've said it.

"It doesn't have to be," he says.

And now I feel exposed. Vulnerable. I'm looking into his eyes now. They are so very deep. Not a bottomless pit like Phineas's but a deep well. It's the kind of thing I don't ever notice when I'm going about my business.

My business.

What am I doing? Have I forgotten why I'm with him? How could I be so careless?

Isaac reaches for me, but I quickly pull away. He does not like that at all. He gets tense. Worried. "What's wrong?"

"You know what's wrong," I tell him, sheathing myself in cool indifference. "I can't stay with you."

"No! You can't leave."

"I can, and I will. You chose to help your grandmother instead of keeping me all to yourself. As admirable as that was, you have to face the consequences."

"Please don't go. . . ."

"If you want to see me," I tell him, "you'll have to make it happen."

He's in a silent panic now. "But where will I find you?"

"Just look in the right places. Be creative. I'm sure you can do that."

Then I stride away, leaving him to the remains of his ice cream, which has already died in the bowl. And no matter how much I want to turn around and go back to him, even for just a few moments more, I don't. I can't.

Find me, Isaac. Please find me. And it troubles me how much I truly want him to.

13

Few Places More Godforsaken

ADDISON

Ivy and I are on a crowded bus with danger ahead. It's taken her long enough, but she's finally cultivated the determination to officially break up with Craig. Thanks to my careful coercion, she hasn't seen him for over a week. I advocate for a phone call, or a text, or even just a social media status change—but Ivy insists on breaking up with Craig in person. I don't like it. Every moment he gets with her is another moment to tempt her, seduce her, lure her off the path and back into the swamp where others can have their way with her. My notorious upline, who always seem to have their way with anyone they choose.

Craig's place is in a sketchy part of town that's not long for this world. A street of small one-story ranch houses that have seen much better days. There are government notices on every door that mark a ticking clock to the end of the world. Perhaps there are places more godforsaken than here, but few have a literal expiration date. Few feel so . . . terminal.

Craig's house isn't a far walk from the bus stop. As soon as we near the house, we hear muffled bass. The cacophony of a crowd. Dozens bottleneck at the door, which seems to leak out smoke like a fire-breathing dragon.

Craig is having a party. A daytime party, no less. Apparently with eminent domain declared on his street, he can trash the place as much as he wants. One last hurrah before the freeway comes through.

Ivy storms inside, and I follow. I can feel her heart rate escalate as her blood surges.

She enters a smoke screen of haze, made solid by fluorescent black lights—and it's like we've crossed over into another dimension. Whomping music. Grungy partygoers who don't seem to actually know one another. Furniture that has burst at the seams. All the class of a landfill. Not my style. Not Ivy's style either—she just needs to be convinced of that.

I can tell that Al has been here. Then again, he's everywhere. Al is like Santa Claus on Christmas.

Ivy is single-minded, moving through the crowd and down the hallway until she locates Craig. He's on his waterbed, wasted beyond cognition, kissing some vaguely attractive, generic girl. The kind who's probably named after a season or a president.

"Easy," I tell Ivy. "Focus your rage. Let it serve *you*, not him."

She heeds my advice, and the fury that ensues is magnificent.

"You scumbag!" Ivy yells. "You brain-dead sleazy sack of shit!"

Craig stumbles to his feet. "Ivy, honey, you made it to the party," he says, like he wasn't just kissing Autumn. "I've been trying to call you."

"Wait, you have a girlfriend!?" says Madison.

"Had," Ivy tells her. "History. And long overdue."

"Ivy, let's not make this bigger than it has to be."

Oh, he's opened himself up for one fine insult there, but Ivy decides it's not worth her time or effort. Good for her.

"Goodbye, Craig. Don't call me again. Ever."

Meanwhile, Summer rolls with the waves of the waterbed, attempting to refasten her bra. "You didn't tell me you had a girlfriend!"

Craig stops Ivy in the doorway. He's so used to her waffling, forgiving ways, he thinks he can just pull on the yo-yo string and draw her back. "C'mon, you know you can't stay mad at me," he says. "So why don't you stay and party with me and Reagan?"

The suggestion has whipped Ivy's fury to a nice stiff peak. So I draw her attention to a dark, cobweb-woven fireplace. And the poker leaning beside it.

She grabs the poker instinctively, knowing what I have in mind.

"What the hell are you doing?" demands Craig.

Ivy storms toward Reagan and raises the poker high above her head.

"No! Don't!" Craig yells.

Reagan screams and cowers.

And Ivy brings the sharp, curved point of the poker down on the waterbed, tugging at just the right moment to rip it wide.

The entire thing bursts. Craig is hit by the domestic tsunami and wipes out, crashing into his dresser, while Reagan sinks into the bed frame, which pools with water.

"You bitch!" Craig screams.

Then Ivy and I march out of that room, her head higher than it's ever been before, a dark smile stretched across her face. "That wasn't hard at all," she tells me.

I burst out laughing. It's been a while since I laughed and actually meant it. I'm proud of her.

We march toward the front door in triumph, on a total high. But when you're in my business, you know that any high is inevitably followed by a low. Nature's way of maintaining equilibrium. And today's fallout comes in the form of something I should have expected. Two guests who weren't exactly invited, but they always show up. Like shit on the sole of someone's shoe.

Dusty and Charlie, their white silk suits and golden chains clashing with the grunge around them.

"Well, if it isn't Addison," says Charlie.

Ivy's already heading for the door. I don't let the brothers know that I'm with her. I approach them, keeping their attention on me, buying time for Ivy to get out.

"Shouldn't you be off helping some acne-ridden adolescent study somewhere?" Both he and his brother offer me disingenuous smiles. No matter how bright their teeth are, their eyes are always dark and glassy. Black holes where light itself is snuffed.

"I go where I choose, when I choose," I tell them. Which isn't exactly true, but they don't care enough to argue.

"Then come join us, little cousin," Charlie says, scratching his neck with a long pinkie nail.

"I'll pass."

"Your loss," says Dusty. "We only want to make your dreary existence more bearable."

Right. As if they can spread their effect on me. For their users, Dusty and Charlie can make a dull conversation interesting. Make you believe that any bad idea is the magnum opus of your life. They make you feel grander than you really are, make you do things you'll regret, and abandon you when things go south. Or worse, they pass you up to Crys.

Then Charlie begins to scan the crowd. "If you're here, Addison, that means you must have a 'ward,'" he mocks. "Who is it?"

"None of your business," I snap, trying to block Ivy from their view without being conspicuous about it.

"That's no way to speak to your superiors," Dusty says, then scans the room, too, if only to spite me. Finally they zero in on Ivy, who's still making her way to the door.

"That one," Dusty says definitively.

Charlie raises his nose and sniffs the air. "Yes, I can smell you in her sweat, Addison."

With their attention on her, I realize I have to play this right. With these two, there is no margin for error. Because when it comes to Dusty and Charlie, the one thing they love more than a plus-one is a plus-one that isn't theirs.

So I shrug and say, "You want her, she's yours. Frankly, she's not worth my time. I'd rather be somewhere else anyway."

Their attention slips from Ivy back to me. "And where might that be?" Dusty asks.

"A library, a classroom, a dorm. You know—a place where I'm much better suited."

They share a derisive grin, both of them dripping such condescension I want to go grab Craig's fireplace poker and shove it straight up their overstimulated nostrils.

"You go, little cousin. Do whatever it is you do. Leave the real action to us."

They glance toward the door just in time to see Ivy exit. And since they think I'm not particularly interested, they're not particularly interested, either. They let her go and give their attention to the partiers around them, dismissing me without as much as a goodbye.

I catch up with Ivy outside. She's crying tears of anger— the ones she wouldn't let Craig see.

"Keep moving," I tell her as we storm away. "And don't look back."

ROXY

I've been to this restaurant before.

Faux Chinese decor. Gaudy golden dragons. Bloodred lacquer over embellished columns. It was actually built by a German restaurateur in the 1950s, when it was much more lucrative to sell something Chinese than German. Toward that end, he hired all Asian staff to maintain the illusion.

It was once the spot to be. Long lines and reservations days out. But, like all things, its time peaked and faded. Then the owner met one of my predecessors, came to the Party, and went out with a bang. He left the place to his adult children, but none of them wanted it, so they sold it to someone who sold it again. Now, under its fourth dynasty, the restaurant looks like a snapshot from history, beauty faded like an old-time movie star. And tonight, beneath the glow of a hundred dusty Chinese lanterns, sits the one person whose name I can't get out of my head.

Isaac.

He's in a red velvet booth with his family.

He doesn't know that I'm here—because tonight I'm not here for him. I have other business. There's a young woman with horn-rimmed glasses that has had enough of the real world and needs a little of me instead. She's here for a date with a junior stock analyst. He's late. She doesn't know it yet, but he's stood her up. She'll realize it soon, however. Then I'll smoothly insert myself into her pity party, and abracadabra, she'll be mine.

"Letting the boy get away, are you?" says a voice from behind.

It's Addison. He leans against a wall painted with plum blossoms, flashing his most presumptuous smile.

"I'm not interested in him tonight," I tell Addison. It's a lie. I'm interested, but tonight he's a distraction. I'm never distracted, and it annoys me.

"Don't take your eyes off the prize, Roxy," Addison taunts. "On second thought, *do*. And I'll take your poolside cabana, while you spend a year . . . elsewhere."

In the booth, Isaac's sister passes a steaming platter to her parents, who sit across from them. I force myself to look away and toward the girl I'm there for.

"Excuse me," I say, and intentionally shoulder Addison out of my way. Then I go to the girl who's finally tired of waiting for her AWOL asshole of a date. I grab her, rip her out of her chair, kiss her till her bones turn to rubber, and I hurl her out the door. Mission accomplished.

"Next!" I say, brushing off my hands and striding back to Addison.

He's neither impressed nor amused.

"That was nasty, Roxy. Not your usual style."

"Yeah, well, maybe I'm changing my style."

Addison shakes his head. "Carefulness counts," he has the nerve to tell me. "You don't want to go the way of 'Lude."

That shuts me up. No one says that name aloud. 'Lude was one of our predecessors. His fall was epic. The stuff of legends. The type of horror story they tell fledglings to keep them in line. *Careful, or you'll end up like 'Lude.* Or, *Better watch out, or 'Lude will come to take you away in the night.* As the story goes, 'Lude was reckless. He overdid it and paid the ultimate price. But there are those who say he's still alive, imprisoned in a cell high above the Party. Able to see the world like the prisoners of Alcatraz but never to be a part of it again.

"Maybe that's what I want," I say to Addison, just to be contrary. "To be just like 'Lude."

"No you don't," he says, his tone dark and deliberate. "I worry about you, Roxy."

And that just pisses me off. Not because he's insincere, but because he truly means it. How dare he condescend—as if I'm the one who needs to be taken under his wing and not the other way around. I don't need his concern. I'm the player here, and he's the wannabe. He'll be soundly reminded of that when I win our competition without even having to try.

But before I can muster something to snap at him, Addison strides to the red velvet booth. He leans over Isaac's sister, keeping her focused on the meal and the conversation the family is having.

And I can't look away from Isaac. He's there with them, but not. He's thinking of me. Wanting to *be* with me. But he can't. Not now. He has to earn it. He has to find me. Those are the rules.

14

Weak**ne**ss Leaving th**e** Bo**dy**

ISAAC

"This wasn't an easy decision," Isaac's parents tell him and Ivy over dinner.

They sit in a tight booth at the Chinese restaurant. They rarely come here. It's a family go-to for special occasions. But "special" doesn't always mean "good."

Isaac squirms in his seat, his body itching on the inside in a way that can't be scratched. And in the synapses beneath his skull, there is only one thing on his mind.

Those pills.

They sing in his head like a song you can't shake, and the tune just keeps getting louder.

It's between the appetizers and the main dishes that Isaac notices his parents clasping hands. He realizes they're about to give them whatever news generated this fancy dinner out.

"We need to talk about Grandma," their father says. "And her situation."

"It's a bit worse than we thought," their mother adds.

Isaac and Ivy steel themselves. "Worse how?" Isaac asks, scanning their faces and preparing for the worst possible news.

"It's the osteoporosis," their mom tells them. "Her bones

have become very brittle. Her hip might never heal properly."

Isaac and Ivy take a simultaneous breath of relief.

"Jeez, Mom," says Ivy. "You guys had us thinking she was dying."

"No," says Dad. "She's not sick, but she's going to have serious mobility problems. And she's going to need more help than we can give her. . . ."

It's Ivy who picks up on the insinuation. "You're putting her in a home?"

"An assisted living facility," their father tells them. "There's a difference. She'll have her own room and can keep her things. It will be just like it was with us, but she'll have medical staff twenty-four-seven."

"And she'll be with other people her own age," Mom points out.

Isaac shakes his head, not liking the idea at all. "Grandma hates people her own age."

"What if she falls again, and no one's home?" their dad levels at them. "And what if the next fall is even worse than this one?"

No one has a response to that. The question just hangs hot and heavy in the air, like the ginger and garlic wafting in waves from the kitchen.

"It's for her own good," Mom finally says.

"No, it's for *your* own good," says Ivy. "Because you don't want the responsibility."

Their dad is about to take the bait and escalate into an argument, but Mom gently puts her hand on his and tries to defuse it.

"Honey, we can't afford a personal caregiver, and that's what she'd need if she stays with us," Mom says. "The only other option would be for your father or me to stop working and stay home, and we can't afford that, either—we can barely keep our heads above water as it is."

Dad sighs, taking a moment, then finally says, "I wish I could snap my fingers and make everything be the way we want it to be. But there are practical considerations. Grandma knows it as well."

"Have you told her?" Ivy asks.

"We've discussed it."

"And does she want to go?"

"She knows it's for the best."

Through most of this, Isaac has remained silent. Because the most awful, selfish thing has occurred to him. If Grandma goes to assisted living, so will the contents of her medicine chest. He won't have access to her pills. He had already sworn up and down that he wouldn't take them from her anymore, but the prospect of their absolute and irrevocable absence has raised that terrible song in his head to a brain-bursting volume. *This is not about me,* he tries to scream over the growing sibilance. *This is about Grandma. How can I be so goddamn self-centered?*

Then the food arrives at the worst possible time, as food in a restaurant often does. No one is in a sharing mood, but it's family style, so everyone must share anyway. Even though the four of them are cramped into the booth, they seem to be practicing a new form of social distancing. Emotional walls instead of physical space. Isaac is reminded of something he learned in science. How space is so cold because a vacuum can't conduct heat. Apparently, neither can an emotional vacuum because the space between them is frigid.

A body in motion tends to stay in motion. Isaac is a living study of Newton's first law as he paces his bedroom that night. He can't sit without feeling like he has to stand. He can't stand without feeling like he has to lie down, and when he lies down, he can't find a comfortable position. There's an empty longing that clings to his ribs, clawing its way up toward his throat. His grandmother's doctor never refilled the prescription Isaac called in, and won't while she's still at the hospital. So on that first day, Isaac had done a deep dive in her room, telling himself he was cleaning it for her—but aware, even then, that it was a lie. He came up with two expired pills in a forgotten bottle in the back of a drawer. He halved the first one, then quartered the second, figuring he could step his way off them, but it's not working. Only now does he realize how much he's come to rely on them. It's as if his heart had been broken, and the splintered pieces have been hidden somewhere outside of himself. Now all he has left is one quarter of one pill.

Maybe it will go away after a good night's sleep, he thinks. Maybe he needs human connection. He's been so isolated these past few weeks. So he picks up his phone to call Shelby. They talk all the time, but it seems to be less lately. And although she's texting again, it seems to be mostly in group texts. He can't remember what they said to each other in their last actual conversation. Did they laugh? Did they argue? Did they say anything to each other that they'd come to regret? How could he regret something if he doesn't remember what was said?

"Hi, Isaac," she says, picking up on the third ring. The tone of her voice is normal. Not cold, but not overly warm, either. But that's Shelby. She's noncommittal even emotionally.

"Hey, what ya up to?" Isaac asks.

"Not much, just homework. How's your foot?"

"All better," he says.

"Well, that's good, right?"

There's something off about this. Not so much like she's walking on eggshells—it's more like she's trying to sweep the eggshells out of sight and out of mind.

"You okay?" Isaac asks, before she asks it of him. But then he realizes she might not have asked him.

"I'm fine," she answers. "Why wouldn't I be?"

"No reason, just asking."

"Well, I'm good, I guess."

"That's great."

"Yeah. So anyway, I really got to get this assignment done before my brain turns to mush. Can I call you later?"

"Sure," says Isaac. They say their goodbyes and hang up, leaving Isaac to replay the entire conversation in his head multiple times, not even knowing, or understanding what, if anything, the call meant. It's like when you get into a texting fight just because you can't read the other person's emotions. You think they're mad when they're joking; you think they're being cruel when they're just being ironic. It's why they invented emojis. His entire conversation with Shelby was like a series of ambiguous texts with no emojis. And now the clawing feeling has gotten all the way up into his head. It's behind his eyeballs, running like rats along his optic nerve. Suddenly, he finds himself crying, and he has no idea why.

. . .

It all comes to a head at his game the next day. He's back on the field, ready to play a full game, at full force, as long as his coach lets him. His ankle is in tiptop shape, and he can pick up where he left off. Isaac knows if there's one thing that can get him out of any rut, it's the exhilaration of competition. Now, all the untamed, undirected energy that has been short-circuiting him will have direction. He'll use it to his advantage. He will be a powerhouse on the field tonight!

Tonight's game is a state qualifier—all the more reason for Isaac to play his heart out. His parents are here. Ricky and some of his other friends are here as well to celebrate his return to the field. Shelby said she kinda sorta might be there, but she had a paper she was procrastinating on. He looks for her on the sidelines but tries not to let it pull his focus.

Just before the game, the coach gives one of his famous impassioned speeches to the team—the kind that always ends with a moral platitude, like you might see on a poster in a gym teacher's office.

Today's is "Pain is weakness leaving the body."

Isaac and his whole team scream it back at the coach like a war chant.

He straps on his shin guards, laces up his cleats, and trots onto the field. Isaac has a weakness inside him that he's determined to purge, and he's going to enjoy it. He inhales the sweet smell of freshly cut grass. Cool early-evening air flows over his body. His leg muscles stretch to their full elasticity. Soon endorphins will fill whatever part of him isn't whole. This will be the end of his suffering.

A whistle blows. The game begins. The ball is passed around. It eventually finds Isaac—but he almost instantaneously loses possession, the opposing team winning out. But it's okay. It's okay. He's not off his game. He just needs to get back up to speed—it might take a minute.

Most of the half is highly defensive, deflecting several tries on their goal. Then Isaac sees his chance and seizes an opportunity, performing a risky slide tackle that dislodges the ball from an opponent. A teammate gets a foot on it and taps it back to Isaac again.

Now he has possession, and God help anyone who gets in his way.

Isaac takes the ball upfield with bestial aggression, eluding one, two, three defenders. He's always been a team player, but tonight he's different. Tonight he has no intention of passing the ball if he doesn't have to.

Isaac knows he's playing recklessly. It's in the way he weaves in and out of defenders. The way he digs his shoulders against his opponents'. He's playing physically. He's playing dirty. And it's working.

The sidelines are electrified. Everyone's cheering him on. His coach is going ballistic. Isaac can score here. He *will* score!

Now he's past the defenders and one-on-one with the goalie, sprinting at critical velocity, with no intention of slowing down—but the ball is pacing ahead of him.

The goalie steps forward with expert timing, well positioned to snatch the ball.

Despite Isaac's impressive display, this is a battle that Isaac is going to lose—and deep down he knows it. But something even deeper inside him doesn't care. That thing scraping on his insides. An entity that is chaotic. That isn't afraid of pain. That welcomes not only the crash but the burn as well.

Isaac bull-rushes forward, thrusting his entire body into the oncoming goalkeeper. But the goalie, with a much lower center of gravity, buries himself into the ball. Still Isaac doesn't stop. He doesn't beg off in the slightest. And when he connects with the goalie, Isaac is thrown violently off his feet by his own momentum, flying over the goalie in a twisting ballistic arc.

And he crashes into the corner of the goal, shoulder-first.

He hears the bone crack—a sound that ricochets inside him like a sonic boom, coupled with a terrible popping sensation.

The human shoulder is made up of three major bones. The clavicle, the scapula, and a third one that Isaac can't remember. That's the one he's busted. That's where ligaments have been torn.

Isaac writhes on the ground, blinded by pain, until the pain becomes too much for him to do anything but breathe and sob. Through his clouded eyes, he sees faces looming over him. His coach. Others he can't identify. Someone shoves a bag of ice on Isaac's shoulder too hard, and he bucks and wails.

The ball never went in the goal. He hardly got to play half a game. And he won't be playing again anytime soon, so no scouts will see him. But despite all that, the scraping, scrabbling thing inside Isaac finally relaxes. Because as much pain as he's suffering, he knows it's only temporary.

Soon there will be relief.

The only question is the dosage.

15

Re**aching** Across the Event Horizon

ISAAC

The emergency room isn't as quiet as it was when they brought Grandma in. Plus, Isaac wasn't fast-tracked by an ambulance, so he's relegated to the waiting room—an anxious purgatory where dozens of people struggle through various stages of contagion and trauma.

Isaac's father paces and rails against the soulless forces of bureaucracy. His mother keeps trying to push Advil on him, but he refuses.

"That's not gonna help!" he insists. The last thing he needs is for some doctor to tell him that he can't get anything stronger until the Advil's out of his system. Isaac feels miserable on so many levels, his emotional exhaustion tips the scale of wretchedness even more than the pain.

When he finally gets taken back into a treatment bay, his treatment is nothing like what his grandmother got. A shoulder injury in a young, healthy kid does not carry the same urgency as a broken hip in the elderly. They don't give him an IV. They don't offer him a magic shot. But after he waits twenty more minutes, a nurse takes his vitals and authorizes medication. A single, beautiful white pill and a soothing cup of water.

"For the pain," the nurse says.

But Isaac's mother stays Isaac's hand as he reaches for it.

"What is it?" his mother asks suspiciously.

"Mom!" Isaac says. "Who cares? I need it!"

"It's called Roxicet," the nurse says.

His mother relaxes and lets him take it. "Okay, good. That's what Nana takes for pain." She pats his arm gently and smiles at the nurse. "Just as long as it's not OxyContin."

"Well, actually—" the nurse begins, but Isaac cuts her off with a well-timed cough.

"I need"—cough—"more water"—cough—"the pill's stuck in my throat."

His mother hurries to the sink to refill his cup.

The pill is not stuck in his throat. He's already swallowed it. But more water will help it dissolve faster—and more important, it gives the nurse a moment to reconsider what she was about to say . . . and that maybe telling Isaac's mother that Roxicet *is* OxyContin with some added Tylenol will just complicate things. The nurse knows what's important. The easing of Isaac's pain. So she doesn't finish her thought, and lets it go.

Isaac feels as if the medication is already working. Of course it's not—he knows it's just the placebo effect—but he'll take what he can get until it really kicks in.

CT scan, an ultrasound, and the threat of an MRI if the first two are inconclusive. The best thing about emergency rooms is that you don't have to schedule tests weeks in advance, and you don't have to wait for results. It all happens right there while you wait—although his father gripes about the inevitability of getting billed by every person in a white coat who glances his way.

More waiting. The TV's on its second installation of a Jason Bourne marathon. All car chases in foreign cities look exactly alike. Especially on painkillers. Finally, the orthopedic doctor on duty comes down with the news.

"Could be better, could be worse," he says. "You've got a fractured clavicle and a torn rotator cuff. The good news is it's not bad enough to need an operation. You'll just need time, rest, and some good physical therapy."

"It hurts," Isaac says. "It really hurts. . . ." Although the edge has already been dulled to a monotonous throb.

The doctor goes over to the little rolling computer and takes a look at Isaac's chart. In old movies, it's always a clipboard, but technology has relegated clipboards to the shelves of history.

"I'll write you a script for the pain," the doctor says, and pulls out a little carbon copy pad—because when it comes to controlled meds, apparently technology holds no sway.

"We'll keep you on the painkillers. Take one every eight hours. I'm giving you two days' worth."

Isaac isn't sure he heard him right. "Two days' worth?"

"You can take it on top of ibuprofen."

"See?" says his mom. "You could have taken those Advil after all."

"But wait," says Isaac. "You're giving me *six pills*?"

The doctor turns to Isaac, and suddenly Isaac can practically see the red flags he just sent up, waving like banners all around the examination room.

"Two days is all you need . . . ," the doctor says suspiciously. "Is that a problem?"

His pen stalls on the prescription form, the part just before the signature. Isaac's heart lingers on a bleak precipice, ready to plunge into oblivion. Then Isaac's woozy brain kicks in, and he pulls back from the edge.

"I can't take six pills," he says, feigning a whine. "Pain meds always make me throw up."

And the doctor finishes writing the prescription. "Just remember to take them with food," he says, tearing off the sheet and handing it to his mother. "You'll be fine."

The doctor leaves, saying the nurse will be in with a referral for physical therapy.

When Isaac's parents see the lost look on his face, they think they know where it's coming from.

"These things happen, honey," says his mom. "It's not the end of the world."

"Life throws you curveballs sometimes," says his dad.

"This was a terrible accident, but you'll put it behind you," his mom says.

But deep down, a part of Isaac knows that this wasn't an accident at all. It was willful. Like letting go of the steering wheel and letting your car go ballistic.

And what bothers Isaac most is not that he did it, but that he did it for six lousy pills.

ROXY

He finds me!

It wasn't easy, but he made his way. He sacrificed so much

for us to be together. It's beautiful the lengths that he would go just to be with me. It was brave—no, more than that.

It was *poetic*.

His friends come over that first night, but I'm the center of his attention. And I give him all of mine. Not just half, but all the attention I can give, and more. He needs it. He deserves it. His friends say they're there to cheer him up, but I can tell he just wants them to leave. It's too taxing. And that Shelby, she's the worst—saying things like "I don't know why you play so hard. It's only a game." If I had the power, I would turn her into a soccer ball, just so I could watch her get kicked over and over again.

What is it like to be me? Isaac's question keeps coming back to me. Not only was I never asked it before, but it was something I never even asked myself. I lived in the moment. I partied. I indulged the rush of the hunt. I took on enough plus-ones to stir media outlets into a frenzy. I prided myself on being a key player in the opioid epidemic.

So what is it like to be me? It's wild. It's frenetic. It's larger than life on a scale too grand to conceive. Yet the word that came to me when he asked was "lonely," and even that's only the tip of it. The word that settles in place now is the full picture.

Unfulfilling.

I don't want to admit that. It makes me angry to even think it. It makes me want to drag a million people to the Party and leave them in ashes. But I know not even that will satisfy me. Not even a little. I am always thirsty, never quenched. No matter how much I get, I need more. To be me—to be *us*—is a curse. Which is why we never stop moving, never stop trolling the depths of people's souls for our next fix. We are addicted to their addiction.

This revelation isn't something I can share with my upline. Hiro would scold me; he is too disciplined to waste time in self-reflection. Because if your soul is an abyss, why would you ever look into it?

But Isaac stands at the brink of the black hole, reaching across my event horizon. I could so easily pull him in . . . but what if I let him pull me out instead?

Interlude #3—Lucy ($C_{20}H_{25}N_3O$)

It's not like I can't remember. I remember it all, just not in what you might call "order," because one memory spills into the next and into the one before until it's all a twisted taffy-pull of things that happened, or maybe didn't happen, because it's like that sometimes too.

But I do know the difference between then and now, because now doesn't need to be remembered, it just is, and "now" means here above the endless Party, on the steep sloping roof where I like to go to get away from the commotion below, because commotion isn't my deal, you know?

But the roof isn't a roof to me. It's a hillside of wildflowers, and the air is a birthday cake fresh out of the oven, and the sky is a swirl of colors that go beyond what eyes are supposed to see. And I dance with him, and with her, and with him, and with them, and it's good to be here still, and to be remembered, and to share the flavorful skies and the painted snails that talk in tongues and even the razorback spiders that will sometimes crawl into your brain and make you scream, because it's like that sometimes too.

The space before me twists and bubbles like a pot being stirred, and in the midst of it is someone I haven't seen before, a young man shivering in wide-eyed wonderment.

"Are you new?" I ask. "I remember when I was new, but that was a long time ago, although sometimes we get to be new again, but not recently, so are you new?"

"Yeah, first time," he says, and I see he's not one of us, but one of them. Just a kid who wanted to experiment. He expected to be somewhere else, but ended up here and thought, *What the* hell. *Why not. It's not like it's going to kill me*—which I would never, ever do. I wouldn't hurt a fly, but I do eat them on occasion—the flies that is, but only the cinnamon ones.

"Lie back," I tell him, gently massaging his neck. "Let whatever comes come."

I feel his pulse in my fingertips, and how it takes me back to the old days! I remember bodies and breath and music played at stretching elastic speed. The distorted words were a spell to open my soul and share it with those who loved me, because then, in those days, love was free.

They would move in moiré circles in the park, so many of them, all slow and loose, their heartache poured out from a rusted can until they felt none of it, and oh! I was beautiful, with a moonflower wreath woven into my hair like an elven bride and my footfalls so light that I could pirouette on a blade of grass, and the dandelion seeds would swirl in the air around me, the rightful center of their worship, while the serious folks would say, "Dandelions are weeds that must be pulled out at the root." But why would they say that when dandelions make everyone happy?

The new boy laughs. "Are you seeing this?"

"I see everything you see," I tell him. "All your dimensions and revelations." Down the hillside now rolls a slow flow of blue lava, not hot, but warm to the touch. You can walk in it. You can lie in it and let it surround you, envelop you. "This can be our secret," I tell him, "or you can tell the whole wide world. I won't mind."

He laughs and cringes, shivers and laughs again. "It all makes sense now. Everything."

Which is what they always say when their trip isn't of the spider or snake variety. They think for a sparkling moment that the cow has a perfect reason to jump over the moon and that the Answer to Everything is woven into the lace of their left shoe.

Who cares if the answers aren't real? Reality is overrated—but they'll remember *thinking* they knew the secrets of the universe. Except, of course, when they don't remember, because it's like that sometimes, too. Enlightenment'll cost ya, baby, like maybe a few gazillion brain cells blown out like Christmas bulbs in a thunderstorm.

Now he's gone pale. His breath rapid and short. He wiggles his fingers in front of his face. "I think I'm seeing my hand from yesterday," he says. They are so cute when they get like this, and it makes me laugh. It makes me forget that the old days are gone and my long hair has turned gray. Well, maybe so—but my eyes are still full of more things than are dreamt of in your philosophies, to quote what's-his-name, who must have had a little of me in him, even though I wasn't born when the Bard was doing his thing.

"You're not what I expected," the boy says.

"Am I better? Am I worse?"

"You're different," he tells me.

"Like . . . you ordered a burger and got a lightbulb instead?"

"Kind of, I guess." And then he confesses. "I feel so . . . strange. I'm a little scared. . . ."

"Just a little?"

"Maybe more than a little."

"Maybe it's because you know something you shouldn't know," I whisper to him. "Maybe it's because you know you can fly."

"I can fly?"

"Can you?"

"I don't know."

"What if you could?"

I caress him harder, reaching into his brain, my fingernails deep into every fold of his cortex, because more than anything in the whole world, I want to see him fly and to know that I was the one—*it was me*—who made it happen and prove to the others that I am not just a silly throwback to a time that was both bloody and innocent but mostly bloody.

"I can fly!" he says.

"I know you can."

Maybe this will be the one with the conviction to do it. And all the others at the Party will see and know. They will fall silent in awe and recognize that I am their goddess—and finally, finally they will all bow to me and repent for how they've treated me, and I will be gracious and forgive them because a goddess can afford to be magnanimous, and all it will take is for this sweet, doe-eyed boy to take flight.

"Will you jump?" I ask. "Will you jump into the sky? Will you soar for me?"

And he looks at his arms and sees wings, and he looks to the horizon and sees the clouds become a hand beckoning him to be one with the sky, which now opens to receive him like a lover, and he knows in his heart that this is the answer to all his questions in his life, so he strides to the edge, and without the slightest hesitation, he leaps into the sky, and I squeal with the absolute joy of it.

But gravity flatly refuses to release him.

He arcs like a diver, plunging out of sight in an awful spider-brained scream like the others, like all the others, not becoming one with the sky but becoming one with the earth far, far below. I didn't want him to fall. I really and truly wanted him to fly, and I really and truly believed that he would. That I could give him that power—or at least open him to a power within himself. Was it worth it to him? I wonder. Was that moment of absolute belief worth what he has lost?

And I am sad, but not too sad, because from way up here, I never hear him hit bottom, but still sad because I am alone again, and I'm still the funny little mascot of the Party. That curious girl who twirls in the corner, just some vague-minded enchantress of light and dreams with no substance but the substance that melts on the tongue like a snowflake. No powers to change what's real, only what's unreal.

And so I sit in the wildflowers, by the blue lava river on the sloping hill of the roof, listening to the Party rage, and wishing, wishing, wishing that the next one will be the one who can fly.

16

Just Another Distraction

IVY

Ivy is getting more attention these days—and from everyone. Guys at school. People she chats up at coffee shops—even from her own friends.

"Are you doing something new with your hair?"

"You're working out more, aren't you?"

"Those jeans fit you so well!"

But it's not any of those things. It's her attitude. The way she interacts. Her quips are quicker and more clever, and there's a bounce to her step, even when she doesn't want it. The "FUTURE" is no longer a screaming accusation. Now it's just the future, and it's fine. She's fine. And she will *be* fine. She no longer feels overwhelmed by life, and that changes everything.

And the attention is nice. Or at least it was at first, until it started to get annoying. It's a side effect, just like the weight loss. It's all water weight anyway. The medication is technically a stimulant, which can make you dehydrated and take the edge off your appetite.

No big deal.

It's been her motto these days.

She's been crushing it in school, so how can she complain?

But just because new paths are opening, it doesn't defuse the minefield that still exists between those paths and Ivy.

Ivy's at the bus stop after school. She could ride with Isaac, but he has eighth period and she doesn't. More often than not, she doesn't have the patience to wait around. Patience is not a virtue her new regimen allows.

Grant Maldonado is at the bus stop too. He's in Ivy's science class. Lately they've been pairing up as lab partners. A month ago she probably wasn't even on Grant's radar—or if she was, it was as a UFO. Not anymore. Grant seems to have taken an interest in the new Ivy. This is a good thing. Grant is good-looking and smart and popular in an unobtrusive way. Unlike the "popular" kids, he doesn't have to try, and he feels no need to wear popularity like a cologne.

Ivy's not quite sure what to do with his attention. Well, she knows what she'd *like* to do with it, but right now it seems like too much effort.

He's a distraction, a voice inside her says. *You just broke up with Craig—you don't need another distraction.*

As much as she wants to be into Grant, there's a part of her that can only see his flaws. Like his Adam's apple, which moves a little too much when he talks. It's hard to focus on what he says when you're always following the bouncing ball. And then there's his gaze, which is the tiniest bit unnerving. He's fine when he's got something to focus on, like when they're doing a lab together, but when it's just her and him, it's like he doesn't know where to look. It's like he's afraid that eye contact is too intimate, and he's worried that any downward glance will make her think he's looking at her breasts. Not that he's actually doing that, but he's afraid she'll *think* he's looking at her breasts. And then he'll know that she thinks that. And *she'll* know that *he* knows. And suddenly they're lost in a hall of social mirrors with no viable way out.

It's not that he's nervous around her. It's more like he's nervous that he might *get* nervous, which is just as unsettling.

It annoys Ivy to no end that this is what she's focusing on—because the guys she usually ends up going out with have so many flaws, they blend together, so she doesn't even bother counting them, even though she really should.

"Hey, Ivy. So how do you think you did on that quiz?" Grant asks.

"Passed," she says, although she's pretty sure she did better than just passing.

Grant continues to make small talk. About teachers, about other kids. About her hair and how cool he thinks it is. She doesn't hear much of it—she's too busy following the bouncing ball. But then he gets that *I'm-not-looking-at-her-breasts* look.

"Listen, I was wondering," Grant says. "Some friends and I are getting together on Friday night, and I thought maybe—"

And then a car rudely honks.

"Hey, Ivy!" Tess yells out of TJ's passenger window. "What are you doing hanging out with these loooosers? Come with us."

Terrible timing. Perfect timing. Ivy now stands at a junction of who she was and who she might be. And it's too scary a place to be right now.

"Gotta go," she tells Grant. "See you in class tomorrow, okay?"

"Yeah, yeah, sure, in class," his Adam's apple says.

Ivy hurries into TJ's back seat, and they spirit her away just as the bus arrives behind them. Ivy finds herself irritated that Tess has ruined the potential date but relieved that she's been spared having to make a decision either way.

You don't need another distraction.

Yeah, well, maybe she does.

"So," says Tess, turning fully around to face her. "You and Grant Maldonado? No wonder you haven't been hanging with us."

"We're friends, that's all," Ivy says. "He's my lab partner. We made latex together."

"Yes," says TJ, "but do you have any plans to *use* that latex?"

Tess smacks him. "TJ, that's rude!" Then she turns back to Ivy. "But do you, actually?"

"Undecided," Ivy tells her. "You'll be the first to know if we do." Which is a lie. Tess is the school's megaphone of private matters. Always fun when it's someone else, but when it's you, not so much.

TJ turns in a direction that isn't toward any of their homes, and Ivy has to ask, "Where are we going?"

"The Pinewood Mall."

"That old place? Who goes there?"

"No one. Yet."

Apparently the mall is so uncool that it's cool again, and Tess wants to be on the trend's leading edge.

"Not to ruin your plans, but I really need to get home," Ivy tells them.

"Fine. I guess we could hang at your place instead," Tess says, not realizing it wasn't an invitation. But how does Ivy tell her that without turning this into an insanely awkward ride? Ivy has homework that she's determined to actually complete, but Tess has a way of making things like homework seem ridiculously unimportant.

Old patterns are not your friends, Ivy.

Instead of telling them outright that they're just her transportation today, Ivy lets it sit and changes the subject, hoping a solution will present itself before they arrive at her door.

"Hey—so how was that party?" Ivy asks. "You never told me."

"It was nuts," TJ says.

"Like seriously," Tess confirms. "I mean, it was wild, but normal-wild for a college party. But then right around midnight, this guy jumped off the roof."

"He was aiming at the pool," TJ says.

"He wasn't anywhere near the pool."

"Someone said he was on acid."

Ivy grimaces at the thought. "Was he okay?"

"Don't think so," says Tess.

"How could he be?" says TJ.

"But we never found out. We bailed, like most everyone else. I mean, we weren't supposed to be there anyway." And then Tess reaches back and grabs Ivy's hand. "Ivy, you were right not to go. I should listen to you more often."

It's enough to elicit a smile from Ivy, but not an invitation inside when they get to her house. Or at least not a *sincere* invitation.

"Come on in," Ivy says. "You can meet our new cat!"

"Cat?" says Tess. "You have a cat now?"

"Kitten, actually. We got it for my grandmother, but she's still in the hospital."

"You know I'm, like, super allergic to cats, right?" Tess says.

"Shit, I forgot."

Tess sighs, then gives Ivy an apologetic smile. "No worries."

And it's back to the original plan. The cool/uncool mall. They take off, leaving Ivy in her driveway.

There is, of course, no cat. But Tess and TJ don't have to know that.

17

The Keeper of the Cauldron

ISAAC

Isaac's grandmother is moved to a step-down unit, then stepped down again, then stepped out. The search for assisted living is like trying to find an apartment in a big city. In the interim, until she's fully healed, she's been relegated to a skilled nursing center. Half the people there are recovering from something. A fall, a stroke, an operation. They do their time and get out in a month or two. The other half are there for the duration, awaiting a different kind of exit.

Isaac would have visited his grandmother without an agenda. He tries to remember that. It goes a long way toward assuaging the guilt for his current agenda.

This is supposedly one of the better facilities. Fake plants abound, in large, shared rooms with respectable TVs. But nothing can conceal the stench of disinfectant and decay.

"Doesn't this place make your flesh crawl?" Grandma asks as Isaac keeps her company for the afternoon. She glances out of the door at a nurse pushing a hunched, vacant-eyed old man down the hallway—clearly one of the long-term residents. "Poor bastard. If I ever get like that, promise you'll roll me out in front of a bus."

"Grandma!"

"I know, I know—I'm just kidding with you. But really, do it."

She and Isaac had already had that *What-the-hell-happened-to*-you? conversation about his shoulder, because it's not like he could hide the sling his arm is in. "Sports injury," he told her, and didn't elaborate.

She scoffed. "When I was your age, sports were more about pleasure than pain. We're raising a generation of masochists coached by sadists."

Grandma shares the room with a woman who has the bed by the window and calls for the nurse every five minutes. She doesn't just hit the call button. She yells out loud over and over again.

"She's like that neighbor's goddamn barking dog," Grandma says, whispering as if not to be heard by the woman but loud enough to make sure she does.

"They treating you okay?" Isaac asks.

Grandma pulls herself up slightly in bed with a mild grimace. "As well as can be expected."

"And the pain?"

"It varies day to day."

Isaac nods. "I hope they're giving you something for it."

"Yeah, yeah, the usual," she tells him. "And they don't leave you alone. You could be sleeping, and in comes the nurse with her stupid little cart and her stupid little plastic cups. They wake you up, make you take your meds, and then you stare at the ceiling, trying to get back to sleep."

"Nurse!!" yells the woman from the next bed. *"Nurse!!!!"*

Grandma sighs. "I really don't like old people."

Medication arrives shortly after four o'clock in the afternoon. Just as Grandma said, the med nurse rolls in with a cart, on which rests an organized array of little plastic cups.

"Ah, here she is," says Grandma. "The keeper of the cauldron."

"Hello, Mrs. Ramey. I've got your afternoon meds. And who's this handsome young man?"

"My grandson. He gets his looks from me."

"I'm sure he does."

The medication nurse has a protocol. She scans the barcode on Grandma's wristband, checks the screen for the medications listed, then double-checks the little cup to make sure the medications are correct. The cart comes into every room with her. It's never left unattended.

"Here you go, Mrs. Ramey." She gives her a little plastic cup with several pills and a cup of water.

"Nurse!!" yells the woman in the next bed.

Grandma sighs. "You got a muzzle somewhere on that cart?"

"Now, be nice," says the nurse. "You got your grandson to keep you company. Ms. Kosmicki, she doesn't get visitors."

Ms. Kosmicki wants the curtains adjusted so she can see out from the bed. Not much of a view, but Isaac supposes some view is better than none at all. Then she wants them closed, because it's too bright.

Isaac watches as the nurse gives Ms. Kosmicki her pills. He watches the old woman swallow. He watches the nurse watching her swallow. It's all part of the protocol. The patient must be seen taking the medications.

But even if they were just left on the nightstand, Isaac isn't going to steal medication from someone who needs it. But there are other ways. Ways in which it can be a victimless crime.

Crime.

He stumbles over the word. Yes, snatching meds that aren't yours is a crime, but only technically. Sort of like a white lie. It's a little bad now for a greater good in the long run. But to accomplish it, he needs a plan.

"Turn on the TV, Baby-boy," Grandma says. "Watch something if you like."

"No, I'm good."

He shifts his shoulder and can't hide his grimace. Grandma catches it.

"How the hell do you hurt your shoulder if you play soccer with your feet?"

Isaac laughs. "Well, the rest of your body comes along."

She reaches over to the bedside table and picks up a brochure. "So, your parents have been giving me the lowdown on assisted living places. The whole thing sucks to high heaven, but those places don't seem so bad after being here." She hands him the brochure. "See this one? It has a pool, lounge chairs. You can come visit when my hip is better, and we can go swimming." She smiles. "Remember how I used to take you swimming?"

"Yeah, Grandma, I do."

He hears the medication cart somewhere in the hallway, rolling from one room to the next, to the next. He hands her back the brochure. "I'll be back in a sec—I've gotta go pee."

"There's a bathroom right here in the room."

"Yeah, and the sign says 'patients only.'"

"You and rules!" Grandma scoffs. "Careful out there. This

place is a maze. I hear they make stew out of lost relatives."

"*Nurse!!!!*"

The need to pee was legit. But afterward, Isaac does some critical reconnaissance and finds the room where the meds are kept. When no one is looking, he slips in to find shelf after shelf of industrial-size pill bottles. He's amazed that there's no lock on the door—but quickly realizes why. The glass-faced cases that hold the meds are all locked. No one can get to the meds but the keeper of the cauldron. He stares at the bottles, reeling from this unexpected failure, when he hears—

"Can I help you?"

It's one of the aides, standing in the doorway and looking at him with a fair amount of suspicion.

Rather than stammering and broadcasting his intentions, he takes a moment, puts on his best clueless teenager face, and delivers the following:

"Yeah—I wanted some ice cream for my grandma, but the fridge is locked." He points to the locked refrigerator in the room—the one for perishable meds.

"That fridge isn't for food," the aide says. "Come, I'll show you where it is."

Isaac takes a quiet breath of relief and wonders how actual criminals get through life without shitting themselves every three seconds.

When he gets back to the room with a little cup of vanilla ice cream—the kind that comes with a wooden spoon— Grandma's asleep.

It's beginning to get dark now. His parents don't want him driving in the dark with his shoulder like this. As if it's easier to keep both hands on the wheel in daylight. "You're not sup-posed to be driving or operating heavy machinery on those meds," his mom had complained.

"I promise I'll leave the forklift at home," he had told her. The compromise was that he wouldn't drive far, and he wouldn't drive after dark. But he can't leave until he figures this out . . . and then he gets an idea.

He kisses his sleeping grandmother goodbye, throws his backpack over his good shoulder, and heads out of the room—all the while listening to the far-off sound of the medicine cart's squeaky wheel. He turns a corner. It's closer now, moving in his direction.

He hesitates. Slows his pace, then at precisely the right moment, he kicks it up into a power walk, just as the cart emerges from around the corner, and *bam!*

Isaac runs right into the cart at full speed. He grabs on to it for balance. It goes down. He goes down with it. Hundreds of little pills scatter on the linoleum floor. Isaac's bad shoulder hits the ground, and he yelps in pain. It's real pain. It makes this whole crash and burn all the more authentic.

"Oh my God, are you all right?"

"I'm fine," Isaac says, through the anguish of his red-faced grimace. His shoulder hurts so much, the pain seems to shoot all the way to his toes, but he can't let that slow him down.

"I'm so, so sorry." He begins to gather the fallen pills as best he can, sweeping his forearm across the floor to pull them in.

"No, no, don't worry," the nurse says. "We'll have someone clean it up."

"No, it's my fault," Isaac insists, hurrying to clean the mess. "It's my fault. I'll do it."

He puts a handful of pills on the cart.

"Please," says the nurse. "We'll just have to throw them away anyway. Really, it's all right."

But Isaac isn't listening. He gathers more. Puts them on the tray. "I'm really, really sorry."

The nurse smiles at him, reluctantly accepting his misguided assistance, because what else can she do?

"Well . . . thank you," she says. "Are you sure you're okay?"

"Yeah. It serves me right. My grandma always says I need to look where I'm going."

Then Isaac leaves . . . with no one having seen the two handfuls of pills he shoved into the hollow of his sling.

With the door to his bedroom locked, Isaac sorts the pills into different piles, then goes online to identify them.

Pink, round, W 1 = warfarin blood thinner.

White, round, M E16 = enalapril for blood pressure.

Yellow, oval, P 20 = Pantoprazole for acid reflux.

His piles are a veritable rainbow of random chemicals, most of which are useless to him. But some are not.

Pain being a constant in a nursing home, there are eleven pills that are various versions of what he needs. Quite a haul for a single subterfuge. Of course, he'll have to find a more permanent supply, but that's not something he needs to think about today. Don't they say you have to live in the moment and let tomorrow take care of itself?

ROXY

I despise family reunions. Especially when it's my own family and especially when it's unexpected. Isaac's ploy at the nursing center, as daring as it was, is nothing but a pain in the ass for me.

Right now, Isaac lies on the living room couch. He's supposed to be icing his shoulder, but the ice pack has slipped off, and he's a little too out of touch to notice. While I'd like to say it's just the two of us here, it's not.

"This is *your* fault for being so ridiculously unattainable," says a voice behind me. My brother Vic. I knew he was here, but I wasn't sure exactly *where* until he spoke. Now I can see him in his slick suit and power tie, which make him seem oh so important—although sometimes I think it's just to make him *feel* important.

Vic and I are not close. Perhaps because we are both so fiercely independent. Sharks in an expansive ocean, we don't have to compete because there is plenty of prey. Still, we're territorial and too much alike to be comfortable with each other's presence in the world. So we each pretend the other doesn't exist. It's gotten so we can be invisible to one another—unless one of us chooses to draw the other's attention.

"Rest assured your sister and I will do our jobs," says Vic, "and be out of your hair as soon as we're done."

"Wait—sister? Which sister?"

Then Dillie comes strolling out of the woodwork and settles in next to Isaac, too cozy for comfort.

"Hello, Roxy," Dillie says with a nasty smirk. "You're looking rather . . . *generic* today."

I haven't spoken to Dillie in years, but here she is, ham-handedly massaging Isaac's shoulder.

"Don't start thinking you can jump my claim," I tell her, not daring to suggest that maybe Isaac is more than just a "claim" to me now.

"I don't see the problem," she says. "Share and share alike, right?"

She knows I'm not big on sharing, but I don't take the bait.

"Don't forget, Roxy, I'm here by invitation."

"No," I tell her, "you're not. You're here by *desperation*. Because someone would have to be seriously desperate to have anything to do with you."

And then Vic comes between us. "Girls, girls, can you at least pretend not to despise each other? Can we, for once, try to get along?"

I can't stand his condescending tone, but Dillie plays right into it. She pouts and says, "Maybe if Roxy stops acting like she's Pharma's gift to the world."

"She's right, you know," Vic says to me, proudly adjusting his tie. "We can do everything you can do."

"That's right," says Dillie. "Maybe I'm not as quick as you, and I don't have your stamina, but that doesn't make me any less capable."

Then Isaac shifts and groans beneath Dillie's indelicate touch, proving her wrong. I sigh. "Maybe instead of arguing, you should just focus on Isaac," I tell her.

"Isaac—is that his name?"

"You don't even know his name?"

And again Vic intercedes. "As entertaining as this soap

opera is, we all have other clients, whether we know their names or not, and the more you two bicker, the longer we have to linger."

That's Vic, always the logical one. All business. Even when he's at the Party, he hangs in quiet places, engaged in professional conversation. "Clients" instead of marks. I wouldn't doubt he's exchanged business cards with new-and-improved Mary Jane.

"Fine," I tell them, and say no more. I will endure this, but only because I have no other choice. I wonder if either of them truly see Isaac the way I do. Are their thoughts wandering as they keep him company, or are they honestly focused on the job they've been temporarily given? The quelling of his pain. The feeding of his need.

Frankly, I don't think they are—which is one reason I don't like to work in tandem.

Isaac has already realized he needs to come up with a better solution than this dismal soiree, and I hope he does it soon. Even as a stopgap measure, it's unsustainable for him, and intolerable for me.

At Your Door in Two Days or Less

ISAAC

Isaac has been skipping out on his friends at lunch. He has
plenty of reasons. His shoulder injury, for one. And all the work
at school he's fallen behind on. Which is why he has spent the
last few lunches in the library.

Surprisingly, he finds his sister there, with her nose in a science textbook. Isaac and Ivy haven't seen much of each other
at home. Different schedules. Closed bedroom doors. And ever
since that last time Ivy tried to pry into Isaac's business, his own
door has been closed more often than not.

He actually brightens when he sees her there.

"Wow, you're really walking the walk, aren't you."

Ivy looks up from her textbook and gives him a genuine
grin. "Yeah, well, don't tell Mom and Dad, but I actually do want
to graduate." She glances at his sling. "How's the shoulder today?"

"Still there." They were both so good at non-answers, they
could have zero-sum conversations that felt completely satisfying. Sometimes it's not about the content anyway.

Isaac sits down across from her. "So I've got to do a full
analysis of a dystopian novel that hasn't been made into a
TV show or a movie. Any suggestions?"

"I'll have to get back to you on that." Ivy ponders her textbook for a few seconds, then looks up at him. "So, I broke up with Craig."

"Again?"

"No, I mean for real."

And this time Isaac can sense it's true. "Should I text you some confetti?"

Ivy sighs. "It still pisses me off that everyone was right about him—and that he doesn't even care. He's already off dating a character from Adult Swim."

"Traditional or digital animation?" Isaac asks.

"Crayon," Ivy responds without a microsecond of lag time.

Just then the library door opens, and Shelby steps in. Ivy follows Isaac's gaze to the door and smirks.

"Don't say it," Isaac tells his sister. He's not sure what she's going to say, other than that it won't be kind to Shelby.

Ivy puts up her hands in surrender, and Isaac puts up his good hand to get Shelby's attention.

"There you are!" she says when she sees him.

Ivy grabs her textbook and gets up.

"Hi, Ivy," says Shelby. "Am I . . . disturbing something?"

"Not at all," Ivy says. "I was just finishing up—he's all yours."

Ivy saunters away, and Shelby sits down in her place, then leans forward and whispers, "I don't think your sister likes me much."

Isaac shrugs his good shoulder. "If she did, I'd be worried."

"Speaking of worry . . . ," Shelby says, then looks at Isaac as if hoping he'll finish her thought and save her the trouble.

When he doesn't, she sighs and lets her shoulders sag, as if dropping a facade in favor of a better facade. "So . . . is it okay to say that we're maybe a little worried about you?"

Isaac's touched, but that's tempered by the fact that she said "we," not "I." As if Shelby was the friend voted to be the one to check in on him, because of their kinda-sorta-ship.

"You can tell everyone to stop worrying," he tells her. "I'm doing fine."

"We haven't seen you out for lunch all week."

"Yeah, and I also don't hit the hallway until just before the late bell," he points out. "Too many bodies out there not looking where they're going. I already had one dude ram into me, and once was enough. I'd rather just be someplace less crowded until my shoulder's feeling better."

She reaches out and grabs his hand across the table. "I get it—I really do. Just don't forget you have friends, okay?"

Isaac smiles warmly at her. "I won't."

"And if you need to talk . . ."

And she waits for Isaac to finish her thought. This time he does. "If I need to talk, I promise I'll call you."

Then she's gone before Isaac could say more, even if he wanted to.

The next day, Isaac does go outside for lunch. Because he does miss Shelby and the rest of his friends. And because he wants to show them, and maybe himself, that he's fine. They're pleased to see him. Shelby makes room for him at the table, but Chet deems it's not enough. He takes charge of reorganizing them so that Isaac is at an end where no one will bump his shoulder.

Isaac does his best to be in the moment, but it's a chore to stay tuned in to the conversation. They're talking about Rachel's birthday, which is coming up. It has been a tradition that Rachel celebrates her birthday with her friends at Six Flags—and regardless of whoever else comes, that group must, without question, include Isaac, Ricky, Shelby, and Chet.

"If you don't all come, then life as we know it will end," according to Rachel—and it might actually be true, because life as they know it always revolved around the five of them being a constant. Any one of them absent from some major event could signal their fellowship in decline. And no one wants to be the first to leave a party.

"Maybe we should do something else this year," Ricky suggests, which is basically burn-at-the-stake sacrilege as far as Rachel is concerned. "I mean, we want to include Isaac, right? And it's not like he can go on the rides. . . ."

Although Isaac knows Ricky is trying to be thoughtful, it only makes Isaac feel like a problem they have to solve.

"It's not about the rides," Isaac tells them. "It's about being together for Rachel's birthday."

Chet nods at him. "I couldn't have said it better myself."

When the bell rings, Isaac waits for the crowds to thin. Chet hangs back with him. Then, when they're alone, Chet turns to him.

"Listen—Shelby was telling us you're in too much pain to even walk down a hallway," Chet says. "Is that true?"

"Uh . . . no, that's not what I told her. . . ."

"Did they give you pain meds?"

Chet has no idea what a loaded question that is. "You

know how doctors are with prescriptions," Isaac says, and doesn't elaborate.

Chet shakes his head in commiserate annoyance. "I hear you, man. Doctors think they know everything, when most probably can't even do first aid." He takes a moment to ponder, scratching his head as if to activate his brain. Then he leans closer to Isaac, lowering his voice. "So I know this website. It's got all these links. . . . It's like a crazy-ass doorway to the dark web."

"And how do you know about it?"

"That's not important. What matters is that you can find anything you want there. You need meds, you got 'em, no questions asked and no control-freak doctors telling you what you can and can't have. You pay in Bitcoin, and boom, there's a fake Amazon box at your door in two days or less. No mess, no problem."

Isaac finds it equal parts tempting and terrifying. "Thanks, Chet, but—"

"I know this kind of thing isn't your style, but when the system's screwing you over, you gotta improvise, yeah?" Then he scribbles down a URL on a scrap of paper and hands it to Isaac. "Rachel'll hound you about herbal remedies, but pain is pain— and that site can get you what you need until you don't need it anymore. Just think about it, yeah?"

"All right, I'll think about it."

Then, as they get up to go inside, Chet says, "Just remember I'm your friend no matter what." It seems like an odd thing to say, but Chet's famous for saying odd things.

Once they're inside and have gone their separate ways,

Isaac crumples the scrap of paper and drops it in a trash can. But getting rid of it won't be that easy, because he's already memorized the URL.

IVY

Ivy has upped her dosage.

She didn't consult Dr. Torres, or any doctor for that matter. She just doubled the daily amount. Double the dose, twice the efficiency. The pills were there—they were practically *begging* her. How could she say no to more of a good thing?

The only problem with that much medication is when it wears off. Late in the day, Ivy is still just as restless, but with none of the ability to focus. And as affable as she is earlier in the day, in the evenings, in those twilight hours, when the meds are fading, she feels flooded with social anxiety.

Stupidly, she goes on a date with Grant Maldonado knowing this, and she's twitchy and awkward all evening, then silently curses herself all the way home. She never feels "off" like that. She's off in different ways, but never like that. And his kiss good night before she gets out of the car clearly feels like a kiss-off. They won't be going on a second date.

The next evening, she tries to engage her brother—but by that time of the day, she has no patience for him, and he clearly has none for her.

"Why are you just lying around like that?" she snaps when she sees him lounging on his bed, doing a whole lot of nothing.

"My shoulder hurts. Cut me some slack, okay?"

"Well, shouldn't you be doing physical therapy or something to help it heal?" Ivy doesn't intend to be so combative, but this time of day every thought goes through a distorting lens. She means to be concerned, not annoyed.

Isaac labors to sit up. "The swelling has to go down before I do much of anything," he tells her. His eyes are slightly drooped. His voice sounds sluggish.

"What have they got you on?"

He shrugs, but his shrug elicits a grimace. "I don't know. Something for the pain."

"Well, obviously," she says, and silently curses herself for being so unsympathetic.

"What's with you?" he asks.

"Why does there have to be something 'with' me? Can't I just show concern for my brother?"

This is definitely not going the way Ivy intended it to. She takes a deep breath. "It's just . . . It really sucks what happened to you, and it makes me mad, okay?" she says. "So get better." And she storms off to her room, where she dolphins onto her bed and releases a primal scream into her pillow, promising herself to never speak to another living soul when the meds are wearing off.

Trying to sleep has been increasingly difficult, but that night, it's entirely futile. Ivy's whole body feels like an electrical tower. High tension wires buzzing through her but no electricity she can actually use. She's going to need something to calm her down. The other night her mother suggested chamomile tea. Didn't work.

Her father said she should try melatonin—but that stuff sucks, because, yes, it makes her tired, but doesn't make her sleep.

So at around half past midnight, making sure her parents are asleep, she quietly goes downstairs.

Used to be during Ivy's worst days, her parents had a lock on the liquor cabinet. She would have thought by now they would have constructed a titanium vault, or have surrounded the area with red laser sensors to alert them of her proximity to alcohol. But there's this thing that Ivy remembered hearing about circus elephants . . . how, back in the day, before animal rights activists kicked the collective three-ringed asses of every circus, baby elephants were kept chained to a stake in the ground. They weren't strong enough to pull out the stake—but here's the strange thing. When they grew up and could easily pull that stake out of the ground, they never tried, because they remembered being too weak to do it.

Just as Ivy never bothered to check the liquor cabinet, because it was always locked. Except that today, it's not.

Imagine that shocked elephant suddenly realizing the stake isn't holding it back at all. That pachyderm would be like, "Adios, Barnum," and be out of there.

So, do Ivy's parents see her like an elephant, or do they trust her now that she's turned over a new leaf? Or were they simply careless? She chooses to believe it's because they now trust her—and because she's won back their confidence, she doesn't go for the hard stuff. No gin, no whiskey. Instead, she takes something more mature. A bottle of cabernet. Don't doctors say that a glass of red wine here and there is good to prevent blood clots? And it's full of antioxidants, right? Why, it would be unhealthy *not* to drink it. So Ivy finds a classy wineglass and brings the bottle into her room to uncork it, and does so in her closet to make sure her parents don't hear—because even the tiny squeaky sound of a wine bottle uncorking can be loud in the dead of night.

The secretiveness of it all makes her feel like a delinquent, which pisses her off, because the last thing Ivy wants is to get drunk. She just wants a decent night's rest.

ISAAC

The box shows up at the door in two days, just as Chet said it would, with a slightly off Amazon logo and a cluster of shrink-wrapped, unmarked pills inside. They were more expensive than Isaac thought they'd be—almost thirty bucks per pill. Remembering what Chet had told them about old video games, Isaac dug his out and put them up on eBay. And when they didn't sell right away, he went online and dipped into the money his parents have put aside for him, since he knows his father's passwords. He'll replenish it before they even know it's gone, once he makes the eBay sales.

He tries not to think about how much money it is—which was easier once he converted it to Bitcoin, which feels like imaginary money anyway.

Now he can breathe easy. He'll use the meds sparingly, and only when he needs to. Only when he feels the previous pill wearing off. Now he'll have the freedom to catch the pain before it comes back full force. If he times it right, then it won't even wake him up in the middle of the night.

He swallows the first one dry. A whole one, rather than the halves he's been rationing. He's actually come to like the bitterness lingering in the back of his throat. It tastes comforting. Familiar.

And it all seems to be working out—because two days later, all of his old games have sold, and he dutifully ships them off to their respective buyers. But he doesn't put the money back into his college fund just yet.

ADDISON

I'm working extra hours for Ivy, and she's getting a little wired. Kind of panicky. It's true her head hurts more often than not. It's true she's having trouble sleeping. And it's true that Al, bless his inebriated little heart, has been helping her with the insomnia that comes with my high-end brand of efficiency. But if I'm going to keep a solid hold on her and beat Roxy's momentum with Isaac, I must get Ivy past this. I must convince her that it's all for the better. Which it is, until the moment it isn't.

Right now it's the morning before school, and she's tidying her room in a Marie Kondo sort of way. Everything she can't find a place for goes straight into the trash.

"I think we're spending too much time together," she says as she picks stray lint from the carpet with her thumb and forefinger.

"I thought you loved to clean your room."

"No, *you* love to clean my room." She's frantic, as if all her circuits are in danger of blowing. But they're not. They're just highly taxed, but her brain can handle it. She just needs to be reassured.

"But look at the result! Your room is what a healthy room should look like. Your room, your closet, your life."

And with impeccable timing, her brother shuffles past, arm in a sling, eyes half-closed from either sleep or his affair with Roxy, or both. He takes a bleary look into her spotless room, turns his gaze to Ivy, and says, "Wow. Who are you, and what have you done with my sister?"

Ivy doesn't dignify him with a response. She just closes her door in his face. Still, it doesn't help my case.

"After everything I do for you, Ivy, don't you think a bit more gratitude is in order?"

Ivy scratches the skin on her elbows. They're beginning to get raw from her doing that compulsively. "You know what you are? You're a control freak!"

"And you're a thankless, privileged baby. Do you know how many millions of people need the benefits of what I give but are never offered my friendship? You should be down on your knees, thanking me."

"I'm already down on my knees picking up lint from the freaking floor!"

"And look at what a spectacular floor it is."

She breathes an exasperated sigh and stands up. I expect her to continue the battle, but she looks at the clock and caves. "I have to get to school."

"And you'll be on time—because suddenly you care. Who gave you that?"

She takes a deep breath and closes her eyes. "You did."

"And who gave you an A-minus in science?"

"You."

"And who gave you the confidence to kick Craig to the curb?"

"You."

I nod in approval. "Now, let's get out there and kick the world's ass."

Ivy opens her eyes, resigned, rejuvenated. She grabs her backpack and heads downstairs to begin her day. I have to admire what a strong will she has. But mine is stronger.

19

All Orbits Are Spirals

ROXY

My vexatious siblings are gone. It's just me and Isaac now. The way it should be. The way it *needs* to be.

His driving has been careful ever since the accident, but with all the construction in town, the streets are troubled. He feels every bump in the road, but I am his shock absorber. His shoulder, which would otherwise ache with every dip and pothole, is safely cushioned by my anesthetizing embrace. I am his secret passenger, and in a very real sense, I am the one driving. This is how I like it—having someone wrapped around my finger so many times, I could wear them like a ring. Even so, something feels wrong. I'm both in my element but outside of it somehow—as if the boundaries of my comfort zone were moved when I wasn't looking. It makes me angry and irritable to feel that way.

I'll admit there's a part of me that hopes, each time I go out in search of someone new, that I'll make a different kind of connection. That I'll find someone who makes me feel something more than my own pervasive numbness. The practical side of me knew it would never happen. The practical side is wrong.

"I can't believe how easy it was," Isaac says. "These offshore pharmacies, or whatever they are, don't ask for anything but the money."

"I'm glad you worked it all out."

Of course, he's getting emails, phone calls, and texts from some very troubling spammers, but I suppose that's part of the price too. Sending your personal information out into the abyss means the abyss knows who and where you are. Not a problem as long as you don't fall in.

It will be my mission to make sure the only direction he falls is mine.

At this moment in time, there's no one else he'd rather be with than me. Right now there's nothing in the world but him and his secret passenger. But there should be other things, shouldn't there? There used to be. I never stop to think about what came before in the lives of those souls I collect. What would be the point? All I see—all I've ever *wanted* to see—is the pressing moment. The all-powerful now . . . But I can't help thinking about who Isaac was before I pulled him into my orbit. And there's an undeniable truth lurking there in the simple physics of my gravity. All orbits decay. All orbits are spirals.

He reaches for me, and I surprise myself by pulling back. "You've had enough for now." Did I really just say that? When have I ever told anyone to slow down? I think about my bet with Addison. The tortoise can beat the hare when the hare gets cocky, but that's not what's happening here. So then what is? What's happening to me?

Chastised, Isaac turns back to the road. His cheeks redden just enough for me to know he's struggling with the idea of "enough."

"But I don't have to ration anymore," he says. "We can be together as much as we want. Now I just need to work out the money."

"You will," I tell him, getting myself back on track. "I have faith in you, Isaac."

He shifts his shoulder and purrs slightly, appreciating his lack of pain.

Isaac hurt himself for me.

It's not the first time I've been the object of desperate devotion. People break themselves in so many ways. They brawl with bruisers twice their size, knowing that they'll take a beating. They pull teeth because they know the dentist and I are such good friends. Once, while playing the handsome Adonis of her dreams, I told a woman that if she loved me, she'd hurl herself off a bridge for me. She did. And all I felt was annoyed, because now I needed to find someone else to bring to the Party.

Sympathy, empathy, I save those plush, downy sentiments for the likes of Isaac's grandmother. I save them for hospitals and the nobler side of my calling. But mostly I feel nothing. Because it is my nature to quell that which we choose not to feel.

"The money's a problem," he mumbles. "Maybe there's a better solution. . . ."

And hearing that unsettles me. Again, I react in a way that isn't like me.

"Better than what?" I ask. "Better than *me?*" The thought of Isaac climbing over me to get to my upline infuriates me. *I'm* the one who takes them in my arms and chooses when to push them out, not the other way around. *I* hold the power in this relationship, not Isaac. So why am I suddenly so worried?

"Do you expect me to just hang on your shoulder until you decide you're done with me? Is that it?"

"No, no, of course not," he says. "But things are getting so . . . confused."

And all of a sudden I think about Addison. This is the way *he* reacts when plus-ones trade up. I am not like him, damn it! I am above that.

Isaac gives me that forlorn expression I've seen so many times before in others. But coming from him, it cuts through me like one of Dusty and Charlie's razors. How is that possible? I am unwoundable. How dare he wound me with his longing?

"Do you *need* me, Isaac? Or do you *want* me?" I ask him. "And you'd better be careful with the answer you give."

"I . . . I don't know. . . ."

"Well, you won't have any peace until you do."

He's so focused on me now that he completely misses the red light. I would have warned him if I had seen it myself, but prevention has never been my bailiwick. And so we barrel into an intersection that promises a world of pain for all.

ISAAC

Entropy, the third law of thermodynamics, posits that order flows relentlessly into chaos. We can paddle upstream for a time, but eventually our arms tire. Eventually we must sleep. And when we do, entropy makes up for lost time.

Isaac had learned all about entropy in physics—along with quite a few other basic laws of existence. In one lab, Isaac had to devise an experiment that would measure the force of two billiard balls colliding at various angles and speeds. It had to be precise, and it had to be reproducible. His solution was to build a wooden ramp with adjustable height, illuminate it with a strobe light, and record the event with an overhead camera to capture the data. He received an A in the lab.

Automobiles do not behave like billiard balls.

There is nothing controlled or reproducible about a car accident. Each one is like a fingerprint—similar, perhaps on the surface, but unique in outcome and its various vectors of misery. On some level Isaac has known that his life was in danger of a crash and burn. It looks like today that might become literal.

Isaac's airbags never deploy. Perhaps it's the angle of the crash. Perhaps the sensors are faulty, or maybe it's because of all of Ricky's tinkering.

Isaac had seen the Honda about two seconds before he hit it. Not enough time to stop the collision, but enough to alter it. He had slammed on the brakes, turned the wheel, and hit the Honda at a forty-five-degree angle, turning what would have been a terrible T-boning into an oblique broadsiding.

The impact is not what he expects. It's less of a crunch and more of a dull thud, like a padded clapper on a bell. But the scraping is much louder. A tooth-rattling screeching of metal against metal that goes all the way down the driver's side of his car.

And all Isaac can think about are the billiard balls. Ballistic physics has taken over. Now he will either die or not die. The outcome is imminent and out of his control.

His car careens wildly. He expects it to leap the curb and smash into the window of the nail shop in the corner strip mall. When his car finally does come to a stop, though, he's surprised to see that he's not even near the curb. Both cars are still in the intersection. They've hardly traveled at all. What would his physics teacher say about that?

Now that it's over, he grips the wheel and takes a few deep breaths to confirm that he's not in the process of bleeding out. He isn't even bleeding at all, although his shoulder is throbbing from the jolt of the crash, despite the pain medication.

Isaac opens his door—although it doesn't open as easily as before—and steps out. He takes stock of the scene in a dazed, disengaged kind of way, one beat out of step with reality. It's as if he's watching himself watch himself assess the situation.

Unlike his own car, the Honda has curtain airbags, which have come down over the passenger-side window—which is the side that has sustained the damage. He has to go around to see who's in the car and how bad it was for them.

It's only the driver in there, no passengers. He sits behind the wheel, window open—a man in a suit, with a tie that's a bit too loose. He can't stop cursing. He doesn't seem to see Isaac there; he just keeps cursing.

Isaac knows this is his fault and that he ran a red light. He saw it an instant before the Honda eclipsed his view. He wants to apologize, but Isaac's father always told him that he should never admit fault at the scene of an accident. "Leave that to the insurance companies," his dad said. "Tell what happened, where, and when. Be truthful, then leave it to them to decide whose fault it was."

"Are you okay?" Isaac asks, interrupting the man's angry litany.

The man turns to him. His eyes are a bit lost, but he doesn't seem injured. "No," the man says bitterly. "No, I'm not okay." But rather than explaining himself, he just goes back to cursing at the dashboard.

Other people are stopping now to see if they can be of any assistance. A woman is on her phone, giving the location, clearly talking to a 911 dispatcher. A large man in a large pickup pulls up and gets out to help. The kindness of strangers.

Then the man in the suit gets out of his car and does the strangest thing. He stumbles a bit, gets his bearings, and tries to run away.

"Whoa, fella," says the large man, who steps in front of the driver, foiling his attempt to bolt. The man in the suit doesn't even struggle. It's as if he can't. There's something wrong about him. He's rubbery—as if the crash has loosened all of his joints. The other man helps him to the curb, where he sits with his head in his hands and his loose tie dangling toward the drain.

The police arrive. A fire truck. An ambulance with paramedics. Flares are set to divert traffic around the accident. It all seems to happen very quickly. Cars pass around the scene, people slowing down to see how bad it is, looking for the corpse under a sheet that they will regret having seen once they have. No corpse today. They're both relieved and disappointed.

The paramedics check Isaac out but spend much more time

with the other driver, who seems despondent and defeated.

A policeman comes over to take Isaac's statement, but before he gives it, Isaac has to ask, "Is the other guy okay?"

"Yeah," says the cop with the slightest smirk. "He's feeling no pain, if you know what I mean."

Then the other driver, instead of going off in an ambulance, is handcuffed and put into the back seat of a squad car. And Isaac finally gets it.

"He's drunk?"

"As a skunk," the officer says. "The Breathalyzer puts him at three times the legal limit. You're both lucky to be alive."

Isaac is shaken by this new spin. Another billiard ball rolling in from a blind spot.

"But . . . it was me," Isaac said. "I ran a red light."

The officer pauses. He closes his pad. "Are you sure about that? He thinks *he* ran the light."

"No, I'm pretty sure it was—"

Then the officer puts up his hand. "Kid, I'm gonna stop you right there." They both glance at the man who sits dejectedly in the back of the squad car, watching as a tow truck arrives to take his car away.

"Believe it or not, you did this guy a favor," the officer says. "If this didn't happen, he likely would have killed a whole family at the next light, or the one after that. He was literally an accident waiting to happen. So maybe you're the one who's got it wrong. Don't you think that's possible?"

Isaac opens his mouth to say something but realizes he has no idea what to say, so he closes it again.

"Listen, if you want me to write you a ticket for running

a red, I will—but taking that guy off the road was a public service. I would say those two things cancel each other out."

"But the streetlight cameras . . ."

"What about them? They don't come into play unless there's a subpoena. But in an open-and-shut like this, that's unlikely. Insurance'll just cover it."

Never look a gift horse in the mouth. Wasn't that the expression? And this horse came with a bow around it. He should be grateful, but all he feels is . . . numb.

"And look," the cop says, "your car looks like it's still drivable. Sometimes the universe smiles on you."

So Isaac gives his report, not mentioning the red light. Then he goes to his car, which starts up just as well as it did when Ricky fixed the spark plugs, and he drives home.

All the while, right next to him on the passenger seat is the little leather coin purse of pills that the police never bothered to look for.

20

A Fallen King

ADDISON

I wonder if Rita knows how much I hate sitting with her on park benches. She's always so content to do her endless knitting, while I just bounce my knees, wishing I could be anywhere else in the universe.

Today we're in a park in a crowded city. It doesn't matter which park; it doesn't matter which city. I couldn't tell you if you asked.

Rita's kids are on the playground—several of them today. Mothers and fathers and nannies sit or stand nearby, mostly on their phones, playing games or posting on social media, and paying attention only if someone on the playground gets hurt. If you ask me, I think they need Rita more than their kids do, but as Rita is so fond of telling me, that's not our call to make.

Today her scarf stretches like a pale yellow ribbon, weaving in and out of the play apparatus like a web of caution tape.

She reaches over and puts a hand on my left knee to stop it from bouncing. "You should go to your boy," she says.

I glance over at him. His knee has just stopped bouncing at the same moment mine has. What can I say? My wards and I are always in perfect tune.

"He doesn't need me right now. He's not playing yet."

"He will be in a few minutes," Rita points out.

The kid is on the high school chess team, which, on sunny days like this, likes to come out to the park. There are several concrete tables with chessboards built right into the surfaces. Right now their faculty adviser—a math teacher who takes the team far too seriously—is gently trying to convince a homeless man to vacate one of the chess tables so the team can have them all to themselves. But the man is being obstreperous and refuses to be displaced.

"Why don't I challenge your best player for the table," the man says. "One game."

The kids snicker at the thought of this wild-bearded vagrant attempting to play chess against a member of their nationally ranked team. They see the man a pawn sacrificed to larger pieces. It makes me angry.

"Sir, I don't think it would be appropriate," says the teacher in a long-suffering way.

"Then how about I play against you? Would *that* be appropriate?"

The kids start to whisper about the prospect, to the teacher's chagrin. "Come on, Mr. Markova," my ward says. "Let's see you play him."

So their teacher reluctantly agrees. And as they set the pieces up, something suddenly hits me.

I know this man with the wild beard. Not as a man, but as a boy. It was twenty-some-odd years ago, when I was pretty young myself. What was his name? I helped him through high school. I stayed up all night with him for the prom. I watched him walk at graduation. Then he went off to college, and we parted ways.

There's a pang of regret in seeing how far he has fallen from the launch I gave him. And what of the boy I am here for today? He has his hopes and dreams too, just as this man had. His parents started his chemical assistance young. He hasn't known life without me, or Rita, or Dex, or any number of my siblings on duty. What are the chances he'll become this man in twenty years?

And why do I care?

Yes, it's my job to care, but only so long as I'm employed to do so. It's all transactional.

Just as it is between me and Ivy.

Or as it *should* be.

Ivy is by no means an innocent . . . but she has no idea that I have ulterior motives.

"What's bothering you, Addison?" Rita asks. "Spit it out. Don't just sit there stewing."

I could tell Rita the usual. That I'm irked by Dusty and Charlie. That Crys is thankless and heartless. But Rita knows my gripes with our upline. She doesn't know about Ivy, though. And in a moment of weakness, I open up.

"There's this girl," I tell Rita. "I've been brought on to help her get through her last months of high school. . . ."

"Go on. I'm listening," says Rita, the mistress of multitasking. Her eyes are on the playground, her fingers don't miss a stitch, and her ears are attuned to me.

"She's . . . been having trouble at night, so she's brought Al into the picture to help her sleep."

Rita stiffens at the mention of Al. "Ugh, he's such a nuisance! I can only stand that man in small doses—but he never comes that way. He's always right there, in your face." She shudders. "Well, if you're having a problem with Al, you must be direct with him. He only responds to directness."

"Al's not the problem."

"Then what is?"

I sigh. "This girl . . . She's beginning to abuse our relationship." But then I have to correct myself, because if I'm being honest, I need to actually be honest. "I mean to say, I've been . . . *encouraging* her to abuse it. She's on her way to being a plus-one."

Rita turns to look at me in that awful judgmental way she has. "So you're roping this girl into the Party? Just so you can hand her off to the Coke Brothers or Crys?"

"No! That's the point. She's on a classic self-destructive path, but I don't plan on handing her off to anyone. I'm all in. I'll be there for her to the end."

"For *her*? Or for *you*?" Rita asks, cutting right through to the meat of it. I can't answer. She knows my answer.

Rita thinks about it and shakes her head. "No. If you're looking for me to absolve you of guilt, I won't. Sorry, Addison. I'm not in the business of forgiveness. Especially for something as underhanded as this."

"There's nothing to forgive—I haven't brought her to the Party yet."

"But you *will*. Because Addison *gets* what Addison *wants*," she says, poking me with her knitting needles to emphasize her words. "You're so spoiled, Addi—you've always been. Spoiled, self-centered, egotistical—"

"Enough, Rita! I didn't confide in you to get a lecture."

"Then why did you?"

I don't answer her because I'm not entirely sure. Maybe it was just to test my resolve. Because if I can withstand all of Rita's pokes and jabs and still stick to the plan, then maybe I'll go through with it. Maybe I'm one step closer to making it happen.

"I'll continue to do my job for Ivy," I tell Rita. "Right until the moment comes to take her up."

"Do you expect a medal for doing your job?"

Once Rita's got a bee in her bonnet, there's no talking to her, so I don't say another word. She returns to her knitting and her observation of the playground. Meanwhile, there are cheers and applause over at the chess tables. At first I think the teacher must have won, but it's the opposite. He has just toppled his king in defeat, and the kids are thrilled that their high-and-mighty teacher has been bested by a homeless man. Yet even though he won, he gives his table over to the team, because it was never about the table.

Drake! That's his name—I remember it now. But I can't help him, because he's not my ward and hasn't been for many years. I will probably never see Drake again. But at least I remember his name.

I turn back to Rita. I can tell that her anger has sublimated into concern, which is actually worse.

"At some point, Addison, you're going to have to decide who you are," she says. "Just because so many of your wards are adolescents, that doesn't mean you get to be one forever."

IVY

When Ivy told Tess her grandmother was in rehab, Tess wondered what drug she was trying to kick. That's where everyone's mind automatically goes. Or at least the minds of the people Ivy knows. She wishes there were a better term for her grandmother's hip situation. Officially, the place is called a "skilled nursing center," but that sounds too much like "nursing home." Rehab, with all its connotations, is still better than that.

The place is on a bus route, with only one transfer to get Ivy there. She's visited Grandma with her parents, who go several times a week. She would go with Isaac, but now that his car is in the shop, he'd have to get a ride or take a bus himself. And anyway, she doesn't want to be just a tagalong. She wants Grandma to know she cares enough to make the effort.

When Ivy arrives, Grandma is in the lounge—a multipurpose room that serves as a mini cafeteria and recreation area. Grandma's halfheartedly eating from an institutional tray and watching an unidentifiable sitcom on a TV that's hung too high for anyone's comfort. She brightens up the instant she sees her granddaughter.

"Ivy! Over here." She tries to roll her wheelchair out to Ivy, but she's wedged in by several others parked at her table. Ivy goes over and manages a hug.

"What a surprise," Grandma says. "Is it just you?"

"Yeah, I had some free time today, so . . ."

Grandma glances down at her half-eaten plate. "Can you believe this shit they give us?" On the plate is something that must be chicken with a rounded orange lump that must be sweet potato. "It probably makes your school food look like lobster thermidor."

And in response, Ivy presents the bag of chocolate éclairs she brought. "At least there's good dessert."

"Contraband!" says Grandma. "I love contraband. Especially the kind where you get to eat the evidence." She peers into the bag, delighted. Several of her tablemates rubberneck, trying to get a view too. Grandma closes the bag and whispers, "Come—we'll eat them where we don't have to share."

In Grandma's room, the shade is down against the late-afternoon sun. The woman in the bed by the window is now on oxygen, and fast asleep.

Grandma positions her chair next to her bed and lowers the side rail. "I don't need your help," she says before Ivy offers it. Grandma gets out of her wheelchair with a grunt and onto the bed on her own. "Wheelchair-to-bed. I made that milestone last week. Now I'm a pro."

The woman by the window coughs, fogging up her oxygen mask.

"Should we be quiet?" Ivy asks.

"For her? She's never quiet for me." Grandma waves her hand dismissively. "Anyway, she's so doped up these days, nothing can wake her. I really hope I'm out of here before she buys the farm."

Ivy doesn't mean to laugh at the poor woman's misery, but it tickles Ivy that her grandmother is so cavalier about it.

Grandma sighs as she gets comfortable in bed. "I hate this place. A few years back, COVID ripped through here like a category five. Not that it could happen now, but there are more bad bugs in a place like this than a cheap horror movie. The sooner I get out of here, the better." She tells Ivy that a spot opened up for her in her first-choice assisted living facility.

"Shady Oaks. Sounds like a cemetery, I know, but it's actually not bad. Two more weeks here, and I move in there."

"I'm sorry you won't be coming back to be with us," Ivy says.

Grandma puts up her hand. Not a topic she wants to get into. Then she reaches over to her bedside table, full of greeting cards and fading flower arrangements, and grabs a card.

"A lot of people love you," Ivy comments.

"Or feel obligated," Grandma says. "Either way, it's reassuring." Then she shows Ivy the overly flowery card she picked up. "From Mr. Burkett, across the street. He had the big C—but he's in remission. Just goes to show you, not everything goes south." She looks at the card and laughs. "You think he's interested in me?"

"Isn't he a minister?"

Grandma chuckles. "Yeah. If he's interested, he'd better realize I'm too old to be a good girl."

That makes Ivy grin. "I definitely want to be like you when I'm your age."

"What, divorced and incapacitated?"

"Stop—you know what I mean."

Grandma smiles. "You've got a lot of living to do first." Then she gets a bit more serious. Looking at Ivy. Really looking. It makes Ivy realize that aside from just wanting to see Grandma, she wanted Grandma to see *her*. Not just her facade, like her friends. Not her flaws, like her parents. More than anyone else, Grandma always sees *her*.

"You've lost some weight. Not that you needed to, but I can see it in your face. Is that from the meds?"

Ivy nods and breaks eye contact, but Grandma won't let her look away for long.

"Listen to me," she says. "I know you've had problems in the past, but you're a strong girl. Meds suck, but if you use them right and don't let *them* use *you*, you'll do fine."

This is what Ivy needed to hear; straightforward, simple Grandma wisdom.

Then she takes Ivy's hand. "I will be there for your graduation. Hopefully not in a wheelchair, but I'll be there. Wild horses couldn't keep me away."

"Thank you, Grandma."

She puts the card back on the table, and it makes the rest fall like dominoes. Ivy reaches over to fix it, but Grandma stops her. "Just leave it. They all fall when the air conditioner comes on anyway." She hits the button to raise the bed a bit more.

"How's your brother?" she asks. "He used to come by all the time, but I haven't seen him for more than a week now."

"He's just busy with school," Ivy says, hoping Grandma doesn't grill her.

And she doesn't. Instead she says, "Look out for him, Ivy. Your parents are all wrapped up in their own troubles now. Maybe you could turn a third eye his way once in a while."

"I will, Grandma."

Grandma smiles, satisfied. "Good. Now let's inhale those éclairs."

ADDISON

I have no patience for sentimentality today. Elderly platitudes are all well and good, but I'm not sure whether Ivy's encounter with her grandmother has helped or hurt my cause. I must be diligent in dealing with possible threats.

"You have to take everything your grandmother says with a grain of salt," I tell Ivy on the bus ride home.

"I know, I know."

"Do you, though? That garbage about using versus being used? This is not a struggle, Ivy. It's a partnership. If you fight against me, we fail. *You* fail."

"I'm not fighting. I'm just—"

"Scared, I know. There's no room for scared. You are a girl of action, not deliberation. Rise to your strength and *do*. Don't just *be*."

"So what do you want me to *do*?"

"Doesn't matter," I tell her. "As long as it's productive."

And so she pulls out her phone and starts speed reading a book she needs to finish for English class. Good. She needs to abhor wasted time as much as I do. And if all goes according to plan, Ivy will never have to be a cranky old woman in a hospital bed.

21

The First to Leave the Party

IVY

Ivy's been more than aware that her brother hasn't been himself lately. On the surface, it's obvious. She can see it in the impassive emotionless look in his eyes, the bags that collect underneath—even his skin is pallid, like someone's been sucking the life out of him. And when he moves, the lethargy is ever more present, because he looks like he's pulling himself through gelatin just to get to his bedroom.

Ivy tries to rationalize. Maybe it's insomnia. Maybe it's the misery of losing the rest of the season because of an injury. Understandable. Explainable. But those things are hard to buy when her brother has been sleeping long past his alarm every day—sometimes to the point of missing school. Ivy might be hyperfocused now, but she's not so self-absorbed that she can't see these things. There's this weakness about him, as if he were an animal off licking his wounds—but it's more than just the physical injuries. A messed-up ankle or shoulder doesn't weigh someone down like this. This is heavier.

It's becoming increasingly clear to her that Isaac has secrets.

Perhaps he always had, and she'd been oblivious, but Ivy doesn't think so. Siblings set themselves in opposition to each other. Since Ivy has always been so intentionally opaque, Isaac was transparent to a fault. He lived who he was inside and out, everything illuminated.

So the fact that he now has something to hide—something enough to lie to their parents about his phone being dead that night he was on the boat—has Ivy deeply intrigued. And maybe a bit worried. She's been spending so much time hyperfocusing on her own concerns. Perhaps it's time to shine some of her pharmaceutical-grade amphetamine light on her brother and see if he actually does cast a shadow. Use that third eye Grandma talked about.

Ivy pushes into Isaac's bedroom without even knocking—hoping to startle him enough to tip him slightly off-balance. But he's not fazed at all. He's sitting on his bed, watching You-Tube videos and eating snacks. He chuckles at something on the video.

"Check this out," he says. "This guy was doing a fly-along with the Blue Angels and accidentally ejected himself at, like, ten thousand feet. Then his parachute gets stuck on the side of a building, and he hangs there for hours until they can get him down."

While Ivy is not beyond a little schadenfreude, Isaac's choice to take pleasure in other people's misfortunes at this moment in time just doesn't add up.

"Since when do you just sit around watching cat videos?"

"It's not a cat video. I told you it's—"

"I don't care. They're all cat videos, okay? Just with humans." She tries to calm herself down. It was Isaac who was supposed to be off-balance, not her. But he's calm as can be.

Calm to the point of being numb. What the hell is it with him?

Ivy pulls up his desk chair and takes a seat, making it clear she's not going anywhere. That makes Isaac seem a little prickly. Good.

"Isaac, do you remember when we were kids? That time we all went doorbell ditching and that old man threatened us with a broom? Or the time we cannonballed people at the pool? Or how about the time we rearranged the neighbors' Christmas reindeer so it looked like they were humping?"

Isaac shoots her a sidelong glance. "No, I don't. . . ."

"Of course not. That's because *I* did those things, not you. Because *I'm* the bad kid. *You're* the good one, in case you've forgotten."

"What the hell is this all about, Ivy? I really don't need you making this day worse than it already is."

Ivy shrugs. "You've saved my ass countless times. I figure maybe it's time I save yours."

Isaac offers up a weak smirk. Noncommittal—like Shelby, who hasn't been around much lately. Ivy idly wonders if they officially broke up, but realizes that Shelby won't commit to a breakup any more than she'll commit to a relationship.

"Ah, so this is a rectal exam," Isaac says. "Well, you can stop. I appreciate your concern, but my ass is perfectly fine."

But Ivy isn't buying it. She looks right into his eyes, refusing to look away. "I know you lied about your phone being dead that night you were on the boat. And I know there's something you're not saying about your car accident. I know, because I know *you*."

He doesn't answer right away. He just turns back to his

computer as the next video comes up. But Ivy can tell he's not actually watching anymore. His thoughts have turned inward. She wonders if he's about to tell her the truth or invent a convincing lie. Turns out it's neither. He closes the computer and turns to her.

"Don't take this the wrong way, Ivy . . . but it's really not your business."

And boom. Just like that she's shut down. She wants to be angry at him, but all she feels is forlorn. Like she's lost something she might never get back and didn't even recognize its value until it was gone. She can keep pushing him, but she knows it will do no good. He's made his decision. He's closed that door.

So Ivy gets up to leave, but before she goes, she offers him a final parting shot. "Word to the unwise, Isaac . . . Bad shit will always come back to bite you. This I know from experience."

Isaac says nothing, just watches her as she leaves, letting her have the last word—but his eyes are screaming. And for the life of her, she can't tell whether it's a scream of rage or despair.

ISAAC

Rachel's birthday finally arrives, and Isaac knows from the moment they enter the amusement park that coming was a mistake—not just because he feels a disconnected distance from everything going on around him, but also because his friends can sense the "apartness" he's feeling and are already making accommodations for him.

NEAL SHUSTERMAN AND JARROD SHUSTERMAN

"We don't have to go on the roller coasters," Rachel says. "At least not right away."

"Sure," Chet agrees. "There are plenty of other things to do."

And Shelby just looks at him with a sad, sympathetic smile, which is worse than anything she could have said.

"Guys, really, don't change things up for me," Isaac tells them. "It's not like I didn't know what I was getting myself into. We're here for Rachel's birthday, so let's be here. I'll wait in line with you. I just won't ride." Which was the wrong thing to say, because they just looked even more guilty.

"I'll hang with you, Isaac," says Ricky, coming to his side. "We can ride the slow rides and make fun of the old people."

"This is not a big deal!" Isaac insists. The last thing he wants is for this to be all about him. Finally, Shelby breaks them out of the feedback loop.

"Well, I don't know about the rest of you, but I'm heading for the Skull Crusher before the line gets too long." And that gets them all moving.

Sadly, the line for the Skull Crusher is already too long, and so they play quiz and charade phone apps that seem specifically designed for waiting in line at amusement parks. Then, when they finally reach the front, Isaac steps across the brightly colored train to the other side. Shelby gives him that sympathetic smile again before screaming as the train is pneumatically expelled out of the station at eighty miles per hour.

It's the same for each ride, and finally the others seem to stop feeling bad for him. Isaac honestly doesn't mind not riding—but there's something else bothering him, and it bothers him more with each ride.

On the Skull Crusher, Shelby sat with Rachel. Then with Ricky on the Viper. Then with Rachel twice and then with Ricky again. Not once did she sit with Chet. Not on a single ride. That couldn't have been coincidental. Which means it must have been planned. It couldn't have been more conspicuous if they had ridden every ride together. What was it Chet had said that day? *Remember I'm your friend no matter what.*

Isaac tries to tell himself he's being ridiculous. But then, when they break for lunch, it all comes crashing down. Literally.

The amusement park is on a mesa, so everything is either uphill or downhill. There's even a Swiss-style funicular that they try to pass off as a ride, but it's really just a diagonal elevator to save people the walk. With hilly terrain, few things are at precisely the same level, which is why the food concession they chose for lunch had a seating area just about a dozen concrete steps downhill.

Chet and Shelby volunteer to wait in the burger line while Ricky takes a call from a classmate who needs engine work but wants it at classmate prices. Isaac waits with Rachel, whose head is down on a table, because she's still dizzy from the Cyclotron, as she is every year. That's also tradition.

Then, on the way down with the food, Shelby steps on a ketchup packet as lethal as a banana peel. It pops, Shelby loses her footing, and she begins what promises to be a bone-breaking wipeout. Isaac leaps to his feet, then grimaces in pain from the sudden move. Even if he weren't injured, there's nothing he can do—he's too far away.

It's Chet who takes quick action.

As Shelby's tray falls, Chet hurls his away, too, freeing him to perform a lifesaving maneuver. Chet grabs her around the waist in the nick of time. She throws her arms around his neck to regain her balance.

And there it is.

It's in the easy grip Chet has around her. It's in the way her hands linger on his shoulders, as if it's second nature. It's in the way they hold that position two instants too long. It might as well be written on matching T-shirts.

And the cherry on top is some middle-aged woman behind them on the stairs who witnesses the whole thing and says to Shelby, "He's a keeper, honey!"

Shelby glances to see that, yes, Isaac was watching. She gives Chet the shoulder tap, and he lets her go. She looks down at the food fail: burgers that have rolled head over heels like Slinkies, leaving bits of beef and bun all the way down, amid a debris field of fries.

"Well, that sucks," says Chet.

"You can tell them what happened," Shelby suggests. "Maybe they'll replace it if we make a stink."

It gives Chet a legitimate escape. "I'm on it." He bounds back up to the concession—but not before throwing a guilt-ridden glance at Isaac.

Shelby approaches Isaac as if he hasn't just seen what he has. "That was fun and a half," she says.

"You okay?" Isaac asks. Clearly she is, but clearly he needs to ask.

"Yeah, it was just stupid. I should have been looking where I was going."

"And . . . is there something else you want to tell me?"

Shelby finally meets his gaze for an uncomfortable beat. "Really?" she says. "I almost die, and you want to do this now?"

"Yeah. Yeah, I do."

"In the middle of Rachel's birthday?"

Rachel looks up at the mention of her name, takes one look at Shelby, and puts her head back down. Rachel knows. Of course she knows; she's Shelby's best friend.

Shelby pulls Isaac away to make their conversation private, or at least as private as it can be in a crowded amusement park. Ricky is there, having just gotten off his call. Sensing something, he gives them plenty of space. Does he know, too? Is Isaac the only idiot?

"Are you going to give that 'it just happened' bullshit?" Isaac asks. "Because things don't happen unless you make them happen."

"We were waiting for the right time to tell you."

"When did it start? Was it that night at the beach?"

"Excuse me, but you and I were never officially a thing? So maybe I don't owe you an explanation?"

"That's low, Shelby." Does she expect him to be okay with this? To just bow out and shake Chet's hand?

Shelby takes a deep breath. "It's not like you've been emotionally available. I don't even know where you are half the time."

"I'm right here!"

"No, Isaac," she says. "You're not."

And it kills him that she's right. This might have happened anyway, but he made it so much easier.

"Is that the best you've got? He's 'there'? Mountains are *there*. Dog shit is *there*. Half of Chet's brain cells have been sucked into his hair like fertilizer, and he's the one you want?"

"At least Chet's fun to be with. He's got a joie de vivre that you don't have anymore."

"He wouldn't even know what that is."

"And it wouldn't matter to me."

Isaac finds he has nothing else to say. For a split second he wishes she had fallen down those stairs, then hates himself for thinking that, and then hates himself for hating himself.

Shelby takes both of his hands in hers, and he doesn't pull away because he knows this is the last time she'll ever do that.

"Isaac, I love you. You *know* I love you. And I'm sure in, like, seventy years, we'll be sitting together in rocking chairs kicking ourselves that we waited so long to get together. . . . But right now there are other considerations."

Chet returns with two full trays, having successfully replaced both lunch—and Isaac. "Who's hungry?"

Isaac storms away, wishing he could be on any roller coaster but this one.

Ricky finds him sitting on a bench near the entrance. He'd prefer to nurse his wounds alone, but Ricky won't have it.

"C'mon, let's get the hell out of here," Ricky says.

"Don't be dumb—you can't just leave them here."

"It's already decided. They're gonna take an Uber home later."

"If you leave, Rachel will be stuck as third wheel on all the rides."

"Actually, no," Ricky says. "Chet might be a douche, but he's a considerate douche. I guarantee you that Rachel and Shelby will sit together, and Chet will be third wheel. Which means that me leaving is the only surefire way to make sure Shelby and Chet *don't* sit together on the rides."

And that's just satisfying enough for Isaac to accept it.

It isn't until they're on the freeway that Isaac asks the question that's weighing heavily between them. "Did you know?"

"If I knew, I would have told you," Ricky says. "I suspected, though. I'm sorry it played out the way it did." Then he adds, "Besides, anyone who uses 'joie de vivre' in conversation isn't worth the effort."

"You heard that, huh?"

Ricky laughs.

The thing is, with all the mix of emotions that Isaac feels—anger, humiliation, betrayal—there's a connective tissue between them that he's almost afraid to admit. Relief. As much as he didn't want this to happen, part of him is relieved that it did.

"You know," says Ricky, "just because the two of you looked good together doesn't mean you were right for each other."

Isaac nods, then reaches in his pocket and pops a pill, not even thinking about it. But Ricky takes notice.

"What was that?"

"Just ibuprofen," Isaac says. "800 milligrams." And the lie is so smooth, he doesn't even register it himself.

22

W**here**ver Freight Trains Go

ROXY

Thanks to me, Isaac's worst days are over. Although his car's still in the shop, physically he's more mobile. He doesn't fear being jostled, and his neck isn't constantly strained because he has to hold his shoulder just so. And with Shelby out of his life, there's nothing that can come between us.

"She was a waste of your time and a drain on your energy," I tell him.

"I know, I know," he says. "But it's still hard."

We sit together on a railroad overpass across town. It's a place Isaac likes to come when he feels a need to gain perspective. His feet dangle while we look down at a passing train. Soot-covered engines drag an endless line of old, rusted freight cars. He has his backpack with him, and it's heavy—because he's filled it with various and sundry items that remind him of Shelby. It's very literally baggage he wants to get rid of. But while he's mourning the loss, I feel an effervescence within me that makes everything feel new.

"There's an open-top coal car coming," I point out. "You could just hurl the whole thing in and let the train carry it to wherever freight trains go."

I caress his shoulder with so much more skill than Dillie had that day, massaging his pain away from the inside out. Isaac is a wounded warrior. He thought he was invulnerable, but now even his armor aches. I must be gentle. I must be sincere. He tilts his head back while I run my fingernails through his scalp, tracing a billion neurons that light up inside. It matters to me how he enjoys it. His pleasure has become my own.

The moment wears off, but we're still touching. Still connected. Then the coal car passes, but he doesn't toss the backpack or dump out the items into its bed. Instead, he gets up, and we leave, his special place of comfort not a comfort to him today.

"I could just hop on a train and go . . . ," he muses as we make our way to the nearest bus stop. "I wouldn't have to think about school, or Shelby and Chet . . . or college. It all seems . . . just too much right now."

"So do it," I dare. "Get on a train. I won't stop you."

"Would you come too?" he asks.

"Of course I would, Isaac. I'm here for you. I won't leave your side."

Making promises is nothing for me. I make them and break them with ease. But this is different. This time I mean what I say. And it scares me as much as it excites me. I've always been calculated. I've had every line memorized. I've always known exactly what to say to produce whatever result I wanted. I know the perfect look to give in just the right moment. I've kissed a thousand marks and made them fall for me. But this is entirely new. What then, if our train-to-anywhere veers violently off the rails?

We take a shortcut, crossing through a construction area that isn't fenced well. There's evidence of vagrants living in the concrete shadows of a freeway under construction, but no one's here now. It feels dangerous. It feels exciting. And I have an idea.

"Open your backpack," I tell Isaac, but he's reluctant.

"I just want to get home," he says. "I don't like this part of town. Ivy's old boyfriend lives around here."

But I am persistent. "We don't have to stay for long. But there's something you need to do, and you need to do it before you go home. You know it as well as I do."

He nods. Yes, he knows. He opens his backpack and starts taking things out. A birthday card. An anime bobblehead. A copy of Shelby's favorite book. A stuffed elephant, because she's been all about elephants since her safari. Isaac piles it all up, takes a deep breath.

"I don't want to do this," he says.

"If you don't want to do this, then why did you bring lighter fluid?"

And at my mention of it, he pulls out the squirt can he got from the barbecue in his backyard. "Yeah, but how am I supposed to light it?"

"Check your back pocket."

He does, and he pulls out a lighter. It's his sister's—the one she uses to light her bong. He smirks. "Hmm—how did that get there?" As if he didn't put it there himself.

"Do it, Isaac," I tell him, with building excitement. "Do it before you change your mind."

His heart rate quickens as he squeezes the bottle, squirting the pile of Shelbyness with lighter fluid. Then he takes one final thing out of his backpack. A strip of pictures of him and Shelby making faces in a photo booth. He lights the edge of it, and once's it's flaring, he tosses it on the pile—and it all ignites with a *whoosh* that makes us leap back. I can feel his adrenaline flowing—his sadness surrendering to the flames, becoming a strange elation. He needed to do this, and I know it feels good. Then, suddenly, there's a voice behind us.

"Hey! You there! What the hell are you doing?"

It's a construction worker, and he's hurrying toward us.

"Shit!" Isaac takes off. Between me and his adrenaline rush, he doesn't even feel the jostling of his shoulder as he runs. We put distance between us and the construction worker, whose interest in us ends as soon as we are out of sight. Once we're far enough away, we stop to catch our breath. Now we're behind a concrete pillar that reaches into the sky, ready for the road that will be laid upon it. We're giddy with the excitement of the moment.

"You say you're here for me," Isaac says, his eyes sparkling. "Do you mean that?"

"Of course I do."

And then Isaac does something crazy.

He kisses me.

I feel the electricity. Neural charges barreling over synapses toward connection terminals. Three point five trillion volts of energy that fill the human body. That's a thousand bolts of lightning. That's a nuclear warhead.

We exist not as things but as events in time.

So many times have I played games like this before, but

today is different—because never before have I ever let someone kiss me.

I kiss *them*.

They don't kiss *me*.

But here we are, together, in an embrace that neither of us ever wants to end, with enough energy between us to obliterate the entire world.

"I'm giving you one last chance to pull out of our competition over Isaac and Iris," I tell Addison that night as I stretch out across a private poolside cabana at the edge of the Party.

Addison is flustered. "It's Ivy, not Iris—and I don't want to pull out. I intend to beat you, fair and square."

I give him a chuckle that is as condescending as I can muster. "Addi, can't you see I'm doing you a favor? I'm trying to save you the embarrassment. I won't take any joy in seeing you humiliated—I'm better than that."

"No, you're not," he says. "And I'll take plenty of joy seeing you lose to li'l old me!" Then he offers me a mocking bow. "It will be a service to you, Roxy," he says. "Because deflating your ego could keep you from popping like an overfilled balloon."

I stir my cocktail with my pinkie and gaze into it rather than risking eye contact with Addison. The phosphorescent shades of purple and red bleed together. Apparently, Al is into neon tonight.

"You know what I think?" Addison says. "I think *you're* the one who's afraid to lose, and that's why you want to call it off."

"Do you know how ridiculous you sound?" And that's as close as I'll allow myself to get to an argument. I still won't meet Addison's eyes, for fear he might read something there that I don't want him to see—he's good at that. Instead, I raise my gaze to the glowing pool. My plus-one for the evening is there—the girl from the Chinese restaurant. It didn't take long to get her here. She's off in the pool with someone in Molly's downline—a muscular new designer who's all fingertips and tongue. I couldn't care less. I like having more room in my cabana anyway.

"Maybe," says Addison, "I should float the rumor that Roxy tried to renege on a bet. Nothing our crowd loves more than dirt on someone else."

I put my glass down hard enough to break the stem and in frustration hurl the rest of it away, not caring where it lands or who steps on the broken glass. The Party being what it is, they wouldn't feel it anyway.

"Rumors have teeth at both ends," I remind him. "I'll tell them you made the whole thing up, and you'll be the one who looks pathetic." Then I add, "As usual."

I can see that it gets him a little hot under his perpetually perfect collar, but he tries not to show it.

"Why are you so set on this thing?" I ask him. "Do you think you won't be able to get her up here without the pressure of a competition?"

And I can see in his face that I hit the nail on the head.

"That's it, isn't it! This was never about the challenge—you're using *me* to push *you*."

"I can bring Ivy up here anytime I like."

"So why don't you?"

"You know why. It's not just about doing it; it's about

doing it right. In a way that my upline won't just grab and go."

I think I have the upper hand on this conversation—but then I slip. It's just the tiniest thing—an uncomfortable shift of my shoulders, but as I said, Addison is alert, observant, perceptive. He begins a smile that takes a good long time to stretch wide.

"This isn't about me," he surmises. "This is about you. You and Isaac."

"I have no idea what you're talking about."

But again my body language says otherwise.

"Roxy, are you falling in love with him?"

The very idea is absurd. Beyond absurd. I won't even entertain it. So I don't respond. Instead, I stand in protest. "You're an ass!" And I stride down to the terrace railing that separates us from the earth below. But Addison follows, and although I expect him to make a big riotous deal of his ridiculous accusation, he doesn't. Instead, he says quietly:

"I'm right, aren't I?"

And although I've denied it—not just to him, but to myself—a part of me knows that he is. That what I feel for Isaac has gone far beyond what I should feel. Far beyond what's safe for me to feel. And I know why Addison isn't mocking me anymore. Because he gets how serious this is. How dangerous. How this could change everything for me, and not necessarily for the better.

"Does Isaac know what you *really* are? What you do? Does he know how toxic—"

"Just shut up, okay?" I snap. "He knows as much as he needs to know. And any feelings that I might, or might not, have will not stop me from winning our competition." And I will win. If only to prove to Addison that I am not ruled by something as pointless and passing as feelings.

Addison tries to put his arm on my shoulder to comfort me, but I shake it off. The last thing I want from him is pity. He's right about one thing. I am toxic. And now my own poison burns me from the inside out—because what neither Addison nor the others will ever understand is that a piece of myself now exists down there in the world below. I stare out into the twinkling night, thunderstruck by the thought of it. Every one of us has an expiration date. Maybe this is how my story ends, and soon I'll exist only as the stuff of legends. A shadowy specter imprisoned somewhere high above, like 'Lude. The nightmare's nightmare.

You endure every moment of your existence because you know there's more to you than the purpose you were created for. Then that desire becomes the greater meaning of what you truly are. So what happens when it all twists back on itself, and you realize, with miserable irony, that you exist to destroy the thing you most want?

"Well, I guess I'll see you in the VIP lounge," Addison says. "Or maybe I won't," he adds as a little dig. "But don't worry, Roxy. Either way, your secret's safe with me." Then he leaves me to grapple with this knot of a situation that's quickly turning into a noose.

Interlude #4—Phineas ($C_{17}H_{19}NO_3$)

Do you fear me? Do you shy away from the aspect of my eyes? They are like placid lakes hiding something that lurks in the depths. You fear it, but only because of the dark that shrouds this thing. But truly there is no need to fear. Because by the time you earn the darkness, you are gone. One cannot see what resides in the dark once you've become a part of it.

I am many places at once, but in a sense, they are all the same place. A hospital room here, a nursing home there. Places where lifesaving treatment has given way to hospice and palliative care. A quiet acknowledgment of the dwindling days. All that blooms must wither, and I am here to press the petals into the pages of your life.

The others despise me.

"You disgust us," my cousins say. "You are filthy and vile!"

But they are no better. I am just as addictive as they—even more so—but what of it? When addiction will pass away with life, it is of little consequence. No one cares if a terminal patient is addicted to that which brings them respite.

Still, my cousins see me as a vulture. A peculiar creature feasting on the bones of the dying. But they are wrong. I bring only relief to those I visit. I do not devour them. I merely breathe them in. I dissolve them one breath at a time, helping them to melt peacefully into their beds, allowing them to become one with white linen comfort. No, I am not an angel of death—I am the sandman, sprinkling sleep into their troubled eyes. I anoint them. I prepare them for that inevitable process that must come to all. Even my name means sleep. *Morphine.* See how it flows so smoothly off the tongue? Like fog off a mountain.

I don't care if the others hate me. I have been here, doing what I do, long before most of my cousins were even conceived. Let them have their party. Let them meddle in the hustle and bustle of people in their prime, fishing with ever shinier lures. Their indulgences are not mine. My place is here in the wards and warrens of infirmity. Labyrinthian places where the corridors wind in upon themselves, leaving no exit, save one.

Far away, in an elder care unit, a proud man refuses the hard therapy that might extend his life for a few more months. "Enough is enough," he has told his loved ones. "I am ready." I am there for him, the Prince of Palliative Care, to watch over him. To witness the petals as they fall. There are still several left on this bloom. His time might be short, but not as short as he thinks. I will be with him through it all.

Elsewhere, a woman old before her time has been lied to. A room in her son's home has been turned into a sickroom. A nurse attends her at all hours. The woman has been told that she's getting better. That it will all be okay, because her family cannot bear to tell her, or themselves, the truth. The treatment she now receives won't make her better. It is merely the medical equivalent of fluffing her pillow. Comfort, nothing more. I do not tell her. It is not my place. Instead, I smooth the lines of worry on her forehead and lighten her burden so that she doesn't have to think on these things. I whisper to her in the deepest of tones. My voice is a slow rattle. A resonance deep in the chest that only those in the twilight can hear.

And just like that I am called elsewhere. Come with me this time. Come see what it is that I do, and do not shrink away.

Now I move through the liquid air of a nursing home where currents of decay swirl into an antiseptic fog, like two fronts converging, promising a deluge. So laden is the air, it feels gelatinous. Such a struggle to push through.

This place is optimistically labeled "a rehabilitation center," and for some it is. Some shall leave this place with a new lease on life, having healed from their falls and their accidents and their strokes. Others will not.

There are two women in the room I have just entered.

I have been called to the one closest to the window.

"Nurse!" she calls. "Nurse!"

But the staff have tired of her crying wolf. She wants the curtains opened. She wants the curtains closed. What she really wants is for someone to acknowledge she still exists. That she's more than an inconvenience.

"*Nurse!*"

"Shhh," I tell her. "You don't need the nurse now."

"But I can't find the button."

"Patience. You'll find it," I reassure her.

The button she speaks of is at the end of a long cord that slipped between her bed and the guardrail. Now it dangles inches from the floor, swinging like a slow pendulum.

"Take the pain away, Phineas. Please . . . ," she says. "Pleeeease . . ."

"I will do what I can," I tell her, "but you must make the first move."

"The button . . ."

"Don't panic," I say calmly. "Search carefully. It's there. You just have to find it."

She moves her hand along the side of the mattress, moving back and forth until she touches the cord. Once found, she closes her fingers around it, pulling it up. Then, once she's holding the grip tightly in her hand, she presses the little blue button down with her thumb. The button releases a measured dose of me into her PICC line, delivering me directly into her bloodstream. I go immediately to work. Warmth spreads through her body. Her drooping eyelids sink another fraction of an inch. Her breathing eases.

"I am here, and will be here for as long as you need me," I tell her, for there is no one else who visits her but me. She catches my gaze and begins to cry.

"I hate you," she says. "I love you."

"Stay close," she says. "Get out of my sight."

Curtains open, curtains closed. Ours is a complex relationship.

Beside her is one flower remaining in the vase of a floral arrangement that wasn't even hers. It was brought for the woman in the other bed by her grandson. But there were too many flowers on her nightstand, so this woman is the beneficiary of the overflow.

I catch the petals as they fall from the flower. I open my book and carefully press each fallen petal between the pages.

"Tell me a story," she says groggily.

And so I oblige.

"Once upon a time there was a young girl who dreamed of being a ballerina. But her father didn't believe in such frivolous things."

"He was a hard man . . . ," she says.

"A hard man," I echo, "who lived a hard life. He said he wanted better for his own children, but instead visited the same harshness upon them."

"The bastard . . ."

All this time, and she cannot forgive her father for his bitter ways. Letting go would have made her life easier. But sometimes people hold on to pain because its jagged edges are so much easier to grasp.

"Go on," she says. "Tell the rest."

And so I weave her life's story—not exactly as it was but as she would want it to be told. I leave out the parts that might paint her as a villain rather than the hero. What point would it do to shine light upon that now? It is that side that has left her here alone. No, she knows *that* story well enough, so instead, I weave a tale lush and layered. . . . Her subjective truth, where she is always in the light, laboring through adversity.

But I stop my tale at the denouement. On the very last page, if you will. The penultimate note.

"Finish it," she prompts. "Make it a happy ending."

"The ending is neither happy nor sad," I tell her. "It simply . . . is."

She finds that unsatisfactory.

"Nurse . . . !" But it comes as barely a whisper now. Her time is close at hand.

"So what happens next?" she asks me, as frightened as the child she once was. The would-be-ballerina who never once attended the ballet.

"I am not privy to that information. I exist only in the here and now, not the hereafter."

I look to the flower. One wilting petal remains, clinging to life. I ready the book. Find an empty page. But still the flower clings. I am patient.

"Now?" she asks.

"Not yet," I tell her.

"Now?" she asks.

"Soon."

But there is no time line for these things. Life is a dance that concludes on its own schedule. And so there we sit, keeping each other company as we wait for the last petal to fall.

23

The Anatomy of an Extinction-Level Event

IVY

What is a hangover, really? Ivy thinks as she strides up to school. For Ivy it used to be just another excuse to blow the day off. Another day to excel at underachieving. But not anymore. That's not the new Ivy. Still, her brain is sufficiently dehydrated and underperforming from a lack of REM sleep. She can practically feel thousands of cytokines shooting up from her liver, inflaming her whole body. Yes, she knows the science of it. By this point in life, Ivy has become an expert at hangovers. She can't let this one get in her way. That's why she shows up at school with ginger-turmeric juice and wearing the darkest sunglasses she owns. Not to mention that she is five minutes early, because, to her own amazement, school is now her main priority.

Math test, science quiz, and despite her hangover, she's pre-pared. Ivy's going to kill it today. And if she starts to lose steam, she has a few extra study buddies in her pocket. She takes an extra one an hour before her first test. With nothing but the hangover elixir in her stomach, it will start hitting her system in forty-five minutes.

And it works like a charm. She feels like a laser burning through the pages of her math test. She's done, twiddling her thumbs and bouncing her knees with nervous energy while the other kids are practically banging their heads against their desks to knock their brain cells into gear.

That's when the phone rings.

Not her phone, the classroom phone. Classroom phones never ring. It jars the kids who are still on edge, trying to finish their tests. Ivy jolts too, but only because her nerve endings are so wired.

Her teacher picks it up with the obligatory "Hello" and listens for a moment. Then says, "Can't it wait? We're in the middle of a test." He listens some more, then hangs up unceremoniously, clearly peeved by the interruption. Ivy watches as he scans the classroom. Then his gaze lands on her, all antsy, flipping her pencil in her fingers.

"You're done, Ivy?" He seems surprised.

"Yeah, a couple of minutes ago."

"Good, because they need you in the main office."

Not what she was expecting. "Why?"

He comes over to take her test paper. "They didn't say," he tells her. "Only that the world must stop revolving until their demands are met."

Ivy smirks. "I can do the math on that for extra credit," she says.

She thinks he'll be amused, but he's not. "I'd get there quickly," he tells her. "They didn't sound too happy."

And so she picks up her bag and goes.

Ivy is no stranger to the school's administrative staff. Particularly Mr. Wooley, the vice principal of discipline.

"What low-level demon did you have to piss off to get named the vice principal of discipline?" she once asked him on a previous visit. "Is that a real job title, or do you just call yourself that?"

It hadn't gone over well. Neither did her pointing out that discipline was hard to take seriously from a man named Wooley.

But those days of bad behavior were behind her now. Of course, whatever this was about, she'll still be as cavalier as hell. Can't let the VP of D see you sweat.

And she's pretty sure she does know what this is about. Her grades have shot up suddenly and remarkably—and, as is always the case, the powers that be will assume the worst possible version of you. They'll think you cheated or plagiarized. That you got someone else to do your homework, or even hacked the school computer to change your grades.

Let them make their unsubstantiated accusations; Ivy doesn't care. The truth will prevail, and the truth is that she will graduate on time with a Hail Mary last semester. Because her new leaf is big and green and soaking up the sun.

Once in the main office, she heads past the school secretary toward Wooley's office, almost like muscle memory, but the secretary stops her.

"Not there, hon," she says. "Principal Payjack's office."

"Wait, Payjack wants to see me?"

"Better hurry. She hasn't got all day."

Whereas Wooley is a tired joke in a cheap suit, Ms. Payjack is a commanding presence, as intimidating as her name. She rarely gets involved in piddling disciplinary issues. She has bigger fish to fry. Suddenly, Ivy's swagger misses a beat and stumbles. Is she now a bigger fish? Then, just as Ivy gets to the door, it swings open, and her friend Tess comes out, clutching her books, her eyes swampy with tears.

"I'm sorry," she says when she sees Ivy, then bolts out of the main office to the hallway.

"What the hell?"

"Come in, Miss Ramey," she hears Payjack say from her office.

Ivy enters to find it's not just the principal in there. The school security guard is there as well. "What's going on?" Ivy asks with building concern. "Why is *he* here?" Then she takes a second look at the rent-a-cop, only to realize that he's not a rental at all. This isn't the school security guard. It's an actual police officer.

"Sit down, Ivy," Principal Payjack says.

Ivy sits down. Then Payjack hits the remote on a TV built into a bookshelf that seems much too fancy for a school administrator's office.

It's a surveillance video.

The image is fish-eye distorted, but Ivy quickly recognizes herself. This is the Walgreens where she got her prescription.

Her brain is buzzing; her legs are bouncing. She's trying to put two and two together. She just aced a math test, didn't she? She ought to be able to put two and two together. She forces her knees still, but it only lasts while she's thinking about it.

"Watch closely, Ivy," says the principal. "Although you know as well as I do what comes next."

But Ivy doesn't. All she remembers is getting her prescription. Because the moment in question was nothing but a blip on a day that had too many other things weighing on her mind.

But when she spots Tess at the end of the aisle, it all clicks. She knows what this is about. They want her to stand witness against Tess. Verify that Tess did, indeed, steal some booze.

"That camera is all the way at the end of the aisle," Ivy says. "You can't prove she did anything."

But Payjack says nothing. Just watches the video. So Ivy crosses her arms and watches, waiting for it to be done.

And then she sees the real reason why she's here.

Because from this angle, and at this distance, there's only one thing that comes across clear as day.

Ivy handing a bottle of Vodka to Tess. Who then stuffs it in her jacket.

"No!" Ivy shakes her head so hard it brings back her hangover. "No, that's not what it looks like."

Then the policeman chimes in. "Are you telling me the camera's lying?" The officer is so smug, she wants to rip his mustache off and shove it down his throat.

"Yes! I mean, no! I mean, it's not showing the whole picture. I wasn't giving it to her to take. I was giving it *back* to her, because I *didn't* want to take it."

"So you made Tess take it instead, and risk being caught?"

"Is that what she told you?"

Payjack and the officer look at each other.

"Not in so many words," Payjack says.

"You mean 'no,'" Ivy says. "No, she didn't tell you that. Because that's *not* what happened."

"We're not going to let you mire us down in the details, when the big picture is crystal clear."

"No, it's not clear. It's fuzzy and black-and-white and distorted. I was there to pick up a prescription. I can prove it!"

But Payjack is done arguing the point. She stands and leans a bit closer to Ivy. She breathes in. "Ivy, did you know that when a person drinks large amounts of alcohol, you can still smell it on them the next day? It's called diacetic acid. And you reek of it."

"What does *that* have to do with . . . ?" And suddenly Ivy's self-preservation instincts kick in. She shuts up. She needs her whole mind now to assess the situation and take critical action. Flapping her lips in frustrated, furious panic is not going to help her. So she bites back everything she wants to say and waits for Payjack's endgame.

The principal sits back down. She lifts the remote to turn off the TV.

"So, Ivy," she says. "What are we going to do about this?"

Ivy looks at the cop, then back at Payjack, who is clearly asking the question rhetorically. Whatever they're going to do, Payjack has already made up her mind about it. But by keeping her silence, it allows Ivy's thoughts to condense enough to come to her own crucial realizations.

"If I was going to be arrested, it would have already happened. You let Tess walk, which means you have to let me walk too."

"Very astute," says Payjack, perhaps a bit surprised by Ivy's sharp analysis. She turns to the cop. "Officer Pedroza, could you please wait outside?"

Pedroza flashes Ivy a stern law-enforcement kind of glance, then steps outside, closing the door behind him. And suddenly Payjack starts playing the good cop. "Whether you believe it or not, I am not your enemy, Ivy. Neither is Officer Pedroza. He could arrest you both, but I think there's a better option."

So is this blackmail? thinks Ivy. *I choose whatever Payjack dishes out as an "option" or be arrested for something I didn't do?* If she lets herself get arrested, the charges couldn't stick, could they? But there's enough doubt and distrust in Ivy to make her unsure of anything.

Payjack now gives Ivy a mournful gaze before delivering plan B. "Ivy, it's clear you have issues that are beyond this school's ability to handle."

"What is that supposed to mean?"

"I think it's pretty clear."

Then Payjack waits for Ivy to put it all together. Which doesn't take long at all.

"I'm being expelled? No—you can't do that! I know my rights. It's against the law to expel a student for something that happened outside of school."

"That's true," says Payjack, with practiced calm. "Which is why I'm asking for your voluntary withdrawal."

Ivy has no answer to that. Her principal is not stabbing her in the back—she's asking Ivy to stab *herself* in the back.

As Ivy recalls, Dante said there were nine levels of hell. She wonders which one she's in now.

"Rosewood Alternative has a much more comprehensive counseling program than we do," Payjack tells her. "I've already contacted them. I'll be happy to set up an appointment for you and your parents there."

Her parents! The idea of bringing her parents into this makes her already pounding head practically detonate. She feels she might have an aneurism on the spot. Death by principal. Must happen all the time.

"I don't need counseling," Ivy insists. "I just need to finish my classes and graduate!"

"I'm sure you will," Payjack says. "But you won't be doing it here."

ADDISON

This is not my fault.

I did everything I could possibly do for Ivy. I got her zeroed in on what really mattered and spent every waking moment reinforcing that.

This is not my fault.

It is a confluence of bad luck and even worse timing. That surveillance video was taken before I began working with her—and it only told the story they wanted to see.

This was not my fault!

Yet the more I say it, the less exonerated I feel. Denying guilt only brings it circling back. And it makes me furious. If I am to be Ivy's one and only to the bitter end and beat Roxy at her own twisted game, then I can't let this derail me. The truth is, I can be with Ivy no matter what the circumstance. She doesn't need school as an excuse to be with me. I refuse to allow my propensity to help get in the way. Not this time. Not anymore.

I turn my attention to Ivy, focusing on her frustrations instead of my own.

"This is a glitch, nothing more," I tell her as she storms down the hallway so fast I can barely keep up.

"A glitch? This is not a glitch! This is an extinction-level event."

"It only feels that way now."

She laughs at that. "What will be different tomorrow? Or the day after that?"

"It's simple," I tell her. "You can do one of three things.

One: You finish up the semester at Rosewood Alternative School—you might still graduate on time if you keep up the hustle."

Ivy just groans.

"Two: You study with me and we get your GED without ever having to sit in a high school classroom again. Except to take the test, of course."

She hardens her jaw and won't even look at me.

"Three: You take a break, work on getting your head back in gear, and go to Rosewood in the fall."

"Or option four: I just give up and drop out."

"No," I tell her. "I will not allow that to happen."

Then she turns on me with a vengeance. "I can't go to the alternative school!"

"There are worse places."

"Not for me, there aren't!"

Then she turns and kicks open the entry door to bright sunlight.

I follow her to the street, where she stands, nowhere near a crosswalk, looking out into bustling traffic, as if she might launch herself into it. Would she do it? I wonder. If she had her heart set on it, would I be able to stop her? But instead, she turns and goes to the public bus stop farther down the street, where Tess sits alone waiting for the bus with a trash bag full of junk from her locker.

When Tess sees Ivy, she wipes mascara from her runny eyes, trying to hide the fact that she's been crying, but the smears just highlight it, like tape around a body.

"God, she looks like a horror movie," I say, but Ivy ignores me. Ivy has yet to let a single tear fall. I still can't tell if that's good or bad. "You don't have to talk to her if you don't want to," I tell Ivy. "You don't even have to sit with her."

But that just makes her sit next to Tess anyway, out of spite.

"I'm sorry," Tess says. "I told Payjack you had nothing to do with it, but she didn't listen."

I try to whisper words of encouragement in Ivy's ear, but she closed herself to me the moment she sat down.

"It doesn't matter," Ivy says. "What's done is done."

Tess rubs her eyes, making a Rorschach across her cheeks, then offers a wicked grin that doesn't jive with her watery eyes. "At least now you can come to Desert Swarm with us," she says.

"You've just been expelled, and all you can think about is that stupid music festival?"

Tess puts her nose slightly in the air. "Not expelled. 'Voluntarily withdrawn.'"

Farther up the street, the light turns green, and a bus approaches. "Don't get on the bus with her, Ivy," I tell her. "Walk home today." Anything to keep these two from conspiring.

"Rosewood won't be so bad," Tess says. "I know some kids there. And besides, we'll have each other." Then she takes Ivy's hand, and Ivy lets her. "We'll definitely have some fun there," Tess says with that same nasty grin, then stands as the bus pulls up.

When Ivy doesn't follow her to the curb, Tess turns back. "Aren't you coming?"

"Nah—it's a nice day. I think I'll walk."

Good for her. A small victory is better than none at all.

Once Tess is gone and the bus pulls away, Ivy looks down at her feet. "Now do you get it?" she says. "Wherever Tess goes, she brings a bucket of bad habits. *My* bad habits. If I'm in that school with her, there's nowhere I'm going but down the drain."

"You know how much I hate defeatist talk," I tell her. "If you ask me, I think Rosewood will be good for you. It will give you a place to rise *from*. When expectations are low, your successes will be greater. The teachers there will be rooting for you to win, not betting on you to fail."

"Blah, blah, blah."

"I'm serious. When you're at an alternative school, everyone who picks themselves up by their bootstraps is lauded as a triumph."

"Not gonna happen. I know myself. I thought you knew me too." Then she gets up to leave.

"Don't walk away from me!"

"You can't order me."

"I'm not ordering you, Ivy. I'm begging," I tell her as honestly and as plainly as I can. "Please. Please don't walk away. Don't leave me. I promise I'll do better."

Then she shakes her head sadly, and I can't help but sense it's pity that oozes from her now. It feels like a stake through the heart. But not as painful as what comes next.

"Maybe you can't do any better," she says. "Maybe I need someone a little stronger."

24

Guts on the Kitchen Table

ISAAC

Is everything okay?

That seems to be everyone's favorite question to ask Isaac lately. From his friends to his teachers. It always comes with an air of arrogance, because whoever is asking it assumes they have all the answers to the problems they don't even know about. It's presumptuous. And it pisses Isaac off.

The next in line to ask is his guidance counselor.

"Is everything okay?" Demko asks at Isaac's next academic meeting.

"Yes. Everything's fine. More than fine." And it's true as far as he's concerned. In some ways, even better than ever before.

"I only ask because your attendance record is showing a lot of absences lately. . . ."

"They're medical," Isaac informs him. "I messed up my shoulder recently."

"Isaac, you've missed seven days this month. And I can see your grades are down. That could hurt your chances of getting into your choice of schools." Demko looks into his eyes earnestly.

"Thank you for your concern. It'll all work out."

The counselor smiles warmly. "I hope so."

Isaac hurries out, aggravated. A vexation he'll turn into fuel to prove Demko wrong. If there's anything that irritates Isaac more than his plunging grades, it's the fact that someone doubts that he can take control. *Everything will work out, like it always does,* he repeats to himself. It's true whenever Isaac hit turbulence with schoolwork, he always managed to find a cruising altitude that would eventually land him high grades. Why should this time be any different?

So right when Isaac gets home, he cleans his desk and sits down to do his homework. There's a lot of catching up to do. But his head is so cloudy, he doesn't even know where to start. He doesn't even remember what chapters he needs to work on because he didn't get the makeup instructions from his teachers.

He finds himself overwhelmed, his mind thickening like soup with every passing moment. It's that time of day. The time of day when he usually takes his second pill.

But aren't these pills part of the reason he's missed school in the first place? Still, he reaches into his coin pouch, going for them anyway. Even when his head tells him no, his body says yes. And that troubles him. Isaac has always been logical—and this is the first time the commands firing in his brain aren't being executed by his fingertips.

Do you want it, or do you need it? he remembers asking himself once as he stared at the pill in his palm. Maybe he's not in as much control as he thought. Maybe this isn't just the older equivalent of sneaking around your parents to get into the cookie jar. When he was a kid, he wanted that cookie. But he didn't need it. Now he knew the answer. He *needs* these pills.

There's a voice in his head telling him that he can't live without them, and it would be pointless to try.

And the thing is, his parents always knew he snuck those cookies. Not because they were particularly observant, but because Isaac himself would either tell them, or telegraph. He'd leave crumbs. He'd leave the lid slightly ajar. At the time, he thought it was just carelessness, but later he came to know that part of him did these things on purpose. Because crimes should not go unpunished. And secrets needed to come out.

That's why Isaac decides that he is going to tell his parents the truth. That he's been taking pain pills. That he's been self-destructive just to get more of them. That he's developing a dependency. And he has to tell them now, before the pills themselves change his mind.

Isaac steels himself for the conversation with his parents. Will they be surprised? Shocked? Angry? Some combination of all three, most likely. Will they blame Grandma? He hopes they don't do that. He doesn't even plan to tell them that it was her pill that got him started—but they'll want to know where he got them in the first place. He could lie, tell them it started after he hurt his shoulder—that it was the ER doctor's prescription that did it. But lying in the midst of coming clean? That's a nonstarter. He was never a good liar anyway. Although lately it's a skill he's developing.

He slowly heads downstairs, then doubles back, then goes down again. How does one start this kind of conversation?

Mom, Dad, I think I've developed a dependency on painkillers.

He could just come out and say it like that—spill his guts

right there on the table. They'd stare at him and say *"What?"* and he'd have to repeat it. It would have been hard enough to say the first time. He's not looking forward to repeating it.

Or maybe he can just work it into conversation over dinner.

Hey, so my shoulder's starting to feel a little better. Funny thing, though. Those pills. They're kinda hard to stop taking. How hard? Like really *hard.*

Or what if he takes a more passive approach and sends them a link to an article about kids his age addicted to pain-killers? There's no shortage of those. Both kids and articles. He could text them the link with no explanation and let them come to him.

But no matter how many simulations he runs in his head, none of them are any less awful. Even so, he knows he must go through with it because the situation has become untenable.

Why do you need to do this at all? the meds tell him in a voice that's hard to ignore. *This is between you and me, Isaac. Let's keep it that way.*

He knows that voice will prevail if he overthinks this, so he forces himself to complete his journey to the kitchen, where he can hear his parents talking.

From the moment he arrives, he knows something is off. It's the smell that hits him first. The acrid stench of burned food. There's a pan lying in the sink like a shipwreck, its contents black beyond recognition. Mom sits at the table, elbow down, head resting in her hand, in standard headache position. Dad's cleaning up the range, where something else boiled over. Clearly dinner turned into multiple casualties of their conversation.

As for the conversation, he heard a little bit of it before he stepped in. It's one of their "financial straits" conversations. There have been plenty of those lately. Which of their workers do they lay off? Where can they cut corners? What magic hat can they pull new paying jobs out of? They fall silent the moment Isaac makes his appearance, as if they hadn't been talking, but they know as well as he does that it's not going to fly. He came to spill his guts, but it looks like theirs are already sprawled out on the table.

"What's going on?" Isaac asks.

Heavy sighs. His father continues to clean the range, not volunteering anything.

"You want to tell him?" his mother prompts.

"Not really, no."

"He's going to find out anyway."

Isaac hates when they talk about him in third person—like they can hit his pause button while they talk among themselves.

"The yacht job is dead," his father finally says.

"What? How? The guy fired you?" Isaac immediately wonders if it was because of that night he passed out in the main cabin—like maybe the guy had a security cam on him the whole time. But it turns out it's something entirely different.

"The boat was seized by the government," his father tells him. "Turns out that asshole owes millions in back taxes."

"They can't do that!"

"They can, and they did."

"But . . . but he paid you, right?"

Their silence gives Isaac the answer. He knows how it goes. Fifty percent up front, and the rest on completion. They were pretty close to finishing—and with all their attention on this one big job, there are no other irons in the fire.

"We can sue, but it would be pointless," his dad says. "He already filed for bankruptcy. We won't get a penny."

His mom lifts her head from her hands. "We'll figure this out. It's not your problem, Isaac."

But of course it is. It's all of their problems.

"Does Ivy know?"

That brings another heavy sigh. More like a deflation. As if the air in his parents' lungs were the only thing holding them up.

"Considering her current situation," his father says, "I don't think it's on her radar."

"Wait—what situation?"

His father turns to his mother. "You want to tell him?"

"Not really, no."

"He's going to find out eventually."

Then his mother hits him with the second of their one-two punches. "Your sister and your school have decided to go separate ways."

Isaac has to repeat it in his mind to make sure he heard right. "What? Ivy was expelled?"

"That's what she told us," his mom says. "So we called the school. Turns out it isn't that simple. She was . . . well, she was caught with liquor. And so she 'voluntarily withdrew.'"

"In other words," said his father, "rather than face the consequences of her actions, she dropped out."

It's like a nuke in Isaac's head. "She can't do that!"

"She can and she did."

"She's eighteen, Isaac," his mother points out. "She can ruin her life any way she wants."

"But she was doing better! Her grades were up. Why would she do this?"

Isaac's father returns to cleaning the range. His mother answers, but it's not an answer at all. "Why does your sister do anything, Isaac?"

"Let me talk to her."

"You can't," his mother informs him. "She stormed out in a rage, and we couldn't stop her. She's gone to some music festival in the desert."

"Was she the one raging," asks Isaac, "or was it the two of you?"

His mother deflates even more at the thought. "There was plenty of anger to go around."

His father throws down the sponge, giving up on the range. "If she's with that worthless boyfriend of hers—"

"No, she's not," Isaac tells him. "They broke up. For good."

To that, his mother says, with barely any conviction, "Thank heaven for small miracles."

Isaac is halfway back up the stairs before he realizes that his entire reason for going down there was derailed.

He pauses. Considers. Don't they say bad news comes in threes? (1) Your biggest job in five years is up shit's creek, (2) your daughter dropped out of school with two months to go, and (3) your son has a thing for painkillers.

No—how could he spring this on them now? They don't need a triple whammy. They couldn't handle it. But he can.

He can handle this without them. He *will* handle it.

It's better this way, that voice in his head tells him. Right. He can wean himself off the pills. People have always told Isaac that he can do whatever he wants to if he sets his mind to it—and it's always been true. Why should this be any different?

The voice in his head offers no comment.

ROXY

I have been through this before, but Isaac hasn't. That puts me at a distinct advantage. So why am I so worried?

I follow him to his room. He closes the door, but doors mean nothing to me. You can't shut out what you bring with you. He paces, trying to get his head in gear for this thing he believes he must do, and I lay into him, determined to chip away at his resolve.

"After everything—after all we've been to each other— you're just going to throw it away?" I tell him. "How could you, Isaac? How could you be so cold, so cruel?"

"You're not good for me," he mutters. "I see that now."

"Oh, so this is just about you? How about what's good for me? What's good for *us*?"

"There is no us!"

My whole essence clenches when he says that. I have gone through these motions thousands of times. The manipulations, the coercions, they are like muscle memory to me. They are rote, like a multiplication table. It's all math. I know exactly how often my equation works and how often it doesn't. But today those numbers don't comfort me, and the same tried and true words don't feel like simple battle tactics. They feel honest. They feel real.

And the truth I can't admit is this: his determination might be stronger than my hold on him. It happens. And when it does, it usually just bruises my ego. Then I'd be on to the next one, even more determined to bend them entirely to my will. But this time I can't imagine losing—and I don't just mean to Addison. The stakes are far beyond that now. I can't even begin to think about losing Isaac. What does that mean? How the hell did I let this happen?

Isaac takes the little coin purse and heads toward the bathroom. I know what he's about to do.

"Stop this, Isaac! Stop now and . . . and I'll forgive you. I promise." I wrap my arms around him lovingly. Possessively. But it's not enough to stop his momentum.

ISAAC

Isaac and Ivy share a bathroom, although the two sides are as different as can be. Ivy has her toiletries arranged neatly; Isaac's are a mess. Until recently, it used to be the opposite.

Before he changes his mind, Isaac unzips the coin purse and pours the pills into the toilet. All of them. They sink into the water and slide down the porcelain slope to the bottom, glinting like pearls in a wading pool.

He almost reaches into the water for them. Almost. But they're already starting to dissolve. In toilet water.

NEAL SHUSTERMAN AND JARROD SHUSTERMAN

But you can still save them!

That voice scares him. Scares him to the point that he reaches for the duck-necked bottle of toilet bowl cleaner beneath the sink and squirts a heavy dose of its blue caustic gel into the water. There. He can't save them now. They're poisoned. He feels relieved. He feels foolish. And there's that voice in his head telling him something he already knows.

You're going to regret this, Isaac.

Even so, he reaches for the little silver lever, closes his eyes, and flushes.

ROXY

I tried. I tried with every ounce of my being to stop him.

"You're just going to send everything we have down the drain?"

"I already did," he says. "It's done. I don't need you. I don't want you. All I want you to do is leave."

It hurts more than I want him to know. But I will have the last word. I always do. And so I lean in close and whisper my prophecy into his ear.

"You will suffer, and I will not be there to comfort you. You'll cry out for me, and you'll receive nothing but silence. You will have no comfort at the very worst moment of your life, and you will understand the true meaning of loneliness."

Then I leave without saying goodbye. Because I never say goodbye. To anyone. For any reason.

Only after I am gone do I let my tears flow. I am so full of fury, I feel like I could combust like a star in the night sky.

I hate you, Isaac!

But from that same sky, a million other stars blaze out a greater truth that proves my fury to be nothing but an ember.

I love you, Isaac, those heavens say.

For I am the one who now knows true loneliness, lost in the space between galaxies.

25

Children of a Wasted God

IVY

A fast car can outrun anything, Ivy thinks. Which doesn't help because TJ's uselessmobile is not fast. In fact, it's barely able to outrun its own exhaust. So anything and everything that Ivy's trying to outrun has no problem clinging to the bumper and coming along for the ride.

There are four of them in the sunbaked car heading to the Desert Swarm Festival. TJ and Tess are in the front. In the back with Ivy is an occasional member of their crew who everyone calls Stone Cold Jimmy, because (a) he's usually stoned, and (b) his hands are always cold.

He eyes Ivy and tries weak attempts at charm and humor, clearly hoping to make some inroads—as if being stuck together in a back seat of a car is something romantic. Ivy resolves that if he tries even the slightest move on her with his frosty little hands, she'll snap off a finger like an icicle.

She reaches into her bag and pulls out her bottle of pills. She wasn't going to bring it along, but it was there on her desk, calling out to her. *You need me,* it said. *I'll keep you awake until the last hours of the festival.* She supposes it's true. It is, after all, an amphetamine. Her study buddy can keep her alert and focused for things beyond studying.

Stone Cold Jimmy watches her press down to open the childproof lid, and he offers a grin that inexplicably makes one of his nostrils slightly larger.

"What you got there, Ivy?" he asks.

"Not your business," she tells him, and she pops a pill dry.

"Ooh, can I have one?"

"You don't even know what the hell it is. Could be anything. It could be cyanide, and I might start frothing at the mouth and die."

"Well, you're not, so can I have one?"

She closes the bottle and puts it back into her bag, making sure it's deep. "No, and don't ask again."

"Ah, you're no fun."

She turns away to look out at the arid landscape baking in the late-afternoon sun. *This is my tribe,* Ivy has to remind herself. The children of a wasted god.

It doesn't have to be, says that irritating voice in her head. So she tells it to take a flying leap. This is where Ivy has always belonged, and any attempts to exit have been met with extreme force. The universe has spoken. Like it or not, her place is here in the back seat with a pothead with cold hands.

ADDISON

Fine. If this is what Ivy wants, then this is what she'll have. I don't know why it should aggravate me—this is a win. It ups my game in a major way. I don't have to keep her nose in the books anymore; now I can focus exclusively on getting her to the Party. She'll be my plus-one in no time—and, damn it, I will feel no guilt, because it's *her* doing, not mine. It's my job to facilitate, nothing more. I can facilitate her journey to wherever she wants to go—and if it's to oblivion, so be it. I'll be with her to the end, and I'll be there before Roxy. Then we'll see who's not strong enough.

As the hours wear on and the sun sinks low, we find ourselves in a long line of cars inching toward the festival grounds. We finally pull into a massive makeshift lot on the desert hardpan. As we get out into the sweltering heat, we're greeted by the sickly sweet smell of Mary Jane's perfume and the arrhythmia of competing beats—multiple bands playing simultaneously.

"There are, like, five stages," Tess says. "A huge amphitheater for the headliner bands, three medium-size ones for up-and-comers, and a little baby stage for no-name acts with potential. But they usually suck."

I remind Ivy to take her bag before TJ locks the car.

Once we cross through the gate, it's clear that this is more than just a music festival. There are carnival rides, booths selling anything this crowd might desire, and a whole avenue of food trucks.

"It's like the county fair fell through a sinkhole into happy-ass hell," Ivy observes.

"Yeah, it *is* hot, isn't it?" Tess says, entirely missing Ivy's point, and begins to wander in the direction of the main stage.

"Don't get lost," TJ says. "I've heard the cell towers here are all overloaded. Phones won't work, and we'll never be able to find each other."

That makes Ivy laugh. "Right—before cell phones, humanity was just a mob of wandering people searching for one another."

"I know, right?" says Tess.

I sigh. "Don't waste your breath," I whisper to Ivy. "Sarcasm dies a lonely death in there."

I had reminded Ivy to download the festival schedule before we arrived, so even without service, we'd know which band was where and when.

They pass the garage band pavilion, where a wannabe K-pop band that does not look at all Korean performs for a sad smattering of people who are mostly just there for a place to sit.

Tess and TJ are all about food right now, and they look in the direction of the food trucks, but Ivy wants to explore.

"Wutever Werx is on the north stage at seven tonight— that's less than an hour, and they're the only band I really want to see," she tells the others.

Tess smirks. "As if I didn't already know you have a thing for Coleman Werx."

"Why don't we meet there at six thirty?" Ivy says. They all agree, and Tess goes off with TJ. As for Stone Cold Jimmy, he's talking to some Beet Red Betty, who seems to be a natural fit for his particular charms.

"Good," I tell Ivy. "Now that the others are out of your hair, we can have some fun!"

I take her down to the midway carnival games, where all the prizes relate to the festival and the band lineup. We single out a row of Whack-A-Moles—mortal competition between five contestants for a prize, which means there's always a winner.

Ivy takes a seat, the buzzer goes off, and I slow down time just enough for Ivy to prevail. She asks for an autographed poster of Wutever Werx that's hanging above the booth, but instead gets handed a small plush figure that looks like a tall, thin turd with a sewed-on face. Sandy Swarm, the festival mascot.

"You can trade three Sandies in for a T-shirt and three T-shirts in for an autographed poster," the carny tells her.

"What a rip-off!" Ivy says, and strides away, putting Sandy Swarm into the hands of someone else who doesn't want him.

Then her eyes are drawn to a concession featuring frozen cocktails spinning in glass-faced drums. The drinks have names like Neon Nirvana, Orange Oasis, Soundgarden Slush—a rainbow of inebriation and alliteration. And who is there beckoning Ivy like a carnival barker? Al.

"Leave her alone tonight," I tell him.

Al just smirks. "Honestly, Addison, do you really think you can keep her on a leash?"

Ivy pulls out her fake ID and shows it to the server. "I'll have a Blue Oyster Bomb—the biggest you have."

"For an extra two bucks, we serve it in a cowbell," he tells her.

"Sure, why the hell not?"

"She's made an excellent choice," Al comments. "Blue curaçao, vanilla vodka, peach schnapps, and rum." Then Al leans over to her and whispers into her ear, "Ask for an extra floater of rum."

And she asks not just for one extra shot, but a double.

"You see, Addison," says Al. "Like you, I live to serve."

"Your interference is not appreciated," I tell him.

"Interference? Banish the thought! I'm here to help you get her to the Party."

"And take her yourself when I'm not looking?"

"Come now, Addison, when have you ever known me to poach? I just grease the gears."

As the twilight darkens and the desert begins to cool, Ivy heads over to the north stage, nursing her bright blue drink, its strength hidden in the sugar.

The others never show up. Big surprise. Wutever Werx is Ivy's favorite band, not theirs, and besides, her so-called friends have never been all that reliable. "Don't wait for them," I tell her. Finally she gives up, finishes her drink in a long sip that gives her a brain freeze, tosses the plastic cowbell into an overstuffed trash can, and heads into the amphitheater. It's one of the secondary stages, with maybe a thousand seats and a standing area down front. A muscular security guard—one of many—stands at the entrance to the standing area, only letting people in who don't look too wasted. With the drink still not taking its full effect, Ivy makes it through just as the band takes the stage to the roar of the crowd. They begin with their seminal number, "Love Like a Mantis." It's the one that almost made it onto the charts. Like most of the bands Ivy likes, Wutever Werx is on the cusp. They haven't hit it big yet—and I know Ivy would prefer if they didn't. She's the type who loses interest in bands that become too popular.

"Is it evil of me to hope they break up before they sell out?" Ivy asks.

"Not at all," I tell her. Tonight the stands are only about two-thirds full, but the front area is literally jumping with die-hard fans. One thing I can say is this band's fans are fiercely loyal. "Keep your eyes open for gaps," I tell her.

Bit by bit she negotiates herself closer to the stage until she's right up against the rail, where several guards keep the fans in their place. She whoops and dances to every song, and I dance with her. Her body language begins to take on the physical slur of a person whose blood alcohol is on the rise.

"No inhibitions," says Al, who I thought we ditched, but he's never too far away. "Shout out to the band!" he says. "Say what you mean and mean what you say!"

And she does. She screams to the lead singer as they're about to start a new number. "I love you, Coleman!"

It actually gets his attention—and then the wildest thing! Coleman Werx nods to one of the guards, and suddenly they're hoisting us up onto the stage, where Coleman dances with us. Ivy is in heaven. And although Werx is not much of a dancer, Ivy kills it. Such moves! I didn't even know she had it in her. The crowd cheers. This is your moment, Ivy! Live in it! Make no apologies, and when you take your bow, try not to fall off the stage, because none of these shitheads will catch you.

A few more bars of the song, and Werx glances to the security guards, who quickly mobilize to get Ivy off the stage.

"Well," says Al, "that was exhilarating."

The band finishes their set much too soon, they do a quick encore, then the lights come up, and people are herded to the exit like cattle. But I can see that Ivy has a look in her eyes both mischievous and calculating.

"Ivy . . . what are you thinking?"

"I'm thinking I'm gonna go backstage."

I start to get worried. The green room, as they call it, will be a cesspool of the worst of *us*, mingling with the worst of *them*. "I don't think that's a good idea," I tell her. "You'll never get in without a backstage pass anyway. Wouldn't you rather get something to eat instead?"

"No," she says unequivocally. "Thanks to *you*, I'm not hungry."

Al laughs. "She's got you there."

The greenroom is a canvas tent with a bouncer who stands there like an executioner to keep out the riffraff. Or at least the riffraff who weren't invited. A gathering of hopefuls tries to convince/beg/bribe him to let them in. But this isn't his first rodeo. He's not budging.

Ivy pushes forward for her shot at the prize.

"Your pass," demands the bouncer.

"I was the one who danced with Coleman onstage."

He pauses, not dismissing her outright. "That was you?"

"Yeah."

"You were good."

"Thank you. Can I go in? So I can thank him personally?"

He considers it, then pulls back the rope to let her pass, while the unanointed cry foul.

"Once more unto the breach!" raves Al, and we're in.

Inside, the members of the band lounge with chosen groupies and invited VIPs. As I surmised, there's also a whole host of familiar faces. Everyone from Molly to Mickey. It looks like the touring company of the big Party.

And there, in the middle of it all, are Dusty and Charlie. I knew they'd be here. They sit on either side of Coleman Werx like twin consigliere, their white silk suits defying the desert grime.

"Ivy, we should go," I tell her. "We should go right now."

"Leave me alone," she says, pulling away from me. "I'll do what I want."

Then Dusty spots us and raises a multi-ringed hand in a royal wave. He turns to whisper into Coleman's ear, drawing his attention to Ivy as she approaches, and there's nothing I can do to stop her. All I can do is trail in her wake, hoping this doesn't go the way it always does.

"Addison!" says Dusty. "A bit out of your element, aren't you?"

"Keep away from her! She's with me," I tell him, not mincing words. I wonder if they recognize her from our last encounter.

"No," says Charlie. "Seems to me she's with our boy Coleman."

"He's on his way to being a star," Dusty says. "We're helping him with that."

Coleman has made room for Ivy to sit down, and she does. I can't help but notice, now that he's not in the glare of stage lights, he doesn't look all that much different from the guy who rode in the car with her. Coleman Werx is just Stone Cold Jimmy with talent.

Meanwhile Dusty and Charlie press closer like bookends on either side.

"Ah, well," says Al with a shrug. "The upline always prevails. No sense in fighting it."

But then I get an idea. . . .

"*You* can stop them, Al."

The suggestion surprises him. "I told you, I grease the

works, not gum them up. What could I possibly do, and why would I want to?"

"Because you hate Dusty and Charlie, Al. You hate them as much as I do!"

I look at Ivy. She's starry-eyed as the lead singer of her favorite band makes her the center of his attention. I don't hear what Werx says to Ivy, but it makes her giggle. Then Charlie reaches out to brush his multi-ringed hand on Ivy's cheek, and I know I'm running out of time.

"Think about it, Al," I say. "That Blue Oyster Bomb she drank was twenty-four ounces. . . ."

"Yes . . ."

"And it had two extra shots of rum."

"Yes . . ."

"On a completely empty stomach."

"Ah—I see your point."

"You can take hold of this entire situation, Al . . . if you want to." Because the quickest way to make someone chaste is to make them suddenly undesirable.

Al thinks about it and sighs. "Don't say I never did anything for you."

Then Al pulls Ivy to her feet and delivers a powerful punch to the gut.

IVY

As far as Ivy is concerned, she's living the dream. Sitting with Coleman Werx, talking about his lyrics. Hearing firsthand where her favorite songs came from. The world seems to be spinning around her, but she doesn't care. And Coleman—"You can call me Cole"—extends his upturned pinkie toward her, fine white powder resting is his long nail. So nineties. It makes her giggle.

Then suddenly the world seems to be spinning in the opposite direction. She gets up, realizing what's about to happen. It hits her gut so quickly, so suddenly, she can't stop it, much less control its direction. She tries to open her mouth to give Coleman warning, but it's not words that come out.

In an instant, what was arguably the coolest moment of her life flips into the most horrific. Ivy blasts Coleman Werx with a ballistic blue deluge, and it seems to Ivy that so much more comes out than went in.

Coleman starts screaming to have her taken the hell out of there, demanding towels, a change of clothes, completely ignoring the fact that she hasn't stopped puking. There are others who try to help, but Ivy can't look anyone in the face. She tries to apologize but can't catch her breath, and she thinks, *Please, for the love of God, please let me black out so I can't remember this.* Gentle but firm hands lead her away, while behind her she hears Coleman say, "I can't believe that bitch barfed on my blow!"

ADDISON

I have been witness to many things, but nothing in the history of my existence has been as satisfying as seeing Charlie's and Dusty's white suits covered in bright blue vomit. They came so close to having their way with her. But Al delivered. I'm going to owe him big.

While Coleman Werx screams an endless stream of obscenities, Ivy is quickly spirited off to the nearest portalet. Her legs have given out now—she can only kneel, and I'm there kneeling with her as she retches. There's nothing left for her to purge, so she dry heaves and cries while I comfort her.

"It's all right," I tell her. "It will all be fine. You have me. I'm here, and I'm not going anywhere."

26

Standing at the Edge of a Storm

ISAAC

Isaac isn't stupid.

He knew from the beginning that this wasn't going to be easy. That withdrawal from any substance is supposed to be the hardest thing you can ever go through short of giving birth. With his family in turmoil, this is the worst possible time to do this, but it's not something he can put on hold. So, while his sister crosses the desert to her music festival, Isaac does the necessary research and plots his own journey. One that won't take him any farther than his bedroom but hopefully can provide him a much more important sort of distance. He may already be in bad shape, but he has to hold it together long enough to do this right.

The internet offers some help but no magical revelations to ease the way. Isaac comes to realize that this is going to be like preparing for a hurricane without hope of evacuation. He is going to have to buckle down and ride this—and given the last time he took the pills, he has less than two hours before the storm hits.

Isaac has a laundry list of items that he'll need to get through this. Then, with his car still under repair, he takes off on his mountain bike, pedaling as fast as he can to the closest 7-Eleven, wobbling all the way, because he can only hold on with one arm. He's already beginning to feel the achiness and encroaching anxiety. It's like a piece of him is missing. Or is about to be. Like he's in the sights of a lurking alligator that's waiting for just the right moment to attack.

He scans all the aisles, piling various items into his arms, his sense of impending doom building. Even the Muzak love song playing on the store radio reminds him that he's all alone in this. The young couple filling their Slurpees remind him of the completeness he used to feel. Isaac snaps out of it. He needs to stay focused. Gatorade for dehydration. Dramamine to control the nausea. Imodium for the diarrhea.

Then Isaac approaches the counter, his hands shaking as he dips his debit card. These aren't like your typical caffeine jitters. His hands are trembling so violently that he drops the card. Now Isaac knows the gator's getting close. *Gator, Gatorade. What a croc. Ha!* Well, at least he can still laugh. For the moment, anyway.

"Are you okay?" the woman at the checkout asks, concerned, but not really.

"Yeah, fine." He picks up his card, takes the receipt, and leaves, riding off into the fading twilight.

As soon as he gets home, he goes straight to his room, closes the door, setting a bucket at the base of his bed, then spreads a bath towel beneath it, in case he misses. He knows his parents won't bother him if his door is closed. They have enough on their plate. But if he starts retching, they might hear it and come to check on him. He'll have to be quiet about it.

He turns on his TV and prepares for a Netflix binge he knows he won't have the strength to watch, but maybe it will provide moments of distraction. And as it begins to get worse, he takes a double dose of melatonin, hoping that he'll hold it down. He thinks that maybe, just maybe, he'll be able to sleep through this. He thinks it right until the moment the jaws finally clamp down.

"Honey . . . you're burning up."

Isaac awakes to the sight of his mother looming over him, her hand against his forehead. Didn't he lock his door? He thought he locked the door. It's morning. His night was beyond tormented. The Dramamine made him drowsy, the melatonin tripled the effect, but the chills, the shakes, the aches, and the cravings of withdrawal kept him in a hellish twilight state all night. Unable to wake up but unable to truly sleep.

"Stomach bug," he manages to get out. "S'been going around."

He doesn't tell her about how his bones are aching and itching on the inside, like a thousand black widows are nesting in his marrow.

"We should get you to a doctor."

"No," he says. "Please, no. It's a twenty-four-hour thing. It'll pass."

"Isaac . . ."

"If I'm not better tomorrow, I'll go, okay?"

His mother is not pleased. She touches his forehead again, then goes out, only to come back a few moments later with a thermometer—the kind that you jam into your ear. Although she doesn't press too deep, it hurts like she's punctured his eardrum.

"Ow!"

"Hold still." She waits for the beep, then checks the readout. "102.4—have you taken Advil?"

He has, but he can't remember the last time. "It's on my dresser," he tells her. She gets it, shakes out two, and hands it to him along with the Gatorade container sitting on the floor, next to the empty trash can. Although the night was beyond miserable, he hasn't hurled.

"You should wash your hands," he tells her. "You don't want to catch this."

At the mention of that, her expression darkens even further but then eases. He knows what she's thinking: there are worse things to catch than a stomach bug. Put in perspective, this is nothing. And now that she's done something to help him, it's easier for her to let him be.

He listens for the garage door opening and closing. He had heard his father leaving earlier. Now he's alone in the house, which he finds comforting, because he can let his guard down, but also terrifying, because if he was alone before, he's truly alone now. What if something goes wrong? What if he has a seizure and goes into convulsions? Those things could happen. What if it happens now, when there's no one else in the world who knows what his body is really going through?

His phone is on his nightstand, but it's too far to reach. It's not plugged in. Did he charge it last night? What if he needs it? What if he has to call 911? He sits up so that he can reach for it and feels something stir within him. Muck at the bottom of a stagnant pool. It grows into a bristling—a rising in his belly, like the heavy churn of butterflies that lift off at a roller coaster's peak, just as the law of gravity takes over.

He reaches for the bucket, but his hand knocks it over. He uprights it just in time, and he pukes his guts out again and again. His stomach knots, and he vomits things he didn't remember eating. Even when there's nothing left, he keeps heaving and heaving until it feels like his organs are going to come spewing out into the bucket. The god-awful feeling—that biological need to purge—never goes away, but his body becomes too exhausted to continue the pointless dry heaves. He collapses into a fetal position on the bed and tries to tell himself it will be over soon. This is the worst of it. It has to be. It's not.

ROXY

The Party is too loud. The music that always provided me a pulse—the one that could almost resemble the beat of a heart—now does nothing for me. It feels more like a rhythmic shock to my frazzled system. Electric paddles on something that refuses to come to life. When have I ever been frazzled?

In the midst of the mayhem, there's a hand on my shoulder. Not firm, not weak, just there. On any other day, I wouldn't have noticed it, and that tells me exactly who it is.

My brother Vic.

"Hiro's asking for you," Vic whispers into my ear. It annoys me because I just managed to forget he exists again.

"Sorry, can't hear you. Music's too loud," I say, without even turning to face him.

"I said Hiro's looking for you."

I heard him the first time, but I wanted to make Vic say it again, because talking to me is so unpleasant for him.

"Tell him I'm busy."

Vic takes his hand from my shoulder. "Just passing on the message. Next time I won't bother."

And he's gone. I glance behind me, but he's already dissolved into the crowd. Or he's still standing right there. As I said, this game we play is very effective. I wonder if Isaac has ever tuned out his own sibling's existence. Suddenly, I get angry that I even thought of Isaac.

I try to distract myself with the commotion around me, but to no avail.

No point in stalling the inevitable; I push through into the VIP lounge, striding down the colonnade to the hallway at the back. I see Nalo over by the dance floor, tending to someone who was left on the ground, abandoned by their partner when their dance ended. He cradles the limp figure, weeping, while the shadows of paramedics do their work, oblivious to our world—seeing what *they* see, but never what *we* see.

I don't stare. It's not my business, and right now I don't want to be reminded of what goes on here. So I leave it behind, marching down the long, dim hall at the back, and slowly push the door open, stepping into Hiro's office.

The chandelier of spoons tinkles in the breeze of my entrance. The candles illuminate him and his desk, but not the things taking place in the periphery of the space. Moans of delirium and the slow escape of final breaths—but all out of view. If you didn't know better, you'd think he was alone, but Hiro is never alone. Although everyone with him is.

When he sees me, he closes his ledger and crosses his hands on top of it, interlacing his fingers.

"Where is your plus-one today, Roxy?"

"I bring you plenty," I remind him, maybe a little too defensive. "I'm entitled to some time off."

"Entitled," he repeats slowly, chewing on the word like an old, flavorless piece of gum. "What makes you think you're entitled to anything?"

I don't have the patience for this today. "What do you want, Hiro?"

He's taken aback by my lack of respect. He demands such obedience, but what can he do if I don't give it to him? Nothing. He didn't hire me, and he can't fire me. Our hierarchy is controlled by forces beyond our control. Decisions made in laboratories and secret closed rooms that are our nurseries. Strange to think that the very humans we dominate are also the ones who gave rise to our power. A circle of irony too uncomfortable for most of us to consider.

"Sit down, Roxy."

"Your chairs are too uncomfortable. I prefer to stand."

"As you wish."

He holds my gaze in an attempt to intimidate me with silence. All it does is waste both our time. Finally, he speaks.

"You've been putting too much attention on a single mark," he says. Then flips open the ledger to confirm the name. "The one named . . . Isaac Ramey."

I say nothing.

"You know as well as I do that narrowing your attentions is counterproductive. You need to be casting a much broader net."

"I disagree. I've been using him to sharpen my approach."

"Why? Your methods have always worked for you before."

"Times change," I tell him. "If we don't change with them, we fall out of favor. We become yesterday's news."

Hiro waves it away. "Yes, yes, footnotes in the larger narrative, I've heard it before. There's truth in the argument, but not in how you're using it. You're lacking sincerity."

"I can't help that," I tell him. "When have you ever known me to be sincere?"

He ignores my logic. "You may lie and dissemble for your marks, Roxy, but do not insult me by treating me like one of them."

I give in. I let my shoulders drop. I tell him the truth, as much as I hate to speak the words. "You can stop worrying. Isaac Ramey is no longer a concern."

Hiro shows the slightest bit of surprise, which becomes the slightest bit of a smirk. "He showed you the door?"

"He showed himself the door."

"Did you at least trip him on the way out?"

I don't answer that. I just wait to be dismissed.

"If he hasn't wandered too far, perhaps I'll send Vic after him. Or Phineas."

The thought of Phineas, with his bony, languid fingers, even touching Isaac makes me sick, but I don't show it, because I know Hiro only said it to see how I'd react.

"Do what you want," I tell him. "I've got better prospects than him. I promise I'll bring you quality offerings tomorrow."

Hiro raises his eyebrows. "What is tomorrow but the lost opportunities of today?" Then he waves me off, and I leave, trying not to show how badly I want to be out of there.

ISAAC

Time moves differently in withdrawal. Isaac knew it would, but he couldn't imagine the dimensions of it. It's not that hours feel like days—they feel like a completely different measure of time. One that weaves in different directions, like a leaf flowing downstream, caught in eddies and currents. There are moments when he slips from his twilight sleep and feels certain that time has doubled back on itself. He remembers his mom coming in, but not when it happens, only later. She took away the bucket and brought it back clean. Replaced the towel. He remembers multiple times there was pressure in his ear. How many times has she taken his temperature? She hasn't called in the national guard or forced him to take a bath to bring it down, so it must not have spiked too high. It's just steady. Did he say things in his delirium? Things to make her worry even more than she already was.

"You're overreacting" is the one phrase he hears his father say. They must have been arguing about what to do.

It's daylight now. Morning? Was that conversation last night? Ten minutes ago? Or was it going to happen in ten minutes? Lazy, soulless little eddies. And through it all, that screaming, burning NEEEEEED. That hollowness in his gut, in his head, in his heart. It spikes and wanes, but it never wanes enough, and the spikes seem higher and higher each time.

"Isaac?"

He opens his eyes to see the last person he expects standing there in his room. His best friend, Ricky.

"Hey, bud—I heard you're having a tough time," Ricky says with a hollow smile.

The angle of the light through his blinds says it's early morning. His parents haven't left yet. They must have let Ricky in.

"Yeah," Isaac responds. His voice is raspy, but he's surprised that he has a voice at all. "Keep your distance, man. I don't want you to catch this."

But Ricky doesn't heed Isaac's warning. Instead, he closes the door behind him and moves in closer. He pulls up Isaac's desk chair and sits down.

Ricky always bragged to the world that he had a superior immune system—which Isaac and his group of friends found eternally amusing, because when they were kids he seemed to be the vector for every cold and flu. "That's how you build up your immune system," he always said. "Get sick a lot when you're little, then you get superpowers."

But the air between them now doesn't feel tinged with contagion. There's something else there.

"You haven't been yourself for a while." Ricky's gaze is fixed. He doesn't blink. Isaac tries to think up excuses, but his mind is too muddled to sell a lie.

Ricky knows. No one told him, but he knows.

"My dad's side of the family is pretty messed up—you

know that, right?" Ricky says, trying to find the right words. "My mom always told us to stay away from my cousins. Because when I was younger, I saw some things I shouldn't have. It was enough to know exactly what's happening to you right now. . . ."

Fear spikes up Isaac's spine, sending him into a moment of fight or flight, but he doesn't have the strength to do either. And suddenly he feels so small, so ashamed, that he can't meet Ricky's gaze. The judgment and disappointment that must be in Ricky's eyes. But that judgment never comes. Instead, Ricky's demeanor is soft, compassionate.

"Here," Ricky says, and tosses Isaac a little black plastic bag.

Isaac peers inside, finding, of all things, candy. Chocolates, sours—a candy store's worth of sweets.

Ricky reaches into the black bag and hands Isaac a Kit Kat. Isaac's shaky fingers labor a little too hard to peel the wrapper, so Ricky helps him, all the while trying to hide how disturbed he is, but it shows. "I know these are your favorite," he says, choking up a little.

Isaac scarfs the bar down, suddenly realizing that he's starving. Then he reaches for some red licorice.

Ricky grabs a licorice too, studying it rather than eating it. "Remember back when we would go to the movies and you and Ivy would always fight over these? And if our parents bought us the black ones, we'd throw them at the people in the front row?" Then Ricky pulls out a bag of gummy worms. "And remember how back in grade school, Ms. Abogado would give these worms out to whoever got the highest quiz scores? So you always got them."

Isaac strains a grin. "At least until they banned candy as rewards." Isaac bites one in half. It hurts to chew the rubbery thing, but maybe it's a good hurt. "They're not even that good."

"You said they tasted like victory," Ricky says. "And you would always share them with me, 'cause I never got any."

"Yeah—meritocracies suck."

"Consider the favor returned," Ricky says. And suddenly it occurs to Isaac that the candies Ricky chose were not random, or even because they were Isaac's favorites. Everything in there came with a memory attached. Ricky was that thoughtful, that mindful, of the things he picked. This was truly a meaningful gift.

"So, withdrawal is all about endorphins," Ricky explains. "The cells of the brain get so accustomed to the drugs that they can't work without them. Right now your brain cells are beginning to shut down."

"And sugar helps . . . ," Isaac realizes.

"Short-term, but yeah. Pleasure endorphins. Gotta love 'em." Ricky takes a deep breath. "Not sure what you were doing, but I have an idea. Anyway, I imagine you got a lotta brain cells to fix."

"A hundred billion in the average human brain," Isaac informs him.

Ricky lets out a subdued guffaw. "Not a test, bro . . . but my point exactly." Then the warm moment fades, leaving the two of them with their chilling reality.

Isaac gets a lot more serious, then asks, "Is it that obvious?"

"Yes and no. Red flags are only there if you know to look. It was your mood swings I noticed first. Then you started just randomly disappearing on us. And every time I saw you, you were practically falling asleep. But the biggest giveaway—it's how your pupils are always constricted." Then he points to the red patching on Isaac's arms. "Then I did a little research, and it turns out itchy red skin is another giveaway. I'm probably the only one of our friends who knows, though—and I haven't told anyone."

"Don't," Isaac says, grabbing his wrist. "Please, don't."

"Beat this thing and I won't have to," he says. It's neither a yes nor a no. There's an understanding between them, and Isaac is comfortable with it. Comforted, even. Now Isaac has a safety net. He hates putting a friend in that position, but he can't change it now. He lets go of Ricky's arm, realizing that he's still holding it. The white marks on Ricky's wrist attest to how tightly Isaac had been gripping him, but Ricky doesn't say anything about it.

"I'll be checking in on you," he says. "But if your family's around, I'll make it seem like I'm just bringing you home-work."

Then he leaves, closing the door behind him. Isaac goes into the bag and slowly eats the candy, trying to savor the memory attached to each and every one.

27

Questions We Shouldn't Ask, and Places We Shouldn't Be

ROXY

I don't know what to feel after my audience with Hiro. The fact that I have to feel anything about it boggles me. My range of emotions has always been narrow because I honestly never needed much bandwidth. There was the triumph of the hunt and compassion for the suffering people I actually help. All I ever needed were those two emotions—one thrilling, the other tedious but necessary. I always saw my moments of compassion as a counterbalance to keep me stable. We know our fate if we ever lose that grounding. Our nightmare has a name—always spoken in a whisper, with a superstitious upward glance. *Better be careful or you'll end up like 'Lude.*

I find myself wandering the Party in a daze, finding the revelry slipping into the background, and instead, seeing what our human marks see. Crack houses and back alleys. Lonely rooms and bathroom stalls where they commune with us. Those scenes are always there, but so easy to render invisible when you focus on the Party. Who sees dirt on the window when there's such a spectacular view beyond? And so I try to refocus myself on our endless celebration, but I'm only partially successful. Reality has become a burden.

And weaving through all of it is a desire that goes against everything I've said I want. A new color in my fabric that can't be removed, and I'm not sure I'd even want it to be. The thought that has been lingering beneath my consciousness finally emerges so powerfully, I nearly say it out loud.

I Must.

Save.

Isaac.

Save him from the Party, save him from Hiro. Save him from me. *No! Not me,* I remind myself. *The me I was before.* The me who would make frivolous, capricious wagers with the likes of Addison, with no thought for the lives we affected. Could Isaac and I be apart just enough to miss each other and at the same time together enough to satisfy our desire?

"You look out of sorts, Roxy. Not enjoying the Party?"

I'm startled to see Al has been watching me. He can't know what's on my mind, but he knows that something is. He seems genuinely concerned—and although he's like the bartender you spill your woes to, he can't know about this. He would never understand. None of them would.

"Just not in the mood today," I tell him as casually as I can.

He's taken aback—and not just feigning it as he often does, but truly shocked. "Roxy? Not in the mood? I never thought I'd see the day." He staggers closer and puts a comforting arm over my shoulder. "If there's anything I can do, you'll let me know, won't you?"

"I will, Al."

He sighs and shakes his head. "Both you and Addison are off your game these days. I'll wager it's your wager."

At Al's mention of Addison, I look around for him, but he isn't here. He's out somewhere with Ivy, micromanaging her life.

"Yes, that's probably it," I tell Al, hoping he'll stop probing.

But then Al gives me his classic smirk. "I daresay he's taken the lead," Al says. "Rumor is that your young man Isaac left you high and dry—or shall I say, low and wet. You're still just a little damp from the 'Sayonara Swirl.'"

I push his arm from my shoulder. "Addison will never get his sister here without her being stolen along the way," I tell Al. "And if no one wins, then no one chalks up a loss, either."

"No," admits Al. "But Addison has been single-minded of late, overachiever that he is. As much as I'd love to see him get some glory, I'd hate it to be at your expense."

Then he turns to a set of new arrivals, leaving me to question the wisdom of my resolve to save Isaac. I know that I'm the only one who can—the only one with the strength and the will. But to save him, I must get him back. Right now he's vulnerable. He could be lured by any of the others. He would become their prize. I must keep him with me. *On* me. Just enough to protect him.

I need a place I can think, so I leave the Party proper and go through the padded doors of the VIP lounge. It's not as crowded in there, but still, the sights and sounds don't help me. That's when I take a moment to consider the massive ayahuasca vine in the corner of the lounge. It's an impressive sight, but it tends to go unnoticed by those engaged in other pursuits—which is just about everyone in the lounge. It has slowly grown through the vaulted ceiling and through the roof. In fact, climbing its twisted stalk is the only way to get to the roof.

Before I can change my mind, I grab hold of it and climb

all the way up. I tell myself I'm going to the roof to get away from the commotion. But deep down, maybe I already know the real reason I'm heading there.

The roof is a moss-covered slope so severe a mountain goat could lose its footing. It's only inviting to those in a gravity-shifting state of mind. I suppose that's why I find Lucy up here. She's one to whom reality is never a burden. Even so, there's an intangible melancholy to her that has always made me uncomfortable. Lucy dangles her bare feet over the edge, absently kicking them back and forth and gazing at the ever-changing shapes of the moonlit clouds. She glances at me with eyes as mystical as a Ouija board.

"He couldn't fly, Roxy," she says. "Why can't they ever fly?"

I sit beside her, having no idea what she's talking about, and no answer, even if I did. In spite of her graying hair, she seems like a child who lost her favorite toy. I feel a need to cheer her up.

"I've heard you're gaining popularity again," I tell her. "At least that's the rumor."

She sighs. "Just waves in a pond. It'll never be like it used to be." And then she adds, "You're still young, but someday you'll know how that feels. In the end we all . . . fall out of style."

The thought of that makes me turn and glance at the steep slope of the roof, stretching up and up until it disappears into a cloud bank. When I listen closely, I can hear a faint screech high above us. Few things give me the shivers, but that sound chills me.

"Have you ever gone higher?" I ask Lucy. "Have you ever climbed to the very peak of the roof?"

She turns to me, uncertain, maybe a bit worried. "No," she says. "There are some places we just shouldn't go."

"Just because we shouldn't doesn't mean we can't. . . ." And then I lean in closer. "Is it true what they say, Lucy ? Is . . . *he* . . . really up there?"

"There's *something* up there," Lucy says. "Can't you hear it?"

I close my eyes. I would like to believe that the universe has mercy on ones such as us. That when we're done, we're done. That we simply disappear. On earth they fear the thought of oblivion, but for us, it would be a far better end than the alternatives.

In that moment, I realize that I have to see the truth of it. I have to know. Then, as I stand, Lucy grabs my hand. I think she's going to warn me, or try to stop me, but instead she says, "If you're going up there, then I'm coming with you."

Because maybe the places we shouldn't go are the places we most need to.

We trudge our way up the steep slope. The moss gives way to shingles slick with condensation and the kind of slime that only grows in dark, forgotten places. I don't question how this roof can be more like a mountain. Our world is not bound by the same rules as the human world. We reach a cloud bank, cotton thick, and I can't see a thing.

"This was a bad idea," I mutter.

"Yes," Lucy agrees. "But bad ideas are so much more exciting than good ones."

After what seems like forever, we break through to a clear, star-filled sky. Below us lightning volleys in the clouds, punctuated by ominous rolls of thunder. Above us the roof comes to a sharp peak. And there's something there at the pinnacle. Some*one*. A figure silhouetted against the moon.

We both stop short.

"Are you scared?" Lucy asks.

And I have to answer honestly. "Yes."

"Good," Lucy says. "Because scared divided by two makes us both half as scared."

We slowly make our way toward the figure at the peak, and as we draw closer, it becomes clear exactly what we're looking at.

The figure has his back against a lightning rod and is held there by two iron snakes wrapping around him, constricting him. Their fanged mouths are open, and their jaws have clamped down onto his shoulders—not to swallow him, but to hold him in place. Forever.

I know this image intimately. The staff and the winding snakes. The caduceus. It's a sign so many of us were born under—but there's something wrong with this picture. The medical caduceus has wings. Where are its wings?

The figure caught in the double helix of the iron serpents shifts his head—the only part of him that can move—in our direction.

"Who's there?" he says in a raspy voice. "Come closer. Let me see you."

Lucy grasps me tighter as I lead us toward him, and she hides behind me, as if she's afraid to be seen.

The figure ensnared by the caduceus is barely a figure at all. He's a sickly gray shadow. A spirit in ruin. He tries to move, but the serpents constrict tighter. He grimaces. He groans. He accepts it.

"Are you . . . 'Lude?"

He gasps, as if I've just reminded him of a name he hasn't thought of in ages. "Do I know you?" he asks.

I shake my head. "I came after you were gone," I tell him. "They call me Roxy."

"Roxxxy . . . ," he says, drawing it out in a serpentine hiss— as if the boundary between him and the caduceus has been lost. I hate hearing my name on his lips. "Are you a bringer of pleasure or pain?" he asks. "Do you raise up or bring down?"

"Neither," I tell him, feeling so uncharacteristically timid. "I . . . I numb."

"I see," he says. "You're from Phineas's clan. He's not my favorite."

"He's not mine, either. . . ."

I can't stop staring. I forget why I'm here, and then I realize that I never really gave myself a reason. Just that I had to see. As if seeing would somehow fill the gaps I've just discovered in myself. The ones Isaac has exposed.

Then Lucy dares to step out of my shadow, and 'Lude grins when he sees her.

"Now, there's a face I remember."

"Hello, Q," she says, meek as a laboratory mouse. Like all of us, he has many names. 'Lude, Q, Drax. It all depends on who you ask.

His voice gets a little gentler as he speaks to Lucy. "Glad to see you're still around. But you sure have gotten old."

Lucy doesn't deny it, but she doesn't like the observation either. "Good to see you, too, Q."

"We were a thing once," he says, reminiscing. "Lucy and 'Lude, the life of the party."

Lucy can't look him in the eye. "It was a long time ago."

"You were so carefree," he says, wistful and nostalgic. "And I was so beautiful. . . ."

I know his story. Quaalude was born to help insomnia. He took work as a masseuse to relax the tightest of muscles. But he came to see the power he had. And he began to party. For a time there was nowhere you could go without him being at the center of it all. Then it all came crashing down. He was not just exiled, but *withdrawn*. His formula was erased by those who first gave him life.

There's a piercing screech from high above. A flash of something in the sky, but then it's gone. Whatever it is, it turns 'Lude's demeanor dark again.

"Are you two here to mock me? To torment the tormented?"

"No, Roxy just wanted to see . . . ," Lucy says.

"So you came to gawk," he hisses. "Come closer, then. For a better view."

It feels like a command, and I can't help myself from inching closer to him—until he suddenly lunges—but the snakes react quickly, squeezing him tighter, shifting their heads so they can dig their fangs deeper. He wails in pain, but his wail resolves into laughter.

"They never tell us that these talismans of our creation are also the shackles of our eternity."

"I'm sorry," I tell him. "I'm sorry for what happened to you."

"Are you? Or are you just happy it wasn't you?"

"I don't take any pleasure in your suffering."

"And yet you wished to see it. To witness what it's like to

be denied your very existence and yet to still exist," he says. "You want the wisdom of the damned? Here it is: there is no hope of paradise awaiting us at the end of our road, Roxy. All that awaits us is the cold iron of the caduceus. In time you'll know. In time you'll join us."

"Us?" I ask.

And in a strobing flash of lightning, I see them. Others affixed to caduceus on identical roofs all around us, dozens and dozens, stretching as far as the eye can see. I don't recognize them, but Lucy's vision, twisted as it is, sees things in dimensions the rest of us don't.

"Is that . . . ? Is that Meridia?" she asks. "And over there—I think that's Darva . . . and little Fen-Phen. . . ."

'Lude gives me a toothless, lascivious smile. "Here it is, Roxy—a glimpse of your own future."

I shake my head, refusing to let this terrible vision worm its way any deeper. "No! It doesn't have to end this way for us. Look at Al! He's been around forever. So have Nico and Mary Jane and . . ."

"Yes, yes, the *naturals*," 'Lude says, dripping disgust enough to rust his serpents. "They'll stumble their way through history until history's end. But not us, Roxy. We are of a moment. Just ask Lucy. She knows."

But Lucy just purses her lips—and I know what she's thinking. *If I don't say it, then it won't be true.*

Again, there's that bloodcurdling screech above us and a flash of something metallic soaring overhead.

"What is it?" I dare to ask.

"The wings of my caduceus. They've grown into a beast that

patrols the sky. Every night it comes to devour me, but I don't die."

And suddenly Lucy, rather than sharing my horror, perks up. "It can fly?"

'Lude ignores her, focusing on me, narrowing the embers of his eyes. And he reads me.

"You've seen something you shouldn't, haven't you, Roxy . . . ?" Then he smiles. "No! You've *felt* something you have no business feeling! That's it, isn't it?"

I take a step back, feeling invaded. Violated.

"You've fallen for someone you feed on. You're in love with one you meant to destroy!"

At that moment I realize I can't escape. He holds the heart I never knew I had in the palm of his hand. He could constrict it like the iron coils of the caduceus . . . but he doesn't. Instead, he gives it back to me.

"My advice is this, Roxy: if you've found something beyond your purpose and beyond the cravings that consume us . . . then grasp this thing you've found and don't let go. Maybe then you won't end up like the rest of us."

And then the patron saint of excess takes a moment for deep reflection. "Maybe if I had left the Party for a smaller, quieter life, I'd still be out there. I wouldn't spend eternity paying the price of my indulgences."

Just then, an iron wing flashes past, and I get a glimpse of the creature that had grown from the caduceus wings—an eyeless gargoyle with razor-sharp talons. I know what it truly is. It is the embodiment of the wounds we leave behind and the chaos we cause. The blind fury of vengeance. Like us, its appetite can never be sated.

"Let's go, Lucy. We've seen enough."

But Lucy shakes her head. "I'm staying."

It's not what I expected to hear. "What? Are you sure?"

She nods and takes a deep breath, steeling herself. There's an excitement in her I haven't seen in all the time I've known her. "I'll catch the winged beast when it comes! I'll hypnotize it. Then I'll climb on its back and fly to the farthest corner of anywhere!"

And although it's only a fantasy, I can't deny that fantasy is the core of Lucy's power.

Hearing her, 'Lude laughs. "In-a-Gadda-Da-Vida, baby!" he says. "If anyone can turn the beast into a butterfly, it's you, Lucy."

She smiles at him coyly, and he grins back, like the lovers they once were.

I wish her luck, then I leave them, the dreamer and the prisoner, and descend back down the mountain-sloped roof toward the Party. But before I get there, I hear a wail of absolute joy streaking across the sky. It's Lucy! I can't see her up there, but I can hear her voice trailing off into the distance. She's found wings to carry her far from this place! And it gives me a powerful surge of hope. Because if she can escape, then so can I!

And I'll take Isaac with me! So we can be together in a world that won't punish us for even trying. Only then will we have saved each other.

Interlude #5—Vic ($C_{18}H_{21}NO_3$)

I am not without compassion. I am not without substance. That others abuse my substance is their business. Who am I to question their choices?

Yes, I may lure people, like my sister, but I have chosen a very different narrative from Roxy. I do not see myself as an angler, my line cast into the water with a cleverly concealed hook. Instead, I see myself as an irresistible light. Does one blame the light for attracting the moth? Of course not; it is the nature of light. And it is the nature of the moth to tempt incineration. In this way, all humans are Icarus. Thus, I am blameless.

I contend, however, that my glow is more like that of the moon. A comforting beacon in dark hours. Moonstruck lovers, lunatics, and werewolves all share the same light.

Before you judge me, remember that many have found true refuge from pain in my company. Some for a short time, others longer. My relationships are not like the ones Roxy fosters, though. Mine are professional. I do not dress in a flashy style as she does. I am subdued. Quiet. Always in a tailored suit and silk tie.

To my clients, I am a trusted confidant. A therapist, one might say, because I am a very good listener. Feel free to spill your troubles to me. I will most assuredly ease your burden if you do. And if you become accustomed to a lighter load on your shoulders—a fractional gravity to all your woes—you have my permission to enjoy it. Come walk on the moon. And if the air is sucked from your lungs, well, don't say I didn't warn you.

No, I am not without compassion. Even for my sister. Which is why I choose to help her.

I am there in his bedroom, in a fragment left over from his ploy at the nursing center, lost in the carpet. He has the faintest memory of having seen it fall, before being distracted by something else. The memory is so slight, it's little more than a nagging suspicion. It's just enough to give me access to his thoughts. And so I go to this boy Roxy has been courting. I keep my distance, though. I linger in the periphery of his thoughts. He lies in his bed, shivering. He misses her so. I feel for him, really I do.

"Is this what you expected?" I ask him in the faintest of whispers. "This willful withdrawal from the very thing that eased your pain?"

"It's terrible," he says. "It's worse than I could have imagined. . . ."

"Hmm . . . ," I say, passing no judgment. "Might it always be like this, Isaac? Unending misery? Have you considered that from this moment on, you will never know happiness again?"

"No!" he protests. "That's not true!"

"But does it *feel* true?"

"It doesn't matter how it feels," he insists. "I'm not thinking right. The truth is . . . The truth is . . ."

"Could the truth be that your life is not worth living without her?"

He shudders at the suggestion. I give him a moment to consider before I whisper again, all the while being careful with my words. I never lie to him. I merely suggest trajectories of thought. I allow him to draw his own conclusions. In this way, I never once compromise my integrity. Once more, like the moon, I am but a mirror.

"Trust your gut," I tell him. "How could it possibly steer you wrong?"

"No, no, no," he whimpers. "My life is good."

"I can see how you might think that," I tell him, giving him validation and support. "But do you actually *remember* feeling any better?"

He has no answer.

"What if I were to tell you that you have always felt this way? What if I were to tell you that you always will? Would that move you to change this course of action you've undertaken?"

"I . . . I have to see this through," he says, his voice weak and airless. "Everything depends on it. And it will get better . . . if I . . . if I only . . ."

"Lost the thought, did you? Don't worry. I understand."

He closes his eyes. Pulls the blanket tighter. I pull it off him gently and let it slip to the floor. He doesn't have the strength to retrieve it.

"I believe you were contemplating ways to ease your torment." Then I move closer so that he can feel my voice tickling the small hairs in his ear. "She's waiting for you, Isaac. She still wants you as much as you want her. All it takes . . . is for you . . . to make . . . a choice."

"Leave me alone. . . ."

"You're strong, aren't you, Isaac? Show how strong you are. Make the choice."

"Choosing . . . *that* . . . isn't strength. It's weakness."

"It all depends on your perspective, does it not? Is it weak or is it strong to admit what you need? It takes strength to humble yourself and admit that you need her. Because maybe, just maybe . . . she's the only one who loves you."

And from there I sit back and let his thoughts take over. Roxy will never know what I've done for her today. But that's all right. I do it as a kindness. I do it because I am generous and altruistic.

"Save yourself, Isaac. You know how. . . ."

Those are my parting words as I leave him. In the end, all I did was nudge him down the easier path. The wide and well-trod path is that way for a reason. So what if it leads to a cliff? All roads come to an end eventually—even the narrow, difficult ones. They disappear deep in icy mountains or wind down to an unrelenting sea. And although they might seem to lead to that false light on the horizon, none of them will ever reach the moon.

28

A Study **in the** Architecture of Doom

ISAAC

Isaac struggles to keep the blanket wrapped around him, but it seems too small. It keeps slipping to the ground, and it aches to reach for it.

I'll never be happy again.

Isaac knows it's a complete lie, but he can't help thinking it. It keeps coming to him. Even when he blocks the thought, it still comes through, not in words, but in a silent wave of despair.

There's no point in living.

He could list a thousand reasons to live, but he doesn't have the strength to think of them. His only coherent thoughts are the noxious ones. The ones telling him that not only doesn't he want to be here, but he doesn't deserve to be here.

I always have and always will feel like this.

He rolls around in bed, wishing he could rip off his own skin. How long has it been since Ricky came? Does he really know how awful this is? He only saw—he never actually went through it himself. There must be people who have. People he can talk to. Talk to about what? What was he just thinking? Wait. Hold on. He can pull the thought back out of the abyss if he tries. He was thinking about . . . He was thinking about . . .

You were thinking about how to end your suffering.

No! That wasn't it! He wants the suffering to end, but not that way. He'll ride it out. Weather the storm. That's the way to end this.

It will take forever. You'll suffer forever and ever andeverand-everandeverand—

This is hell. Isn't that the definition? Eternal suffering? All those medieval versions of fire and brimstone have it wrong. Who needs flames burning you from the outside when a fire inside is so much worse?

Or you could find a way back to it. To them. To her . . .

This will peak at seventy-two hours. That's three days, and he's only halfway there. This time, when his parents come home, they will know. They will take him to the emergency room, and the doctors will know the instant they see him. His parents won't believe it at first. But his blood work will have all the evidence needed to shatter their image of him.

You won't be able to bear the shame.

No! You will! They'll be there for you. They love you and will always support you and help you.

Out of obligation. Any love will be snuffed by their disappointment.

And Isaac bursts into tears, because he can't resist the thoughts. A dragon of lies that bullies the truth, crushing it like a bug, then standing in its place with such mass, it cannot be moved, and Isaac can't see around it.

His thoughts become hazier. The world fades. And now he's in a misty labyrinth, covered in vines. A dream? No, a hallucination, because Isaac comes to realize he's wandering through the hallways of his house. The night has passed, and the sun is beginning to rise. But the voice still echoes, pulling him down the hallway as if in a trance.

Hallucination is the last step before death, he remembers. What if withdrawal is too much for him? What if he's in the process of becoming just another statistic? Is this how he's going to die?

Save yourself. You know how.

And so he stumbles toward salvation. The bathroom at the far end of the hall. His eyes are as dry as his powdery lips. In the bathroom, he gets on all fours, searching around and behind the toilet. Yes, he flushed the pills, but what if he missed when he dumped them in? What if one of them bounced off the rim and onto the floor? It's possible, isn't it? More than possible, it has to be true. It has to be, because this insatiable desire won't accept the alternative.

Behind the toilet Isaac finally finds something small and white, but it crumples in his hands. It's just toilet paper. He slams a fist into the tile. There's pain, but it feels far away. Then he sees something protruding from the trash can. The little coin purse where he kept his pills. *What if . . . ? What if . . . ?* He grabs it, clawing his fingers inside.

No pill in there . . .

But to his absolute delight, he finds little bits and pieces. Crumbs of white, left from the times he broke pills in half to conserve his supply. As carefully as he can, he turns the coin purse over and shakes the powdery fragments into his palm. The ghosts of salvation.

He licks them off his palm, then turns the coin purse inside out and licks its lining, getting every last drop. It's not nearly enough, but it will give him the strength for what he knows he must now do.

A public bus is nothing but a courthouse on wheels, Isaac decides. A trial by a jury of questionable peers. Sure, everyone seems to be minding their own business, but what they're really doing is passing judgment on everyone around them.

Your kid is too loud? You must be a terrible mother.

Your shopping bags are in the way? You're a selfish and inconsiderate ass.

Your deodorant has worn off? You're the filthy scum of the earth.

And the only thing that can lift the verdict is if you give up your seat for someone else. Then you're a saint. Because there is nothing between guilty and not guilty on a bus.

Isaac is not a saint today. He's not giving up his seat for anyone. He leans his head back against the window because his neck struggles to support its weight, but every time the bus rattles, pain shoots through his skull like lightning, so he has to pull his head from the glass. His withdrawal is in a trough. The pill fragments have buffered it just enough to allow him to function but nothing more.

While some buses have seats that face forward, limiting eyelines, and thus judgment, this one has all the seats facing inward, to leave more standing room. A woman across from him looks at him—something longer than a glance but shorter than a glare. She goes "Hmphh" in disapproval and clutches her purse tighter in her lap.

Isaac has no idea what about him she finds so disagreeable.

His look? His smell? His slouch? Or maybe it's a blanket rejection of the whole package.

You don't know me, he wants to say, but he can't muster the strength to say it. Thus, the verdict stands.

He's in and out of awareness as the bus trudges along. Not quite dozing, just slipping into a fog that only clears when the bus squeals to a halt or hits a brain-rattling pothole. He almost misses the stop and has to lurch out of the closing doors at the last instant, where he trips on the curb, tumbling into a patch of mud so miserable even the weeds have taken their own lives. When he gets up, the bus has moved on. He takes a moment to get his bearings and shuffles in the direction of Birch Street.

He knows this neighborhood is sketchy, to say the least, but when he arrives at Birch Street, he knows that it's the true heart of darkness. He had been here once before, but it was night, so the worst of it was hidden in shadows. But under the diffused light of an overcast afternoon, the truth is splayed before him, naked and unashamed.

There are no birches on Birch Street. There aren't any trees at all. There used to be, but all that remains are stumps. There are one-story homes on both sides of the street. Many of them seem vacant. These homes are beyond mere disrepair; they are a study in the architecture of doom. All have a red *X* spray-painted on their cracked stucco facades, as if tagged by a graffiti artist with no soul or imagination. Doors and windows have been removed from the homes that have already been vacated. An exterminator company works on one of them. Its truck features a picture of a cartoon rat being flattened by an anvil. Its slogan: WE KILL RATS DEAD™. As if there's any other way to kill them.

At the second house up the street—one of the few that has yet to give up the ghost—sits a woman in slippers and a faded flowery house dress, in one of those lawn chairs that's too low to get out of without great effort. Random objects are spread out around her on the lawn. YARD SALE is written in Sharpie on a cardboard sign.

"Looking for something?" the woman says, not realizing—or maybe completely realizing—how suggestive that sounds. "I'll give you a good price on anything you see."

Isaac just walks past, not wasting his meager energy on a response. The house he's looking for is five houses up, on the left. Blistering stucco, a weathered blue door, and a big red X like all the others. There's a U-Haul out front, and there he is. Craig. Ivy's ex-boyfriend.

He's carrying a TV from the house to the truck. A girl of maybe nineteen, who looks like she'll one day evolve into the woman in the lawn chair down the street, watches Craig with lazy anxiety, telling him to be careful of the cord but not motivated enough to help keep it out from under his feet.

As Craig deposits the TV in the U-Haul, Isaac hitches up his pants and straightens his collar, waiting to be seen. When Craig does see him, he stops short.

"You?" he says.

"Can we talk?" Isaac asks.

"Nothing to talk about," Craig says. "I want nothing to do with you or your psycho sister, you hear me?"

"I'm not here about her," Isaac says.

Craig looks him over. "You look like shit," he says.

"Sports injury," Isaac says—and for some reason, hearing himself say that makes Isaac laugh.

"Who's this guy?" asks the girl, who's come over to investigate just in time to hear his laugh, which Isaac admits sounded as creepy as it felt.

"This is the loser who broke my nose." Only now does Isaac realize it's still a little bruised nearly two months later.

"You oughta break his back," suggests the girl.

"Maybe I will."

The girl looks Isaac over, gives him a "Hmmph" like the woman on the bus, and goes back inside.

Craig puffs his chest out, striking a confrontational pose. "So, what the hell do you want?"

Isaac doesn't have the time or the patience for posturing, so he gets right to the point. "I need painkillers, and I'm willing to pay for them."

It takes a moment for Craig to register that Isaac has gone from enemy to customer. Once he gets it, he gives Isaac a gloating Cheshire grin. "Pain meds, huh? Feeling that certain yen? Jonesing for the angel of easy nights?"

"I can pay," Isaac says again.

"I don't know—I kinda like seeing you hurt."

Isaac knew this would be tough. He knew he'd have to jump through hoops, and some of them would be on fire. But as long as there's relief waiting on the other end, he'll jump, if Craig is willing to tell him how high.

"What makes you think I even sell that shit?" Craig asks.

"If you don't, you know who does. I'll pay for information, too."

Craig scratches his neck for a moment, considering. Another U-Haul passes, abandoning the doomed neighborhood.

"Come inside," Craig finally says.

Isaac sighs with relief. "Thank you, Craig."

"Shut up. I haven't done anything for you yet."

The house is in shambles. Most of the furniture has already been removed. Boxes are stacked up everywhere.

The girl is now taking the claw end of a hammer to the wall, pulling out nails where pictures once hung.

"What are you wasting your time for?" Craig scolds. "No one's gonna care."

"These are good nails," she says, and gets back to the task.

Craig leads Isaac down a hallway. "You're lucky you caught me," he says. "Whole street's been condemned. They're tearing it all down to build a freeway—this is the last week to get out."

"What if you don't want to leave?"

"You think they care? They'll bulldoze it anyway."

Craig leads to a bedroom that smells of mildew, where the planks of a dismantled waterbed still lean against the wall, ready to be taken out. There's an old desk that doesn't seem worth the effort to move, a broken-backed chair to keep it company, and stacks of plastic storage boxes labeled REC ROOM, as if all of Craig's recreational activities took place here.

The sliding door to a closet is open, revealing pill bottles and Baggies strewn in the corners. Not so much a dragon's hoard as much as a dragon's leavings.

"Don't bother with that," Craig says. "Needle in a haystack. And there might actually be needles."

Instead, Craig turns his attention to the storage boxes, unstacking them until he gets to the one with the subheading "various and sundry." He opens it to reveal it's full of various and sundry prescription bottles, far more organized than the leftovers in the closet. If Isaac weren't dehydrated, he would drool. They look legit, except for the fact that the labels are all handwritten. Craig starts sifting through the bottles, looking at the labels.

"No . . . no . . . no . . . Ah! Here we go!"

He pulls out a pill bottle. Not a small one, but a fat one— the kind that can hold maybe a hundred pills, although Isaac has no idea how many are really in there. Craig smiles at Isaac and shakes the bottle in his hands like maracas, creating a beat.

"Ready to dance?" says Craig.

Isaac reaches for it, but Craig holds it back. "Money first."

"How much?"

"All of it," Craig says. "You're in no bargaining position, so don't even try."

And so Isaac takes out his wallet and gives him all that's in it. "Three hundred. It was all I could take out at the ATM."

Craig counts it, nods, then says, "Now the money in your socks."

Isaac's eyes must register shock, because Craig laughs. "How stupid do you think I am? Nobody wears tube socks anymore unless they're hiding something in there."

Isaac bends over, trying to hold his balance as he pulls an additional $120 out of his socks. Still, Craig doesn't give him the pills. Because the hoops haven't been lit on fire yet.

"Now tell me you love me," says Craig.

And when Isaac doesn't respond, Craig shakes the bottle to a bossa nova beat. "Papa's waitin'."

"I love you," Isaac says.

"Aw, say it like you mean it."

"I *love* you, Craig."

"Good. Now say that your sister is a bloodsucking whore."

Isaac clamps his lips together. He knows it's only words, and although he's willing to humiliate himself, he won't humiliate Ivy. Even if she's not here to hear it, he just can't do it.

"Say it," demands Craig.

Isaac bites his lip until he tastes blood and shakes his head so hard his brain feels like it will explode through his ears.

"No?" says Craig. "Aw, too bad."

By now the girl has come into the room, drawn to the sound of drama and maybe the smell of blood.

"Okay, then, how about this?" Craig grabs the hammer from the girl. "Sit down." And when Isaac doesn't move, Craig says, "I promise I'm not gonna hurt you."

Without much choice, Isaac sits in the broken chair.

"Now put your hand out on the desk."

Again Isaac hesitates.

"Like I said, I'm not gonna hurt you. This is about trust."

Isaac can't stop from shaking as he splays his hand, palm down, on the old desk. Then Craig takes the hammer and puts it in Isaac's other hand. "Now smash your hand."

"Craig . . . ," says the girl, getting a little spooked.

"Either leave or watch," he tells her, "but don't get all up in my business."

The girl chooses to watch. Somehow Isaac knew she would.

"I . . . I can't," says Isaac.

"Well, then call your sister a bloodsucking whore. It's got to be one or the other."

Isaac thinks that maybe with a weapon in his hand, he can use it on Craig, grab the pills, and run. But Craig was already anticipating this and positioned himself far enough away that Isaac wouldn't get a good swing at him. And even if he did, he didn't have the strength to run.

He looks at his hand. He looks at the hammer. He knows it's going to hurt. A lot. But if he gets those pills, it will only hurt for a while. So he closes his eyes, grits his teeth, and brings the hammer down.

And at the last second his arm is pushed to the side. It's just enough to make him miss. He hears the heavy *THUNK* as the hammer hits the desk. He opens his eyes to see the crescent moon it made in the wood an inch away from his fingers. He thinks it must have been the girl, but when he looks up, he sees that it was Craig, who's still gripping Isaac's forearm. Craig's grin is gone. Now he looks shocked—almost scared.

"You'd rather smash your own hand than disrespect your sister?"

Isaac can't even answer him. All he can do is nod.

"Just give him the damn pills, Craig. We've gotta finish packing."

Then Craig gets his swagger back. "No," he says. "We don't have to pack. Our friend here is gonna do it for us. Then he'll get his pills."

And although Isaac feels like the Walking Dead deep in the rot, he grabs box after box after box, loading them into the U-Haul until it's almost sunset. And when Craig keeps his word and gives Isaac that glorious bottle of pills, Isaac finally cries. Because at that moment he truly loves Craig.

29

Somewhere Between Limbo and Lust

IVY

I will now and forever be the girl who threw up on Coleman Werx.

"It's not a big deal," Tess said when Ivy first gave her the grim details.

"Yeah," TJ added, smirking. "I'm sure he gets puked on all the time."

The festival has gone on for two more days, but for Ivy, it's all been overshadowed by that one thought, which she can't get out of her head.

On the last night, after the festival closes, they wander the massive parking area for what seems like hours, unable to find the car. TJ is convinced it's been stolen, until Ivy recognizes a vehicle that was parked nearby: an old, refurbished school bus painted like a Mondrian canvas. Mondrian. Not her favorite artist, but she supposes it's better than a Jackson Pollock bus. All that visual randomness might make her puke again. Thank goodness for new world hippies and Mondrian's cold, hard geometry.

It's past 1:00 a.m. when they find the car. The endless tailgate party has now become a mass exodus. Everyone is trying to get out of the one entrance to the one highway that cuts through this godforsaken corner of nowhere. Ivy's only consolation is that Jimmy passed out the instant he got into the car, saving Ivy from any unwanted advances.

But still . . . I will forever be the girl who threw up on Coleman Werx.

It's an unwanted mantra that will plague her for a long, long time.

Although it doesn't feel like it, at some point Ivy must have slept, because when she opens her eyes, it's suddenly dawn. And TJ is asleep at the wheel. That doesn't matter, though, considering that the engine is off, and they're not moving. They're on the highway, but traffic is at a standstill. Not even inching forward, just stopped dead.

"What's going on?"

"Waze says there's a big accident up ahead," Tess says with a yawn. "Whole road's shut down till they clear it."

"How far have we gotten?"

"I don't know—five, six miles, maybe."

"That's all?"

Ivy looks over to see that Jimmy, still asleep, is a study in drool and mucous on his side of the back seat. That alone would be enough to propel Ivy out the door, but she has other concerns.

"I've gotta go pee," she tells Tess.

"Yeah, good luck with that."

Ivy gets out to a wave of heat. The sun hasn't risen past the far-off mountains yet, and the temperature's already rising.

"Roll down the windows," Ivy says. "You'll roast in here once the sun's all the way up."

"Yeah, yeah." Tess shifts, leaning on TJ, and goes back to sleep.

Ivy decides that Dante was wrong—hell has more than nine levels. This one exists somewhere between Limbo and Lust. Stalled traffic in a featureless desert seems the perfect metaphor for her life. *Why even bother going home?* she thinks. *What's waiting for me there?* Nothing but another wasteland—but even worse than this one. The fused sands of her atomic detonation. Sure, she escaped it for a few days, but it's all still there waiting for her.

Home means facing the bottomless pit of her parents' judgment. But where else can she go? She supposes she could stay with Tess for a while. Tess's mother won't care. She actually says Ivy is a good influence on Tess—proving that everything's relative. But she can't forgive Tess for getting her into this mess to begin with. That would not make for a cozy situation.

Ivy steps off the road into the dry brush. There's nothing taller than knee-high, which means there's nowhere to relieve herself without having to squat in full view of every single car on the road. How screwed up is it to be so dehydrated and yet have to pee so badly?

Then, up ahead, she spots the Mondrian bus—which clearly has been remodeled into an RV, so it must have a bathroom. She's found her urinary oasis.

As she approaches, she hears music playing inside. Not loud, though—it's kind of an early-morning metal. Even so, it still hurts her head. Outside, a guy and a girl sit in folding chairs, like they've decided to set up camp right there on the stalled highway to wait out the apocalypse. They pass a joint between them, taking hits, making it hard to talk to them as they hold their breath.

"Hey, do you have a bathroom in there?"

A pause, a smoky exhale. "Yeah, but we're chargin'," the girl rasps.

All Ivy has on her is her phone, with her ID and debit card slipped into the case. She doubts they take plastic. "Seriously? I really need to go."

"Sorry," the girl says.

Ivy tightens her thighs and tries to woo them. "So . . . who's into Mondrian?"

"Monty who?" the guy asks.

"Mondrian—the artwork on the bus."

"That's the Peacock Family bus," the girl says.

"Partridge," the guy corrects.

"Whatever. It's the actual bus from that TV show in the seventies."

"Never heard of it," Ivy says.

The girl shrugs. "Me neither, but Owen got it cheap."

"Owen gets everything cheap," the guy says. "So now it's the Owenbus."

Through the bus's windows, Ivy can see some others moving around inside.

"What are you guys, like some millennial Manson clan?"

"Nah," the girl says. "We don't kill no one. Not intentionally anyway."

"Listen," Ivy says, with as much sincerity as she can muster. "I really do need to go. . . ."

Then the guy's eyes seem to find focus as he looks at

her. "Hey—aren't you the girl who threw up on that guy?"

"Wait—you were there?"

"No," he says, "but it's a meme now." He pulls out his phone. "Wanna see?"

There are so many more levels to hell than anyone can possibly realize. "Absolutely not," Ivy tells him. Like everything else from the past few days, she'd have to process this informational tidbit later.

"Well, if you're the vomit chick," the girl says, "that's different. You're practically royalty." She gets up and gives Ivy a regal, if somewhat imbalanced, bow. "Our crapper es su crapper." And she leads Ivy in.

Inside are several others, some asleep, some trying to reconcile with the morning. The one playing music is in the far back. He offers her a smile. It's more of a leer, but as far as leers go, it isn't all that unpleasant. In fact, it's almost kind of charming. She leers right back.

"The can's to the left," the girl says. "If you have to hurl again, let us know—we could post about it. 'Trail of the vomit girl' sort of thing." And she gives Ivy a sly grin, making it clear she's joking. It actually makes Ivy laugh in spite of herself.

The charming leerer has to shift his knees to let Ivy open the bathroom door. "Enjoy," he says. "All the comforts of home without the baggage."

Instinctively Ivy knows this must be Owen, the alpha of this crew. She offers him a sly, almost flirtatious grin before closing the door, and Ivy wonders why she's always drawn to guys who are no good for her.

And then a thought comes to her. A crazy thought that, at

this jagged juncture of her life, doesn't seem all that crazy.

What if I go with them?

It's outlandish. It's insane. But is it any more insane than going back home? She doesn't need her parents, and they don't need her. An extended road trip with total strangers might be precisely what she needs. A cooldown period. She can reconcile with her parents later, once she's had time to make sense of her life and they've all had time to miss one another. Let them lavish all their attention on Isaac—who, come to think of it, might actually need it. He has been acting a little sketchy lately. Imagine that! Her baby brother actually has issues! What could they be? she wonders. Did he flunk a test? Did he get Shelby pregnant?

He wrecked his car, for one.

Right, but he'll be fine. They'll all be fine if Ivy is out of the picture for a while.

She can't believe she's actually entertaining this wild thought—but the more she does, the lighter that crushing weight on her shoulders feels.

ADDISON

I knew even before we got on the bus. There's an aura—a certain light that you feel rather than see. I knew before we set foot inside that Crys was on the Owenbus.

Ivy doesn't see what I see as she moves toward the bathroom. The light is too dim and her mind too shot to see how pale some of the others on the bus are. How their eyes are recessing into ever-deepening sockets. They've been dancing with Crys. He's been draining them. They're not sucked entirely dry yet, but they will be soon enough.

"Ivy, do what you have to do, and leave!"

But she takes her time, all the while fantasizing about an escape that is just another trap. If backstage with the band was the frying pan, this is the fire.

"These people are not what you need."

Ivy should know better. She *does* know better, but her sense and senses have been dulled beyond the point of reason. This Owen is just another Craig. Better looking, more charismatic perhaps, but on the inside he's the same—nothing but foul air and empty promises.

And right beside him sits Crys, like he's the one who owns the bus—although it's likely he's the one who bought it for Owen. He's relaxing, taking an uncharacteristic break. Crys eyes me with an unreadable gaze.

"Dusty and Charlie are looking for you, Addison," he tells me. "I've never seen them so mad."

I try not to show how unsettled I am to see him here. To see him so close to Ivy.

"Let them look," I say, shrugging it off.

Crys nods to the bathroom door. "That one seems ripe."

I can't tell if he's baiting me or if he's actually going to make a move on Ivy. If he does, I'll have no defense. Crys is in a class by himself. Too powerful for me to stand a chance in any sort of confrontation.

"She's hardly worth your time," I tell him.

He smiles at that. "Come now, Addison, everyone deserves to dance."

Finally Ivy steps out of the cramped bathroom, and although I try to impel her toward the front of the bus, her eyes immediately settle on Owen. They introduce themselves. He comments how their names just roll off the tongue together. Ivy and Owen. He invites her to sit. She does. Crys smiles.

"Let's see if I have a new partner."

And although I know I mustn't disrespect the head of my upline, I can't allow this to happen.

"Ivy," I say. "You can't stay here. You did what you needed to do. Now you have to leave."

But she's already caught in a web of banter with Owen.

Where are you from?

Here and there.

"There" is where I'm trying to get.

Too bad, I'm beginning to enjoy here.

Such banal flirtations, but they serve their purpose.

"Ooh, the dance has already begun," says Crys.

And Owen pulls out a tiny plastic zip bag with what looks like a little uncut blue diamond inside.

Good for what ails you. What ails you, Ivy?

Everything.

So let's make everything nothing.

And she considers it. She doesn't go running from the bus screaming—she actually considers it.

"Ivy, no! This is not what you want! Can't you see that?"

Crys runs a finger down her cheek. Her eye twitches slightly. "She'd be a waltz," Crys says. "No! A tango!"

Owen shakes the bag. The blue crystal inside catches sunlight streaming through the window.

And then I suddenly remember something. "Ivy! Your friends! They never opened the window—and the sun is over the mountains now! They're going to bake in that car if you don't do something! You have to go to them before it's too late!"

She might not be able to pull out of this nosedive for herself—but maybe she can for others.

She holds eye contact with Owen for a moment more, then pats him on the knee.

"I'll be back," Ivy says. Then she gets up and makes her way to the front of the bus. I breathe a sigh of relief. Because I already know she won't be back. Once she's freed from this moment—once she realizes what she almost did—she won't return. She'll be far enough from Crys's gravity to resist it.

I expect a scolding from Crys, but he just looks at me and laughs. "You certainly do have a way with this one, Addi."

"Sorry, Crys. Maybe you're just not her type."

"Of course I am," Crys says, his voice patronizing. "The truth is, I let her go—as a gift to you, because it pleases me to see Charlie and Dusty so aggravated." Then Crys gets serious. "But you *will* bring her to me eventually. You know that, don't you?"

"Not everyone becomes your plus-one," I remind him.

"No, but *she* will. I smell it on her." Crys leans back as Owen puts his Baggie back into his pocket. "And when you do bring her, you'll do it willingly and without hesitation. Or I will be very, very angry with you."

I leave without another word, trying to escape Crys's gravity. But who am I kidding. I am forever trapped in orbit.

30

This Kind of Thing

ROXY

I was so deathly afraid Isaac was gone forever—that the very determination that endeared him to me would be the thing that ripped him away. They say gratitude is the most powerful of all emotions. I understand that now, because Isaac is back, and gratitude has just about swept me away. I won't fight the current.

Isaac knows a place where we can be alone, where we can plan our future together and plot our escape.

He takes me there.

A glorious palace in the sky!

It sits nestled in the soaring limbs of all the decisions Isaac has ever made, each one branching and dividing until bringing him to the delicate green shoot that is this very moment.

The windows of our palace look upon the canopy of a forest lush and green. The triumph of life over decay. We can't keep our hands from one another as we sweep up the grand staircase to our private haven, where gossamer curtains as impossibly delicate as hummingbird wings flutter and shimmer in a gentle breeze.

We are far from his family and friends. Far from Hiro, who

would punish me, Vic who would mock me, and Addison who would accuse me of what I already know. That I am in love.

I have never felt such joy, such relief. These are things I've always known I must never feel, and yet I do. The addiction has become addicted. There is a symmetry to it, a perfection in that closed loop.

"I missed you," he tells me a hundred times, and I never tire of hearing it. "I never want to leave you again."

"You don't have to."

"I can't think about anything but you," he tells me.

"And I can't feel anything when you're gone," I tell him. "I never thought . . ." But I hesitate, afraid to say the words.

"You never thought what?" he prompts.

"I never thought that I could . . . *need*, too."

From the moment I entered this world, there was nothing I needed. My whole existence has been about desire and conquest. But to need someone as much as they need you? It's both an acceptance and a surrendering of power. It unites you so completely that you can't tell where you end and they begin. How transcendent, how exquisite to lose your boundaries to one another.

Through my entire existence I have known only purpose and predation. I've known the satisfaction of saving life and the thrill of ending it. But I have never, never known the sheer joy of connection. If I could stop time like Addison, I would. I would halt its flow forever and let us stay cocooned in this moment until time itself forgets us.

"There is no one else in the world but you and me, Isaac."
And although I've said these words countless times to countless

others, this is the first time that it's not a lie. Because in this sanctuary, we are so alone as to be in our own universe. We need nothing but each other.

We hold each other close upon a feather-down bed, more luxurious than any either of us has known. A fire flickers in the hearth, and I feel I'm near the moment of release. And if I try hard enough, I can forget, if only for these moments, that the rest of the world is still out there. That his glorious palace is just a brief respite. A way station on the way to our freedom.

"I know there are others," he says, "but am I the only one you've ever loved?"

"You are," I whisper, and again this is true. Truth is foreign to me. So foreign that it frightens me. There is terror in all this intimacy, and more than anything, I want it to go on. The vulnerability of it! I have bared myself to him—if he chose to, he could strike me down, just as I could strike him. We are each other's saviors. We are each other's victims. I want to be forever in that moment where our kiss is also a knife poised at each other's throats.

"I will never let anyone else hurt you," I tell him.

"I will never let anyone take you away," he tells me.

And now the moment finally comes. He breathes me in, and I revel in it.

"I've never known anything could feel like this," I tell him, but he's in the throes of such euphoria he can't respond.

In the wake of release, I press my ear to his chest, listening to the racing of his heart. The perfect union of muscle and will. If I could only have a heart that beats like his. But maybe I already do. Because if Isaac and I are now one, as so many lovers claim to be, maybe I can share this beat that counts out the seconds. Maybe his heart could be mine, too. And maybe then I will understand the mysteries to which my kind, by our very nature, have always been blind.

"I love you," he finally says; then his eyeballs roll back, and his lids flutter closed with contentment. That just feeds me further. What I fed on before—the desperation, the weakness of prey—it was nothing compared to this. Yes, breathe me in, Isaac. Let me be your everything just as you've become mine.

IVY

When Ivy gets back to the car after her urinary mission, just as she had suspected, TJ, Tess, and Jimmy are still asleep inside with the windows closed. Opening the door releases a wave of clammy heat. She has to wonder if this road is about to become yet another statistic in the long, sad annals of concert tragedies. She rolls down all the windows, bringing in air that is, while not cool, not sweltering, either.

And now that she feels like the savior—or more accurately, the babysitter—of her sorry little crew, thoughts of returning to the bus are gone as quickly as they had intruded upon her. What was she thinking? She's way too old to run away to join the circus.

The stalled traffic begins to wake into a tortoise crawl. TJ can't stay awake for the relentless stop-and-go, so Ivy offers to drive, and he's more than happy to let her.

Half an hour later, when they finally come to the accident,

it's mostly moved over to the shoulders. Multiple totaled cars and an RV that's ripped open and eviscerated, its various amenities strewn about like so much roadkill.

According to social media, the accident had multiple fatalities. There are also asinine rumors that it was intentional and politically motivated—proving that social media is nothing more than a bad game of telephone wired into the Matrix.

"They say it could be the CIA, or maybe China," Tess announces. "I'm not saying that it is; it's just what they say."

This is the same nebulous "they" that claim vaccines are government mind-control, and that lizard people secretly rule the world. To Ivy it's just proof that idiocy is alive and well. The misinformed mob never changes; it just replaces torches and pitchforks with iPhones and Androids.

It could have just as easily been the Owenbus in that accident, Ivy thinks. *Next time it might be.* She shakes her head to chase away the thought and the memory of her little flirtation with destiny. She knows that Owen had been holding out a bag of crystal meth—and how close the scale came to tipping toward the promise in his smile. Best not to linger on it.

The pace starts to pick up once they're past the accident, and, still fighting her own exhaustion, Ivy takes one of her pills so she can focus on the road. But even before it hits her bloodstream, she knows that one is no longer enough. They call to her from her purse, reminding her that if she's going to be sharp enough to make the trip home, she'll need a second, maybe even a third. *More is better, Ivy,* the pills seem to tell her. *Especially right now when you need to be alert.* And relatively speaking, that's nothing compared to the shit Owen was offering her, right?

So her pills, plus a hefty dose of ibuprofen to combat the hangover, is her cocktail for the day. And she muses that whoever makes Advil and Adderall ought to sponsor music festivals, with all the money they must rake in from them. Music makes the pharmaceutical world go 'round, both over and under the counter.

At around eight o'clock that morning, still nearly two hours from home, she gets a text from her mom, and then another one.

Ivy we need to talk to you.

Ivy please call us.

Then, when her phone vibrates with an actual call from her mother, Ivy turns her phone off. She'll face her parents when she faces them. She doesn't need a coming attraction of the new family drama that will surely stream on an endless binge once she gets home.

There's a police cruiser parked in the driveway. Ivy's first instinct is that this must be about her. That the powers that be were not mollified by her involuntary "voluntary withdrawal" and have decided to arrest her after all.

TJ had taken the wheel again half an hour before. They've already dropped Jimmy off, so it's just Ivy, Tess, and TJ now. Tess, seeing the squad car, has reached the same conclusion that Ivy has, because she asks, "Should we just keep going?"

But Ivy's rational mind inserts a thumb in this rancid pie to test the temperature and forces Ivy to consider that this couldn't be about her. You don't send a police car to sit and wait for a girl accused of petty theft. Especially when you have no clue when she's coming home.

"It's fine," Ivy says, even though it clearly is not.

"Text me," Tess says, eyeing the squad car nervously and offering no argument. Then she and TJ take off like Bonnie and Clyde, even before the car door is entirely closed.

Ivy heads toward the front door, counting her steps and controlling her breathing. The last few days have been a series of trapdoors. She's not ready for another one, but what choice does she have? If there were something truly wrong, her mother would have done more than just send enigmatic "we need to talk" texts, right? But she had called, hadn't she? In fact, her parents may have called more than once, but Ivy wouldn't know because her phone's still off.

When she steps in the door, her parents are there in the living room, standing with two officers. One has a tablet, taking a report, and the second is apparently there for moral support.

The fact that both her parents are there and alive lets her cross one item off her list of terrible reasons for a police presence, but there are still hundreds of other horrific things to consider.

The moment her parents see her, they register instant disappointment. This is nothing new, but it seems to be more than just their standard dissatisfaction.

"What's going on?"

"Ivy, do you have any idea where your brother is?" her father asks.

"Isaac?" she says, as if she has another brother. "No . . ."

"Have you heard from him at all?" asks her mother.

She pulls out her phone to check, but it's still off. "I don't think so." She turns it on, but it takes forever to power up. "Will someone tell me what's going on?"

The moral support officer answers for them. "Apparently your brother's been missing since last night."

"Last night?" Ivy is floored. "And you're just reporting it now?"

There's a look of shame, guilt, and maybe self-loathing in her parents' expressions. Another day, another time, Ivy might have found that satisfying, but not now.

They give her an abbreviated version of the story, which they've already told the officers. Isaac had stayed home sick yesterday, for the second day in a row—but he seemed to be feeling better by the time their parents got home in the evening.

"Still a little weak," Mom said, "but looking much better."

He had taken dinner up to his room, closed the door, and hadn't come out for the rest of the night. They had heard his TV on, so assumed he was there—but when the TV was still on at 5:00 a.m., Dad peeked in to find him gone. There was no way to know when he had left, where he had gone, or why.

"And he's not picking up his phone?" Ivy asks.

"It goes to voicemail," Dad says. Then has to add, "Just like yours."

"There's a logical explanation for all of this," Ivy insists.

"Your daughter's right," the cop with the tablet says. "We see this kind of thing all the time. Nine times out of ten it's nothing."

Dad bristles. "What do you mean 'this kind of thing'?"

"Well, teenage boys have a tendency to—"

"My son is not one of your statistics," Dad snaps.

The other officer opens his mouth to say something but wisely closes it again. The fact is, Isaac isn't "that kind of kid" who does "that kind of thing." Ivy is. But she's the one who's here, and Isaac is not.

"Have you contacted his friends?" the first officer asks.

It had been the first thing her parents had done. Word was out to all of Isaac's close friends, but none of the ones who responded had anything to say—except that they hadn't seen much of him lately. And nothing at all from Shelby. "But it's still early," Mom is quick to say—even though it's pushing eleven.

One of the cops suggests that he and Shelby could have run off together, which just pisses Dad off again. To Ivy, it seems in the realm of possibility—until her mom's phone dings with a curt Nope haven't seen him text from Shelby. Probably the most declarative statement she's ever made.

"That's it?" Dad asks. "She doesn't even sound worried."

And all at once Ivy realizes, *That's not the text of a girlfriend. It's the text of an ex-girlfriend.*

"He's been acting funny," Ivy blurts. "And don't act clueless about it, because you've seen it too."

They don't deny it. "It's true he hasn't been himself," Mom admits. "He's been upset over his injury."

That snags the officers' attention. "What sort of injury?"

Instinctively, Ivy knows where this train is going. Her first instinct is to join her parents and say "not my brother," but the cops are the only ones with enough objectivity to follow the tracks all the way off the rails.

RICKY

Ricky can't stop cursing himself for sleeping in. While he had been up half the night binging TV, Isaac was out there binging something else.

He should have told someone what he found out the other day. He should have made this a "situation" instead of just a secret between friends. Isaac would have been furious at him for breaking their confidence, but his anger would fade once he was clean. Ricky should have done something. But instead, he kept it to himself. And now it has shot past "situation" to "crisis."

He had planned to check on Isaac this morning—but when he checks his phone after waking up, there's a message from a number he doesn't recognize.

"Ricky, it's Isaac's dad—is Isaac with you?" the voicemail asks. Then he can hear Mr. and Mrs. Ramey arguing about what else to say in the message. That muffled argument makes everything clear. *"Just call us, please, as soon as you get this."*

Isaac bailed. He couldn't handle the withdrawal and bailed.

Ricky is about to call them back, but he can't bring himself to do it. How do you tell your best friend's parents that their son has become an addict? Definitely not by phone. So he pulls on his pants and is out the door before his mom can insist he sit down for breakfast.

As he starts the car, he thinks about his cousin Mike. The one he told Isaac about. It wasn't just Mike's life that had been ripped apart by his habit—that whole side of the family was like a gaping wound that wouldn't stay closed long enough to heal, or even properly scar. Once every year or so, Mike would have what his aunt Jen called a "flare-up." They'd track Mike down, find him at the bottom of the lowest barrel, and then get him into rehab. He'd come out of it a self-professed new man. Until the next flare-up.

Ricky takes some comfort in knowing that this is Isaac's first time. Sometimes one trip to the pit is enough to scare somebody clean. It's not a cycle yet. Once it becomes a cycle, it gets much harder to break.

If anyone could get through this, Isaac could, Ricky had told himself. Ricky always admired Isaac—envied him, even—for his ability to commit and see a thing through to completion. Sometimes, although Ricky never admitted this to Isaac, he would "borrow" some of Isaac's determination for himself. Pretending, if only in his head, that for a moment, he was Isaac. He could, just for that moment, leave his own baggage behind and accomplish things he'd otherwise talk himself out of. "What would Isaac do" was often his secret mantra.

So maybe that's why he felt okay leaving Isaac to his own devices. Because he knew exactly what Isaac would do. Isaac would fight his way through this and come out the other side, humbled but wiser.

But that's not what happened.

It's only a five-minute drive to Isaac's, and Ricky is already regretting this decision. He should have called. He should have called.

The second he turns the corner and sees the police cruiser in the driveway, he's convinced of the worst. But when Ivy answers the door and he sees how agitated she and her parents are, he's actually relieved. They're in crisis mode, but they're not falling apart. Which means they're in the same holding pattern they were in when they called. They are in the dark. He's going to have to be the one to enlighten them.

"Ricky, please tell us you know where Isaac is," Mr. Ramey says.

Ricky takes a deep breath. "I don't know where he is," Ricky tells them, "but I'm pretty sure I know what he's doing. . . ."

IVY

Even though her parents are in a wild state of disbelief, Ivy stays silent, accepting what Ricky tells them—because this is the first explanation that actually makes sense to her. And the dots would have been so easy to connect had it not been her own brother. But just like her parents and their "not my Isaac" mentality, she couldn't consider her brother and drugs in the same hemisphere of her brain. But now hindsight bursts in, and it makes her want to hurl again. Even when they were kids, Isaac was the one who looked out for Ivy, not the other way around. And although Ivy made a big show of resenting it, she had come to rely on it—and to take it for granted. And now, when he was the one who needed her, she hadn't been sharp enough to help. She hadn't even been present.

Ricky tries to calm her parents down, but everything he says just slices deeper. "I think this started before his shoulder injury," he tells them. "That shoulder thing—it might have even been intentional. To get more meds."

Ivy's dad just keeps shaking his head, speaking in short blasts of denial that come out of him like Morse code. "No. Can't be right. No. No. Must be more to it. Someone else. Someone did this to him. Someone." And then he looks at Ivy—and although she knows he's grasping at straws on the edge of a cliff, the fury she feels at that glance of implication makes her explode.

"What? You think this is *my* fault?"

"Nobody's saying that, honey," her mom intercedes.

She stares her father down, and he folds. Really folds. His posture contracts into a question mark. He looks defeated and years older in a matter of seconds. He looks away—or more accurately looks inward, and clearly doesn't like whatever he sees. It deflates Ivy's anger, because that's something she can relate to.

Ricky tells them that the "flu" Isaac had over the past couple of days was withdrawal—that he was trying to get himself clean.

"So you knew, and you didn't tell us?" her father says, finding a new target of blame.

Now it's Ricky's turn to fold, but before he can respond, the police officers, who were more than happy to watch the drama play out, step in to stop the blame game.

"We'll report this and make sure to keep an eye out for him," one of them says, while the other one talks in code into his radio. To Ivy, it seems that the search priority has just been downgraded. Self-destructive behavior clearly isn't prioritized over other worst-case scenarios.

They leave, and Ivy, her parents, and Ricky are left to grapple with what the hell to do now.

• • •

They split up to search for Isaac. Ricky leaves first, and Ivy's mom next. Her dad agrees to stay home, just in case Isaac comes back, and lets Ivy take his car—which he's never done before, but priorities change. Even Ivy's. Suddenly being expelled and the prospect of the alternative school doesn't feel like the world's biggest problem.

With his car still in the shop, Isaac either went on foot or took public transit.

Ivy's head is still pounding, and her exhaustion has kicked into survival consciousness. She throws back more Advil and another Adderall to keep her focused and alert.

"Did you say he was acting better yesterday?" asks Ricky. He and Ivy are keeping a running phone conversation as they search. Ricky's on his way to their school; Ivy's on her way to the soccer fields. It's not like she thinks she'll find him there, but they've got to check all the familiar places first.

"That's what my mom said," Ivy tells him.

"It's too soon for him to be over withdrawal. Which means he found himself a fresh supply—which explains why he looked better when your parents saw him last night," Ricky deduces. "He probably just came home to grab a few things and took off when he knew no one would notice he was gone."

Nothing at the soccer fields but little kids in neon uniforms. Ricky says there's no sign of Isaac at school. Mom reports that he's not at the pier, and she's going to walk the beach to see if he's there. As if you can ever find someone at the beach. Ricky starts reaching out to other friends to help in the search.

"He's gonna be so pissed off when he finds out that everyone knows," Ricky says.

"Who cares, as long as we find him?"

Ivy tells Ricky she'll check the malls next, but Ricky makes a good point.

"Why would he go to the mall?" he asks.

"Why would he go to any of the places we're checking?"

"Let's think about this for a minute," Ricky says. "If he went somewhere to get wasted, then it's someplace where he thinks he can be alone and no one will find him."

The first place that comes to Ivy's mind is the boat his parents were working on—and it finally hits her what Isaac was really doing that night he fell asleep there. Could he have gone there? No, because the job had been killed, and the yacht's long gone. But there are plenty of other boats in the marina. Would Isaac hop on a random boat to indulge his habit?

It's this line of thinking that leads Ivy through a chain of associations that may have been the same ones Isaac made. . . . *Wood veneer yacht cabin. Wood cabin. The woods.*

"Ricky," Ivy says, "do you remember that tree house you and Isaac built?"

31

At the Divergence of Two Sturdy Boughs

IVY

As Ivy recalled, the skeleton of the tree house was already there, like a relic from another age, when her brother and Ricky found it five years ago. Just a weather-warped platform and foot-long two-by-fours nailed into the trunk to serve as a ladder. The platform was secure, though, as it was wedged at the divergence of two sturdy boughs.

The original kids who built it left no trace of who they were.

"Could be dead," Ivy was happy to tell Isaac and Ricky at the time. "Could be haunted." Which just made the real estate even more valuable.

Ivy was thirteen and Isaac twelve the summer the boys claimed it, and remodeling began. Isaac had put together a typically overambitious design, adding actual stairs, walls, and a roof, and since Ricky had the know-how to build it, it took less than a month to complete. Isaac did up the interior with indoor/ outdoor carpeting and bits and pieces of leftover wood veneer from their parents' remodeling jobs. Ivy had spent an afternoon there helping them saw wood but decided the whole endeavor was too Norman Rockwell for her. A mildly creepy portrait of preteen Americana.

She came back once when it was done, and Isaac gave her a tour of the one-room space, like a realtor at an open house. It was no Taj Mahal, but Ivy had to admit it was pretty impressive for a couple of twelve-year-olds. But by the following summer, it got infested with spiders, and Ricky, in spite of his macho pretentions, didn't do spiders. Then a skunk wandered up the stairs and decided to nest. Isaac walked in on it, it sprayed, and that was that—because although the stench eventually left Isaac, the tree house was history.

The sky is ominous and thick as Ivy drives along the road at the edge of the forest, not even sure where the tree house is. The "forest" is just a few acres of designated wilderness surrounded by neighborhoods. It would take maybe ten minutes to cross it, but when they were kids, it had all the semblance of Mirkwood. She finally spots Ricky's car off the side of the road and pulls over. It looks like he's just arrived too, and now peers down a gap in the trees that, once upon a time, was a path.

"You really think he's here?" Ricky asks as Ivy arrives.

"I don't know . . . but look at that." She points to a stretch of tall grass that had been flattened by someone who had come this way recently.

Ricky, who's always beating himself up over one thing or another, says, "Damn. I should have thought of looking here."

The overcast sky is all but blotted out beneath the lush spring canopy as they enter the forest, making it all the more dim. Ricky leads the way, and Ivy has the increasing sensation that they're traveling through a tunnel—one that leads to another world entirely.

"Are you sure you remember where it is?" Ivy asks.

"Positive," Ricky tells her.

They finally come to an enormous weeping willow that has no business being here among the oaks and sycamores.

"Left at the willow," Ricky says.

The tree rustles in the wind, its narrow leaves singing in a deeper, more mournful pitch than the rest of the forest, and Ivy realizes it must be called "weeping" not just for its limp, languid profile, but also for the sorrowful song of its leaves. A brooding threnody for all things lost.

They leave the path into thick underbrush that doesn't reveal whether or not someone passed this way before them. Then, just a minute later, they spot the tree house up ahead.

It has not fared well. After only a few years of neglect, it looks once more like a relic of a bygone age. The roof has caved in, and it lists horribly, looking like Dorothy's house, if it had landed in a tree instead of on the witch. Ivy shudders. This is where childhood goes to die.

"My God," Ivy mumbles.

"Yeah, right?"

The stairs are mostly intact, and there's the hint of a footprint on the first step, but there's no way of telling how long it has been there.

"I'll go first," Ricky says, but Ivy stops him.

"No. He's *my* brother."

She climbs the stairs and lingers at the threshold, peering in.

"Is he there?" Ricky calls from the bottom of the steps.

The scene reveals itself to her in bits and pieces. The fallen roof partially blocks her view. Behind it is an old moldy mattress—no doubt brought here by any number of vagrants using the place for shelter over the years. The smell of skunk is long gone, replaced by the stench of urine. No. Isaac's not here. She doesn't know whether she's more disappointed or relieved. She's about to head back down, when she sees a sneaker poking out of the shadows, and she follows it to a figure sitting propped up at the head of the mattress in the darkest corner. She gasps.

"Isaac?"

Ricky bounds up the stairs behind her as Ivy negotiates the debris to get to her brother. It looks as if he had fallen out of an airplane through the roof and landed here—and now that she's had that thought, she can't get it out of her mind.

Isaac, eyes half-open, lolls his head in her direction. "You shouldn't be here . . . ," he says, his voice a lazy slur.

She kneels next to him, "Isaac, what are you on? Look at me!" She grabs his chin, forcing him to look at her. "What are you on, and how many did you take?"

"Go home," he mumbles. "I'm good. I need to sleep."

She sees the pill bottle beside him and picks it up. The bottle has four letters written right on the plastic in Sharpie: ROXY. It catches in Ivy's mind. Something she'll have to consider later. Right now, her full attention has to be on Isaac.

Then Ricky picks up something Ivy hadn't noticed in the detritus around them. A bong.

"He's been smoking it," Ricky says. "Shit, he's been smoking it."

"How the hell did he learn to do that?"

"Googled it," Isaac mumbles, and he lets out a weak giggle.

The bong is Ivy's. She didn't think Isaac knew where she

324

hid it, but she should have known better. Between siblings, some things can never be kept secret.

"You said you wouldn't tell," Isaac says. "Why'd ya tell her, Ricky?"

Ricky doesn't answer. Instead, he pulls out a water bottle and brings it to Isaac's lips. "You're dehydrated. Drink."

"Not thirsty," Isaac says, but the second the water is over his lips, he begins to suck it down, much more thirsty than he realized.

"Help me get him up," Ivy says, and together she and Ricky pull Isaac to his feet.

"No . . . we want to stay," Isaac protests, but too weakly to matter.

"He's delusional," Ricky says.

"Ya think?"

Isaac's legs are like rubber, and his head rolls from side to side as they clumsily negotiate him around the debris. The structure of the tree house is so rickety, it's all they can do to keep from splintering the wood with their weight.

"Is this really necessary . . . ?" Isaac says, and then runs out of resistance, surrendering his will to theirs.

ROXY

They pull him right out of my arms! They drag him away from me! We were content. *I* was content—something I can't say I've ever truly felt before. How dare they intrude on our perfect, private world? These fools! Thinking they can save him, when I'm the only one who can! How could they not see that? How could they not realize what Isaac and I are to each other? How well we fit?

I hate them! That sister of his and that "friend." If I had the power, I would enter their hearts and minds and turn them to mush. I would destroy them. Not for sport, but out of vengeance. I would leave them so beyond hope that not even Naloxone would waste his time trying to save them. But I can't. I have no power unless they invite me in, and they're not about to do that now. Never have I felt so completely helpless.

They drag him down the grand stairs, leaving me alone in our palace in the sky. Almost alone. Because lingering there on the stairs is Addison. At first I think he's there to gloat, but instead he seems somber. That, in its own way, is even worse.

"You came with *her*?" I ask.

He nods. "Ivy cares about her brother a great deal. I couldn't stop her even if I tried."

"Did you try, Addison? Or are you so intent on winning our bet that you pushed her here? You kept her focused on the task of finding him, doing that miserable thing you do with time so that she'd get here quicker."

He doesn't answer me, but he doesn't have to. I know the answer. Of course he's here to serve his own interests.

"I'm sorry it had to be this way, Roxy." As if he didn't have a choice in the matter.

He turns to look down the grand staircase when he hears the three of them down below. It's still a grand staircase to me, but in a moment of weakness, I see what humans see: the wretched rotting room that sits wedged in a tree.

I force the vision away. I will see what I choose to see! I will not let their meager reality cut into mine!

"I have to go," Addison says, as if it's an apology. If there's anything I despise more than failure, it's pity.

"If you're leaving, then leave," I snap. "And when you do get her to the Party, make sure she suffers."

He's clearly uncomfortable at the suggestion. Good. If he wants to be like his cousins, then he'll have to sacrifice that precious little conscience of his. If the act of intimate obliteration makes him queasy, let him go sit in a rocking chair and knit with his sister.

What is there for me to do now? I could try to pull myself up by easing the pain of some poor tormented soul. Soothe another broken hip or infected molar. Spend time with someone who would truly be grateful. Or better yet, I could indulge myself in some boastful brainless frat boy or sorority sister, luring them in with lust, then kicking their ass right up to Hiro—if only to punish the entire human race for stealing Isaac from me. But none of that would be even remotely satisfying. There is only one thing I want. One thing I need. And I resolve right here and now that I will not let them take Isaac away from me. I may have lost this battle, but there's a much larger war. I will steal Isaac back, and once I do, I will find us a place where no one can separate us ever again.

32

Shred Your Head with Blender Blades

IVY

The moment Ivy saw that orange pill bottle, with ROXY scrawled in black Sharpie right on the naked plastic, she knew where it had come from. Craig always named his drugs, like children name their toys. That Isaac and Craig have struck up a relationship over painkillers is as mind-blowing as is it is disgusting. It doesn't just make Ivy sick, though; it makes her furious. Because had it not been for her, Isaac and Craig would never have met.

Ivy and Ricky work to get Isaac out of the woods, having to stop more than once because Isaac is so easily winded. He trips, and although he doesn't fall, he scrapes his arm against the rough bark of a tree. Ivy can see that it's bleeding slightly, but he doesn't even seem to notice it. No pain. It's as if his entire nervous system has curled in upon itself and given up.

As soon as they reach Ricky's car, Isaac, without an ounce of fight left in him, hurls himself across the back seat and lies there like a rag doll.

"Maybe I should take him to the hospital . . . ," Ricky says.

"No!" Isaac insists. "I just wanna go home."

Ivy nods. "Take him home. My parents will decide what to do from there."

At the mention of their parents, Isaac groans.

"Do they . . . know?" he asks.

Ricky looks to Ivy for guidance, but she has no words of advice for anyone right now.

"When you disappeared, I had to tell them, man," Ricky says.

Then Isaac's face pinches tight. He turns away, and they can hear that he's crying. Stifling it as best he can, but still, when sobs go that deep, there's only so much of them you can hide. For the life of her, Ivy can't ever remember seeing her brother cry. Not even when they were kids.

"They're not angry, Isaac," she tries to tell him. "They're just worried. I texted them, and they're thrilled that we found you."

"I don't want them to see me like this. . . ."

"I know," Ivy tells him. *I never wanted them to see me like that either,* she wants to say. But instead she says, "Believe me, they've seen worse." Then she closes the door and turns to Ricky.

"I'll meet you there," Ivy tells him. "There's something I've got to do."

Because the fury inside Ivy needs a release.

ISAAC

Shame. Isaac has never felt such shame. Now everyone knows what he's done to himself. They see what he truly is inside. Who he's become. *What* he's become. Ricky offers him under-standing and encouragement as he drives, but all Isaac hears is judgment. Isaac refuses to sit up—not only because it's an effort, but because he's afraid he might meet Ricky's eyes in the rearview mirror, gazing back at him.

Ricky might be telling him that everyone is there for him, but that doesn't matter. Isaac feels more alone than he's ever felt in his entire life. Until he realizes that maybe he's not alone. Maybe he's not alone at all. . . .

ROXY

I will not be left behind! I will infiltrate and subvert this so-called rescue.

Instead, *I* will be Isaac's salvation.

Even now I am with Isaac in the back seat of his friend's car. I can tell it will be hours until my influence wears off and he becomes sick, desperate for my touch. But by then he won't have access. He'll be at home under twenty-four-hour watch. Or worse, in rehab, where I'd have no hope of getting close to him.

If I am to save him—if I am to fulfill both our destinies—I need to make a move now. And so even before he knows I'm beside him, I plant a most necessary doubt.

"They'll make you suffer, Isaac," I tell him. "They don't know what you really need. They don't care like I do. . . ."

"It's gonna be okay," his friend says.

"Yeah . . . ," Isaac mumbles. "I know it is, Ricky." He's too beaten down now to resist.

"It was too much for you to do alone," his friend says. "I should have realized that. I should have been there for you, but I'm here now. We all are. And we'll be here for as long as it takes."

I'm disgusted by his greeting-card platitudes. If he starts reciting the Serenity Prayer, I may just scream.

"This is just a hiccup, that's all," his friend says. "Everybody has hiccups. No biggie."

So now I'm being dismissed as a "hiccup." As if my existence is a mistake to be corrected. As if I serve no function in this world. Never mind the millions I've saved from excruciating pain. So what if I exact payment for my services—who doesn't? Sure, they're all happy to use me when they need me, but then they shun me when it's convenient. Such hypocrisy.

But not Isaac. He's seen the error of his ways.

"You won't shun me, will you, Isaac?"

Isaac takes a deep, shuddering breath. He's so fragile right now. So uncertain.

"You tried to leave me before, and it just made things worse," I tell him. "That's because we were meant to be together, Isaac. You can't deny it."

He closes his eyes. He hears me deep in his bones, but will he listen? He's receptive now. Open. I lean in and I whisper.

"Save us, Isaac. . . ."

I can feel the moment he decides—the moment he takes what little agency he has left and chooses *us* over *them*. It is the most important decision of his life. I'm so grateful he made the right choice.

RICKY

The fact that Isaac is safe, if not sound, is an immense relief. Ricky had really blown it, and now he's being given a second chance to do right by Isaac. Get him home. That's all he has to do to redeem himself. But the task is fraught with obstacles. With the new freeway going in, through roads no longer go through. There are miles of detours, and they're caught right at the leading edge of construction. Getting to the other side of it is like trying to cross a river, where bridges are few and far between.

"There oughta be a law against this much construction," Ricky gripes. "We need another freeway like a hole in the head, right?"

Isaac just grunts behind him.

"You okay?"

Stupid question. Of course Isaac isn't okay.

Then Isaac sits up—Ricky catches sight of him in the rearview.

"Can you put on music?" he asks.

"Sure. What do you want."

A pause, then Isaac says, flat as can be, "Death metal."

That makes Ricky guffaw. Isaac has always had eclectic taste in music, but that's not exactly in Isaac's wheelhouse.

"Really?"

"I need something loud. Something to shut out the noise in my head, you know?"

Ricky nods. "Yeah, I get it," and at the next stoplight, Ricky fiddles with his phone, trying to pull something up on Spotify.

Death Cab for Cutie . . . no . . . *Death Note* soundtrack . . . no . . . "Ah! Here we go—I found the perfect playlist!" Suddenly the speakers just about hemorrhage with *Crimson Hurl*, complete with vocals straight from the left armpit of hell.

"Plague Pustule," Ricky says with a chuckle. "Gotta love 'em."

The light changes and Ricky moves through, but he has to slam on his brakes as another car cuts through the rerouted intersection. Some asshole in an Alfa Romeo who doesn't understand the concept of traffic cones and detour arrows.

"Look at this guy," says Ricky. "Some people just shouldn't be behind a wheel."

"SHRED YOUR HEAD WITH BLENDER BLADES. VOMIT BLOOD AND DIE!" screeches Plague Pustule.

The hapless driver gets caught in the middle of everything, having to do a three-point turn, to a chorus of honking horns. Then the pickup next to Ricky moves forward just enough to make it even more difficult for the stuck driver to maneuver.

"As soon as we get past all this, it should be a straight shot to your house," Ricky says.

"HEART IMPALED ON A RUSTY NAIL. VOMIT BLOOD AND DIE!"

When Ricky glances in the rearview mirror, Isaac is out of sight.

"Isaac?"

At first he thinks Isaac has just lain back down again . . . until he turns around to see that the door is ajar. Not just ajar but open. And Isaac is gone.

IVY

Ivy's head is in overdrive with all the things she might do to Craig when she gets to his place. Kick him repeatedly in the nuts. Gouge out his eyes. Drown him in his own diseased pool. All those options are on the table. She has to find some way to make him suffer.

Did Isaac's addiction start with Craig? she wonders. Yes and no. It started with that fight that sprained Isaac's ankle. After that, the path that brought him back to Craig must have been a strange one. The kind of path that makes you think you're going straight until you find yourself back where you started.

Kind of like the path she's taking now to get to Craig's place. In the weeks since she'd seen him, his whole neighborhood has become an extended construction zone. Roads that used to go somewhere are now bleak dead ends. Heavy equipment and demolished pavement paint everything in shades of Armageddon. And her phone is useless, insisting that she drive through intersections that are just plain gone. She has to turn around more than once, blazing her own trail.

Craig had told her the entire street was about to be torn down. A quarter mile south, concrete was already being poured for the freeway that was slowly heading in Craig's direction, inch by inch burying Birch Street without a trace. Hundreds of homes supplanted by a need to bypass his part of the world entirely. "A corridor, they call it," Craig had said. "Like it's nothing but a home-improvement project. Like your whole neighborhood's gotta go because your asshole neighbor needs a hallway." When Ivy asked when he had to be out, Craig was never specific. "Eventually" was all he said, like maybe he'd be pulling up his pants and running out the door when the wrecking ball showed up.

She finally finds a route to the north side of the construction zone—and makes her way down side streets toward Craig's place. Part of her hopes that he's already gone, but a bigger part hopes he's still there so she can rip him a new one.

Her heart is racing, but it's more than just adrenaline, more than just anger. She had taken another pill just before heading into the woods to fight the exhaustion and to make sure she was sharp enough to face Isaac. Now she feels a battle raging inside her. Her body's need to rest at war with the chemicals demanding alertness. She finds herself sliding into moments that are almost hallucinogenic while she's driving. Not safe. She needs to be careful. She only needs to be awake and focused a little while longer. But her heart—it feels like it's about to burst out of her chest like an alien and stare her in the face saying what the hell did you do to me?

There's an unpleasant electricity shooting through her. She's felt it before. She's become used to it even, but now it's been dialed up into the red. It makes her think of her grandmother's house—the one she lived in before her first fall. An old Victorian with an electrical system that could have been installed by Edison himself. The fuses would constantly blow, plunging the whole house into darkness. It used to scare Ivy when she was little.

"Never have the TV and the drier and the air conditioner on at the same time, sweetie," Grandma would tell her.

But now every appliance is on and running in overdrive,

and as she turns onto what's left of Birch Street, she feels the fuses begin to blow, one after another, *Bzzt! Bzzt! Bzzt!* in a relentless cascade.

She pulls over to the side of the road but jumps the curb. Then she looks at the vial. Not Isaac's but hers. It's empty. When did it go empty? How many of those pills had she taken? Oh shit! She begins to panic, and her heart, as fast as its beating, quickens. She shuts her eyes. She can't catch her breath. *Just calm down. Just calm down.*

She tries slow deep breathing but can't get enough air, so she's back to taking sharp, jagged breaths. *This is just a moment,* she tells herself. *Just a moment. It will pass.* She's not even sure where she is anymore. Is she still in the car? Did she make it to Craig's place? *Bzzt! Bzzt! Bzzt!*

Ivy feels like she's rising out of herself, shooting upward faster and faster. And as her eyes roll back, she hears a strange voice that's also familiar. And the voice says:

"Welcome to the Party. . . ."

33

Farther Than Anyone Else Dare Go

ROXY

I'm with Isaac on a street paved with every hope I've ever had, glittering silver and gold. Buildings on either side flash with chasing lights like the Las Vegas Strip, while jewels of every cut and color dangle from the memory of trees like ripe fruit. They twirl and twinkle, catching the eye—the quintessential shiny objects that might steal the focus from distractibles like Isaac's sister—but not from Isaac. He takes it in but doesn't let it pull him away from the center of his attention. Me.

We move down the street toward his destination.

"You saw Craig's place," Isaac says. "You saw that closet! All those bags and bottles! It was a mess. He must have left something behind. I'm sure of it."

I grip his hand, letting my nails press gently into his skin. Not enough to hurt—he couldn't hurt now if he wanted to—but to be my silent promise to him that in spite of the dazzling spectacle and blinding lights, I won't let go.

And finally there we are, standing before the open elevator, its peach-toned mirrors and golden fixtures so inviting. His world has no choice but to fade into shadow behind the powerful luster of mine.

Isaac is confused, but only for a moment, as his mind slips into the easy, rolling logic of dreams.

"Are you excited, Isaac? Are you as thrilled as I am?"

He answers by being the first to step into the elevator. This is clearly the most exciting moment of his entire life. The doors close behind us, he hits the button, and we begin to rise.

I am wary about what comes next, for I am not bringing him to the Party. I will take him *beyond* the Party. But to get past it, we must go through it. Lucy showed me the way! She blazed a path across the sky to freedom—to a place farther than anyone else would even dare go. All Isaac and I have to do is follow her lead.

"When the doors open, don't listen, don't talk to anyone, and whatever you do, don't dance."

"I won't," he says. "I don't want to dance with anyone but you."

I smile. His sincerity is enough to cut the most jaded of us. I'm glad it's me he found.

"I love you, Isaac," I tell him. "Do you believe that?" I ask, because I desperately need validation of my own sincerity.

"I believe it with all my heart," he says.

"And do you trust me?"

"You know I do," he says. "Do you trust me, too?"

I'm about to respond, but I have to stop myself. I realize I can't give him the answer he wants. Because as determined as he is to stay true, there are things stronger than resolve. The Party is a treacherous affair. There are simply too many ways for him to be pulled off course. Too many pitfalls, too much hunger. And too many sharks.

"Just keep your eyes on me, and don't look away."

The elevator slows, and we are blasted by music and lights as the doors slide open. Like always, Al is there, a glass of something high proof in either hand.

"Roxy! Welcome!" he says with his casually ingratiating slur. "And look who you've brought with you! A pleasure to finally meet you, Isaac. It was well worth the wait."

"Ignore him," I tell Isaac.

"Roxy, don't be rude," Al says.

And since he doesn't step aside, I push past him, sloshing out most of his offered drinks, and yet they don't seem to lose any volume.

The Party rages at full-bore. Marrow-killing bass vibrates in Isaac's bones, making him giddy, the spectacle muddling his mind more than I've already muddled it. I know how it is. The Party makes one receptive. It tenderizes the meat for those who would devour it.

Molly brushes by, her fingers intentionally grazing Isaac's shoulder and neck, making him shiver. "Oooh, I like this one, Roxy. He's hot. Will you be sharing?"

"Out of my way, Molly."

"Touchy, touchy," she says, and breezes past, but not without a parting stroke of Isaac's cheek. "Your loss, cutie."

It's enough to weaken Isaac's resolve, and he looks toward the open deck, where revelers bob in the infinity pool.

"What's over there?" he asks.

"It doesn't matter," I tell him. "That's not where we're going."

I forge our way through the crowd and take a deep breath

as I push through the padded leather doors of the VIP lounge. Anyone watching will think I'm simply doing my usual thing. Taking my plus-one past the point of no return. But the only way out is through those doors. To the place where the aya-huasca stalk grows. If we can get to the roof, we'll be out of danger's way. I'd thank Lucy if I could for opening my mind to our escape. Because there's more than one iron-winged beast patrolling the skies, and if she can fly free, then so can we.

ADDISON

Success! Ivy and I step into the Party like celebrities. Like we are the center of the turntable on which the music spins. In all the times I've been here, I've never felt anything but peripheral. Maybe because I always knew my plus-ones were just using me to get to my upline. Everyone knows you study with Addison. Everyone knows he's just there to keep you awake long enough to find some real action. "He's nothing but a lukewarm latte," I've heard others say behind my back. Well, look at the latte now! Tonight they'll finally see what I'm capable of.

"I'm not supposed to be here . . . ," Ivy says, confused and disoriented by the sudden blast of sound and light.

"Of course you're supposed to be here, Ivy. Where else would you be?"

"I was doing something else. What . . . what was I doing?"

"Must not have been important."

I refuse to feel guilt or remorse over this. The fact is, Ivy would have ended up here eventually—and with someone who didn't care about her the way I do. She deserves better than that. She deserves to meet her destiny with a friend. Someone who truly knows her heart. I am that friend. Not like those idiots she rode home with—the ones who ditched her at the curb at the first sign of trouble. No, I won't be ditching you, Ivy. I will be there with you right to the very end, which is so tantalizingly close, I can taste it.

I watch her chest heave as she struggles to get enough air.

"Takes your breath away, doesn't it?" I tell her, and I point out the highlights. "Pool deck to the left, dance floor to the right, bar straight ahead, and the VIP lounge—because you're my very, very important person."

I catch sight of Dusty and Charlie in their usual booth—and I turn to Ivy, making sure she looks me in the eye. "Don't forget who you came with," I tell her. "Promise me that."

"Yeah," she says. "Yeah, I promise, but—"

"No buts! This is the time of 'and.' As in 'you and me,' 'rock and roll—'"

"Rum and Coke!" says Al, appearing as he always appears, with big red Solo cups in each hand.

"Welcome, one and all!"

"Not tonight, Al," I say, staving off his offerings. "I'm all Ivy needs tonight."

Al heaves a histrionic sigh. "Will no one accept my hospitality? First Roxy, now you."

"Wait—Roxy's here?"

"Yes, she practically hurled my best tequila right onto the floor." Then he leans in and whispers, "She arrived just before you." Then he winks. "With you-know-who."

I bristle, and that makes Al grin.

"It doesn't matter," I say, and pull Ivy away before Al can rile me with subtle taunts. When I last saw Roxy, she was the very picture of failure. Isaac was being spirited home—and probably to rehab. But I was foolish to count Roxy out. She's wily and resourceful. But she hasn't won yet! And even if she finishes first, the fact that I might finish at all will be victory enough. Still, I want the whole thing if I can get it. After all her conceited condescension, it is not enough that I win but that Roxy lose.

I can see her on the other side of the Party as she impels Isaac through the throng, toward the VIP lounge. I won't let it rattle me. I will finish what I'm here to do.

"Wait!" Ivy shouts over the music. "Is that my brother? I think I see Isaac!"

"You think too much, Ivy," I tell her. That's partially my fault, I know. "You're here now. Focus on that. I don't even have to stop time for you to be in the moment."

Turns out her brother's presence isn't a bad thing—because now she pushes even faster toward those red padded doors.

But just then Dusty catches sight of us and alerts Charlie. They both look in our direction. I tighten my grip around Ivy's waist to make it clear that she's with me, and for once, it's staying that way.

"I have to get to my brother!"

I try not to be exasperated by her single-mindedness. It's one of the things I like about her. "Yes, let's follow him," I tell her, moving her ever forward. "But remember—he's not why you're here. This is Ivy time."

Then, when I look back at the Coke brothers' booth, Dusty's still there, but Charlie isn't. I hate the fact that he's mobilized and I don't know where he's gone or why. I take a moment to track Roxy and Isaac. They've pushed through the doors ahead of us.

The moment she's out of sight, Ivy's focus gets foggy. She looks around at the trappings of the Party. She wavers. Waffles.

"I can't *be* here!" Ivy gasps. "Not now!"

"And yet you are, so you might as well make the best of it," I say as jovially as I can muster. "Play this right, and everyone will remember you."

"I don't . . . I don't give a shit . . . about being remembered!"

It's getting harder and harder for her to catch her breath, but I can't slow down now. "Don't be silly. Everyone wants to be remembered."

And just then I see trouble. Crys is making a beeline toward us, with Charlie in his wake. Damn Charlie! The weasel. He knew I wouldn't let him and Dusty have their way with Ivy, so he went straight for the big guns. And I can't move fast enough, because the crowd doesn't part for me the way it does for Crys.

We're intercepted. Crys stands right in front of us, blocking our path, with Charlie and his slimy, sleazebag smirk like icing on the cake.

Crys doesn't even spare a glance at me. He's zeroed in on Ivy. He grabs her hand in that glittery vise grip of his. "Dance," he orders, and begins to pull her away. And I think, here it is, again. Here it is as it always is, and I am powerless to stop it. And then—a miracle!

"No!" says Ivy, and she pulls her hand away.

It stops Crys cold. Once Crys has his hands on you, you don't refuse. You couldn't slip out of his grip if you tried. If Crys says dance, you dance.

Now Crys glares at her. The aura of his indignance swells, absorbing all the highs and lows of the music, leaving only the narrow muffled bandwidth between.

"I told you to dance."

"And I told you no." Then Ivy looks to me. "I'm with him." And she grips my hand tighter.

Crys takes a long moment before he responds to that. Charlie's smirk turns a satisfying sour.

"You're with him," Crys echoes in disbelief.

"You heard the lady," I say, for the first time standing up to Crys. And I see the exact moment where he caves. Crys caves! To me! It's more than I could have ever hoped for.

"Fine," says Crys. "Then be with him." Then he narrows those soulless ice-blue eyes at me. "You'd better finish what you started, Addison."

And as quickly as he arrived, he's gone, with Charlie tagging along at his heels like a neglected pet. And although I'd love to bask in the moment, I can't. I've got work to do. I cut us through the crowd with a confidence I've never had before, pushing us through the padded doors into the lounge. I don't see Roxy, but that can't matter. I can't let it distract me.

"This way," I tell Ivy. "The dance floor in here isn't as crowded, and the music is so much better." Because even though she won't dance with Crys, she can no longer deny that it's her destiny to dance with me.

ROXY

"You haven't told me where we're going," Isaac says.

I haven't told him because I don't really know. There's no destination, just a trajectory.

"Away from all of this," I tell him. "Across both of our skies to a place where no one from your world or mine can hurt us."

We're halfway to the corner where the ayahuasca stalk grows. And then something pulls my attention. Addison. He's with Irene, or Ida, or whatever the hell her name is. I watch him smoothly guide Isaac's sister to the dance floor.

Well, I don't care. Let him win our bet—I never plan on coming back to the Party anyway. He can have his triumph, as long as I have mine too—and the sooner Isaac and I are free from here, the better.

It was only an instant that I was looking away. The tiniest moment of distraction. But when I turn back to Isaac, he's gone.

"Isaac!"

But I can't hear him answer. He's been swallowed by the shadows of the lounge. And so I begin a frantic search, desperate to find him before those shadows digest him.

ADDISON

I swing Ivy onto the dance floor, pull her close, and begin a breathless tango.

"I can't," she protests. "I don't know this dance."

NEAL SHUSTERMAN AND JARROD SHUSTERMAN

"Oh, but you do," I tell her. "You've been doing it for years."

And sure enough, she follows my lead perfectly, like a hand in a glove, into a smooth Media Luna. Her surprise is lost behind her exhaustion. I quickly step things up. A series of rapid *ochos*, in an embrace that would crush her spine in clumsier hands.

Seeing us, the band switches up the music. Fiery flamenco guitar, with a powerful cajón drumbeat, and the percussive purr of castanets, dangerous as a rattlesnake.

I push her back into a *colgada*, leaning away, then I pull her into a tight *calesita* spin. Our feet could set the floor on fire! We are cheek to cheek, so close there's no telling where she ends and I begin. So close I can smell her adrenaline breaking down into cortisol right there on her breath.

A crowd has begun to gather around us—more than is usual for this most intimate of dance floors. The others of my kind now on the sidelines are watching us—watching *me*. In this shining here and now, Ivy and I are the only couple that matters.

"Stop . . . Please . . ."

"No stopping now, Ivy. Not when everyone's watching."

I've been waiting forever for this. I have been ignored and hazed, disrespected and disregarded. Dismissed as a classroom tool no more functional than a ruler to measure one's worth. An eraser to wipe out one's shame. Do you all see now? Do you see what I really can be? What I'm truly worth?

The Coke brothers are there, miserable with defeat as they watch us own the dance floor, knowing I will soon be above them. I will be the higher rung in their upline. And Crys! He stands with his muscular arms folded, yet with a smile on his face. I recognize that look. It's pride. Pride to see me, little Addi, center stage, coming into my own.

Ivy is so out of breath she can't speak anymore. But her eyes do the pleading for her. *Don't you see, Ivy? This was meant to be. You are so special. You are the blaze of glory turning our dark sky bright as day.*

I whip her into a dramatic *cruce forzado*, then suddenly switch direction in an *ocho cortado*, leaving her barely knowing left from right, up from down. Is Roxy watching? I wonder. Is she there in the crowd to witness this victory? I don't know why it should matter, but it does.

The music crescendos in that penultimate moment before what will be the grandest climax I've ever experienced. I hurl her away, tightly gripping one hand, then spin her back into me like a yo-yo and trap her in a tight *mordida*. The crowd gasps at each move.

The evolution of what I was into what I can be requires this sacrifice. But each time I catch sight of Ivy's eyes, they tug at my soul just as powerfully as I tug at her body. I feel her desperation— her helplessness. She has never been a helpless girl. Even when she loses control, she has always been the leader of the dance. But not today. And as thrilled as I am, I can't help but feel I've stripped her of her dignity. She deserves better than the heartless losers here that would exploit her and leave her. But isn't that what I'm doing? Isn't that what I am about to become?

The final steps of our dance. I hurl Ivy down into a perfect death-drop dip. Our arms extended, her body inches from the ground, her eyes fixed on mine.

Finish it, Addison, I can hear Crys say in my mind. *Finish it and earn your place.*

And it's so very easy now. . . . All I have to do is let go. . . .

ROXY

I was looking away for only a moment—Isaac couldn't have gotten far. Yet even as I think it, I know that's not how things work here. Time and space stretch and contract as they do their relentless business, like worms burrowing in the darkness. But Isaac is still here. He has to be! He couldn't have left the Party without me knowing—I would have felt it.

Did he go through the doors, back to the crowded outer party? If he did, I'll never find him before Molly or Vic, or any one of a hundred others get their claws into him. I swear if they try, I will crush them into dust. I must find him, and I must find him *now*!

I bump past two of the new designer drugs. They're not working on humans, but enamored with each other, hands all over one another, as if they've just discovered they have bodies.

"I'm looking for a boy," I tell them, trying not to sound as desperate as I feel. "His name is Isaac. Tall. Good-looking. Vague expression. Or at least it's been vague lately."

One of them laughs. "You just described, like, every plus-one here."

I storm away, with no patience for these self-absorbed idiots.

"What's up with her?" I hear one of them say.

"What's ever up with her?" the other responds, and

laughs—as if this frantic search is something they've seen from me before. Well, screw them. They're as useless as they are lethal.

There's a gathering now around the VIP dance floor—where Addison is, no doubt, putting on his little puppet show. If Isaac saw his sister, he would have gone over there—but before I can make a move toward the dance floor, I feel an icy hand on my shoulder. I turn to see the last face I'd expect to see in this place.

"Phineas?"

"A good evening to you, Roxy," my lugubrious cousin says in that distant, submerged voice of his.

"Why are you here?" I demand. Phineas never comes to the Party, much less the inner sanctum. His presence anywhere is never a good omen.

Phineas regards me with a mournful, lonelier-than-thou expression that I so despise. "I've heard of your competition with Addison," he says. "I've come to bear witness."

"There's nothing to witness," I snap.

But Phineas is unfazed. A single narrow eyebrow arches like a dark, lightless rainbow. "You seek your young man," he says. "I have seen him."

"Where! Where did you see him? Tell me!"

And far too slowly, Phineas raises a bony hand, pointing to the last place I want to think about. The last place I want to go. He points toward the hallway that leads to Hiro's office.

I take off so quickly, the pillars themselves seem to bow in my wake.

The hallway is littered with souls too weak to reach the door. I step over them, on them, kick them out of the way. Their fates are not my concern. Finally I reach Hiro's door and turn the knob, but I pull too hard, and it comes off in my hand. So I kick the door and kick it again and again until the jamb splinters and the door flies open.

Isaac is there. He is lying on the floor, limp like a rag doll, and Hiro stands over him, holding up Isaac's arm, scrutinizing it as if looking for a good vein.

The doorknob is still in my hand, so I hurl it at the chandelier to create a distraction. A rain of spoons clatters to the ground—but I should have known nothing distracts Hiro.

"Get your hands off him!" I snarl.

"I was just checking to see if he still has a pulse."

Then Isaac blinks and looks at me. He offers a lazy smile. "There you are!"

Hiro lets Isaac's hand flop down. "You were supposed to bring him to me. Instead he wandered in here on his own."

"He's not for you!" I don't care if Hiro is the head of my upline. He has no power over me.

Hiro sighs, like it's nothing more than a minor nuisance. "Must we go through this again?"

I kneel down, grab Isaac's face, and make him look into my eyes. "Did he . . . ? Did he *do* anything to you?"

Isaacs eyes finally find focus in mine. "Did who do anything to who?" he murmurs.

"You don't have to worry, Roxy," Hiro says. "You never introduced us. You know I don't do business without a proper introduction."

"You're not getting one," I tell Hiro. "Not now, not ever!"

"As is your prerogative," Hiro says, with such casual disregard it unnerves me.

I have nothing more to say to Hiro. Instead I give all my attention to Isaac. "Stay with me, Isaac, and I'll get us out of here."

"With you," he says with that same weary smile. "Always with you."

Which is just what I need to hear.

He's so weak now, I just about have to carry him out of Hiro's office—and now the hallway seems impossibly long and is no longer straight. Instead, it winds back in upon itself like an intestine. The very walls fight me every step of the way, but I will not yield an ounce of my determination.

At last we emerge in the VIP lounge, where all the attention is still on the dance floor. Good! That means no one will get in our way! I hold Isaac tightly, not daring to let him go as I move us to the corner, where the towering ayahuasca—and freedom—waits . . .

. . . Only to discover that the ayahuasca is gone.

It's been hacked down. All that's left is a jagged stump where it had been. I look upward to the hole in the roof—still there, but now there's no way to reach it.

"Sorry, Roxy."

I turn to see a beefy security guard, the safety-seal insignia on the breast of his black jacket.

"Roof access has been prohibited. Too much funny business going on up there."

"You can't do that!" I demand, panicking. "We can go wherever the hell we want! That's always been the rule!"

He shrugs. "Not my call. Orders came down from the highest level."

I don't even know what that means. I know that Hiro

answers to someone, who answers to someone else, and so on, but none of us can see that far up the chain.

And then I hear a voice behind me—a voice I never expected to hear again.

"Too bad," says Lucy. "The roof was the grooviest place to be."

I turn to her, shocked. "Lucy? But . . . but you're gone! You flew away on the caduceus wings!"

"Did I . . . ? Oh, right, now I remember. Wow, what a trip."

"You said you wanted to be free."

Lucy shrugs. "Well, yeah—but there's just a whole lot of nothing out there. Turns out this is the only happening place for us."

I suddenly feel dizzy, disoriented.

"Forget it, Roxy," says the guard. "Why don't you take your plus-one to the Jacuzzi. There's plenty of room."

"He's not a plus-one!" I scream at him.

That's when Isaac, burning through the final fumes of his energy, falls to the ground—and now I see what Isaac sees. Not the blood-veined marble floor of the lounge, but a moldy, mottled carpet. Not the dead ayahuasca stump, but a warped, hammer-dented desk in a dark room that is the very epicenter of abandoned hope.

ADDISON

Finish it, Addison. Finish it and earn your place.

Everyone watches. Everyone waits to see what I do. The flourish with which I finally step into greatness.

I hold Ivy in the death-drop dip.

All I need to do is let go. All I need to do is release my hands from her wrists, let her body drop to the floor, lifeless, and then step away, striking a final conquering pose. There will be applause, so much applause, and all for me. If I just let her go.

But Ivy's eyes . . .

Yes, I know it was her choice to abuse me, but isn't it my choice now to abuse her abuse?

Finish it, Addison.

But I can't.

As close as I am to everything I thought I wanted, I can't do this. I won't.

I pull Ivy up from the death drop and into my arms, to the collective gasp of the crowd. Her arms weakly wrap around my shoulders, and my hands hold her around the waist, not to manipulate her into another step but to support her. To keep her from falling. And I know, I know, I know I will never be Dusty. I will never be Charlie. I will never find favor in Crys's eyes. Because after this moment I will forever be the one they laugh about. The one who could have been.

But when I look at Crys and his shock at this choice I've made, I realize that this is its own victory. I stand in defiance of everything Crys is and everything this Party stands for. And I smile—because for one shining moment I stole the Party . . . and then hurled the entire thing into a death drop and let go.

I rush off the dance floor with Ivy in tow. She still can't catch her breath, but at least she still has breath to catch.

Then Ivy suddenly pulls against me.

"But I saw Isaac!" she says, remembering. "He's here! I can't leave without him."

I keep our forward momentum. We are still in the tango, after all, just a different one. I must lead, if only for a few more crucial steps.

I sweep us out of the lounge and into the raucous beat of the outer party. The crowd parts for me now, the way it does for Crys. Because, for once, my determination surpasses his. We're at the elevator in seconds. The doors open. I move her in, and I step away, our dance finally over.

"You have to go, Ivy. You have to go now. Press the button."

But she doesn't do it.

"My brother . . ."

"There's nothing you can do for him."

"I have to try."

"No, you don't."

How can I make her see? There's a body bag with her name on it, just waiting for her if she doesn't get out of here. But if she's going to come down, she has to be the one to choose it.

"I can't push the button for you. You have to do it yourself. Please, Ivy!" This is her one and only chance to get out of here, but how can I convince her when she won't leave her brother behind? And so I take a deep breath and make a decision.

"I'll find him," I tell her. "I'll save Isaac. I'll bring him home."

"You will?"

"I promise."

Her eyes linger on mine. Her hand reaches for the button that will take her away from here, but she still hesitates.

"You really mean that? You'll bring Isaac home?"

"I swear it. And I would never lie to you, Ivy, never. You know that."

And finally, *finally* she presses her finger to the button. The elevator doors close, and she's gone.

I take a deep breath and let my shoulders relax.

"Well," says Al, suddenly beside me. "That was entertaining. Almost as entertaining as that crash and burn on the dance floor. Truly epic. I would almost call it selfless."

"Just shut up, Al." And I take one of the flutes of prosecco from his hands, downing it to the last drop—but not in consolation. Instead it is a proud toast to what I've just done. I may have just saved Ivy's soul. Which means, if there's the remotest chance that I have one, then maybe I've saved mine, too.

"So what now?" Al asks. "Are you off to save her brother, like you told her?"

I shake my head. "I couldn't if I tried," I confess to Al. "I lied to her."

And Al offers me his broadest drunken smile. "Now, that's something I can respect."

34

Tears of a Predator

ROXY

I kneel over Isaac, holding his focus, knowing how tenuous it is, knowing how easily I could lose it. I don't see the lounge at all anymore. All I see are the shadows of the ruined room Isaac brought himself to.

"Isaac, I need you to get up. We have to get out of here."

And he tries—he genuinely tries—but those legs that have kicked a hundred goals have no strength left in them. He gets halfway up, then slides back down into the corner.

"Legs aren't working right now," he says. "Let me rest a bit."

"No! You can't rest! Not here, not now."

I can't control my tears. They fall on his cheek, dribbling toward his mouth. He licks them off his lips, relishing them. In fairy tales, the tears of love can cure blindness. They can save a life. They can even bring someone back from death. But mine do nothing but bring him closer to his end.

Then Hiro's there. He actually left his office to watch this, and it makes me hate him all the more.

"Roxy, be sensible," pleads Hiro. "Where do you think you can go with him?"

"I don't care! Anywhere but here!"

"Every path you take, every stair you climb, every door you open will lead you back here. To this room, to this moment. It can't be avoided."

"I don't care! Isaac, get up!"

He tries once more, and once more he slumps back down. And he laughs weakly at his own inability to do anything to help himself. Damn it!

When I look up, I see others beginning to surround us, like I'm caught in some kind of nightmare. Dusty. Charlie. Mary Jane. I don't want them here. This is none of their business. But still they keep coming. Molly and Crys stand side by side with Lucy and Phineas.

"What are they doing here?"

"We're here for you," one of them says.

"To see you through this," says another.

"It would be so easy to mock you."

"But we won't."

"We're here to support you."

"Who else will if we don't?"

I grip Isaac tighter, as if I can protect him from all of them. But they keep their distance. They don't try to interfere.

Hiro smiles and shakes his head. "As vexing as you can be, Roxy, I have to admit, I admire this side of you. It's always refreshing."

"What do you mean?"

"The way you fall in love, of course," Hiro says. "Time and time again."

And the miserable chorus behind him agrees.

"Never fails."

"She's a hopeless romantic."

"Hopeless."

"Restores my faith in the power of futility."

I feel a knot in the pit of my stomach. Worse than a knot. A black hole. Something inside me so dark, nothing can escape. *What the hell are they talking about?*

"Roxy," says Hiro, in his most patronizing tone. "Do you think this is the first time you've fallen for one of your marks?"

He's lying. He has to be. Hiro's a master trickster. He gaslights and distracts. He misdirects with sleight of hand. It won't be true if I don't believe it.

"Of course it's true," says Hiro, reading my thoughts. "You just don't remember. You were not blessed with much of a memory, Roxy. But if you need proof, I have it all here."

Then he produces his huge ledger out of nowhere, slams it down on the desk, and opens it. He knows the exact page to turn to. I don't want to look, but I can't help myself.

The top of the page is marked ROXY, and there's an endless list of names divided between five columns. He points out each column with his ash-stained finger and speaks in a singsong voice, like it's a nursery rhyme. Like he's counting piggies instead of lives.

"These are the ones you brought to me . . . and these are the ones you kept. These are the ones who got away . . . and these are the ones you helped. And these? These are the ones you opened your heart to and loved into oblivion."

That last list is in red ink, like a tally of accounts overdue. Name after name and not a single one can I remember. I can't recall a single face.

"You've brought them all to the lounge, with the same dream of escape. And tomorrow, when the ayahuasca is tall and lush once more, you'll do it again. And again. It's who you are, Roxy. Who you've always been."

I can't tear my eyes away from those names. Every single one of them is crossed out, except for the last one. Isaac Ramey.

"The cost of living in the moment is the loss of all those moments before," Hiro says, suddenly the philosopher. "It's how you thrive, Roxy."

I squeeze Isaac tighter. What does he make of all this? Does he see it? Does he hear what I'm being accused of? Or does he see nothing but an empty room, and me?

I shake my head, still in denial. "No! I will never forget him."

But all the others scoff, and Hiro smiles at me with pity. He doesn't say the words, but I hear them anyway.

You will, Roxy. You will.

I ignore Hiro. I ignore them all. I focus on Isaac. Everything depends on this moment. What I am, what I did, what I remember, or what I forget doesn't matter. What matters is what I do in this moment.

"Isaac, I need you to do something for me."

He purrs a gentle, submissive response.

"I need you to take out your phone. I need you to call nine-one-one."

"Don't know where . . ."

"Your pocket. Focus just long enough to do this, Isaac. Reach into your pocket."

His arms are like lead and his fingers rubber, but he does it.

He angles it toward his face long enough for it to unlock. In a grid of apps, he struggles to bring up the right one. Finally, he gets the number pad.

"Roxy . . . ," says Hiro, but I put up a hand to shut him up. Isaac dials. A single ring, and the operator picks up.

"Nine-one-one, what's your emergency?"

And then Isaac drops the phone. Shit! It's inches from him that might as well be miles.

The operator waits. "I'm still here . . . ," she says. Good. They're trained to wait. She must have heard the phone fall.

"Speak to her, Isaac."

Isaac swallows. He tries to gather strength.

"Are you there? I won't hang up until you've disconnected."

"Say it, Isaac. You know what you have to say."

It takes so much effort for him to force the word out of his throat, but finally he does.

"O-o-overdose."

And then his whole body caves with the admission of that singular, terrible word.

"Sir, can you tell me where you are?"

Another gathering of will. Like pushing a boulder up a mountain.

"Sir, can you please give me your location?"

"B-Birch . . . ," Isaac says. "Eleven twenty-nine—" And right then, in that instant, his phone abruptly dies. It's as if the universe itself has chosen to turn its back. But it's okay. It's okay. Because he got out the number. He got it out and they heard. Maybe I'm wrong. Maybe the universe held its breath, keeping the phone on just long enough for him to give that house number. I want to believe that. I so desperately want to believe that.

Isaac turns to me, his eyes narrow slits.

"I love you," he says. "I need you. I want you more than anything in the world."

And Hiro kneels next to me. "Embrace this, Roxy," he says. "Take what he gives you, and walk away."

I turn to Hiro and the others in fury. "This has nothing to do with you. Leave!"

But they don't. They just watch. They wait. They bear witness to this great failure that they will insist is a success.

Is this all I am? In the end, is this all I am capable of? *No!* I want to scream out to them. *I brought relief to his grandmother, didn't I? I bring relief to thousands. Millions! It's right there in Hiro's damn ledger.*

But I also take for myself.

Even when I don't mean to. Even when I don't want to. Because it's not only *in* my nature. It *is* my nature. That undeniable truth finally begins to bore into me. There is nothing new under the sun for us; we are habitual. Predictable. Repeating the same pattern over and over until we fall from disrepute into disfavor. Until we end up chained to a caduceus with no wings.

But that won't be today.

And if what Hiro says is true—if all my yesterdays vanish and my tomorrows never come—then all I have is this moment. All I have is right now. And right now I am in my prime. It's the only thing I can take comfort in.

"You've done well, Roxy," Hiro says. And the others agree.

"Every life you take makes us stronger."

"All of us."

"We are your family."

"We are your friends."

"We are the ones you love."

"And who love you."

"The others fall like flies."

"But you are still here."

"We are still here."

"He is nothing more than prey."

"And you are the predator."

Hiro puts a comforting hand on my shoulder. "Be the Roxy I love," he says. "The Roxy I'm so proud of. Do what you do like no other, and take away the last of his pain."

So I pull Isaac close and give him one final kiss. And as our lips touch, I can feel it—the moment he goes past the brink. I can sense that silent instant when nothing can stop what's coming. There's too much damage to overcome. Too much of me.

And the moment he slips past the point of no return, something changes in me. A release. A freeing. Like an anchor has been unchained from my feet. I was suffering, but now I'm not. It's amazing how quickly an open wound can zip itself shut. Maybe it wasn't a wound at all. Because I don't feel any of the pain I just felt a few moments ago. I feel . . . numb.

The sound of distant sirens spill in through the naked windows. It doesn't matter. I already know the medics won't get here in time. Isaac can barely move at all now. He can't find the strength to either open or close his eyelids. They stay fixed at half-mast.

"Naloxone will be along soon," Hiro says.

"He'll be too late," I tell Hiro.

"Yes," Hiro agrees, "but I won't scratch out this one's name until it's official."

The thought of running into my cousin—of seeing the accusation in Nalo's eyes—is enough to get me moving. I lay Isaac gently down on the filthy floor and back away.

No . . . Stay with me, he mumbles—a weak subvocalization only the keenest of ears can hear. *I don't want to be alone.*

I hesitate, but only for a moment.

"Roxy, you know the rules," says Hiro.

Please . . . Please don't leave me. I'm scared. . . .

Yes, I know the rules. We can bring them here. We can caress them and seduce them. We can comfort them, and we can even give them joy. We can be their everything.

But when they die, they die alone.

The others have already left. It's just me and Hiro standing over him now. His world is fading—I can once more see the lounge and the ayahuasca stump, which is already sprouting new shoots.

"Goodbye, Isaac," I say.

Then I turn away and leave with Hiro, refusing to look back.

I am good at what I do. More than good, I am the best. I need moments like this to remind me not to look back and to always move forward. I am more than life and death. I am the fire that burns through the world. All their attempts to contain me have failed. Why should I feel shame at that? Why should I feel remorse for that boy who lay dying in a dark room? He's the one who came to me, after all. *He* abused *me*. So why should I weep another tear? He reaped what he sowed.

As I leave my latest conquest behind, I bask in the knowledge of what I am and in the power that comes with my position. All of life, all of death, is a mirror that reflects back on me, and so I preen at my own reflection, sated and self-satisfied.

I step out of the inner sanctum of the VIP lounge, and the Party explodes around me. The bass drops and begins to resonate the last of my self-doubt away. Unwanted memories have no place here. They sail off like embers and die. The others who had been there to support me have gone their separate ways—all but Mary Jane, who's waiting for me. She puts a kindly hand on my shoulder.

"I'm sorry about what happened," she says. "If you want to talk, I'm here for you."

I'm confused. What a weird thing to say. "Talk about what?" I ask.

She smiles and takes her hand back. "Never mind, Roxy."

She turns and goes, and once she's gone, I move deeper into the press of bodies. I am so hot right now, and everyone knows it. It's like I own the world. It has no choice but to yield to my gravity.

35

The Tail End of Twilight

ISAAC

Isaac's breaths are slow. Measured. Although there's no one there to measure them. He can't call this consciousness or unconsciousness; he doesn't even know what state it is.

But he knows he's in trouble.

There were pills hiding in Craig's closet, just as Isaac hoped there'd be—and some of them were the right ones. He didn't take many. Just two. One he chewed, but his mouth was too dry to swallow, so the other he mashed into a powder on the desk and snorted. It felt bad until it felt good.

But only after doing it did he remember how much he already had in him.

And now he's definitely in trouble.

Did he call 911, or was that just a dream? He told them where he was, didn't he? But now he can't even remember that himself. He can't focus his thoughts or his eyes. Everything is diffused through half-closed lids. It's as if his lashes have taken on immense weight, too heavy to fight against. His whole body has become too heavy to move. Like gravity on the surface of the sun. But there is no light to this sun, only gray shadows swimming around him. For the briefest moment he felt surrounded by eyes both dispassionate yet intense. He dreamed he was the center of attention, only to see it evaporate with the last of dusk, leaving him the center of no one's attention at all.

He can't feel his hands or his feet, but he hasn't lost his sense of smell. Mildew and mold. The reek of a dying forest. Is that where he is? The tree house, where he hid from the world? But then wouldn't he hear the rustling of leaves?

This is bad. He should call 911.

Images worm their way through his mind now. His life doesn't flash before his eyes. More like a random box of old photos tossed up into the wind. Brief twisting glances of moments carried off, forgotten the instant they're remembered. He doesn't have hands to grasp them, so the wind sucks them all into the sky.

But then, in the silence of this wretched place, he hears the approach of sirens, and it gives him relief. He *did* call. They are coming! They're almost here!

Good. Now he can move past this. He can bring his grades up. He can regain his standing with the team. He can earn back his friends. He imagines his parents, unable to bear the sight of him now, but he will redeem himself. He will go on to college and a career. He will design the most amazing things—airborne wonders that will take him soaring toward his shining future.

He relaxes, letting go as the sirens grow louder, and finds one more thing in which he can take solace.

He feels no pain.

Not the slightest bit.

The last thought he has, before all thoughts cease, is that he has finally been healed.

IVY

Ivy is dragged back to consciousness by the sirens. Her headache feels lethal. But it wasn't. It isn't. Still, it pulses in her skull
with every beat of her heart. Veiny streaks blur her vision like
lightning on her retinas, and a million hornets buzz between
her ears.

The sirens make it worse, but they pass. Spinning lights illuminate abandoned homes, making it clear that Craig couldn't
possibly be here anymore.

She came to exact some sort of revenge, but now she feels
foolish. That bastard doesn't deserve a moment more of her time.

She looks to her empty pill bottle on the passenger seat
beside her, and her fury shifts from Craig to herself. Those pills
were helping her! They were! But even that she abused. What's
wrong with her? What is it about her wiring that can't understand how less can be more?

She rolls down her window and hurls the bottle out to
join the detritus in the street. It's a symbolic gesture at best. She
must find a way to make it more than just a gesture.

She starts the car. And takes long, slow breaths. The deeper
she breathes, the less the pulse of pain in her head.

How long has she been here? It was the tail end of twilight
when she passed out. Now it's night. Isaac will be home by
now. She's glad he went with Ricky. Because now he must be
with Mom and Dad. They'll know what to do. And knowing
that helps her to relax. This could have been so much worse.

And so Ivy drives off, ignoring a gnawing feeling of dread
that haunts her the whole way home.

Interlude #6—Hyde (CH₂O)

Shhhh.
  Hush now.
    No need to rush.
      All the turmoil and travails,
        all the passions and pantomimes
          are done.

It was all **for** naught,
  moot as moot can be.
    But not to worry.
      Time to let all **t**hat go.
        This plac**e** is,
          as is silence itself,
            peaceful by its very nature.

And *my* nature is to denature.
  Carbon, hydrogen, oxygen—
    such versatile elements!
      They comprise the bulk of **who** you **are**,
        of who I am.
          We are no**t** so di**ff**erent,
            you w**h**o mo**v**e in **a** circle,
              and I who seals the circle closed.

I am not like those others
  and their endless raging rave.
    Their concerns, their actions
      are not mine.
        We exist on different planes.
          I have no interest in the games they play.
          I exist for one reason
            and one reason alone.
              The tender preservation
                of those in my care.

I seep slowly into them,
  replacing the blood of life
    with my restful embrace.
      I am here to hold every cell in place.
        Gently, gently.
          Although there is no longer a need
            for such loving care,
              but respect compels it.
              And I am all about respect.

As for the boy
  whose flesh I now embalm,
    I know neither who he was,
      nor what he did before he came to me.
        It is not my place to know.

He is younger than most of those I serve,
 but the task is the same,
  large or small, old or young.
   And although I do not frequent the Party,
    there is an event I do attend.
    Far more somber.
     With music, perhaps,
     but not the kind
      one might dance to.

For this event, he is as he was.
 But only on the outside,
  arranged for the eyes of the living.
  Inside, I have changed him.
  I have prepared him
   for what is to come,
    turning his flesh
    to supple armor,
    impervious
     to the ravages
     of decay.
Bent in grief,
 the gathered now rise,
  a slow processional,
   to pay their last respects.

The weeping.
　So much weeping,
　　and so many.
　　　The boy was well loved.
　　　　The young almost always are.

There, there,
　I whisper to those who come to view.
　　Weep not for him;
　　　he is beyond the reach of your tears.
　　　Weep instead for yourselves,
　　　　and for the wounds he leaves behind.

His parents
　force themselves to look
　　for as long as they can bear.

His grandmother
　rises from her wheelchair,
　　refusing anyone's help,
　　　and labors to the casket.
　　　　She purses her lips, and
　　　　　behind her veil
　　　　　　refuses to let tears flow in his presence.
　　　　　　　"Goodbye, Baby-boy," she whispers.

His sister,
  eyes flooded,
    but silently so.
      She is not a wailer
        like so many in the rows behind.
          She **give**s him a note.
            Slips it **u**nder hi**s** hand.
              And whispers **th**at she loves him.

The note will never be read,
  any more than the boat**s**
    entombe**d** with the pharaohs
      under **p**yramids
        will sail the Nile.

It's n**o**t the note that matters,
  but the act of placing it the**r**e.
    A spell to bin**d** memory
      just **as** I **b**ind flesh.

Ma**y** I share what she has written?

She will do for herself,
    what he was unable to do for himself.
        She will go to rehab.
           For both of them.
                She will free herself
                    from the chains he could not,
                        and make it stick,
                            as a sworn promise to him.

If that is so,
    then she will not meet me
        for a long, long time.

This is good.
    I have no enmity toward the living.
        I do not crave or covet
            or endeavor to entice
                as the ones who stole this boy's life do.
                    I am genuinely pleased to not be needed.

The grief comes in waves
    as friends and family rise
        with reluctant fervor
            to give testimonials.
                In their faces I can parse not just sadness
                    but guilt.
                      Everyone feels this is their fault
                    our fault
                      my fault.

If only I saw,
   if only I acted,
      if only I listened,
         if only I heard,
            if only,
               if only.

How often I have seen this.
   Even those
      who furiously point
         the finger of blame
            secretly blame themselves.

Psalms recited,
      the ritual moves to a close.
         He and I are returned to the silent dark,
            where I am most comfortable.

And by and by,
      the last of his tenure here has passed.
     I seal the circle closed,
         and we are committed to the earth again.
           He has only one task left to him now:
              to fulfill that commitment.

Shhh. *Hush*, now.
   There is no hurry.
     None at all.
       For we have all
         the time
           in the world.

36

Never Seen Roxy so Radiant

ROXY

How can you feel anything but bliss when you are worshipped by millions? When they hurl riches at your feet? When they give up their lives for you? It reminds me that I am more than the limited vision and limited mission of the minds who created me. I am the beginning of relief and the end of suffering, and I am still the rising star of the Party.

"Roxy!" says Al as I arrive, glittering in sequins. "I've never seen you so radiant as you are right now." And although Al is a sycophantic little lech, he speaks the truth. "Alone tonight?" he asks.

"Just building up an appetite," I tell him with a grin.

I make my way out to the deck, so I can look out over the world. All the possibilities, all the opportunities. Souls that glimmer like a spatter of stars down below.

Have you ever had that sense that the world was waiting for you? That all you have to do is reach out and grab it? Even if you haven't, I'm sure you can imagine it. That fleeting feeling of confidence. That, just for a moment, you've mastered it all, and you feel invincible. It's a feeling that makes life worth living.

Except, of course, when feeling pushes you just a little too far.

Like when you fly down that black diamond ski slope you weren't quite ready for and shatter your leg. Or you speed around a corner on your bike in the rain and your wheels lose traction, sending you in a flesh-tearing slide on the pavement. Or maybe it wasn't even your fault; maybe your car got rear-ended just a few weeks after you got your license, and now that relentless throbbing in your neck just won't go away.

But it's all right. I swear to you, you don't have to worry—because I feel your pain. I hear all your cries of anguish. Rest easy, because I will be there for you. To ease your suffering. Because that's what I do.

And maybe we'll get to know each other in a special kind of way. And maybe I'll stay a little longer than you planned. And maybe we'll fall for one another.

Did you call for me? You must have, because I'm there by your side right now. There's chemistry between us—do you feel it? Do you feel the small hairs on your arms start to rise as I move even closer?

Open for me. Let me in. Don't be afraid, because I promise not to hurt you. I promise never to lie. I promise that you can trust me.

And if a tiny, tiny voice tries to tell you to run as fast and as far from me as you can, you mustn't listen.

Because I'm here.

And I love you.

And I won't let you go.

ACKNOWLEDGMENTS

Roxy is a labor of love that would not have been possible without the friendship and support of everyone at Simon & Schuster. Particularly our publisher, Justin Chanda, who personally edited *Roxy*, and assistant editor Alyza Liu, for all her hard work on *Roxy*.

But there are so many people at S&S who go above and beyond! Jon Anderson, Anne Zafian, Lisa Moraleda, Michelle Leo, Sarah Woodruff, Krista Vossen, Chrissy Noh, Katrina Groover, Hilary Zarycky, Lauren Hoffman, Anna Jarzab, Emily Varga, Chava Wolin, and Chloë Foglia, to name just a few.

And thanks to Neil Swaab for that amazing cover! Wow!

Thanks to our literary agent Andrea Brown for everything she does, as well as our entertainment agents, Steve Fisher and Debbie Deuble-Hill, at APA; our contract attorneys Shep Rosenman, and Jennifer Justman; and our amazing managers, Trevor Engelson and Josh McGuire.

We're thrilled at all the international sales of *Roxy*, and want to give a shout-out to Deane Norton, Stephanie Voros, and Amy Habayeb in S&S foreign sales, as well as Taryn Fagerness, our foreign agent—and of course all our foreign publishers, editors and publicists. In Germany; Doreen Tringali, Antje Keil, and Ulrike Metzger at Fischer Verlage. In the United Kingdom; Non Pratt, Frances Taffinder, and Kirsten Cozens at Walker Books. In Australia; Maraya Bell and Georgie Carrol. In Spain; Irina Salabert at Nocturna. And in Norway, our friend and Russian translator Olga Nødtvedt, who keeps us connected to our Russian fans.

Thanks to Barb Sobel and Kim Thomason, for all the various life-saving assistant work that keeps critical things from falling between the cracks; research assistant Symone Powell, social media mavin Adam Alonsagay, and Thresa and Keith Richardson, for their marketing expertise, and more importantly, their friendship. Thank you to Kevin Cody, for your support so early in the process. And a special thanks to Elias Gertler, for always being there as a fellow creative, but most importantly, as a friend, considering just how close this story is to our hearts.

Lastly, we are a family of creative souls who support one another, and that love and support makes all the difference. Thank you, Erin, Joelle, and Brendan. Although we're in different places we're never really far apart.

A special thanks . . .

Sofía,

I can't thank you enough for giving me the inspiration and strength to write about this difficult topic—but more so, to tell a story with the potential to heal. Thank you, from the bottom of my heart, for always daring me to be a better creator and a better person. This book couldn't have been written without you, and I definitely wouldn't have embarked on this sojourn of the soul without you by my side.

Con mucho amor,
Jarrod